YEAR 12

A
HALF PAST MIDNIGHT
NOVEL

JEFF BRACKETT

YEAR 12

A Half Past Midnight Novel

ALSO BY JEFF BRACKETT

The Half Past Midnight series
Half Past Midnight
The Road to Rejas
Crazy Larry – *Coming Soon*

Other novels by the author
Streets of Payne
Chucklers, Volume 1: Laughter Is Contagious

Short Stories by the author
The Burning Land
Ghost Story

The most recent information on Jeff's publications
can be found on his Amazon Author Page.
For advance information on new releases, sign up for
his mailing list at http://jlbrackett.com/ww49.
The mailing list is for release notices only – no spam.

For Zachary and Brandy, my son and his hummingbird.
I love you, and am so very proud of you both.

And for Dad. I'm sorry I didn't finish this in time
for you to read it. I hope it finds you, anyway.

ACKNOWLEDGEMENTS

I've often heard it said that writing is a solitary endeavor — that it's just the author and the computer, sitting for hours at a time, hammering out the story until it's completed and ready for publication. Well, any of us who have done it, know for a fact that the saying is wrong. A book may begin as a story in the author's mind, but it is influenced by many others along the way as it grows from original concept to finished product. In the case of *Year 12*, there were discussions with friends and loved ones, and encouraging messages and words of advice from other friends, fellow authors, and fans in my social media groups. I want to thank you all.

But there were some of you who went above and beyond, and you guys deserve a special shout out. So to Meloney, my better half, thank you for standing by me... for being my sounding board and inspiration, and for putting up with the long months while I got my act together.

James Husum, my brother from another mother — you've also listened to me work through various plot problems, and I can't tell you how much I appreciate you.

My beta readers for this one... James, Jeanette, Linton, Carol, Brenda, Chrissy... I thank you all for your time and tolerance as you waded through the rough draft on this one.

For Lynn McNamee at Red Adept Author Services, always a friend, and one of the best editors in the business, thank you.

For Sarah Carleton, editor at Red Adept, who did an amazing job editing the book, thanks for your patience in working with me to make this book so much better than it was when I handed it over to you.

And for Kim H., my proofreader at Red Adept Editing, thank you for your final polish, and your kind words.

There are bound to be others that I've missed here. Please forgive me. So to anyone else who contributed to this work, in whatever way, no matter how small... please know that this book wouldn't have been the same without your help.

Thank you all.

PART 1
LEAVING

CHAPTER 1
THIEF

I WAS ALMOST TO THE BARN when I heard the back door of the house open. Dropping to the ground, I tried to blend into the darkness, hoping the lamplight from the back porch wouldn't reach that far into the night. The old man leaned against the back railing. He looked lost in thought and more than a little tired, and I wondered for a moment what was going through his head.

Several voices in the house rose in argument, and the man cursed as he turned and went back inside. They'd been going at it for more than an hour already and showed no signs of slowing anytime soon. I slipped around back, dropped my pack on the ground, and then swung the barn door open, freezing for a second as an extraordinarily loud burst of shouting came from the house. And though I could make out a few distinct words, they might as well have been spoken in a foreign language for all the meaning they held for me.

Solar-synchronous orbit? I had no idea what that meant, but it really didn't matter. As long as they kept quarrelling, I didn't have to worry about being discovered. While the drone of old men and women carried through the night air, no one would be paying any attention to the horses.

It was a warm summer night, and the full moon illuminated my way as I slid through the shadows into the barn. I left the door open, needing the moonlight, as I slowly stepped inside and smelled the rich scents of horse and fresh hay. Moving to the nearest of six stalls, I pulled a slice of fresh apple from the pouch on my belt and held it out to the mare before me.

"There's a good girl." I spoke quietly and cupped my hand around her nose, letting her catch my scent, keeping her calm with my words and attitude. "And there's more where that came from once we get down the road a ways." I stroked her nose as I slipped the bridle over her head then led her out of the stall.

As I turned toward the barn door, I saw the silhouettes of two dogs approaching from across the yard. *Great! All I need is for a bunch of barking dogs to attract someone's attention.* But I was at least partially prepared for them. I pulled several bits of jerky from my pocket and coaxed the dogs to me. They scarfed the meat down in a matter of seconds and sniffed my hands for more. "Greedy little things, aren't you?" I reached into my pouch. "Want some more? Come on." There were leashes hanging on the wall by the door, and I grabbed two as I led the dogs back into the mare's stall. I handed them each another piece of jerky, and they munched happily as I slipped the leashes around their necks and secured them in the stall. "You're good dogs, aren't you?" I emptied the rest of the jerky into a pile and slipped out of the barn.

After saddling the mare outside the barn, I grabbed my pack from where it lay and secured it behind the saddle. More shouting from the house across the yard told me I still had time before anyone missed the horse. I swung my leg up and quietly rode away from the lights of home.

———— ⚹ — ⚹ — ⚹ — ⚹ — ⚹ ————

I rode through the night, armed with some old folding maps I had stolen from the Rejas Library. I felt a bit guilty about that. No one had yet devised a way to make paper as fine and crisp as the Old Days paper in the books and magazines preserved in the library. That meant every bit preserved was precious. I justified it by telling myself I would return the maps in a few months when I came back from my trip. Besides, the library had dozens of the Texas and Oklahoma maps and at least ten other copies of the *Easy-Fold Map of the United States*. And while there was some question as to whether or not the United States still existed, the roads and cities were still there — mostly.

Mother Nature had reclaimed sidewalks as well as most of the smaller roads in the area within a few years of D-day. But she was still working on the larger highways and interstates, so it was easy enough to see the wide, flat, barely covered pathways that meandered across the landscape. They were recognizable enough to use as guide markers for a journey, anyway.

In less than two hours, I was riding north beside Highway 96. The light of the full moon illuminated the road well enough, but a decade of unmaintained blacktop still made traveling it at night a dangerous endeavor. Grass runners and shrubs grew through crumbling concrete and potholes. The overall path was still mostly flat, and the uneven ground was easy enough to navigate during the day, but concrete, whether covered in grass or not, was still unforgiving. Not wanting to risk injury to my horse, I kept to the softer grass that grew to the side of the roadway.

I rode for about three more hours, keeping Tallulah to a slow trot in the darkness. I estimated we'd gone about ten miles by the time I decided to stop. The young appaloosa was in good shape, but I didn't want to push her too hard, especially so early in the journey. Riding a short distance into the forest, I quickly found a good spot near a little stream.

A few minutes later, I had Tallulah tethered to a tree where she would be able to drink, while I climbed one of the trees I'd picked out as a support for my hammock tent, which was, as the name suggested, basically a hammock with a fine-mesh mosquito net over it. It took a little work to hang the tent as high as I liked, but I'd gotten good at it over the last few years, and within a matter of fifteen minutes, my pack and I were settled into it, almost twenty feet above the ground.

I listened to the sounds of the forest as I tried to get to sleep, telling myself that they were the reason for my insomnia. But I knew better. It wasn't the forest, or the crickets, or bullfrogs keeping me awake but rather the excitement, and perhaps a bit of fear, at the sheer audacity of my undertaking. The truth was that the whole thing was more than a little intimidating. What did I know about traveling and the world? I'd lived most of my life in a town of fewer than three thousand people.

But the message had been clear, and while the Rejas City Council sat and argued about who would act as ambassador, I wasn't going to wait. It had taken them two days to decide to send anyone at all. There was no telling how long it would take to figure out *who* to send. *And there's no way they would have chosen me, anyway.*

I was well known in town, though not for anything I had really done. It was more a matter of what had been done *to* me and *for* me. And I was tired of it. I needed to make my own mark on the world and to earn a place in my community for something I actually did on my own. But none of the council would have agreed, not even my own father. Despite the fact that I was the one who had first seen it.

Well, Donna and I.

CHAPTER 2
THE BEGINNING

I PEERED THROUGH THE RAPIDLY DARKENING forest. Donna's hand in my own was warm in the cool nighttime air as I led her through the trees.

"Where are we going?" she asked quietly.

"You'll see." I looked back at her and smiled teasingly.

"Come on, Zach. Tell me, please?"

"Nope. It's a surprise."

I could hear the pout in her voice as she complained. "Not fair."

"Whoever told you life was fair?" I grinned evilly.

She slapped my arm. "You're mean, you know that?"

"Don't worry—we're almost there." I knew that patch of the Texas Big Thicket as if it were my own backyard. I should. Having lived there for more than a decade, for all intents and purposes, it *was* my backyard.

We pushed through the trees and entered the clearing at the eastern edge. I stepped aside, waving my hand in a grand gesture as if presenting her with a special gift, and she gasped at the sight before us.

The clearing was about thirty yards across, an almost perfectly round hole in the huge pines of the Texas Big Thicket that gave an unobstructed view of the stars and Milky Way. That, in and of itself, made it one of my favorite places to go even on cold winter nights. But in the late spring, for a period of a few weeks or so, there was a special magic to the place.

"Oh my God, Zach. It's beautiful!" She stepped past me into the gently flowing clouds of fireflies flickering lazily through the air. This clearing was a breeding ground for them, and every spring it came alive with what appeared to be millions of drifting lightning bugs. Males flew about, frantically flashing their signals in an attempt to attract a mate. The females, who held all the power just as in the world of humans, stayed on the limbs of trees or tall blades of grass, flashing their replies.

Donna held her arms out to her sides, slowly spinning around to see the tiny flashing orbs all around her. Her expression of wonder brought a smile to my face, and I noticed, not for the first time, that she was really quite a pretty girl. She was a year younger than I was, and we'd known each other for several years. Her father had died during the Rough Times after the Doomsday War, when Crazy Larry had rolled into town at the head of a small army. I'd met her a year later when she and her mother had started training with Megan.

We'd always been good friends, but lately she acted as if she was trying to push the relationship a bit farther, and I wasn't exactly sure how I felt about that.

Other girls had tried to get close to me, but they had always turned out to be more interested in my story than in me. Unlike them, Donna had never pushed me for anything more than friendship. She'd never pressured me with the all-too-familiar "Tell me the story." She had respected my privacy, and as a result of her discretion, we'd become close friends.

I followed her into the clearing and lay back in the grass, looking up at the light show. I'd seen the fireflies on many occasions, but the joy on Donna's face brought a smile to mine. She finally realized I was watching her, and she dropped beside me, a self-conscious grin still plastered to her face. For several minutes, we lay there in comfortable silence.

"Zach?"

So much for silence. "Yeah?"

"Why don't you have a girl?"

And so much for comfortable. I hesitated, somewhat anxious about where the conversation might be going. I deflected. "Why don't you have a guy? I know for a fact that Jerry's been trying to get your attention for weeks now."

She chuckled. "Jerry's a dick. He thinks more about his reputation with the ladies than about the ladies themselves." She rolled onto her side and rose onto one elbow. I turned my head to meet her eyes. "I'm not interested in becoming a notch on his bedpost. Especially not for—" She stopped and pursed her lips. It was obvious she'd almost told me something she considered important but had changed her mind.

"Not for what?"

"Wait a minute. You never answered my question." She sat back up. "You always do that."

"Wait. What? I always do what?"

"You always avoid answering my questions when you don't want to talk about something. Then you twist the conversation around to distract me." She frowned. "You think I don't know what you're doing, but I see it. I'm not stupid!"

"Wait a second." I sat up and scooted back on the grass to where I could see her better by the flickering light of the fireflies around us. "How did this go from me asking about Jerry to you saying I think you're stupid?"

"It didn't. It went from me asking *you* about a girlfriend to you avoiding the question just like you always do." She shifted to where she could better face me. Her lips pursed, and I could tell she was upset. "I just don't like Jerry." She looked down, and her hair fell forward like a dark curtain, blocking my view of her face as she lowered her voice. "I don't want him to be my first."

At first I didn't understand. Her first what? Yeah, I could be slow like that sometimes. When I realized what she was saying, my reply was equally inspired. "Oh. So you... um?"

"Yeah." She looked up at me, expression inscrutable. "I *um.* And I don't want some little boy in a big man's britches to *un-um* me."

I chuckled at that. When she glared up at me, I said, "Sorry."

Her expression softened a bit. "It's all right. I guess it's not exactly the discussion you expected to be having tonight."

"Ah, not exactly." *Oh yeah. I'm absolutely eloquent tonight.* "I mean, you just—"

But Donna wasn't finished. "I wanted to see if you might..."

I swallowed. Was she asking what it sounded like she was asking? "If I might... um?"

She giggled. "Or un-um..."

"Wow, Donna. I, ah... I mean..." There I was, Mr. Articulate yet again.

She looked at me directly for the first time since she'd broached the subject. "Look, it ain't like a marriage proposal or anything. I don't expect anything more than what we already have. We're friends, right?"

"Well, yeah. I like to think so."

"So I don't want my first time to be with some dick like Jerry."

I snickered at the double entendre, and after a second, she must have realized what she'd said. She laughed and slapped my shoulder. "You know what I mean!"

"Hey! You're the one making bad jokes here." I rubbed my shoulder in mock pain.

Her smile faded, and she steered the conversation back to the subject. "I also don't really want to be all clumsy and bumbling when I finally do get married, either. I want my first time with my husband to be wonderful, and that won't happen if I'm so worried about the pain of my first time, and being all clumsy and wondering what a man likes and doesn't like."

What she said made a certain amount of sense. And I'd be lying if I didn't admit that it was all I could do not to roll her onto her back right then and there.

"And I sure as hell don't want to go hop into bed with someone I don't even care about or who doesn't care about me. And you do care about me, right?"

"Well, yeah."

"So then..." Her voice trailed off, and she looked at me.

I didn't know what to do. Was she finished talking? Did she need to talk it through some more? If I let her keep talking, she might talk herself out if it. But did I want to risk ruining a good friendship for the sake of sex?

When I didn't do anything, she took a deep breath and leaned in toward me. Her lips were soft and warm as she kissed me. Stunned for a second, I didn't react. But she didn't stop, and after a few interminably long seconds, I reached up, cupping her cheek as I kissed her back. Her tongue brushed my lips, and I opened, reaching forward with my own. She moaned, or maybe it was me. I wasn't sure. All I knew was that the situation had gone from trot to gallop in a matter of seconds, and I wasn't entirely sure what to do about it.

I felt like a clumsy child, not knowing what to do with my hands, lips, or tongue. Should I bite her lip? I'd heard some girls liked that. Could I get away with touching her breasts, or her butt, or even her... *um*? It might be too soon.

My mind spun with the typical insecurities and questions of a twenty-year-old, and I was almost paralyzed with indecision. *Will I disgust her by rushing things? Does she really want this? Is she going to change her mind? Is there some game going on here I don't know the rules to?* I didn't want to jump to the wrong conclusion. Did she really want to go all the way, or did she just want to neck for a while? If I pushed it too far, I might get slapped. If I did something wrong, I might anger her and ruin a valued friendship.

Donna seemed pretty sure, though. She pulled back for a second, and by the dim yellow light of the fireflies, I saw her pull the loose dress over her head. I swallowed. She saw my hesitation and smiled reassuringly as she slid the straps of her bra over her shoulders. Her breasts drew my eyes like magnets. She twisted the bra around to where she could get to the clasp.

"Donna?" My eyes refused to pull away from her breasts as I spoke. Distracted, I realized my hands had somehow become attached to them. Wasn't I about to say something?

"What?" she murmured.

"Hmm?"

She pressed my hands tighter on her breasts and moaned. The sound broke the spell her breasts held on me, and I looked up at her face. Eyes half closed, she licked her lips. We were both panting as she spoke. "You said my name?"

But those amazing breasts called to me again, and I leaned up, taking a nipple into my mouth, licking it, then pulling gently with my teeth, afraid of hurting her — and even more afraid of not pleasing her.

She gasped again, pressing the back of my head to her then pulling away. She pushed me onto my back and straddled me, and once again, those lovely breasts were in my hands. "You had something you wanted to say?"

I remembered. "Yeah. I..."

She ground back against me. She still had on her panties, and I was still fully clothed. But her center was hot enough that I could feel it against my hard length even through our clothing. Once more, I couldn't tell which of us moaned.

"I... um..."

She ground harder against me. "You what?" she teased.

I gripped her hips, pulling them forward then back, increasing the friction between us. Then I forced myself to stop. I couldn't think while we were doing that. And there was something I needed her to know. "I um." I swallowed, unsure how she would react.

She looked alert again, maybe a little irritated. "What?" she panted. "Oh God, what is so important right now?"

I looked her in the eye.

"I," I said plainly, "*um*."

She blinked, then smiled as she caught on. "Really? You too?"

My face flushed at the admission. "Yeah."

"But I thought you... I mean, there are always girls throwing themselves at you. I sorta assumed you had... umm."

We both chuckled at the term. Then I shook my head.

Donna raised an eyebrow then smiled tenderly. "Then we can both un-um each other." And she leaned forward to kiss me again. There was no hesitation that time. We laughed together as my shirt got tangled over my head. When we finally got it, I pulled her back to me, wanting to feel those gorgeous breasts against my bare chest. Our skin was hot as we ground against each other again, and I reached down to her hips, pulling her tightly against me, then slid my hands around and inside her panties to grasp her cheeks. That time, I *knew* it was she who moaned, and I smiled to think that I could cause such a reaction in her.

She sat back, reaching for my belt, and my hands yet again were drawn to her breasts. I pinched her nipples lightly as she fumbled the buttons on my pants. Her hand grasped my length, bending me painfully as she tried to separate me from my pants. "Ow!"

Reflexively, I pinched her nipples harder, which caused her to hiss.

"I'm sorry!" we both said at the same time. Then we laughed.

I rolled her gently off me onto her back. She smiled at me. "We're a mess, aren't we?"

I nodded. "But they say practice makes perfect." I stood, sliding my pants down, and my erection sprang comically up. The cool night air made me realize I'd been sweating.

"What's that?"

I wasn't sure how to answer her. Surely she knew what it was. It was sort of the point to what we were doing, wasn't it? *What am I supposed to say? My pecker? No, too crude. My penis? Too clinical. My love pole? Just plain ridiculous.* But she pointed past my head, and I turned to see what had interrupted our moment.

At first I thought it was just another firefly, but it didn't flicker. It didn't change direction. It was a steady shining light in the sky, traveling from one side of the clearing toward the other. I stood there like an idiot, penis wilting, pants around my ankles, as I realized what I was seeing. I'd read about them in the library and never thought I'd see one. "It's a satellite!"

Donna stood, still clad only in her panties as she grabbed my elbow. "There haven't been any satellites for years." The pressure of her bare breast on my arm was distracting, and I looked over at her, once more becoming aroused. She turned her face to me, brimming with excitement.

21

My erection began to return at the sight of her nearly naked body, and I was glad to see her grin. Good, we can get back to —

"We need to get back! We've gotta tell your dad!"

"Wait. What?"

She turned away from me, bending to pick up her clothes. The sight of her backside stretching those panties had me fully distracted again, and I realized my chance was slipping away.

"We need to let them know there's a satellite in the sky! Don't you realize what that means?" She clasped her bra and slipped the straps back over her arms, and I nearly groaned with disappointment as her breasts — those gorgeous breasts that I had just had in my hands, in my mouth — disappeared behind plain white cotton. "Someone is rebuilding!"

She slipped her dress back over her head, and I did groan then. She looked at me, still standing in the clearing with my pants around my ankles, and she smiled pityingly. She sauntered over to me. Yes, that was the word. She *sauntered* over to me with a sexy smile. "Oh, Zach. I'm sorry." She reached out, and her touch sent a thrill through me once more.

I moaned.

"It's not fair to leave you like this, is it?"

Hope beat in my chest as she squeezed lightly. Then she giggled. "Then again, whoever told you life was fair?" She squeezed once more, giggled, and ran out of the clearing toward town.

I sighed and dropped my head. Looking down at my confused penis, I spoke resignedly. "Guess we stay *um* for a bit longer."

———※——※——※——※——※

Dad sent me out with messages at first light. Rejas had a seven-person town council. Dad, as mayor, and six others sat once a month to hear and decide on city business down at City Hall. But on rare occasions, someone called a special session. This was one of those occasions, and I spent four hours delivering messages to all six of the other council members.

That night was the first of several meetings at the Dawcett homestead. The initial meeting was immeasurably complicated by the fact that the two ham radios reported they were receiving a signal, apparently from the satellite. Taking full advantage of the fact that I happened to live where the meetings were taking place, I eavesdropped every chance I got. And hearing the content of the message had me more excited than I had been in a long time.

It was actually two messages. The first was a simple recording that played over and over in a loop:

> *To any citizens who are able to receive this message,*
>
> *Be advised that the government of the United States of America is advancing down the long road to recovery. With the destruction of Washington DC as well as many of the nation's largest cities, the government has relocated to a secret location. We also have a new military installation that is working to rebuild some of our technological infrastructure. If you are hearing this message, it means that you have either saved or rebuilt to some level of electronic technology. Please send representatives to discuss what is needed for the reconstruction of our great nation.*

That simple message was accompanied by a set of coordinates in Morse code—35-20-23N / 99-12-02W. They pointed to a town in western Oklahoma, and the message was clearly a kind of call to arms. And when I heard the location was an old abandoned spaceport left over from a ten-million-dollar competition called the Ansari X Prize, I was intrigued enough to visit the library.

According to a couple of magazine articles I found, the Ansari X Prize had been a private space race that took place around the turn of the century. Any private individual or business that managed to build and launch a reusable manned spacecraft twice within two weeks would win ten million dollars. Evidently, several companies tried, but a company called Scaled Composites won the prize in October of 2004 with the second launch of *SpaceShipOne*.

But before their spaceplane roared to victory, several other organizations were also working toward that ten-million-dollar prize. One of them involved a failed and abandoned spaceport near the small town of Burns Flat, Oklahoma. It looked like the US military had taken up residence there and had used it to launch a satellite.

Who knew what else they were building up there?

With that question, my imagination refused to let me rest. I had to get away from Rejas, where I was known as Leeland Dawcett's son — the kid hundreds of people had fought a madman to rescue. I had to make my own mark on the world.

CHAPTER 3
CAUGHT

THE SMELL OF EGGS AND bacon woke me two days later. It was a wonderful scent. The eggs had some sort of herbs or spices mixed in as they cooked. At first, I drifted in and out of consciousness, content with the senses that the wonderful dream sent my way. The whine of dogs shocked me fully awake.

Keeping as quiet as I could, I reached up and pulled at the side of the hammock so I could peer over it at the ground below. I squinted at the scene, trying to make sense of the situation. I was supposed to be alone. No one knew where I was. Yet there were Bella and Cricket, sitting below, looking up at me, tails wagging contentedly. Smoke drifted up from a small campfire, and I saw a hulking figure kneeling beside it, frying pan resting on a small metal camping grill. I had used such grills many times when I'd camped out.

The demeanor of the dogs told me they knew who the mysterious cook was even if I hadn't yet figured it out. It wasn't my dad—the guy at the grill was way too big. The rifle that lay on the ground beside him caused my heart to thump loudly in my chest. It was a bolt-action rifle from the Old Days. There weren't many people who carried those any more since bullets were becoming scarce. Most folks carried simple black-powder rifles or, even more commonly, a bow and arrows like I did. Anyone who carried an Old Days rifle was a person of means and good standing.

He shifted where he squatted beside the fire, drawing my attention from the rifle back to him, and as his size registered, I finally realized who it must be. "I'm not going back."

Mr. Roesch simply looked up from his pan to where I peeked over the edge of my hammock.

"You can't make me. I'll just sneak out again."

"I know."

I waited for him to elaborate, but he had nothing more to say. That was pretty normal for him. Mr. Roesch was one of the least talkative people I knew. Dad had once told me it went back to something that happened to him on D-day, but neither of them ever showed any inclination to elaborate.

Not really sure of what to expect, I slipped my boots on and grabbed the rope I had coiled beside me. I used it to lower my pack then tied myself off to my upper support line while I dismantled my hammock. Mr. Roesch watched as I swung from tree to tree, and I thought I saw him nod with approval as I finally untied my support lines and lowered myself to the ground beside my pack. But he said nothing as I left my gear on the ground and walked over to sit across the fire from the big man. He scooped a pile of eggs and bacon onto a thin shingle of wood and handed it across to me.

"Thanks."

He nodded and began eating the rest of the food directly from the small frying pan. As with most things having to do with Mr. Roesch, breakfast was a quiet affair. I ate, all the while wondering what his appearance meant. At first, I was convinced he was going to try to take me back home. But he could have easily overpowered me and thrown me over his horse if that was the case. I finally figured it out.

"They decided to send you, didn't they?"

He looked up with a twinkle in his eye. He jabbed his fork at me. "Got it in one."

"Alone?"

Mr. Roesch shook his head. "Told 'em I had people I could pick up along the way."

"You knew I was already out here?"

"You'd been hounding them for the chance ever since they deciphered the message. Suddenly you get quiet and disappear?" He scooped another forkful of eggs into his mouth. "Your dad checked the barn and found the dogs leashed up in an empty stall. Didn't take a genius to figure it out."

"But how'd you find me? There's half a dozen ways I could have gone."

He just pointed to the two Catahoula leopard dogs. My girls nuzzled up to me, tails wagging, unaware of their unwitting betrayal. "Shoulda taken them with you."

I sighed at my own stupidity even as I scratched my girls behind the ears. We finished the rest of our breakfast in silence. I broke my last piece of bacon in half and tossed a bit to each of the girls then threw my shingle into the fire. Shortly thereafter, we were strapping our gear onto our horses, and I was still trying to figure out what was going on. Finally, I gave up working on it and just asked, "So my folks are all right with this? With me going with you to the meet?"

"We talked about it when we figured out what you had probably done. Figured you were probably gonna go no matter what. Makes more sense for me to go with you than to let you go on your own."

I couldn't entirely stop the grin. "So I really get to represent Rejas for this?"

"Nope."

My grin died.

"*I* represent Rejas. Your dad got the rest of the council to agree to let you come along for as long as I can put up with you. Figure it'll be a good experience, you being the son of the mayor and all."

"But I can..." I let my words trail off at the look Mr. Roesch gave me.

"I represent Rejas. You're my assistant. Capiche?"

I swallowed. "I don't know what a capeesh is, but I understand."

He grunted as he swung into his saddle.

CHAPTER 4
ATTITUDE ADJUSTMENT

RIDING WITH MR. ROESCH WAS like riding with a statue. He looked like a person, but he was silent as stone and always seemed to be lost in his own thoughts. When I tried to drag him into conversation, I was more often than not answered with grunts, nods, or shrugs. After trying for several hours, I finally gave up. He obviously didn't want to talk, and I didn't need the frustration.

Bella and Cricket scouted several yards ahead of us, and as the sun approached its zenith, I called out, "Bella! Cricket!" They stopped and turned to look at me as I rode toward them. "Hunt."

They scampered off into the forest beside the road, and I finally got a reaction out of Mr. Roesch. He turned to me with a raised eyebrow. "You trained 'em to hunt? That'll come in handy."

I grunted at him, happy to finally be able to turn the tables on the taciturn old man. As I pulled my horse past him, I had to fight hard to suppress a grin.

It wasn't long before the two came back with a pair of rabbits. I dismounted and praised them. "That's my good girls. Put it down." They did, and I scratched them both behind the ears for a moment. But they wanted more, and I needed to oblige them. I grabbed the coneys, pulled out my knife, and quickly gutted them, dropping the heads and entrails for the girls.

I looked up at Mr. Roesch. "Ready for lunch?"

He smiled and dismounted. "Need help?" He jutted his chin toward the rabbit carcasses.

"Nah. I got it." I was pleased to have impressed the older man. "I'm the assistant, right?"

He nodded. "That you are." He took Tallulah's reins and left me cleaning the rabbits as he took care of the horses. "Looks like you're learning pretty fast, too."

He put a quick fire together, starting it with a tinder kit he pulled from his pocket. By the time I had the rabbits cleaned and skewered, he had a good fire going, and it was my turn to be impressed. It usually took me twice as long to get a decent fire, and I made a mental note to pay more attention next time to see how he did it so quickly.

We ate in silence of course. Everything with Mr. Roesch was in silence. I thought for a bit about my plan... my former plan. When it had been just me, I had known my intent. I would travel to the space center, announce myself as a representative of Rejas, and see what the price of admission might be. By the time anyone from Rejas caught up with me, it would be too late to contradict me.

Of course, all that changed as soon as Mr. Roesch entered the picture. And despite the fact that my own plan was pretty much in shambles—not that it had been such a great idea to begin with—I was genuinely curious as to what the council had decided to do. But I knew Mr. Roesch wasn't going to volunteer any information. I was going to have to drag it out of him. So as we neared the last of our meal, I gathered up my courage and asked him.

"Mr. Roesch?"

He looked up at me over the fire. He stopped chewing and raised an eyebrow—the only indications he had heard me. "So what's the plan? I mean, what are you gonna—or I guess, what did the council decide to do?"

He went back to chewing for a moment, and I wasn't sure at first if he was going to answer. But he swallowed the last bit of meat from the bone in his hand and tossed it to the dogs. Bella snatched it out of the air and growled at Cricket, warning her away from the tidbit. "Depends," Mr. Roesch said without looking at me. He stood as if the conversation was over, but I wasn't willing to let it go that easily.

"Depends on what?"

"On what they're after."

"What do you mean? The message said what they were after. They want to rebuild the country."

He began kicking dirt onto the campfire. "Yep. That's what they said."

I swallowed the last bit of my food and absentmindedly tossed the bone to Cricket. I wiped my hands in the grass and hurried to help bury the fire. "Ain't that a good thing?"

"Isn't."

"Why not?"

He shook his head. "I'm not saying it isn't a good thing. I'm correcting your grammar."

I was dumbfounded. "My grammar?"

He shrugged. "I'm the ambassador. You're my assistant. Can't have my assistant come across like an ignorant hick." He climbed back into his saddle without looking at me. "You have responsibilities now. Even as my assistant, you still represent Rejas."

I thought about that as I climbed into my own saddle. The idea that I had a responsibility to the town hadn't really hit me until then. As I thought about it, I realized I'd been approaching the whole thing from a pretty selfish point of view. I'd been so intent on making my mark that I hadn't considered the impact of my actions on other people. A quick moment of soul searching told me something about myself, and I didn't much care for the message.

If you want to be treated like an adult, then stop acting like a kid.

We rode in silence as I thought about it. Everything I had done had been for selfish reasons. Ever since I'd been kidnapped ten years ago, I'd spent nearly every day resenting the fact that I'd had to be rescued... that people had fought and died to save me.

I'd spent my days since then trying to overcome that feeling of inadequacy, trying to make sure it would never happen again. I'd studied hard in the school when they'd finally gotten one running, and I'd excelled in reading and history. I'd done all right in math, but history was my real interest.

I'd trained hard with Dad when he still taught the self-defense classes and harder with Megan when Dad had gotten too busy with town politics and she'd taken over the classes. I trained the dogs and learned to hunt with a bow and take care of myself in the wilderness. I was one of the best around with the throwing knives my dad had given me as a kid. Basically, I'd pretty much lived my life to ensure that I would never have to depend on anyone else again.

But riding alongside Mr. Roesch, I realized that, while independence was a fine thing to strive for, there were more important things at stake. That realization put a new spin on all the things whirling through my mind, and I began to feel the tiniest bit of shame and guilt at the way I'd gone about this whole endeavor.

It wasn't until we were several miles down the road that I realized Mr. Roesch had never actually answered my question. Wasn't the fact that government was trying to rebuild the country a good thing? He had implied it might not be. But all the history books I'd read had extolled the virtues of the founding fathers of the United States. They had taught us in school that the government had been built to be of the people and for the people, and that seemed like a pretty evenhanded way to do things.

I considered asking him what he'd meant again but strongly suspected I wouldn't get an answer. We rode the rest of the afternoon in silence.

CHAPTER 5
FIRST LESSONS

RIDING WITH MR. ROESCH THE following day was suddenly a new experience. Whereas the day before he had been quiet and reserved, now he was more talkative than I'd ever heard him. It appeared I wasn't the only one who had thought more on what was going to be expected of me. He gave the impression that he was genuinely intent on educating me as to what our journey was all about.

It started as we ate breakfast. He had produced a few more eggs and a slab of bacon and began cooking while I once again performed my circus antics, swinging from tree to tree as I broke down my hammock.

I was pretty proud of the way I camped. I'd read about hammock tents in an old magazine from the library. It wasn't black ink on plain newsprint like the Rejas newspaper. The magazine was full color on glossy paper, and I had often wondered how they'd gotten paper to shine like freshly cleaned glass.

The article had shown pictures and detailed descriptions of a method of camping that had evidently been relatively popular back before D-day. I liked the idea and devised my own version of hammock camping. It consisted of a hammock covered with a mosquito net, much like the ones I had read about. But I had added an extra support line above the netting. I could use it as a sort of zip line, tying myself to it and sliding back and forth between trees while I secured my hammock and raised my gear off the ground. It gave me the means to camp much higher in the trees than the hammocks I'd read about would allow.

When I was finished breaking down my hammock and had lowered my last line out of the trees, I walked over to the fire. He handed me a shingle full of food again. As I took my first bite, he asked, "Why do you go to so much trouble?"

I hurried to swallow before replying with the incredibly intelligent, "Sir?"

He jabbed his fork up at the trees where I had slept. "Why sleep up there?"

"It's safer. No wild dogs or wolves can get to me up there, and people usually don't even see me until they're within bow shot." I smiled. "I've had people walk right under me and not even know I was there. Using the hammock means I have to camp in pretty dense growth, and people tend to keep their eyes on their path when they're going through the woods at night. They don't usually look up unless they're near a clearing."

"Smart." He nodded, taking another bite. Then he pointed his fork at me. "But you still haven't really gotten to the why."

"Excuse me?"

"Why do you feel the *need* to sleep in the trees?"

I felt like the older man was testing me in some way, but I had no idea what answer he was looking for. Hadn't I already told him why? Obviously, he was looking for more than a repeat of my claim that it was safer. I shook my head. "I'm sorry. I guess I don't understand."

He looked at me in silence for a moment, and I swallowed nervously. Finally, he nodded. "I'm beginning to think you might work out after all." He chewed another bite, swallowed, and looked up at the trees again. "First of all, I think you're being pretty smart, sleeping up out of sight." He looked back down at me. "And you're smart again to admit to me when you don't understand something."

He finished his breakfast and tossed the shingle into the fire while I hurried to shovel the rest of mine into my mouth.

"But be careful who you admit it to."

"Sir?" There I was again with the witty banter. I swallowed the last of my breakfast and tossed my shingle after his.

"You can always ask me *privately* if you don't know something. That's how you learn. But the impression you make on people will reflect on me." He reached out and lightly grabbed my shoulder, adding emphasis to his words. "It will reflect on all of Rejas. I don't know yet how we're going to play things at this meeting, so you need to be on your toes. Understand?"

I hesitated then decided to be truthful. "No, sir, I don't. Not completely."

He actually grinned. "Good answer!" He stood, and the two of us began kicking dirt over the coals. He continued talking as we worked on cleaning the campsite. "What I mean is, why do you feel the need to sleep up in the trees? I know you said you feel safer, and it lets you avoid animals and people. And I'm impressed you knew better than to just repeat that when I asked you to elucidate."

Elucidate? What in the world does that *mean?*

"But what I'm really asking is why you feel the *need* to avoid them. Not the animals but the people. Don't you trust them?"

"You never know what someone's gonna do. It's better to be safe than get hurt." *Or kidnapped.*

"And if they smile and tell you that you can trust them? What about then?"

I was silent as I saddled my horse, trying to wind my way through the hidden depths of the conversation. It was beginning to feel like one of my dad's lessons, and part of me resented the feeling. But since I didn't want to get shut out of the trip, I figured I'd be better off going along with it. "You can't trust someone just because they smile at you."

"But what if they promise you they won't act up?"

"Still can't be sure." I sighed. "Look, Mr. Roesch, I get that you're trying to teach me something here. But I'm sorry—I just don't know what it is."

He cinched his saddle down and looked at me over the top of

it. Leaning onto the saddle, he asked, "If you go to all that trouble to sleep in the trees just because you can't fully trust people" — he slung his saddlebag over the haunches of his horse — "then why are you in such a hurry to believe a message from someone you've never seen just because they say they want to rebuild the country?"

"But they're the government."

"Are they?"

That caught me. I thought about it for a second. "They must be. The message came from the satellite. No one else would have the resources to launch a satellite." I was proud of that little piece of logic. My pride lasted all of two seconds.

"You think the United States is the only government that could put a hunk of metal in the sky?"

That sent my brain in all sorts of directions I hadn't considered. "Why would another government send us that message? Why send us to a location in Oklahoma?"

He shrugged. "I don't know. But I'm not going in blindly just because someone says they represent the US government." He swung into his saddle. "And here's something else for you to think about. Once we get to the spaceport and meet these people, how will we know if they really represent the government? Would it make a difference if they wore US military uniforms? We both know from experience that a uniform doesn't mean anything, don't we?"

He had me there. Crazy Larry had rolled into Rejas at the head of a bunch of thugs wearing army uniforms. Then he had proceeded to destroy a good portion of the town, kill several hundred people, and kidnap me — all in order to get revenge on my dad for having beaten and humiliated him back on D-day. No, uniforms weren't a guarantee of anything.

I mulled the idea over silently as I tried to follow all the implications and possibilities. Mr. Roesch kept quiet, letting me think, as we broke camp and rode north.

CHAPTER 6
OLD FRIENDS

THE REST OF THE DAY was filled with similar thought exercises as Mr. Roesch began teaching me a new way of looking at things. He repeatedly stressed that I couldn't go to Burns Flat with any sort of preconceived ideas.

"Evaluate the situation," he told me. "Gather as much information as you can."

He taught me that I needed to learn to quickly analyze any given situation, decide for myself how to react—or not react—and never give away my full intent before I was ready. "It's a lot like how your dad taught you to control a fight. Keep your opponent off balance. Don't react the way they expect you to. Try to take control of the situation. And if you can't take control, make them *think* you have control."

I shook my head at the new concepts. I understood that I'd always been pretty linear in my way of dealing with people, but I'd never really had cause to consider treating anyone differently. The idea of dealing with someone I couldn't trust was disconcerting.

"Where did you learn to think like this?" I asked him as we rode.

"Hmm?"

"Where did you learn all this stuff about logic and trust and analyzing situations and stuff?"

He turned his eyes back to the road. "Your dad never told you what I used to do before D-day?"

"No, sir. I never asked."

"Long time ago, I was a lawyer."

I had read about lawyers in various books, but to be honest, stories that involved the law and lawyers had always struck me as pretty boring. I preferred more action. "So lawyering taught you all this?"

"It did. You have to learn to take advantage in a situation where you can find it. And you learn that the truth isn't always as cut and dried as you would think."

"I bet you'd make a mean poker player."

He simply shrugged, giving nothing away and making my point for me.

The sun was fading behind the trees when the dogs began barking. Cricket launched forward, growling and yipping as she raced up the road, while Bella stayed back beside me. The fur on Bella's back was ridged up, and her bark had the characteristic booming volume of the Catahoula breed. Mr. Roesch and I pulled the horses into the trees and dismounted.

"Bella, hush!" I hissed, and she responded as she'd been trained. "Come." Bella dropped back to my side, waiting to be told what to do. "Good girl," I whispered and reached down to scratch her behind the ears. Cricket was out of earshot, and I wasn't going to shout for her and give away my position before we knew what was going on.

To my right, Mr. Roesch grabbed his rifle, and seeing he was taking the reaction of the dogs so seriously, I immediately pulled my bow and strung it. I had a pouch for my arrows that I slung over my back. It wasn't a quiver like the ones I had seen in books. I'd tried something like that before. Whoever came up with that design for a quiver had never had to run through the woods with arrows in it. My design was more like a flat goatskin pouch with a rigid back and a flap over the top. I could easily move through all sorts of brush at a full run and not have to worry about losing any of my arrows along the way.

I grabbed four arrows from the pouch and held them in my bow hand, snug against the bow. Gearing up took only seconds, and when I looked back up from my task, I found Mr. Roesch watching me intently. He nodded approvingly then jutted his chin forward, indicating we should move out. The fact that he wasn't speaking told me he'd prefer that we do so quietly. We slipped through the scrub, keeping as silent as possible as we approached the area where Cricket had charged forward.

We moved quickly, but it soon became apparent that while Mr. Roesch was pretty quiet for a man of his size, he wasn't as quiet as I was. I touched him on the sleeve and leaned in close. "Let me move ahead," I whispered. "I'll wave you up when I see something."

He pursed his lips then nodded reluctantly. "Be careful. Don't take any unnecessary chances."

I nodded and padded ahead, silent as the wind. Beside me, Bella's speckled fur blended into the overgrowth, especially with the dim remains of the day fading by the second. A few moments later, the alarm call of a blue jay told me something had disturbed the wildlife a short distance ahead. The idea that there was a disturbance so close but I didn't hear Cricket barking any longer made my chest tighten with concern for the smaller of my two girls. I nocked an arrow in the bow, holding it in place between the fingers of my bow hand. With my right hand, I quietly moved a branch out of my way.

A quiet rustle from behind told me Mr. Roesch was getting impatient, and I turned to see him easing forward. I held my hand up to indicate he should wait where he was while I moved ahead. It was too dim to see his expression, but I thought he didn't look very happy. Nevertheless, he nodded. I turned to Bella and held up one finger to her. It was the hand signal I used when telling her to *sit*, and I wasn't sure she would obey without the verbal command that normally accompanied the gesture. But she dropped her haunches to the ground obediently and watched me.

I held up an open hand, palm toward her in the *stay* command, and she dropped to her stomach. Pleased that she obeyed so well, I turned back toward the road and crept slowly forward.

The sun was nearly gone at that point, and the calls of various toads, frogs, and other night creatures were beginning to fill the air. Over the rising cacophony, a voice called out, "Would either of you gentlemen in the woods there be Mark Roesch?"

Freezing in place, I blinked at the unexpected inquiry from the road ahead. It was a woman's voice, and I turned to look back at Mr. Roesch questioningly. Unfortunately, he was barely more than a dim silhouette, and there was no way for us to communicate without one of us going to the other. Starting back to him so we could discuss matters, I was surprised when he responded to the mysterious woman.

"I'm Mark Roesch. Who are you?"

"Before I tell you, can I ask you a question?"

"You can ask. Whether or not I answer depends on the question."

"Fair enough." She paused. "What does the little green frog say?"

I thought I had misheard until Mr. Roesch began to laugh. Then I heard him moving through the forest behind me, all attempts at stealth abandoned. I wasn't entirely sure what had just transpired, but he apparently trusted the woman in the road, whoever she was. To my utter surprise, he began to sing, "Blink, blonk went the little green frog one day. Blink, blonk went the little green frog!" It was a tiny snippet of a song. But he walked past me as he sang it, and I could have sworn I heard him sigh wistfully.

A second later, I heard a distinct giggle from the road. "Hello, Mark."

From my cover of scrub at the tree line, I saw Mr. Roesch spread his arms and embrace one of the two women who waited for him on the road. "Hello, Kenni."

CHAPTER 7
ULTIMATUM

WATCHING FROM THE COVER OF a copse of yaupon, I wasn't entirely sure what I should do. For the moment, I was hidden, bow drawn, arrow nocked, watching as the normally taciturn Mr. Roesch smiled and laughed with the woman he had called Kenni in the road while the other one stood by. As he stepped back from the smiling woman, I saw her by the light of the waning moon. Still smiling, she turned her face toward me. And though I was certain I was fully hidden from sight, she beckoned to me nevertheless.

"Come on out, young man. We're all friends here."

I wasn't sure that I was as ready to trust her as Mr. Roesch obviously was, but then again, I wasn't really sure what was going on, either.

My mentor called to me. "Come on out, Zachary."

Still, I hesitated. The second woman looked in my general direction, obviously not quite certain of my location. But not "Kenni." There was absolutely no way she could actually see me — no way! — yet her eyes drilled directly into me, and I had the eerie feeling that despite the darkness, despite the cover of the foliage, she *saw* me looking back. And though it was a warm Texas summer night, my skin prickled into goose bumps.

But despite the strangeness of the situation, there was no indication of a threat — just an uncanny feeling that there was more going on than I could tell. I licked my lips as I weighed my options.

In the end, the deciding factor was the black-and-white speckled bundle of fur that sprang back to her feet, tail wagging as she bumped against the second woman's leg. As if in agreement, Bella let loose a quiet whine beside me. It wasn't fear. It was the whine she used when she wanted a treat but I was keeping it from her. It was her, "Please, Dad, haven't I been good long enough?" whine.

I sighed, and though I eased the tension from my bow, I kept an arrow nocked and pointed at the ground. I whispered, "Bella, come." I heard more than saw her approach in the darkness. Together, she and I walked quietly from behind our cover.

As we cleared the trees, I scowled at the smaller of my girls, who pawed lightly at the leg of Kenni's companion, clearly vying for more attention. "I see you've met Cricket."

She looked back down at the dog. Seeing she was once more the center of attention, Cricket rolled onto her back, inviting the woman to rub her belly. She grinned and knelt to oblige. "Cricket? What a cute name." It was evident that Cricket was enjoying herself. Her tail thumped her pleasure on the grass-covered concrete. Bella trotted past me to nudge the woman's other hand. The overt bid for equal attention caused the woman to giggle. "And what's your name?"

I slipped my arrows back into the pouch on my back. I still didn't know who these women were, but I trusted my girls. "Her name is Bella."

She scratched Bella behind the ears.

"Zachary, I'd like for you to meet an old friend." Mr. Roesch brought my attention back to the woman beside him. "This is Kennesha Anderson. Call her Miss Anderson."

"He will do no such thing! Zach and I are going to be very close friends soon."

Mr. Roesch raised an eyebrow. "You are, huh?"

"We are."

From the look on his face, I could tell there was again more going on with their conversation than I knew. Before I could say anything, though, she stepped forward, presenting her hand to me. She was younger than Mr. Roesch though not by too much—a pretty black woman, slender yet muscular, with close-cropped hair and skin so dark I wouldn't have been surprised to see stars reflecting off it. "You can call me Kenni."

I shook her hand. "Thank you, Kenni."

"And this," she waved a hand toward her companion, who now sat on the ground, rubbing Cricket's belly, "is Robin."

Robin looked up and smiled at me even as Bella nudged her hand with her nose, obviously wanting her share of the attention. The woman scratched the dog behind her ear. Not to be outdone, Cricket wriggled her way halfway into her lap. Robin smiled, looking up from her spot on the ground, and extended a hand for me to shake. "I would stand, but it seems I'm not allowed up quite yet. I'm Robin Scott. Pleased to meet you."

We shook hands, and Bella nudged her again, reminding Robin that she had other priorities and that I was interfering with the attention she and Cricket deserved. Robin giggled. "Kenni said you would have some friends with you, but I didn't know they would be *this* friendly!"

"They aren't always. But when they are, I know I can trust the person they're with." It was true. They were my people barometers. It wasn't usually so overt, but I could always tell whether or not I could trust a person by the way my girls acted around them.

As usual, Mr. Roesch used the moment as another lesson. "The proper response at this point would be 'The pleasure is mine.'"

Chagrined, I slumped my shoulders. "The pleasure is mine." Robin raised an eyebrow, looking from me to Mr. Roesch and back again. "I'm his assistant. It's a long story."

Kenni chuckled. "Well, we have a fire set up in the trees over there by the creek." She pointed to a little clearing just a few yards past the tree line across the road. "Would you gentlemen like to get your horses and join us?"

A fire? I didn't smell any smoke, and looking past them, I didn't see any hint of a glow. I did hear the faint sound of running water, though.

Mr. Roesch nodded and turned to me. "Zach, would you mind running back and getting the horses? We'll be spending the night with friends. Tomorrow promises to be an interesting day."

Interesting. That was a word that always made me suspicious. It implied the potential for excitement or fun, but in my experience, far too many *interesting* things had proven to be more dangerous than entertaining. Still, Mr. Roesch had made it abundantly clear he was the one calling the shots. Morning would be soon enough to find out what was going on.

But for the moment, I was the obedient assistant. I trotted back to get the horses.

When we got to their campsite, I saw why I hadn't seen or smelled the fire. The only indication that it was there was a small mound with rocks on top. The rocks surrounded a top hole, while a smaller hole went through the side of the mound. A bundle of small branches protruded from that side hole, and as we approached, Robin walked over and pushed the branches a bit farther in.

"Zach?" Mr. Roesch's voice reminded me that I still had work to do, but I promised myself I would take a closer look at their unusual campfire as soon as I took care of the horses. I walked them over to the creek where a pair of chestnut mares stood. Moonlight gave just enough visibility that I was able to work without worrying about tripping on anything.

The women's horses were picketed close enough to the creek that they could get to water throughout the night. I nodded in approval as I bent to uncinch the saddle from Mr. Roesch's horse. His was a tall cream and white, nearly seventeen hands at the withers, and strong—as any horse that carried the big man would have to be. Mr. Roesch called the horse Ford. He said he'd always been a Chevy man in the past, but after D-day, he decided to make a change.

I spoke to Ford as I worked, wanting to get him comfortable

with my sound and scent. "Hey, boy. You ready to get this load off?"

I heard Cricket's tail begin to thump in the grass nearby, so I wasn't startled when Robin's voice sounded behind me. "You look like you could use a hand."

I pulled the saddle from Ford's back, set it on a log I'd picked for that purpose, and nodded. "I wouldn't turn it down."

She helped me strip the rest of the tack from our mounts while they drank. "So who are these handsome devils?"

"The big guy there is Ford. He's Mr. Roesch's. And this little lady is Tallulah." I stroked her shoulder affectionately.

"She's yours?"

I shrugged. "She's a good friend who lets me ride on her back."

Robin chuckled, and I was suddenly self-conscious of the way I spoke about Tallulah.

"Sorry. Guess I get carried away sometimes."

"Don't be. It's good to see someone who's not afraid to show their appreciation for animals."

I smiled.

"These two" — she pointed to the chestnuts — "are Cinnamon and Shadowfax."

"Shadowfax?"

Robin chuckled. "Kenni is a big *Lord of the Rings* fan."

I grimaced. "Sorry, never read it."

"Well, don't let Kenni find out, or she'll spend days telling you every detail. All you need to know is Shadowfax was Gandalf's horse."

"Gandalf. Got it." I pulled my hoof pick out of my pack. "If you still want to help, why don't you brush them down while I clean their hooves?"

We spent the next several minutes in a surprisingly companionable silence, she brushing the horses while I picked the hooves clean and checked their legs. Working together, it only took a few minutes.

"Thanks. That was fast." I took the brush from her and slipped the hoof pick into my pocket.

Robin nodded. "I enjoy spending time with animals. I have to say, though, you really seem to have a way with them."

I shrugged. "I've always been good with them. Especially dogs."

As if on cue, Bella and Cricket trotted up beside me. Absentmindedly, I reached down to scratch them affectionately. "There's my good girls." Their tails wagged more fiercely.

"Come," I told them, and they followed as Robin led the way back to the main camp. Now that my eyes had fully adjusted to the darkness, I could see a dim glow from the fire. It wasn't much, but it was enough to rekindle my curiosity. Robin must have seen my interest and led me over to it. "It's a variation of a Dakota fire pit."

"A what?"

She pointed out the anatomy of the pit. "Dig a hole in the top of the mound. Make it about a foot or so wide and a foot or so deep. Then dig the feed hole about half that diameter on the windward side. Angle the second hole so that it intersects the main pit at the bottom so the breeze will blow into it." She lightly kicked at the mound. "It works better if you either find or make a small hill. Makes it a lot easier to make the holes intersect right."

I walked around the pit, and from the opposite side, I could see how the two holes intersected at the bottom of the main pit. "What about the wood sticking out?"

"It's an easy way to add fuel to the fire without disturbing the main pit." She grinned. "The fire burns more efficiently than a regular campfire, uses less wood, and hardly produces any smoke at all."

I nodded, walking around the pit again, memorizing how it was made.

Mr. Roesch and Miss Anderson—Kenni—walked over. Kenni slipped an arm around Robin in a familiar fashion. It was a casual yet intimate gesture that caught me by surprise. I had read all sorts of books in the library, and I knew what lesbians were. But the world had shrunk considerably since D-day, and Kenni and

Robin were the first I had ever met. I was momentarily speechless, not sure how I should react.

Kenni must have seen me studiously avoiding looking at them. She laughed. "It's all right, Zachary. We know it's unusual, especially these days."

Mr. Roesch looked from Kenni to me. Something in my face must have amused him, because he smiled for a second before getting serious. I recognized the look and groaned inwardly. Crap. It was lesson time again.

"You have to learn to conceal your emotions better than that, Zach. You don't have any idea what we're going to run into on this trip. Things aren't always going to be like they are in Rejas, and offending the wrong people might mess things up in all sorts of ways."

"Oh, don't be such an ass, Mark," Kenni joked.

But Mr. Roesch shook his head. "Me being an ass right now could save his life later." He turned his attention back to me. "We have a long way to go, and we're likely to meet a lot of different people between here and there. And I can just about guarantee that not all of them are going to say and do everything the way you're used to. What if we find a whole town where there aren't any men left? You think women are gonna just hole up in their homes, moping, because they can't find a man? No! Some of them will find that it's not so important whether the arms they find comfort in belong to a man or a woman just as long as they care for each other." He looked around for a second then pointed at Bella. "You've spent a lot of time training those dogs, haven't you? Well, what are you gonna do if we run across a town where someone wants to buy one of them?"

I shrugged. "I can be polite. I'll just tell them the dogs aren't for sale."

"But what if they get insistent? What if you notice there aren't any other animals in town? That the people are thin and starving and desperate enough that they'll eat anything, including your dogs if they can get their hands on them?"

I swallowed.

"What if they get pissed off and start yelling at you? Threatening you? Crying because their kids are starving? What would you do then?"

"I-I don't know."

Mr. Roesch narrowed his eyes. "Well, I know. You would do what I tell you to do."

I nodded. "Yes, sir."

"You would do exactly what I tell you, when I tell you, and nothing more than I tell you."

Everyone was silent at that point, and Mr. Roesch must have realized he'd drawn all eyes to himself. He stepped back. "Look, I'm sorry. I'm not trying to be a hard-ass. But the kid needs to realize that as rough as things are, he's still been sheltered. This isn't a picnic. We don't know what we're walking into, and we don't know what we're going to find along the way. And those people might just as easily be desperate enough to eat us instead of the dogs. You can't make any kind of assumption if you don't have all the facts."

I cleared my throat. "Mr. Roesch?"

"Yes?"

"I understand what you're saying, and I agree with you. I've lived in a small town that's mostly cut off from the rest of the world. I know there's a lot that I don't know."

Kenni chuckled again, and I was glad I'd managed to lighten the mood a bit, because what I had to say next just might undo it. "But there's something you need to know, too. And if it means you feel like you have to send me back..." I squared my shoulders and met Mr. Roesch's narrowed eyes with a steady gaze of my own. "Well, you already know I won't go, so I won't lie to you on that count."

He scowled. "Well, what is it, then?"

"Bella and Cricket are not for sale. Nobody is gonna eat them without going through me first. No matter what you say."

He froze, and I couldn't tell whether he was angry, shocked, or simply stunned that I would stand up to him.

"I just figured *that* might be one of the facts you'd want to know before you make any kind of assumption."

Everyone was silent for a moment. Then Kenni chuckled, and Mr. Roesch turned to her. His voice was almost pleading, "Damn it, Kenni. Do you even know what's going on here?"

She stopped, sighed, and laid a hand on his arm. "Of course I do, Mark." Then something happened that caught my attention. Her smile faded, and the same time, Bella and Cricket froze, heads cocked curiously toward Kenni as she spoke. "I can *see* it plain as day."

I'd read about sailboats and seen pictures of them, and I had heard people use an expression about taking the wind out of someone's sails. Kenni's words seemed to have that effect on Mr. Roesch. He hadn't been angry with me. Not really. Neither had he been exactly happy with me. But when Kenni told him she could see what was going on, his shoulders slumped, and his expression told me he was finished with me. He was finished with the whole situation.

"We'll talk about it more tomorrow."

CHAPTER 8
NEW COMPANIONS

ROBIN AND I WORKED THE horses over again in the morning, and I tried hard to avoid Mr. Roesch. But since I was part of a four-person campsite and responsible for grooming the horse of the man I was trying to avoid, well... it was an exercise in futility. To be fair, Mr. Roesch seemed content to leave me to my inner demons while he wrestled with his. But after the horses were ready, we all still had to eat. And that meant sharing a seat around the small fire pit.

As Robin and I approached, Kenni and Mr. Roesch looked up. It was apparent they had been deep in conversation. It was equally apparent that they had stopped their conversation as soon as we got within earshot. *Yeah, nothing like a sudden hush falling over the room to make a person feel awkward.*

Mr. Roesch handed me a shingle of food, just as he had for the last few days, but the gesture seemed hollow and strained. After several minutes of anxious silence, he cleared his throat.

"Look, Zachary. It's sorta been brought to my attention" — he flicked his eyes briefly toward Kenni — "that I might have been a little too hard on you last night. I need you to know I wasn't upset. Not really, anyway. I just want to make sure you're ready for whatever we're going to run into on this trip."

Kenni interrupted. "We also need you to realize that none of us really knows what we might run into." She looked significantly at Mr. Roesch. "None of us."

He had the decency to look embarrassed at that. Then he shrugged. "Look, son, there's still a lot I can teach you. But there's also a lot that I don't know. And I have to be smart enough to admit it, same as you. So as much as it pains me to have to say this, I owe you an apology."

He grinned good-naturedly as he said that, and I had to smile back. And just like that, most of the tension dissipated.

But as we finished breaking camp and got our group on the road again, I couldn't help thinking about some of the implications of everything that had happened. I thought about it in silence as we rode, and for the first time in two days, Mr. Roesch seemed content to let me do so without shoving his lessons down my throat. He rode a bit behind the rest of us, silent and brooding. I rode ahead of him but behind Robin and Kenni, who led the way, chuckling and speaking quietly to one another.

The morning was clear and bright—yet another beautiful East Texas day. Birds called through the trees. Bella and Cricket traipsed in and out of the brush ahead, occasionally bounding off after something they scented then reappearing a few minutes later, tongues lolling and tails wagging at the great fun. Everything seemed peaceful except for Mr. Roesch.

And me. I considered all that had led up to our confrontation the previous night. "You have to learn to conceal your emotions better than that, Zach," he had told me. And there was his reluctance to take the message from the satellite at face value. He obviously didn't really trust whoever had sent it. Not completely, anyway. And the more I thought about it, the more I had to admit that I had been much *too* trusting. There was simply too much I didn't know, and I realized that my lack of knowledge applied to several facets of my current state of affairs.

For the next few hours, I tried to look over what I knew of the situation with some of the impartiality he'd been trying to teach me. There were implications in the fact that my father and the rest of the council had sent Mr. Roesch, a former lawyer, as the Rejas representative to what might or might not be an official representative of the national government.

And ever since he had pointed out that *I* also represented Rejas simply by virtue of accompanying him as his assistant, he had been stuffing my head full of all sorts of what-if scenarios. I tried to think through all the possible reasons.

Okay, so he didn't want me to screw up the meeting with whoever we were going to meet — that one was obvious. And yes, I had to admit that I likely would have done exactly that. But there seemed to be more to it than that, and I needed to figure it out. My learning to conduct myself properly was more than him just not wanting me to embarrass him, or Rejas, or even myself. He seemed to be grooming me. And the more I thought about that, the more it worried me.

Our new companions were yet another mystery. Who were they? How had they known where we would be the previous night? What was their relationship to Mr. Roesch?

I wondered why Kenni's words had swayed him. I'd never seen Mr. Roesch argue too much back home. He was always pretty quiet. But he also didn't really knuckle under too well. Not to anyone.

I had watched him listen to what people had to say on many occasions, and he always appeared to consider their words and value their opinions. But I had as often as not seen him completely disregard their advice after they'd said their piece. It was as if he listened, weighed the evidence, and then did whatever he wanted based on his own interpretation of the facts. *Likely another facet of his training as a lawyer.*

But there was more to his deference to Kenni than just that. He appeared to take her words as absolute. And the more I considered that, the more I realized I was thinking about the situation all wrong. I was concentrating on Mr. Roesch's reaction to Kenni when I should have been examining the question of what it was about Kenni that Mr. Roesch considered so deserving of such regard.

Yes, that felt right. I looked up to where Kenni rode beside

Robin. As if she knew my eyes were on her, she turned to look at me and smiled. Then she jerked her chin, gesturing for me to approach her.

So I reined Tallulah over to ride on Kenni's left while Robin rode on her right. She smiled again in that friendly way she had. "You're awfully quiet this morning."

"Yes, ma'am. I've had a lot to think about. And Mr. Roesch seems to be pretty caught up in his own thoughts too."

She turned in her saddle and looked back at him. Then she nodded. "Yeah, I guess he is. Guess I should have expected that reaction."

"Ma'am?"

She grinned again. "All right. First of all, you're gonna have to drop the *ma'am* stuff. Unless you want me to start calling you *sir*."

"Sorry. It's just the way I was raised. But I'll try."

"That's all I can ask. And as for Mr. Roesch..." She paused as if trying to think of what to say. "Mark and I have a little history."

"I gathered that much. He acts... different around you."

"I suppose." She shrugged. "We were together on D-day. We met under unusual circumstances."

Beside her, Robin guffawed. Kenni sighed. "And yes. Robin already knows the story."

"Must be some story, then."

"It is. But not all of it is mine to tell."

"But Robin gets to know?"

Kenni paused. "Something you'll learn—you don't keep secrets from those you love. It breeds distrust. So I suppose what I should have said is that some of the story isn't mine to tell *you*."

She said it without malice, which made it hard to get upset with her.

"Besides, someday you're going to want me to keep something secret for you too. And won't you feel better knowing that I can be trusted to do so?"

"I guess so."

"But I can tell you that Mark and I went through some life-altering changes together. We lost loved ones, and we made some friends." She looked up the road into the distance, and at first I thought she was going to stop talking. But after a few seconds, she continued. "I guess just about everyone has a similar story in that regard. But most of all, we learned to trust each other implicitly. I haven't seen Mark in more than ten years, but still, I would trust him with my life."

Then she turned those eyes back to gaze intently at me. "And I believe you should do the same. He has nothing but your best interests in mind. Still... let me talk to him." She looked up at the sun overhead. "You two ride on ahead. I'll have a word with Mark."

With that, she pulled her mount back to fall into place beside Mr. Roesch, leaving me and Robin to ride beside one another. I looked at Robin. "Is she always so cryptic?"

Robin shrugged. "She can't always put what she knows into words. Sometimes she gets so much that it's hard for her to tell what's important, so she doesn't really know what needs to be said until it doesn't need to be said any longer."

I just stared at her.

Robin apparently realized how that sounded and laughed. "Yeah, talk about being cryptic. I guess I just topped Kenni, didn't I?"

"Well, I sure don't understand what you're talking about, so I guess so." I laughed along with her.

"You know how she said that some of what happened to Mark wasn't her story to tell?"

"Yeah."

"Well, some of what happened to Kenni isn't my story to tell, either."

"Now, why doesn't that surprise me?" I asked.

"Look, if you want to know what happened to Mark, he has to tell you."

"And Kenni?"

"Once you get Mark's story, I imagine Kenni will fill in her part too."

CHAPTER 9
STORY TIME

THE REST OF THE DAY was a little awkward what with nobody telling anybody else's stories. And since I seemed to be the only person who didn't already know those stories, it basically felt like everyone was avoiding me specifically. I was determined to resolve that problem as soon as the opportunity presented itself, but for the time being, there was nothing I could do about it.

A few hours after lunch, there was a little distraction as we wandered through what had once been a small town. But like so many East Texas towns, it seemed to be completely abandoned. It wasn't a complete waste of time, however, as a little scavenging through Uncle Benny's Quick Stop gained us some powdered-drink mix and a box of dried noodles. Rats had chewed one corner of the box, and a few of the packets inside were ruined, but eight of them still looked good.

The distraction and good fortune seemed to lighten everyone's mood a bit as we got back on the road. About an hour or so before sunset, we found a spot where a small stream had washed out part of the highway. The dogs caught the scent of something and raced ahead, barking excitedly at the edge of the stream. Their barking spoke to me of danger and challenge, and I drew Tallulah up to see what they had cornered.

As I approached, Cricket pounced in and back, dodging back

and forth at something on the bank—something that struck with such speed that she barely evaded it. "Cricket! Bella! Come!" Heart pounding, I grabbed my bow and swung out of the saddle as the girls returned to my side. I didn't bother to string the bow, instead running to the stream and using it as a simple pole to pin the snake that had been resting on a warm rock beside the water.

"Zach? What is it?"

"Cottonmouth!" And with the head pinned tightly, I drew my belt knife and quickly decapitated the thing. I kicked a hole in the soft dirt and tossed the head into it, safely burying it before I brought the rest of the snake back to the others. "Are cottonmouths edible?"

Mr. Roesch shrugged. "I have no idea. Kenni?"

"I don't know either. I know rattlesnake is. I guess we can try it and find out."

So we made camp there. Robin and I tromped around, beating the bushes and overturning rocks to make sure there were no other snakes. Once we felt relatively safe, we picketed the horses. I let Robin do the grooming while I started cleaning the snake for dinner. I kept an eye on Kenni, watching as she dug the fire pit, mentally confirming that I knew how she did it. As I began pulling the skin from the snake, I wrinkled my nose at the smell.

Mr. Roesch must have been watching me. "Something wrong?"

"Just smells fishy. You still want to try it?"

He walked over and sniffed of it. "We can try it, but it might also be a good idea to have the dogs bring in some rabbit. Just in case."

I grinned. "Bella, Cricket, hunt!" The two of them darted into the brush.

"I'll get some water." He went back to his pack to get a small pot, put it over the fire to boil, and took the snake from me. Cutting it into bite-sized chunks, he tossed it into the water along with some of the noodles and a flavor packet that came with them.

The girls returned after a short while with another brace of rabbits that I cleaned, again giving them the entrails as a reward. I gave the rest of the rabbits to Mr. Roesch, who pulled a packet of cornmeal, as well as some salt and dried jalapeños, from his saddlebags. Kenni took out her belt knife, walked over to a nearby shrub, and cut several small branches that held bunches of tiny red berries. She broke one of the berry clusters loose and handed it to him. "Stick these in the meat while it cooks. It gives it a citrus flavor."

Mr. Roesch looked at them questioningly before holding them to his nose and sniffing. "What is it?"

"Sumac."

"Are you crazy?" He tossed it away and wiped his hand on his pants.

"Depends on who you ask. But it's not poison sumac. Different leaves. Different berries. Poison sumac has light-green or white berries in clusters that hang downward, and the leaves have smooth edges." I watched as she held another branch out to him. She pointed. "These leaves have serrated edges. There are a lot of edible varieties, but they all have red or purple berries, and the clusters grow pointing upward." She cut the berry cluster loose and tossed the leaves to the ground. "It should give the meat a nice tang."

"If you say so." He shrugged and skewered the meat with the small branches.

I was intrigued and walked to the shrub she had cut them from. The berry clusters were distinctive, and I realized I had seen them growing along the trail for most of the day. I stripped several of the tiny things loose, rolling them in my hand. I sniffed them, but there was no particular scent. Finally, I popped a few in my mouth, chewing tentatively. "Holy crap." I spat the bitter, astringent mess out. "That's nasty!"

Robin laughed as she stepped out of the brush nearby. "You aren't supposed to chew them. The flavor is in the coating, not in the actual berry." She had a handful of leaves that she stuffed into a pouch on her belt as she walked toward me. She smiled as she took some of the tiny berries from my hand and popped them in her mouth. "You just suck on them for a few minutes."

I followed her example and was pleasantly surprised at the tart flavor.

"Better?"

"Much."

"You can chew the shoots too. In fact, if you get them while they're young enough, you can eat them like tiny stalks of celery."

She pulled a small growth from the base of the shrub and peeled the bark from it. After breaking it in half, she handed me part of it and popped the other in her mouth.

I licked the green shoot and raised an eyebrow at the tart taste.

Robin laughed at my expression. "Go ahead and eat it."

Somewhat tentatively, I bit down on the little stalk. It was tangy, and as Kenni had said, it had a citrusy taste. I nodded. "Not bad." I looked once more at the plant, memorizing it so I would be able to readily identify it in the future.

"Are the leaves good too?"

She shrugged. "I wouldn't say they're good, but they won't poison you."

"Then why save them?"

She looked puzzled until I pointed to the pouch in which she had stuffed the handful of leaves.

"Oh! That's not sumac. There's a patch of comfrey back there." She pointed to where she had emerged from the thicket.

"So comfrey is edible?"

"Yes, but I collect it for its healing properties. It's one of the best medicinal herbs around."

"Robin was a nurse in the Old Days." Kenni spoke from behind me. "She's continued as an herbalist since then."

I was intrigued. Herbal healing had always interested me. I decided to get her to teach me what she could whenever we had enough time.

Half an hour later, we all congregated around the fire, munching the rabbit and some poke salad in silence. After only a bite or two, we decided as a group that the snake and noodles would better serve as dog food. It wasn't inedible, but it wasn't appetizing, either. And we had fresh rabbit that was oh, so much better.

I was picking at my meal, trying to figure out how to start the conversation I wanted, when Kenni gave me the opening I was looking for. "Tomorrow morning, we'll probably get to what's left of Carthage."

Mr. Roesch took the bait. "What's left of it? What do you mean?"

Kenni grunted. "Don't you remember? That was the town where there'd been a fire." She looked at me. "Most of it was gone, burned to the ground."

I seized the opening. "So you guys have been this way before?"

Mr. Roesch sat on a log, quietly studying the fire pit in the evening light. His expression was stoic, stubbornly refusing to show that he'd been manipulated by his friend. Finally, he shook his head and glared at her. "That was low."

Kenni shrugged. "We can't keep talking around it. Carthage is where we have to decide which direction we're going."

"So?"

She gestured to me. "Zachary, you have a map, don't you?"

How did she know that? "Yes, ma'am. Sorry. I mean, yes, I do." I pulled the map out of my pack and handed it to her.

She unfolded the crackling paper and traced a route with her finger. I watched over her shoulder while Robin held a small torch over the map so we could all see it better.

"We're right around here on Highway 59." Kenni pointed to a stretch between two towns. "Uncle Benny's was back at Tenaha." She pointed to a dot. "Now, the stream here is too small to show up on the map, so I don't know for sure exactly where we are, but judging by the amount of time we've been traveling, I'd guess we're just over halfway between Tenaha and Carthage."

Robin nodded. "Looks about right."

Kenni traced a line on the map from Carthage to the northwest. "If we head up 149 toward Tatum, we eventually have to go past East Texas Regional."

Mr. Roesch clenched his jaw.

She continued. "If we keep going north on 59 instead —"

His tone was flat as he completed her sentence. "We go through Marshall."

She nodded. "Either way, it's going to be rough on you." He started to say something, but she shook her head. "You know I'm right. It's only natural."

That was my opening. I cleared my throat. "Sorry, but why is it going to be rough?"

Everyone was silent. Mr. Roesch stared into the fire while Kenni and Robin looked at him. Kenni gently prodded him. "Mark, tell him." She put a hand on his shoulder. "It will do you good to talk about it."

"What about your part? What about what happened to you?"

"So we'll tell him together. It'll do us both good. And it will help him to understand some things."

He sighed deeply. When he looked up at me, I was shocked to see tears in the man's eyes. He began. "Kenni and I met on D-day. I lived in the city of Marshall, Texas, at the time. I was at East Texas Regional Airport to pick up my wife and daughter."

Kenni chimed in. "And I had just flown in to meet my brother. I was on leave and —"

"On leave?" I interrupted. "What's that mean?"

"It meant I had some time off. I was a Marine."

"Like in the army?"

"No, not like in the army." She seemed insulted. "The US had different branches of the military who worked in different arenas."

Now I was really getting confused. "Arenas?"

"We had the Air Force, who specialized in air warfare. The Navy handled aquatic warfare. And the Army focused on land battles."

"So what were the Marines, then?"

"Marines were trained to work in all arenas. Think of the other branches as specialists. They knew a lot about their particular type of fighting. But the Marines did it all. We fought in the air, on the land, *and* in the water."

"And you were one of them?"

"I was."

I was impressed.

"Now, can we get back to the story?"

"Sorry," I said.

"I was on leave to visit home on D-day."

Mr. Roesch picked up the narrative again. "We were both at the airport when the EMP hit." He took a deep breath. "You already know about the EMP and what it did."

I nodded.

"My wife and daughter were in a plane when it lost power." His tears flowed freely now as he spoke. I'd never known he had a family before he got to Rejas. It made sense. So many other people had lost loved ones that day and in the hard times after it. But he'd never spoken of it.

"The plane crashed and set off a chain reaction of explosions at the airport. The crash—" He stopped, unable to continue for the moment.

Kenni came to his rescue. "The crash killed his family. The explosions at the airport got my brother." She took a deep breath. "And my lover at the time."

Robin took Kenni's hand and squeezed.

"Mark and I barely made it out alive."

We all sat in silence for a bit. "Mr. Roesch? Why did you come to Rejas? You said you lived in Marshall."

"Marshall was also where my wife and daughter lived. I couldn't go back there."

And I understood. Once we reached Carthage, Mr. Roesch would have to choose between going back to the place he had once lived with his family and the place where they had died.

CHAPTER 10
BELIEF

THEY WEREN'T KIDDING WHEN THEY said Carthage had burned. I wouldn't have known a town had once been there if Kenni hadn't pointed out some of the remains. Along Highway 59, there was little other than the road itself and a few crumbled bridges to distinguish the town from the forest that had begun to reclaim it. Even the main highway had succumbed to the ground cover in many places. It was pretty obvious we weren't going to find anything worth scavenging there.

We passed a slight depression, and Kenni stopped, looking up and down its length. "Zachary, can I see that map again?"

I pulled it from my pack and passed it over to her.

She sat on her horse for a few minutes, looking at the ditch then back at the map. "Mark? I think it's time to make a decision."

Mr. Roesch pulled his mount up alongside hers. "Not that I'm arguing, mind you, but what did you find that makes you say that?"

She leaned over, holding the map closer to him. I leaned over so I could see as well, shading my eyes against the late-morning sun. "I'm pretty sure this is where we are." She pointed to a spot on the map.

"That's pretty specific. Why do you think we're there?"

She pointed to the right, up the ditch, to where a piece of steel, straight and narrow, stuck out of the earth. It spanned horizontally about three feet over the ditch and seemed to have just been cut off at that point. Mr. Roesch squinted. "Is that a piece of railroad track?"

"Looks like it. And right here on the map is where Highway 59 intersects with the railroad and a small creek in Carthage. I think this ditch is the dried-up creek bed."

Mr. Roesch and I looked up and down the depression much as Kenni had. Mr. Roesch nodded. "Looks about right."

"Which means we're about half a mile from the middle of where Carthage used to be. That means we need to decide what direction to go."

Mr. Roesch sighed. "Okay. I've been trying to think about this as objectively as I can."

"And?"

"Burns Flat is northwest, toward the airport. But if we go that way directly, it takes us closer to the DFW metro area, and we already know for a fact that it was hit hard on D-day."

"So you're worried about fallout?"

"Yeah. The closer we go toward Dallas, the stronger the chances of running into it. No need chancing it."

"So" — she traced a finger up the map — "if we stay on 59, we go up through Marshall and into Oklahoma. Eventually we'll hit Interstate 40, and we could take it west all the way to the spaceport."

Mr. Roesch shook his head. "That looks like it would add at least another week to the trip."

"You on a schedule?"

"Not really. I told the council I'd try to be back in six to eight weeks. But everyone knows that nothing's a certainty these days. Still, an extra week before we even get there seems a bit much." He ran his finger to a point just north of Marshall. "What about if we go north to Jefferson then cut northwest on 49 through Paris? We could get a more direct route without taking as much extra time and still keep far enough away from the DFW area that we should be safe."

Kenni nodded. "Looks like a good compromise to me."

So we continued north, passing through the crumbling remains of a dead town.

We camped that night on the banks of the Sabine River. A nice breeze had rolled in, and cloud cover had cooled us off for the last few hours of the day. All in all, it was one of those summer evenings that just made you content to be part of the world. We found a place to break for the night, and the weather was nice enough that we briefly considered fording the river and pushing on for a bit longer, but Mr. Roesch squashed that idea.

"We can break here, catch some fish, get a good night's rest, and start fresh tomorrow. Or we can cross the river, move on for a few more miles, and camp somewhere up the road in our wet clothes. I vote for sleeping dry with a belly full of fish."

I had to admit he made some good points.

Our routine was pretty well established by then. We all knew our jobs and were learning to do them pretty efficiently. Less than an hour after we'd dismounted, we were sitting around a fire pit, watching a couple of spiced catfish cook on some cedar shingles.

I sniffed appreciatively. "That smells great!"

Mr. Roesch just grunted, never looking up from the fire. I looked over at Kenni, questioning her with my eyes. She shook her head. I took that as a hint to let him be. So we all sat around in awkward silence while the big man brooded over the food.

Eating was more of the same. We sat looking at one another, waiting for someone to break the silence. Bella pushed her head into my lap, inviting me to scratch her behind the ears. Cricket, who was giving Robin a similar treatment, preferred belly rubs. As Robin reached down to scratch her, the dog rolled over onto her back. Robin chuckled and rubbed Cricket's belly.

"She really is a glutton for attention, isn't she?"

"Yes, ma'am," I said. "She doesn't trust people easily. Well, not usually. But when she does, she trusts them completely. She wouldn't expose her belly to you otherwise."

Robin smiled at that, still rubbing Cricket's tummy as the dog grunted in pleasure.

A few minutes later, Mr. Roesch finished his fish and tossed his shingle into the fire. He stared at the flames as they consumed the split wood.

Kenni spoke softly to him. "Having trouble sleeping again, aren't you?"

He simply nodded.

"Nikki?"

Another nod.

"Can you hear her?"

He shook his head. "It's just that damned crash over and over."

Kenni laid a friendly hand on his arm. "I'll see if I can get her to talk tonight."

Wondering what they were talking about, I looked from his face to hers. Then I saw Bella and Cricket roll over and look at her. Their tails had stopped wagging, but I didn't feel they were frightened, either. They were paying close attention as if watching something they weren't used to seeing. Something I couldn't see. I didn't realize I was staring at Kenni until she looked my way and her brow furrowed. "What?"

I looked away, afraid I would offend her. "Nothing. Sorry." I looked back up to find her still staring at me. "I'm sorry. I'm just trying to figure out what's going on. I'm still odd man out, and I know it. You talk about things and people that I don't know, and it's like everybody knows some special secret except me." I looked at Mr. Roesch. "I'm trying to be respectful of what you went through and the fact that we're heading to your old home and the memories it has to be giving you. I know it's got to be like torture for you, so I don't want to… I don't know. I just don't want to make things worse for you."

We all sat in silence for a few minutes. Even the dogs settled back down, acting once more as if nothing in the world mattered except getting belly rubs and ear scratches while they lay beside the fire. Then Kenni spoke.

"Back before D-day, there was a radio host my dad used to

listen to. I don't remember his name, but he always told little stories about famous people. Only he didn't tell you what they were famous for at first. And he didn't tell you what their names were. He would tell you some little side story about how they gained the ambition—or acquired the talent—to become that famous person instead of just an ordinary Joe like the rest of us. At the end, he gave the big reveal about who the person was.

"He called it *The Rest of the Story,* and it was a pretty popular program." She looked at Mr. Roesch and then pursed her lips. "I guess it's time to tell you the rest of our story."

I sat up, letting the dog beside me contentedly warm herself by the fire. I concentrated my entire being on Kenni's words.

"Mark helped me get home after D-day. Shortly after we got there, my mother died."

Now, *that* was an abrupt way to start a story. "I'm sorry."

"Don't be. Death isn't really the end of things." Kenni looked at me, her gaze drilling into me. "That's sort of the point of this little story. Death is just a transition. Do you believe that, Zachary?"

I shrugged. "I don't really know. I know I'm supposed to believe it. Most of the people in Rejas believe it."

But Kenni was shaking her head. "That's not really what I mean. I'm not talking about religious faith." She leaned forward. "No, when I talk about death not being the end, I'm talking about something much simpler than religious belief and salvation. I'm simply asking if you believe that we're more than just a bunch of electrical impulses firing through some chemical soup housed inside a bag of meat and bone. Do you accept the possibility that there's something more to us? Something that's part of that combination of electrical impulses and chemistry and physiology but can still exist without it?"

"Well, I suppose so." I nodded. "Yes, ma'am."

"No—not, 'I suppose.' Do you really *believe* it? Deep down in your gut?" She peered intently at me as if whatever answer I gave were of supreme importance. "Think about it before you answer."

Though not really sure where the conversation was going, I knew it was a turning point in my relationship with Kenni. So I searched my thoughts on the matter, really examining them. I had long since rebelled against my peers' religious beliefs. I'd even gone through a short period where I had decided I was an atheist, eschewing any possibility of a creator. I thought that the idea that someone could tell me there was some supreme being that no one could see or hear was more vanity than faith. After all, who were they to tell me what to believe?

Later, I had realized my *refusal* to believe was just as vain as their insistence that I do so. I had no more proof such a being *didn't* exist than they had that He did. So I had come to accept that there were many things I simply didn't know about the world... things I would likely *never* know. That had been a turning point in my understanding of life. I had learned to accept other people's beliefs as a viable possibility, which had eventually brought me a strange contentment in my dealings with them.

Like Kenni, I didn't begrudge or belittle their faith — I simply couldn't accept it for myself. But she also made it clear that religious belief wasn't the type of faith she referred to. She was asking if I believed there was a possibility of something beyond life as we knew it. And that was a question I had long since asked myself.

"Yes. There's always the possibility."

"And do you believe there may be people who can more easily access this part of themselves, who can see things others can't?"

Once more, the girls perked up, watching Kenni intently. What was it about her that grabbed their attention? Were they seeing something? I'd always heard stories about dogs and cats being able to see ghosts, though I'd never really believed them to be anything more than old wives' tales. But I was starting to wonder if there was something to them.

She smiled and nodded. "I see you do."

What was she talking about? The whole conversation had just gone off track. "Wait. What does —"

"My brother called it 'the knowing.' Mark calls it 'seeing.' I've heard it called second sight, clairvoyance, ESP, or any number of other things. I've even had people over the last few years call me a witch."

I swallowed. "And you say you have this" — I hesitated — "second sight?"

She nodded. "I believe a lot of people have similar gifts to one extent or another. Whether or not they choose to accept or acknowledge them is another matter." She gestured toward Bella and Cricket. "Most animals can sense it. And I've seen how you interact with them. You have a real gift with animals, don't you?"

"Well, sure, but that's just—"

"Just what?" She grinned. "It's something more than most people have—an unquantifiable thing that some have and others don't. It's a gift that can't be explained by normal means."

I looked at Mr. Roesch. She said he had called it "seeing," so he knew about her claim. "Mr. Roesch?"

He looked up from the fire then looked at me and shook his head. "Like she said, it's nothing I can explain. I've seen her predict the future. I've seen her tell me things no one could possibly know." He looked back into the fire. "I've seen her talk to the dead."

Kenni laid a hand on his shoulder and squeezed it before turning back to me. "Now that we don't spend all our time watching television or staring at computer screens, I think we're getting back in touch with that part of ourselves. I think most people, maybe all people, have the capacity for it in one degree or another." She looked keenly at me. "With you, it's an affinity for animals."

"What? What do you mean?"

"You have a touch of it. I've seen the way you look at me when I get a flash. What is it you see?"

I stared at her. "Nothing really. It's the girls. They change. It's like they see something no one else can see."

She nodded then turned to Mr. Roesch. "Mark, what did you see the night Mama died?"

He didn't bother looking up. "You know what I saw."

"But Zachary doesn't."

He looked at me again and shrugged. "I saw Kenni's mother the night she died. She laid her hands on Kenni's head. And I saw a glow. It was a soft golden glow on her hands where they touched Kenni." He smiled sadly and looked over to Kenni. "It was beautiful."

She looked back at me. "In ancient times, people simply accepted that these things existed. Sometimes they called them gifts, and sometimes curses. Sometimes the abilities were embraced, and sometimes they were feared and reviled. But even as recently as half a century ago, most people accepted that they were real.

"Then we grew more educated, learned more about technology and science. We were taught that there was a logical explanation for everything, even what we had once believed to be unexplainable. Science replaced faith." She shrugged. "We lost our ability to believe in anything else."

Mr. Roesch snorted. "Until someone like you comes along and shoves it in our faces."

"So I propose we conduct a little experiment." Kenni looked at me. "Zachary, would you mind participating?"

"No, I guess not."

"Now, I'm going to try to see someone on the other side."

"Other side?"

"Just let me know if you or the dogs see anything."

"O-Okay." Inwardly, I shrugged, but I kept watch. I shifted my gaze between her and the girls, watching for the subtle change in their attitude that I had seen earlier. For almost two minutes, nothing happened. "Kenni?"

"Shh!"

So I shushed. Another few minutes passed, and my eyes were burning. I kept resisting the urge to blink, afraid I would miss something. A few minutes more, and I was tired of looking. And suddenly, Bella's ears twitched. She raised her head, watching Kenni intently. I looked at Cricket. Her eyes were riveted on Kenni as well. "There!" I said.

Kenni closed her eyes for a moment and took a deep breath as if she had just completed some physical task. Then she looked at Mr. Roesch. "You're right. Nikki was trying to get you to see something. She says you need to be careful when you go home. There will be bad people."

"Nikki?" I asked.

"My first wife," Mr. Roesch answered without looking at me.

"And, ah... didn't you say she... I'm sorry, but isn't she...?"

"Dead?" he said. "Yes. But isn't that what we were just talking about?"

I turned to Kenni. "So you're telling me you can speak to the dead?"

"It's like I said. There are some people who have certain gifts that others don't."

I shook my head, not willing to take the leap with her. "I admit I said I thought it was possible, but that doesn't mean I fully believe it, either."

"You aren't willing to believe your own eyes?"

"My own eyes? I didn't see anyone but us. I definitely didn't see a ghost!"

"But you saw your dogs react?"

"Sure, but that doesn't mean anything. Just because they act a little... odd doesn't mean something actually happened."

"It doesn't mean it didn't happen, either."

I knew better than to get drawn into that kind of argument. "So we're basically saying that something might or might not have happened? Do you know how that sounds?"

"Of course. I don't expect you to take my word for it. I just want you to remember it. File it away, and keep an open mind for now."

"About what?"

"About what we've been talking about. About the idea that just because we can't see something doesn't mean it's not there. About the idea that there just might be people who can touch the supernatural."

"What?"

Kenni smiled in that knowing way she seemed to have.

"Supernatural simply means that something is beyond the natural. Just like your gift."

"My gift?" My voice nearly squeaked at the sudden shift in topic. "I don't have a supernatural gift."

"So everyone can gain the same affinity with animals that you have?"

I thought about it for a second. Everyone had always told me I had a special way with animals. It had taken me a fraction of the time to train Bella and Cricket that it took even the best trainer back in Rejas. And I'd always been able to calm temperamental horses and livestock. Everyone had always called it a gift. But I'd never thought anything much of it.

She looked at me, waiting for an answer.

"That's not the same thing at all," I said.

"Why not?"

"Because having a way with animals is..." I didn't know how to finish the sentence.

"Normal?" Kenni asked. "If that were the case, then everyone would have it, wouldn't they?"

"No. Being a good shot with a bow isn't an ability everyone has. That doesn't make it a supernatural ability."

Kenni nodded. "Granted. Are you a good shot?"

"Yes, ma'am."

"And could you teach someone else to become a good shot?"

"With enough time, sure."

"And could you teach them how you handle animals?"

I clapped my mouth shut.

"Zachary, I've had a feeling since I met you that there's something in you that I'm supposed to help. I feel like you have your own gifts and that I'm supposed to help train you."

Great, someone else who wants to start teaching me. I was really getting tired of all the lessons.

"No, I'm not going to start filling your days with lessons like Mark does."

It really bothered me when she did that.

"At least not right away," she said. "All I ask is that you keep your eyes and ears open to anything unusual."

"I guess I can do that."

"And can you try to keep your mind open as well?"

I hesitated. I didn't want to lie to her, but neither did I really believe in some kind of — what had she called it? Second sight.

"I'll try."

"Good enough for now." She sighed. "Now, why don't you and Robin go get some rest? Mark and I have to talk."

Shaken, I took advantage of the dismissal and walked away from the discussion she and Mr. Roesch were going to have. Whatever it was, I had the distinct impression that I didn't want to have anything to do with it. I grabbed my gear and moved away from the river, into the tree line. Spotting a pair of trees that fit my needs, I began slinging my hammock, losing myself in the personal ritual. Fifteen minutes later, I was staring up through the tops of the trees, rocking gently in the breeze.

CHAPTER 11
PERSPECTIVE

WE RODE IN RELATIVE SILENCE. I didn't know what Mr. Roesch and Kenni had discussed after Robin and I had left, but he seemed thoughtful the next day. And her discussion with me had left me more than just a little uneasy as well. The idea that I might have some kind of special powers was ludicrous, but it bothered me that all the others seemed ready to accept that Kenni had them.

I couldn't really put my finger on why it bothered me so much. It wasn't as if she had tried to do anything wrong or pressure me into anything. The more I thought about it, the more it seemed like yet another instance of me not controlling my own destiny — another person who seemed to know more about where my life was heading than I did.

I finally gave up with that line of thinking. There was nothing I could do about it for the moment, so my time was better served by paying attention to the road ahead. The map showed we would more than likely be in Marshall before evening, and Mr. Roesch had mentioned he wanted to go by his old home. Personally, I didn't think that was a very good idea. But putting myself in his shoes, I also realized how hard it would be to have come all that way, gotten so close, and then not gone by to see it.

When we began to encounter rusted hulks of old automobiles, I knew we must be getting close. Abandoned cars were commonplace on the highway, but they were more frequent along the stretch leading into Marshall. I figured it was a good indication that we were approaching a relatively large town—at least by any standard I was used to.

I wondered how big it had really been. "Mr. Roesch?"

He looked at me but didn't speak. His raised eyebrow was the only indication he was listening to me.

"We're passing an awful lot of cars. Does that mean Marshall was a big city?"

He smiled slightly and shook his head. "Not really. I think there were twenty-five or thirty thousand people."

It was my turn to raise an eyebrow. *Thirty thousand? Rejas has fewer than three thousand.* "That's not a big city?"

He chuckled. "I guess *big* is a relative term, isn't it? No. By pre-D standards, thirty thousand was a decent-sized town, but the really big cities usually had millions of people living in them."

"Millions?" That many people living together was almost incomprehensible.

He looked at me quizzically. "Don't you remember anything from before D-day? Your dad told me y'all came from Houston. That was one of the largest cities in the country."

I shook my head. "I was eight years old when it happened. I guess I remember bits and pieces. Little things like riding in a car and having a birthday cake with fancy flowers made out of icing. I remember television. I even remember going someplace with Mom and Dad to see a movie once. But I don't really remember very much."

"You have no idea how sad that makes me."

I shrugged. "I used to think about it. We talk about it sometimes."

"We?"

"Some of us who aren't quite old enough to remember too much of what it used to be like. We talk about what we do remember." I looked at him sheepishly. "It's not very much. School helped some. They kept pictures up and taught us about the Old Days in history classes. But those of us who remember much of it have been out of school for a few years now."

"Don't you go to the library?"

"I do. Not many others my age do, though. It's hard to get time to go there. Everyone has a life to lead, and going into town just to look at books takes too much time away from the farm, or the forges, or whatever it is you have to do during the day. You know how it is."

"I guess I never really thought about that part of it." Mr. Roesch looked at another line of vehicles as we rode past. "So much lost."

"Dad always told me we shouldn't worry too much about it. He said we lost a lot of bad stuff along with the good and that we just have to make sure to appreciate what we have, and not dwell on what we don't."

"Like?"

I pointed to the dogs. "Bella and Cricket. He tells me that if things were the same as they were before D-day, I wouldn't have had the time to train them and spend so much time hunting with them. He says I probably wouldn't even have learned to ride a horse.

"So I guess it would have been cool to learn to drive a car. And I wish the motorcycle still ran. I remember learning to ride that when I was a kid." I grinned. "And I'll be the first to admit just how awesome it was. But the way Dad explained it to me was that a lot of the stuff he misses — and the rest of the people who were around before D-day miss — I *don't* miss because I never really knew it. And I have new stuff that you guys didn't have growing up. He says life's harder in a lot of ways, but at least he doesn't have to worry about paying the mortgage."

Mr. Roesch chuckled. "I've always said your dad's a smart man."

"I like to think so."

We rode on for a few minutes before I asked something I'd always wondered about. "Mr. Roesch?"

"Hmm?"

"What's a mortgage?"

CHAPTER 12
OWEN

B Y AFTERNOON, THE ROAD HAD widened to twice the size I was used to seeing, and bare concrete showed through in the center, though it was in pretty bad shape. The forest hadn't encroached as far as it had in most places, and several buildings were more or less standing about fifty yards from the road. As we passed one, I saw movement in one of the windows, and I wondered if I should string my bow. A man emerged from the darkened interior and waved to us. Mr. Roesch waved back.

"Trade?" the man yelled. "News?"

Kenni and Robin pulled back alongside us. "What do you think?" Kenni asked Mr. Roesch.

"Looks harmless enough. And we might get some information about the road ahead. You get any…?" He waggled his hand back and forth in the air.

Kenni cocked an eyebrow at him. "Is that your way of asking if I had any sort of seeing about him?"

"Well…"

"No, I didn't get anything. I'm not a mind reader."

"Damn close, though." He looked back at the man standing in the clearing before the two-story building. "Give us a second," he yelled.

The man nodded and walked back to the doorway.

"You armed, Kenni?"

"Shift your horse a few feet forward where he can't see me for a few seconds, and I will be."

Mr. Roesch twitched his reins and moved forward. Without moving her head, Kenni reached into her saddlebag and pulled out a bundle wrapped in a dirty white rag. She unwrapped it quickly and tucked the pistol under her shirt in the back of her pants.

"Is that my SIG?" Mr. Roesch asked.

Kenni grinned. "A long time ago, it was."

He looked over her at Robin. "Miss Scott? You armed?"

"Shotgun wrapped up under my leg on the saddle."

He turned to me. "I know you have your bow, but I also see it's not strung. I've seen how quickly you can remedy that, so just keep your eyes open."

I nodded.

"Got your blades on you?"

Another nod.

"Your dad says you're good with them, so I won't baby you." He spoke to all of us. "I don't expect trouble, but be ready if it shows up."

He turned his horse toward the man sitting in front of the building. We followed, eyes open.

The man smiled as we approached. "Welcome, folks. Where you from?"

Mr. Roesch spoke for us. "We're up from Rejas."

"Rejas, eh? Town doing all right?"

"We had a rough time of it for a while, but we're doing all right now. About three thousand strong."

The man's eyebrows went up. "Three thousand? That's fantastic! I'm not even sure there's that many left in Marshall."

Mr. Roesch dismounted, and the man immediately stuck out his hand. "I'm Owen. Owen Jakeman."

"Mark Roesch." He pointed to the rest of us and gave our names.

"Well, it's a pleasure to meet you folks. You looking for any supplies? I got all sorts of stuff inside. Food, gear, even got some artwork my wife painted. She's pretty good."

"We'll be happy to look around, but mainly, we just want to see what news you can give us about the road ahead."

Owen nodded. "Fair enough. First thing I can tell you is that those are fine horses. And if you're going through Marshall, you need to keep your eyes and ears open. There's a shortage of decent livestock in the area, and lots of gangs are popping up. Not as bad as the old days after the bombs but bad enough. One of the main things they're stealing is horses."

We all looked at one another.

"We appreciate the warning," Mr. Roesch said. "We'll definitely keep a close eye out."

"Good. Now, if you want to come inside, I can at least offer you a few minutes rest out of the sun and a cold glass of water." He turned and headed back into the building. "Come on into the front office."

"Front office?" I asked.

"Back before the bombs, this was a hotel. I still keep a few rooms cleaned in case someone wants to trade for a night's sleep, but to be perfectly honest, that doesn't happen very often. So I turned the front office here into a sort of trading post."

"Do you get much business?" Kenni asked.

"Not really. Then again, it's not like I have bills to pay, either. The dollar is more useful as toilet paper than money, and coins are just dead weight. But if you have trade goods, then you can get by all right."

I tied the horses at the long watering trough in front and posted Bella and Cricket outside to watch over them, giving them a firm "stay" command. I didn't know if they would really stay for long, but they lay on the ground beside Tallulah as if they were going to listen. "Good girls," I told them and followed the others inside with only a few glances over my shoulder to make sure they stayed.

Inside, the front office was filled with half a dozen glass cases stocked with all sorts of trade goods. The far wall of the room was a huge mirror, bigger than any I had ever seen. I was a bit embarrassed when I saw how bedraggled I looked, and I snaked a hand up to brush my hair back.

Mr. Roesch, Kenni, and Robin were wandering around inside, looking at the various display cases, and I walked in to join them. One case was filled with various kinds of jerky, labeled according to the kind of meat and spices used. Another was filled with bags of grain and legumes, from pinto beans to some kind of purple-hulled bean called a royal burgundy.

There was even a cabinet with a couple of old rifles and handguns. But the one that caught my eye was filled with all sorts of blades. There were throwing knives, Bowies, daggers, machetes, short swords, and even what looked like a replica of the Japanese-style sword my older sister kept. A *katana*, she called it. She'd gotten it from the father of her fiancé when he'd been killed by Crazy Larry and his bodyguard.

I shuddered a bit at that particular memory and went back to the other knives. I'd worked the forge with Mr. Roesch and my dad when I was younger, and I knew how to look for stress points in the blade. And while some of the ones in the showcase were all right, most of the work was below the quality of what I already carried. There were several knives that were impossibly shiny. My dad had a couple of knives like them from the Old Days. They were made of something called stainless steel, and they almost never rusted.

Something else caught my attention, though. Lying in the case on top of their sheaths was a pair of old handmade long knives. The blades were rusted, and the handle on one of them was missing. But without the handle, I could see that it was made in a sturdy, full-tang design, out of what appeared to be good-quality carbon steel. Whoever had originally made the knives had been an experienced bladesmith. The blades were forged in a trailing-point design, curving up at the tip to a needle-sharp point. It was all I could do to keep the interest from showing in my face.

"Let me know if there's anything you want to see," Owen said to everyone. "I'll pull it out of the case for you."

He was all smiles, as friendly as a salesman should be. But studying the room, I furrowed my brow. He was too easygoing. There were all sorts of valuables in there, and Owen was only one man. Granted, he was visibly armed. He wore a shotgun slung across his back, and I saw others on the wall around the room. But he was still too confident. Too trusting.

"Don't you worry about being in here with four people you don't know, all of us surrounding you? All of us armed?"

Owen's face froze. Mr. Roesch figured it out before I did. "That's because he isn't alone." He held his hands out to the sides in a clearly nonthreatening manner and turned slowly, scanning the room. I understood and also began to look around, checking closely for hidey-holes. But try as I might, I didn't see anything. I stopped and saw Mr. Roesch smiling at Owen. "I assume the mirror's a two-way?"

Owen nodded. "My wife's in the room behind it. She's got an M-16 covering everyone in here, and she's a damn fine shot."

"So are we the ones being ambushed? Or is your wife watching us simply as a guard?"

"Just a guard. We don't plan on doing anyone any harm. But we don't want anyone doing us harm, either."

"You do realize that if something happened, you would be among the first to die?"

Owen shrugged. "Then I guess it's in all our interest to make sure nothing happens, right?"

"I suppose it is."

The two men smiled at one another before Owen spoke again. "So what are you folks looking for?"

I wandered away from the case of knives, pretending interest in some jerky. I felt an itching between my shoulder blades at the thought of some hidden person pointing a rifle at me, but Mr. Roesch seemed all right with it. And if I put myself in Owen's place, I would probably do something similar.

A label in the case caught my eye. "Buffalo jerky?"

Owen walked over behind the case. He pulled a large pair of scissors out and clipped a little off. "Try a bite."

I put it in my mouth and chewed for a moment. "That's really good!"

He smiled. "There's a guy that comes in every three or four months from up north. Says there's a bunch of folks in North Texas that have herds of buffalo. He brings in a few pounds of the jerky every trip."

Mr. Roesch joined me at the counter. Owen offered him a bite as well. Mr. Roesch nodded. "Yep, pretty good. I might be interested in some." He wandered over to the firearms case. "You got any ammunition for the pistols?"

Owen shook his head. "I'm afraid not. That's why they're still in the case. Not much ammo left these days, and a pistol doesn't do anyone any good without it."

Mr. Roesch sighed. "That's too bad. You have some nice ones in here." He peered at them. "They're a nine millimeter, aren't they?"

"Most of them. There's a couple of forty-fives in there too. But the majority are nines."

Mr. Roesch pointed to one. "That's a nice one."

"Yes, sir, it is. It's a Springfield XDm." He pulled it out of the case and handed it to Mr. Roesch, who pressed something on the grip, and part of the handle fell into his left hand. He then pulled the top of the pistol back and looked through a hole that appeared in the side of the pistol. Having absolutely no idea what the various parts of a pistol were, I simply watched and tried not to make a fool of myself by gawking.

Then Mr. Roesch pressed something else, and the top slid back into place with a loud click. He took the piece in his left hand and slipped it back into the bottom of the handle. He handed it back to Owen. "If one were to have some ammo for these, how much would you trade, ammo for the XD?"

Owen smiled and licked his lips. "Well, if someone were to have enough ammo to trade for a pistol, it would probably take about five hundred rounds for such a firearm as the XD. Remember, you're the one who said it was a fine pistol. Your own words, sir."

"I said nice, not fine. And five hundred rounds is totally out of the question. After all, a pistol doesn't do anyone any good without ammo. Those were your words, I believe."

The two men smiled at one another, and I wandered away as the dickering began.

CHAPTER 13
TRADE

WALKING OVER TO KENNI AND Robin, I saw them looking through some old books. Robin was thumbing through an illustrated book of medicinal herbs, while Kenni thumbed through a ratty and torn women's magazine.

They looked up as I approached. "Mark found something?" Kenni asked.

"He's haggling for a pistol."

"What about you? Did you find anything?"

"There's a pair of knives I wouldn't mind having. They aren't real pretty, but they look well made. My dad taught me enough about how to work on them that the repairs should be easy enough."

"So are you going to trade for them?"

"After Mr. Roesch is done. But I think I'll start with something else. Something I can't afford."

Kenni smiled. "So you barter a lot back home."

It wasn't a question. "Yes, ma'am."

"Ma'am?"

"Sorry. It's a habit."

Robin interrupted. "I don't understand," she whispered. "Why try to get something you know you can't afford?"

"Let's go watch him, and I'll explain later," Kenni told her. "It looks like Mark is done."

I looked back and saw Mr. Roesch shake Owen's hand. Owen took the pistol they'd been haggling over and slid it into a holster as I approached. Mr. Roesch turned. "Zachary, would you go to the horses and bring me my saddlebags?"

"I'll get them," Kenni said. "I think Zach wants to look at some of the knives."

Owen smiled. "Do you? Well, I have a fine selection."

"I saw some of them. Could I see the sword? My sister has one sorta like it."

The trader pulled the katana out of the case. "Now, this isn't one of the cheap fakes that you usually see. This is what they call battle ready." He handed it to me, and I pulled it part of the way out of the wooden scabbard. He was right. The sword wasn't just decorative. Everything I could see about it indicated that it was ready to use.

I let enthusiasm show on my face. "This is really nice. What's it worth?"

"I suppose that depends on what you have to offer. I can tell you this, though. It's probably worth more than that pistol your friend just got."

On cue, I let my face fall. "Maybe we should put it back, then."

Owen smiled and took the katana back from me just as Kenni returned with Mr. Roesch's saddlebags. "Why don't you see if there's anything else that strikes your fancy while I settle up with your friend?"

"Sure."

Owen turned to Mr. Roesch, who reached into one of the bags and pulled out three small leather pouches. "One hundred rounds in each pouch."

Owen actually shook as he took the pouches from Mr. Roesch. "You don't mind if I count them, do you?"

"I'd think you were foolish if you didn't."

The man pulled out a wooden block with holes drilled in it and began inserting the ammunition into the holes. I could see that the holes were laid out in rows, and a quick count showed it was a ten-by-ten pattern.

While the two older men worked out their trade, I looked back into the case for another expensive item. There was another sword, smaller but still obviously outside what I could afford. When Mr. Roesch and Owen had exchanged goods and finished their barter, the trader turned to me, smiling. "Did you find something else?"

"Yes, sir. I'd like to see that one."

Owen looked at it, and for the first time, I saw a slight frown touch his face. "I'll be happy to let you see it." He took it out of the case and handed it to me. "But you should know that it will be almost as much as the last one."

"Really?" I feigned disappointment.

He smiled again. "Why don't you show me what you have to trade, and we'll see what I have that's comparable."

I pulled the leather pouch from my belt and peered inside. "I guess I really don't have a lot." I reached in and pulled out half a dozen barbed arrowheads, a few archers' thumb rings, thumb gloves, and some jerked goat.

He picked up one of the barbed-steel arrowheads and inspected it. "This is well made."

"Thanks. My dad taught me."

"You made them yourself?"

"Yes, sir."

He got a speculative look and went back to the pile of items. He looked at the rest of the arrowheads then picked up one of the thumb rings. "What are these?"

"Thumb rings. They're used in archery. They help your speed and accuracy."

"And these?"

"Thumb gloves. They protect the thumb on your bow hand."

He sighed. "Son, I'm sorry, but I don't see much trade value in any of this." He picked up one of the arrowheads again. "These are at least worth something but not enough for you to get a decent blade."

I sighed and started putting it all back in the pouch. Then, as if I had just seen them, I pointed to the old knives in back. "What about those?"

Owen looked at the knives. Not reaching for them, he asked, "How many of these arrowheads do you have?"

"I have about a dozen."

He nodded, still not reaching for the knives. "I tell you what. I'll trade you, sight unseen, your dozen arrowheads for these two knives."

"And the sheaths?"

"And the sheaths."

I pretended to think about it. "All right." I counted out a dozen arrowheads and slid them across the counter.

Owen smiled and pulled the knives out of the case, wrapping them in a rag before laying them on the counter. As he pushed the bundle across to me, he offered his hand.

I shook it. "Done?"

"Done," he agreed. "I'm glad we were able to do business."

"So am I."

"What are you planning to do with them?"

"The knives?"

Owen laughed out loud. "Yes, son. You don't think I didn't notice the blades you have strapped under your sleeves, do you? And the small throwers you have on your belt? And the make of those arrowheads looks like the same quality. A man who knows metal the way you obviously do wouldn't waste time on junk, so you evidently saw something in these that I didn't. What is it?"

I blushed. "They're a good solid design, and the metal looks to be a good quality. I can refit the handles and clean up the blades. With a little bit of work, I can have them as good as new in a few days."

"You can, eh?"

"Yes, sir."

He looked at Mr. Roesch, who nodded. "He can. He was raised working a forge and pounding metal. His dad taught him. Taught me too, for that matter. But Zachary's better at it."

Owen pursed his lips then counted out half of the arrowheads I had traded him. He handed them back to me. "Take these back. Those knives you got from me weren't doing me any good the way they were. If you can fix them up the way you say, I want to propose something to you. I'm trying to set up a kind of coalition of traders in the region. If you folks have a town doing as well as you say, and you have a local forge set up, then I want you to consider setting up a trade route. How many days' ride is it from here to Rejas?"

"Took us five days' steady riding."

"So if we set up a regular trade route, you could figure a two-week trip from Rejas to here and back if you haul a wagon."

I blinked. Owen certainly had high aspirations.

Mr. Roesch voiced what I was thinking. "So you want to trade... what?"

"Anything!" He grinned, suddenly enthusiastic. "You say you folks have a forge and know how to use it? We can start there. People can always use decent metal goods. Son, I've been working to set up a trading hub for the last two years. I think it's gonna be vital if we're ever gonna get back on our feet as a society."

He had me curious. "A trading hub? No offense, but why is that a vital thing for a society?"

"Back before the EMP, we had trucks that ran goods everywhere. If someone made bread in New York, they could sell it in California. If someone in Texas invented a new way to water a garden, they could share the new technology with people in North Dakota. Everybody benefitted. It gave everybody a common bond and interdependence, knitted us together into a more cohesive society.

"These days, it's a lot harder to travel, so we've lost a lot of what bound us together. But if we get traders running regular routes again, we begin rebuilding those connections. It might not be coast to coast, but it's gotta start somewhere. So I got my buffalo trader from up north, a gator hunter from Louisiana that comes in every few months, a couple of scavengers that specialize in finding old tech items that still work, and plenty of local folks trading canned goods and locally grown crops.

"And if you have metal goods like these" — he held up one of the arrowheads—"and those"—he pointed to the knives in my belt—"then we have the beginnings of another trade line."

"So you take what you got here, and remember that I did you fair. And when you get back home, talk to that daddy of yours about maybe setting up a steady trade between us. I figure we can all use goods from other places, and the side benefit is communication."

Mr. Roesch nodded. "That alone would be worth it. We've been isolated for so long we don't know what's going on outside of a fifty-mile radius. Setting up a regular route between us could be huge."

"So will you set things up on your end?"

Mr. Roesch nodded. "We will."

They were both smiling as they shook hands again.

"If this trip goes according to plan, we should be back through here in about a month. After that, a week to get home, maybe another week to clear things with the town council, and another to gather trade goods and people to run the route. A conservative guess would be two months from now before you have your first trade wagon from Rejas."

Owen nodded. "That sounds fine. And while you're on your trip here, think about things you folks need in Rejas. When you come back through, leave me a list, and I'll see what I can do to gather some of them up."

"Sounds good."

Owen looked past Mr. Roesch to where Robin was still thumbing through the book on herbal medicine. He looked back at us. "So are we finished here? I need to see if that young lady needs anything."

CHAPTER 14
MARSHALL

THE SUN WAS BEGINNING TO dim with the approach of nightfall when Mr. Roesch guided us down an overgrown street with tree limbs arcing overhead from one side to the other. Several houses sat in various states of disrepair, and he rode up to one that looked worse than most of them. Every window appeared to be broken, and the front door was completely missing.

He dismounted and, leading Ford by the reins, walked through the front entrance. He and his obedient mount disappeared to the sound of crunching bits of decaying house. I looked at Kenni and Robin, cocking an eyebrow in an unspoken question. Kenni simply dismounted and led her own mount inside, following the big man's lead. Robin and I followed suit.

We found that Mr. Roesch had walked Ford all the way through the house and into a huge backyard through a broken sliding glass door. He was removing the saddle when I entered the backyard to join the others. I gazed around, a bit surprised. The front of the house was nothing spectacular and looked like a stereotypical home in a stereotypical small neighborhood, like so many that still sat empty back in Rejas. But the property in back extended back much farther than one would think based on the appearance of the front, and I could see that there was an acre or more, with a variety of trees and brush starting several yards back from the house.

I was dying to ask Mr. Roesch about the house. I assumed it was his since going there had been his stated goal. But he hadn't said anything at all when we'd arrived. In fact, it had been several minutes since anyone had said anything, all of us knowing how hard the visit had to be on him.

He stripped Ford of his tack without comment as if nothing unusual was going on. But we all knew better. Mr. Roesch never took care of his own mount — not since he had declared me to be his assistant. That night, we all took our cue from him and groomed our own horses. I viewed it as a bit of a break since the majority of the grooming had fallen to Robin and me. But there was also a tension in the atmosphere as though we were all expecting some kind of reaction from Mr. Roesch and were unsure what to do until it happened.

Finally, he turned to me. "Zach, there used to be a big ditch just past that clump of brush. Would you picket the horses where they can drink?" And he turned to go inside without waiting to see what I did.

The ditch was where he'd said it would be, though the years had turned it into more of a stream. It was a lesson we had all learned over the last several years. Nature abhors a vacuum. If there was an empty field, it filled with plants. If there was an empty waterway, it filled with either water or plant life. Without mankind molding things to our will, nature would inevitably reclaim her own. It was just a matter of time.

When I finished tying the horses up and got back inside, I found everyone sitting around an old table in what had been a dining room. Someone had lit a small candle, and Mr. Roesch held a framed portrait in his hands, speaking softly as tears rolled down his cheeks. I walked around the table to where I could see the picture. It was a photograph of a younger Mr. Roesch in a suit, standing beside an attractive young woman in a blue dress. Between them was a little girl in a white dress. A bow decorated the girl's blond hair. Her smile showed two missing teeth in front.

Mr. Roesch touched her face on the picture. "It had been raining all day, and Nikki was worried that Angela was going to get her new dress dirty." He laughed. "And sure enough, she did. We were so worried about it that I didn't even let her walk from the car to the door of the studio. I picked her up to carry her inside while Nikki held the umbrella, and while I was closing the car door, I brushed her up against the dirty car. You can't see it, but that dress has a black smudge right across her butt. I thought Nikki was gonna kill me."

"So technically, *she* didn't get dirty."

"No." He chuckled at my comment. "No, I suppose I'm the one who did that."

Kenni reached over and gripped his hand with a familiarity that spoke again of the friendship they shared. I looked away and saw that darkness had fully fallen. "So what's the plan for the night? Do we cook or eat cold?"

"Considering Nikki's warning and the fact that we have the new supplies, why don't we play it safe and eat a cold meal tonight?"

I was happy to hear Mr. Roesch sounding more normal.

"And Zach? I'd appreciate it if you would keep an eye on the horses tonight. Considering what Owen said, we wouldn't want someone to hear them in the night and decide they're free for the taking."

From what I remembered, the backyard didn't have any trees large enough to hang my hammock. "Yes, sir." *Oh, great. A night outside on the ground.*

CHAPTER 15
ONE OF US

BREAKFAST WAS ANOTHER COLD MEAL. I figured everyone was taking Kenni seriously, and while I didn't have the same faith that the others seemed to have, I didn't see any harm in being a little cautious. After nearly an hour, the horses were saddled and packed, and we were all outside waiting for Mr. Roesch. After another half hour, I looked at Kenni. "Was he all right this morning?"

"He was quiet. Nikki and Angela spoke to him a lot last night."

I was learning to interpret Kenni's mystical observations in a way I could relate to, so mentally, I translated what she'd said to *He had dreams about his lost family*. And considering the fact that he had slept in his old home for the first time since D-day, that was more than understandable. It was, after all, where he had once shared a life with them—a life that had ended tragically and horribly.

Most adults had similar stories. Even I remembered some of the world we had left behind, and I'd only been eight years old when it had happened. And while I didn't recall much about them, I had lost friends and family too. So my attitude might have been somewhat less than sympathetic when I sighed and dismounted.

"You sure you want to do this?" Kenni asked me.

"He keeps telling me I'm his assistant. I figure it's on me to get him moving."

"This isn't really the same thing, Zach," Robin said. "Maybe you need to give him some more time."

But I wasn't in the mood to be patient. I threw my reins around a sapling and marched through the front doorway and into the dim interior of Mr. Roesch's old house. I wasn't exactly sure what I was going to say to him, and I wasn't foolish enough to throw diplomacy out the window. It was, after all, what he thought he was training me for. But I was also learning to get results. For a split second, it actually occurred to me that this might be some sort of test. Maybe he wanted to see how I would handle his recalcitrance as part of his constant training.

When I saw him sitting on the old bed, I knew better. He held that framed photo in his hand, and the grief in his eyes robbed me of whatever words I had thought to say. Immediately, I knew that while I might be able to claim to have also lost friends and family just as he had, I had nothing to compare to the devastation of losing a wife and daughter. The raw emotion on his face looked more painful than anything I had felt in many years.

And as I watched him grieve, all I could think was that I needed to get out unseen before he knew I had intruded on such a personal moment.

"How old are you, Zachary?" His words froze me as I was turning.

I turned back to him, swallowing my embarrassment. "I'm twenty, sir."

He nodded. "Angela would have been just a couple of years younger than you if she had lived." He looked away from the picture, turning to face me. He pushed back most of the grief I had seen just a few seconds before. "I wonder sometimes if you two would have liked each other. I've watched you and some of the other kids, and I've often thought about how she would have fit in."

I had no idea how to answer. I didn't even know if I *should* answer. But his expression begged me for something, and I knew that whatever I had intended to say when I walked in, it wasn't appropriate, considering the man's grief.

I only had to think for a second about what he had said, and I realized that I *did* know what to tell him after all. It had been swirling around in my head as I'd walked into the house, but the framing of the thoughts needed to be changed. "She would have fit in just fine. We all get along, all of us from our general age group. We can't help it."

I walked over and sat on the bed beside him. "You know how yesterday you asked me about what I remember from when we lived in Houston?"

"Yeah."

"I told you how a lot of us talk about what we remember sometimes. What I didn't mention is how formal we've made it." I looked up and saw that I had his full attention, so I continued. "You call us kids. I guess we all think of you as old folks."

He smiled a bit as I said that.

"And I don't think I ever really thought about it until now, but even though we all were around on D-day, our perspectives now are a lot different than yours."

"It's called a generation gap. It's what keeps you kids and us old folks from seeing things the same way. It was there between me and my parents just like I'm sure it was there for my dad and his parents." The bigger man sighed. "I suppose it's been there throughout history. But this gap is going to be bigger than most. I'm part of the last generation to have lived the majority of my life in a high-tech civilization."

I nodded. "And I'm part of the last generation that will even vaguely remember what some of that was like. Those bombs fell twelve years ago, and we were barely old enough to understand what was going on. Some of us remember more than others, and we talk about it sometimes, comparing memories. I guess we're sorta trying to bolster each other's memories because we know that *our* kids will have no idea what we lost. It's almost like we feel we need to..." I trailed off, suddenly less sure of what I was trying to say.

"Keepers of the flame, eh?"

I furrowed my brow. "I'm not sure what that means."

"It's an old saying. It means you don't want the memories to be lost—like a flame going out in the wind."

"Yeah, that fits. But the point I'm trying to make is that Angela would have been one of us. She would have shared what she remembered, whether it's a drive your family took to go shopping or watching a movie on the TV with you. Maybe you went somewhere special that she remembers. Jerry's always talking about how his family took him to that big park, Disneyworld, just a month before D-day. But whatever her memory was, it would have started someone else talking about how they had done something similar, or maybe one of us would have asked what it was like.

"We try to remember because we know that one day our kids will ask us questions about the Old Days, and we want to be able to tell them what it was like. We're the last." I took the picture from him and looked at the young girl smiling at the camera. "She would have been one of us."

CHAPTER 16
SHOT

WE RODE OUT OF MR. Roesch's neighborhood two by two. He and Kenni rode beside each other, speaking to one another quietly enough that I couldn't overhear any of their conversation. Robin rode beside me, patient and quiet. I got the impression she was perfectly content to just watch the world go past, perched in her saddle. I liked that about her. She never put any pressure on me.

Mr. Roesch had let it be known that he had big plans for me, and Kenni had hinted that her hoodoo witchy power had plans for me too. But not Robin. All she wanted was companionship. Maybe it should have bothered me that she seemed to be just as content getting that companionship from the dogs or the horses, but her lack of expectation made me feel strangely peaceful. She was someone who wanted nothing from anyone, including me. For the moment, that suited me just fine.

Bella turned, looking behind us, nostrils working frantically, ears pointed forward. Cricket joined her, growling low and menacing. I reined Tallulah in and turned, studying the area that had attracted my girls' attention. There was a flicker of movement in a window about fifty yards back, gone almost as soon as it registered. But it was enough to draw my attention. I squinted, trying to detect more detail in the darkened interior of the distant structure, but there was no sure way to tell if I had really seen anything.

"Mr. Roesch?" I reined Tallulah back around and called to get his attention.

He looked back over his shoulder. "What?" When he saw I had stopped, he pulled Ford to a halt as well. "Something wrong?"

I never got a chance to reply. Mr. Roesch grunted and slumped forward in his saddle just as a thunderous crack sounded. It was a sound I hadn't heard in a long time. But it wasn't something I would ever forget, either.

Kenni recognized the gunshot too. Her pistol was out in a second, and she spun her horse around, looking for its source.

"There!" I pointed to the house where I had seen the movement. A length of black stuck out from the window, resting on the lower ledge.

Mr. Roesch slid to one side, and I pulled Tallulah up beside him to brace him in the saddle. Kenni fired several shots at the window just as another shot rang out. Whether it was because her shots distracted the shooter or simply blind luck, the mystery shooter missed that time.

Leaning Mr. Roesch against my shoulder, I grabbed at Ford's reins. *Never going to be able to hold him like this.* Not taking time to think it through, I scrambled from my saddle onto Ford's back, landing behind Mr. Roesch. Holding Tallulah's reins in my left hand, I grabbed Ford's in the other and kicked him into a gallop, pulling Tallulah along and struggling to hold Mr. Roesch in his saddle as we fled the ambush.

Robin pulled up on the other side of Tallulah. "Let me have her! You've got your hands full with him. I'll lead your horse!"

I nodded, and with an amazing show of agility, she reached up to Tallulah's bit and snaked the reins from my side to hers without slowing any of us down. Seeing Tallulah was in good hands, I concentrated on keeping Mr. Roesch in the saddle and guiding Ford as we put more distance between our attacker and us.

Robin led us to an intersection and cut to the right. I followed without question, struggling to keep my balance, reaching around my mentor to hold him upright between my arms, and keeping a tight hold on Ford's reins. I couldn't afford to let the horse give in to panic or let my charge fall to the ground, but the strain of trying to keep up the insane balancing act was causing me to slide steadily back on the big horse's flanks. I had to slow us down as soon as we were out of the line of fire or we were both going to fall.

Luckily, Robin slowed before that happened. We didn't stop, but I was able to take a second to reach down to the cantle of Mr. Roesch's saddle and pull myself back up snugly behind him. Looking over his shoulder again, I saw Robin duck as she rode, horse and all, into the open garage of an old house. That might work for her, but Ford was a much bigger horse, and there was no way I was going to be able to lean Mr. Roesch over in the saddle, keep him balanced, duck over him, and guide his massive mount under the doorway. I pulled up close to the open door and called, "Help me get him down!"

But she had anticipated me. She had dismounted as soon as she got the horses inside and was reaching up to help me slide the big man out of the saddle. Kenni was there with us before we got him to the ground. "How bad is he?"

"I don't know. Haven't had time to—"

She pushed me aside before I could finish. It was dim in the garage, but there was enough light to see that his shirt was soaked with blood. She put fingers to his neck, checking for a pulse. "He's still with us."

She looked back up at me. "Do you have...?" She blinked at me. "Are you all right?"

I looked down, realizing with a sick feeling that my shirt was just as wet as his. It was soaked with the sticky warmth of Mr. Roesch's blood. "I... I'm fine. It's his blood." I stripped the ruined shirt off and pressed it against the wound in his chest.

"Good." She looked around. "Where'd Robin go?"

Robin called from across the garage. "Bring him in here." She disappeared back into the house without waiting for us to reply.

"Help me get him inside."

Robin waited inside the door, pointing up a hallway. "Last room on the right." She ran ahead. "In here," she shouted as she ducked into the room. I heard a rustling ahead as Kenni and I struggled to get the big man down the narrow hall. *In here* turned out to be the master bedroom. It was large, and the windows were still intact. Robin had stripped the old sheets and bedspread off the large bed and thrown a blanket over the mattress.

Kenni and I laid him on the blanket as carefully as we could. I looked at his unconscious form. I didn't know if it was the dim light or my imagination, but he looked pretty pale. For the first time, it occurred to me that he might not make it.

"Do you have a first aid kit?" Kenni asked me.

I nodded and started to go get it.

"Get mine too," Robin called without looking up. "It's the red one in my right saddlebag."

I hurried back to the garage to get them. As I entered the garage, Bella and Cricket ran in, tongues lolling as they panted in exhaustion. "Good girls," I said absentmindedly as I gathered gear. The garage was crowded with four horses in it, but I didn't want to risk them wandering off. The outer door was broken, partly hanging off the track. But I was able to force it down far enough that it would block them for the time being. "Come," I told the dogs and ran back inside with the med kits. I tossed them to Robin. "Is he going to make it?"

She didn't even look up. "I don't know. If I can stop the bleeding, he at least has a chance. Doesn't look like it hit a lung, and if they had hit his heart, he would already be dead."

This was a side of Robin I hadn't seen before, but I remembered Kenni mentioning that she had been a nurse. She rummaged through her kit, pulling out bandages and a leather pouch. "I don't suppose you have a sewing kit in your bag, do you?"

"I have an emergency suture kit. Is that what you need?"

She looked up at that. "You do?"

I grabbed my bag and pulled it out. "I also have alcohol wipes and some sterile bandages in a sealed plastic bag in there."

"Thank God. You just tripled his chances." She grabbed the

supplies then handed me one of the wipes and the pouch of leaves. "Clean your hands. Then crush a few of the leaves in the pouch. Just enough to make them limp and moist."

I fumbled the ties on the pouch, but when I got it open, I recognized the leaves she had gathered a few days ago. Comfrey, she had called it. I hurried to follow her directions, noticing that the leaves emitted a crisp, fresh scent similar to fresh cucumbers. When I looked up, she had cleaned her own hands and was just beginning to stitch the hole in Mr. Roesch's chest.

"What do I do with the leaves?"

She nodded her head to the plastic bag of bandages. "Wrap them in a piece of bandage."

As soon as I had done that, I stood over her shoulder, watching her work. "What can I do now?"

"You can stop blocking my light."

"Sorry."

Kenni grabbed my arm. "We'll be right back," she told Robin, pulling me out of the room.

She led me back toward the garage, speaking quietly as we went. "Mark has a rifle. You any good with it?"

I shook my head. "No, ma'am. But I'm a damn good shot with the bow."

Kenni sighed. "That'll have to do." We entered the garage. "Gear up."

Understanding, I went to Tallulah and grabbed my bow. I braced it against my foot and strung it in a quick and practiced move, then grabbed my emergency pouch and quiver.

"You know what I have in mind?"

"I think so. We're going back."

"Good." She went back to Ford, drew Mr. Roesch's rifle from its sleeve, and pulled back the bolt on the side. She dug through his saddlebags and came up with a small box of ammunition. "Not a lot, but better than nothing." She slung his rifle across her back and went to Robin's appaloosa. She grabbed a box of shells and the shotgun I had seen Robin holding at the trading post then led the way back inside.

Back in the bedroom, Robin had finished sewing up the wound in Mr. Roesch's chest and was struggling to roll him over. She looked up as we walked back in. "Good. Help me roll him over. I need to sew him up on his back too. And make sure you don't put his face in the blanket. We don't need him suffocating while we're trying to save him."

I looked at Kenni, who nodded. I leaned the bow against the wall, knelt, and helped roll him onto his stomach, making sure he was still able to breathe. Robin didn't even look up as Kenni laid the shotgun and shells on the floor near her.

"How's it going?" Kenni asked.

"Not too bad." Robin kept her eyes on her work as she continued sewing Mr. Roesch's wound closed. "Having a suture kit is a huge help. Once I get the wounds closed, I can cover them with the comfrey. That should help the skin heal, anyway. There's not a lot I can do for him internally. I think I still have some old antibiotics in my kit, but I don't know if they'll do much good after a decade. I guess it's better than nothing."

Kenni was silent for a second then touched the other woman on the shoulder. "All right. Your shotgun is on the floor behind you. Zach and I have to make sure no one's coming after us. If we're not back in an hour, start getting ready to move yourself and Mark back to our place. If we're not here by the time you have him stable, and you're ready to go, then head back. We'll catch up when we can."

That stopped Robin, and she looked up. "What? No! All you need to do is guard the area. Keep anyone away from us while I get him patched up."

"No, baby. We have to make sure there aren't too many of them. If we're in here and there's a large group, then we're trapped. And if we're trapped, we're dead. You're the only one who can save Mark, so it's up to us to make sure you have the time you need."

I swallowed as I heard her explain this.

"But—"

"No buts," Kenni told her. "And we don't have time to argue about it." She turned away from Robin, not giving her the chance to object any more. "We should be back before the hour's up. Safe word's..." She thought for only a second. "Safe word's *Tallulah*. Got it?"

Robin nodded. "Tallulah."

"Answer with *Ford*. Duress word is *Cinnamon*."

Once more, Robin nodded. "Cinnamon."

"Take care of him." Kenni leaned over and kissed Robin. "I'll see you in an hour."

Kenni turned to me. "Ready?"

"Hang on a second. Let me post the girls."

"What?"

She must not have noticed the dogs come in with me, and they were sitting quietly against a wall, away from where Robin worked on Mr. Roesch. Their demeanor told me they knew something was wrong and they were frightened.

I knelt beside them and rubbed behind their ears. "Good girls. You're good girls."

Bella whined a bit and licked my chin. Cricket sniffed my bare chest and snorted at the blood still smeared on me. I wished I had more time to spend with them and make them feel more at ease. But time was something we were in short supply of. I led the girls to Robin and touched her on the shoulder. Then I pointed at the two of them. "Stay," I told them, reinforcing it with an open palm, the hand signal I used for the same command. Then I closed the open hand into a fist. "Guard."

Bella whined again and started to come to me.

"No." I held up the fist again. "Guard."

This time she sat beside Cricket.

I grabbed my bow and walked out of the room. Kenni raised an inquiring brow at me.

"Are they still sitting there?" I asked.

The question seemed to surprise her. "Yes."

"Good. They should protect Robin and Mr. Roesch once we leave."

"Really? They'll protect her?"

"It's not perfect, but they usually do what they're supposed to."

She looked over my shoulder. "And is there a reason you won't look at them?"

"Sometimes if I look at them after giving them a command they don't like, it's like they take that as an excuse to come to me, and I have to start all over again."

Kenni said goodbye once more, and we went back into the garage to gather our gear. I grabbed a shirt from my bags and shrugged it on. "So what was all that about Tallulah and a duress word?" I grabbed my bow then slipped my quiver across one shoulder and my go pouch over the other so that they crisscrossed over my chest.

"When we come back, we announce ourselves with the word *Tallulah*. She answers with *Ford*. If any of us are in trouble, like with unwelcome company, we let the others know by using the word *Cinnamon*."

I nodded and settled everything into place.

"Ready?"

I shrugged. "Not really."

"Yeah. Me either."

I followed her out of the garage, and the two of us headed back the way we had come.

CHAPTER 17
KENNI MAKES A POINT

WE MOVED BETWEEN ROTTING HOUSES, often slipping through holes in the walls, as we retraced the path we had made from the place where Mr. Roesch had been shot. Kenni led the way, never glancing back to make sure I followed. On several occasions, if she had a clear view through a window, she would raise the rifle and peer through the sight.

We were only a mile or so away from the house where we had left Robin and Mr. Roesch when I heard voices ahead. I tapped Kenni on the arm and put my mouth to her ear. "Voices ahead," I whispered.

She nodded and pulled the bolt back on the rifle, making sure there was a round chambered. Popping the cover off the sight on the rifle, she peered up the road, watching for movement. I pulled my binoculars from my pouch and did the same. We were deep in the darkness of another rotting home, and the smell of mold and mildew clogged my sinuses. After only a few seconds, I caught movement at the edge of my field of vision. Shifting my view to the left, I saw more movement as three men and one woman trotted from one house to the next.

I tapped her on the shoulder and handed her the binoculars. "I just saw four people move between those two houses." I pointed out which houses I meant.

"I saw them." She continued looking for a moment before

returning my binoculars. She watched as I slipped them back into the leather pouch on my hip. "What else you keep in there? Anything that might help us with our immediate predicament?" She indicated the houses, where I saw movement once more.

"Not in this pouch." I touched the quiver on my other hip. "The only thing that might come in handy for what I see coming is in here."

She nodded. "You said you were good."

"I am."

"How good?"

"I once dropped a buck at almost ninety yards with a kill shot."

"Once?"

"It was a lucky shot," I admitted. "But at fifty yards, I can hit a man-sized target almost every time. It might not be a perfect shot, but it'll hit. At forty yards, I can hit the chest almost every time. Thirty yards, and I'll drill clean through their heart."

"Good. But remember that if it comes to that, these people have rifles that can fire a lot faster than a bow."

"You've never seen speed archery, have you?"

She blinked.

"At close range, I can fire four shots in about three seconds."

"Bullshit."

"No, ma'am, it's not."

She looked at me as though I'd grown a third eye. Finally, she relented. "Whatever. Hopefully, it won't come to that." She looked at the houses ahead. "Think you can sneak around and get behind them?"

I nodded.

"Do it. I'll try to bluff them into dropping their weapons, but it probably won't work. If the shooting starts, don't be a hero. Take a shot if you can do it without getting killed. Mark would be pissed if I lost him his assistant."

I was too nervous to smile at the joke, so I slipped out of the house and around the back. As I ran, I pulled four arrows out of the quiver and positioned three of them between the fingers of my right hand, nocking the fourth so it was ready to fire. Only a minute or two later, I heard Kenni shouting, "That's close enough! You have to the count of three to drop your weapons and—"

They didn't wait to hear the rest of her threat. A rifle and two pistols fired while she was still talking. And I wasn't in position yet.

I sprinted to the back of the next house I saw. From the sounds out front, it was obvious that the shooters weren't too worried about ammunition, and it occurred to me to wonder where they got it all.

It sounded like all the shooting was between Kenni and me, so I ran through the broken back door of the next house, intending to come out behind them. The man crouching in the window of the house was just as surprised at my appearance as I was at his, but I was already running and had momentum on my side. He had a pistol and swung it toward me as I slammed into him, knocking him through the rotten wall into the next room. A shot rang out, and my heart skipped a beat. In the next heartbeat, I realized I wasn't hit, but the thunderous roar in such close quarters robbed me of my hearing on the left side. The only sounds that got through were a high-pitched ringing in that ear and faint shouts in the right one. The two of us fell to the floor together, him trying to swing the pistol back toward me while I desperately tried to block it with my left hand. I had lost my bow in the struggle, but my right hand still clutched two arrows. I shoved them through his throat, and his eyes opened wide in shock and surprise. He sprayed at me as his throat filled with blood, and I knelt on his gun hand, looking wildly around to make sure we were alone as the man's struggles faded and he bled out.

The stench of mold and mildew was suddenly overwhelmed as his bowels evacuated, and I gagged at the thought of what I had done. Gritting my teeth, I thought about Mr. Roesch lying in that house with a hole in his chest, and I tightened my resolve. Making sure he was dead, I pulled the pistol from the man's hand and dropped it into my pouch, surprised at the weight of the thing. I knew the basics of how to use one but wasn't practiced enough to try it in a life-or-death situation. Better to depend on the weapon

I was most familiar with. I looked around, gathering my arrows, and found my bow in the other room, where it had been ripped from my hand as we fell through the wall.

Over the ringing in my ears, I heard more shooting outside. It sounded as if the people attacking Kenni were moving away from me, which meant they were angling to get closer to her. I slipped out through a broken front window, crouching as I ran up to the nearest tree. I nocked an arrow, held three more between my fingers, and dashed to another big pine tree. About to dart to another, I froze when I saw movement ahead—two more shooters, and they weren't even trying to be careful but were laughing as they fired at the house in which Kenni hid. They trotted forward, unleashing a barrage of bullets as they moved, in an obvious effort to keep her pinned down.

The bad news was that it seemed to be working. From my position, I could see the window where Kenni had been crouching, and the steady hail of lead was evidently preventing her from peeking up, because there was no return fire. With a bit of panic, I worried that she might have already been hit.

I scanned the trees and buildings, trying to find the fourth shooter, but no other movement gave him away, and there was no more time to look. Kenni was in trouble. I stepped out from behind my tree and drew on my first target. Still, I didn't think I could just shoot them in the back. I yelled at them, "Hold it right—"

They spun, weapons raised, giving me no time at all to think. I fired. Before the first arrow had hit its target, I had nocked and fired my second arrow. Nocking a third arrow as I moved, I spun back behind the tree in case they didn't drop immediately.

I looked up to see the fourth attacker taking aim at me. My bow was pointed at the ground, and I knew there was no way I was going to beat him to the draw. In my mind, I could see his finger tightening on the trigger, and when the crack of the rifle sounded, I clenched my eyes tightly and jumped.

It took me a second to realize I hadn't felt anything. I opened my eyes to see the last thug falling to the ground. Movement to my right drew my attention, and I dropped to a crouch and drew my bow.

"Hold on, Zach!" Kenni stepped out of the doorway of another house.

I looked back at the house where we had started. "But I thought you were back there!"

"So did they." Her grin was somehow frightening. It was a feral thing to behold, and I remembered that she had been one of the Old Days' warriors. Marines. "I moved as soon as they started shooting. Didn't seem like a good idea to stay where they expected me to be."

I looked at the man who had been about to shoot me and swallowed. That had been way too close. "Thanks."

She said nothing as she approached the man, nudging his rifle out of his hands with her foot. She looked around, examining the two I had shot then narrowing her eyes as she scanned nearby houses. "Where's the last one?"

"Back there." I tipped my bow at the house where I had stabbed the man in the throat.

"Dead?"

I just nodded, suddenly feeling sick.

She picked up the rifle at her feet and began stripping the man of any gear he had on him.

"You okay?"

"I guess." I walked over to the two I had shot. Following Kenni's lead, I grabbed the first one's rifle and began removing anything useful he had on him, carefully laying it on the ground for examination. I moved to the second one and paused.

For a brief second, I had a moment of personal satisfaction. Both shots were clean and precise. They had punched straight through the sternums and into the hearts. But when I saw the swell of breasts on one of the two, I froze. I had forgotten that one of the attackers was a woman.

While I knew intellectually that it made absolutely no difference and that she would have killed me if I hadn't shot first, my realization that I had killed a woman somehow made me feel as if I had done something odious. Her eyes stared at me, empty and void of life. But they also accused me, condemning me for ending her existence.

"You weren't kidding about being good with the bow." Kenni's voice from behind made me jump. "I saw how fast you were when you took these two out."

I nodded silently, thankful for an excuse to look away from the judgment in the dead woman's eyes. Kenni must have seen something in my face.

"You've never killed anyone before, have you?"

"No, ma'am."

"It's never easy. At least, it shouldn't be easy. If you have any kind of conscience, taking another person's life is a terrible thing."

"I know all that," I told her. "I've trained all my life in martial arts. I lived through the war with Crazy Larry... saw my sister shoot him in the head while he held a pistol on me." I swallowed at the memories. "You don't go through all that, train for that, without thinking about what it means to have to kill someone."

"But thinking about it isn't the same as having to do it, is it? Look, you did what you had to do. You can't let it get to you. Don't let it make you hesitate. If you hesitate or back down out here, it'll probably get you killed. Understand?"

I swallowed at the ruthlessness of her statement, understanding suddenly just how little I knew about Kenni and wondering if I really wanted to know more.

"Yeah. I just..."

"What?"

I pointed to the woman. "I never thought I would kill a woman."

Kenni looked at me, a dumbfounded expression on her face. "Seriously? That's what has you all worked up?"

"Well... yeah. I never thought I—"

Quick as a snake, she slapped me so hard my eyes watered.

"What the hell?" I shouted.

Before my vision cleared, she did it again.

I blinked hard and staggered back. Movement to my right told me she was going to do it again. I leaned back, parried her strike, and locked her wrist in a quick and practiced movement I had learned many years earlier.

"What the hell are you doing?" I yelled.

She grinned up at me from where I held her, bent at the waist, unable to reach me for another strike. "That's better. Now, let me up."

"So you can slap me again? I don't think so!" My cheek still burned from her strikes.

"I'm done. I think I made my point."

"Point? What point?" But I let her up, shoving her slightly away from me.

She stood and nodded. "You tell me. What point did I just make?"

"That you can hit me? What kind of point is that? You think I've never been hit by a woman? My sister trained me for years! I've sparred with men and women from all over town. Being hit by a woman is nothing new."

"Really?" She stared at me, head slightly cocked, eyebrows raised, a mocking expression on her face. "But surely you know a woman can't hurt you. Not really, right?"

I was slow sometimes, but I eventually figured things out. I sighed. "Okay, I get it."

"Good. Take a piece of advice from on old Marine. You don't go looking for a fight, but whenever one finds you, you hit hard, you hit fast, and you never *ever* back down. I don't care whether your opponent is a man or a woman. I'd hate to see you get killed because your opponent has nice tits." She walked to the woman and began stripping her of her gear.

I started gathering the items I had taken off the man. "Did you really have to slap me so hard?"

She shrugged. "Probably not. But I wanted to make a point. And I wanted to make sure you remembered that point."

I didn't know whether to be angry at Kenni or at myself. In the end, I settled on being happy to still be alive.

CHAPTER 18
SPOILS

WE DIDN'T KNOW IF THERE would be anyone looking for our attackers, so we dragged the bodies into the nearest house and dumped them into a bathtub. Kenni yanked the plastic shower curtain down and threw it over them. "Let's go."

I stared at the lumpy pile for a second then turned to follow her. We gathered up the supplies and hurried back to the garage. The weight of two rifles, two pistols, and all the ammunition that went along with them wore on my back. It made me feel clumsy as we backtracked our way to Mr. Roesch and Robin.

I was concentrating on trying to not make too much noise, with all the additional metal hanging off of me, when Kenni stopped. Jerking my head up, I looked around, frantically searching for danger. Kenni shouted out, "Tallulah!"

There was a delay of only a few seconds before the reply came back. "Ford!"

We trotted the last few yards into the garage to find Robin getting to her feet. Bella and Cricket ran to me, tails wagging as they whined their eagerness to see me again.

"There's my good girls." I rubbed their heads. "Were you good girls?" Cricket's tail thumped against the wall as she licked my hand before Bella rubbed her head against my leg. "Good girls."

Mr. Roesch still lay where we had left him on the floor, pale and sallow. But I was relieved to see his chest rise and fall as he breathed. Robin went to Kenni, and they hugged one another tightly.

"You okay?" she asked Kenni. "I heard a lot of shooting."

"I'm fine. Turns out that Zach is every bit as good with the bow as he said he was."

Robin hugged me as well. "Thanks for getting her back to me."

I shrugged, uncomfortable with the attention. "She saved my ass too. If it wasn't for her…" I trailed off at the look from Kenni. Too late, I realized she probably wouldn't want Robin to think about how dangerous it had all been.

Robin simply smiled tiredly. "It's all right. I knew when you left it was going to be risky. There wasn't any help for it." She turned back to Kenni. "Just don't try to hide things from me, all right?"

Kenni pursed her lips and nodded. "Fair enough." She walked to Mr. Roesch and knelt beside him. "How's he doing? I see you got the bleeding stopped."

"For now. There's no way he's going to make it to Oklahoma, though. We've got to go back."

Kenni was silent, studying him.

I sat wearily beside him on the other side. I looked at his pale face and studied his shallow breathing. "He won't make it back to Rejas either, will he?"

Kenni shook her head. "I don't think so."

"Well, we sure as hell can't stay here." Robin said.

"Owen's," I said. "It's only a few hours' ride. We can build a sling and carry him between two horses."

"What makes you think Owen would take him in?"

"He's a trader." I waved my hands at the weapons we had brought back. "We know he's short on ammunition, and I didn't see anything like these rifles in his stock."

Kenni smiled. She grabbed one of the rifles we had taken off our attackers. "How much ammo did we get?"

I got back to my feet and retrieved the belts and pouches I had carried back from the attack. I set them on the ground, and the two of us began going through them.

When we had sorted everything, Kenni exhaled and nodded. "It'll do." To Robin, she said, "You think Mark will be well enough to travel a few hours tomorrow?"

"I don't know. He's not bleeding. He's not got any blood in his mouth or rattling in his chest. If he's still alive in the morning, we'll have to decide then."

"All right. I'll keep sorting through this." She indicated all the firearms and ammo then looked up at me. "You go keep watch to make sure those thugs don't have any friends coming to check on them."

Chagrined that I hadn't thought of that on my own, I grabbed my bow and quiver, posted Bella and Cricket to guard the garage again, and went outside to find a good tree to climb.

—✸——✸——✸——✸——✸—

Kenni came to find me nearly three hours later. Despite the fact that I was nearly forty feet above the ground and hidden in the thick foliage of a giant oak, she walked within sight and looked directly up at me. *How does she do that?*

"Zach, come on down."

I clambered back to the ground while she waited. "Nothing?" she asked when I was beside her.

I shook my head.

"Good. Let's go inside and get a bite to eat. If nobody's come by now, they're not going to."

We went back inside to the enthusiastic greetings of Bella and Cricket. Tails wagging, they vied for my attention as I entered. I couldn't help but grin as their tails wagged so hard that their entire rear ends shifted from side to side.

"They sure love you," Robin said with a tired-looking smile.

I knelt to their level and let them lick me as I rubbed their fur and scratched behind their ears. "What's not to love? They're such good girls, and they have impeccable taste. Don't you, girls?"

Robin chuckled as Cricket rolled onto her back, presenting her belly to me, imperiously demanding that I scratch her.

"And somebody loves their tummy rubs, don't they?" I smiled, rubbing her belly while I found the spot behind Bella's ear that she loved me to scratch.

Kenni snorted from behind me. "I think they have you trained just as well as you've trained them, don't they?"

"I guess they do, at that. But it's only fair, isn't it?"

I walked over and checked on Mr. Roesch. "How's he doing?"

"His breathing is steady," Robin said. "Still no obvious problems. I'm hopeful."

"That's good news, then. Right?"

"Yes, it is."

Kenni handed me some cheese and jerky. "Eat. Tomorrow's going to be a long day. We need to keep our strength up."

I sat on the floor of the old bedroom and bit a hunk off the jerky. Bella and Cricket sat on either side of me, waiting patiently as I chewed the jerky. I sighed, bit off a couple of pieces, and tossed one to each girl.

Kenni snickered. "Yep. They have you trained well."

I grinned and looked around. Kenni had been busy sorting through all the gear. Everything was grouped into various piles: rifles, pistols, food, medical, and various small pouches that I recognized as those the ammunition had been stored in.

"Looks like we have plenty for a trade with Owen, don't you think?"

"I think so. There's nearly eight hundred rounds for the ARs, more than five hundred for the two nine mils, and three hundred for the forty-fives." She walked to the piles and picked up a pistol. I recognized it as the one I had taken from the man I'd stabbed in the throat. She held it out to me. "This is yours. I'll show you how to use it later, but until I do, just leave it alone and don't point it at anyone."

I didn't reach for it. "It's not loaded, is it?"

"It wouldn't do anyone any good if it wasn't." She raised

an eyebrow at my reluctance to take the sidearm. "Are you that nervous around firearms?"

I shrugged. "I've never had one. Not many people around Rejas do. But I remember what they can do."

"Well, you can hold this one safely. It's loaded, but there's nothing in the chamber."

I looked at her blankly.

"It means it can't shoot anything right now."

I took the thing gingerly and put it on the floor beside me. She shoved several small bags full of ammunition into a larger pouch and put it beside the pistol. I was surprised at how the pouch thudded when she dropped it. Tentatively, I lifted it up, and I grunted in surprise at the weight of it.

Robin must have seen my nervousness. I got the distinct impression she was trying to distract me when she spoke. "I take it you didn't find any other people out there?"

"No." I looked away from the pistol. "Nothing but a few birds and squirrels."

"Good. I'd rather not worry about that on top of having to keep..." She trailed off, looking warily at me.

"Having to keep Mr. Roesch alive? It's okay. You can say it. It's not like I don't know he's bad off."

"Sorry. I don't know how close you two are. Sometimes it seems like you're friends. Then other times, you act like you're mad at each other."

I chuckled. "I suppose so. He's been around so long we consider him family."

"Then why do you always call him Mr. Roesch instead of Mark?"

I shrugged. "I was eight or nine years old when he came to Rejas. He helped my dad build the forges, and they worked them together for years. My dad's a big man, but Mr. Roesch was even bigger. To a kid my size, he was huge... bigger than life. He was always Mr. Roesch to me." I looked at the big man on the bed. "He still is."

I looked back at Robin and found her smiling at me. "What?"

"That's sweet."

I blushed. "Whatever."

Kenni chimed in. "You know, you're every bit as tall as he is. And the years you spent at the forge didn't do you any harm, either."

I shrugged. "I'm not like Mr. Roesch."

"You're younger. At the rate you're going, you'll be as much of a mountain as he is in a few years."

"No way."

Kenni nodded. "Do you see yourself?"

"Okay, I know I'm in decent shape. But he's a solid slab of muscle."

"And I saw you when you took your shirt off this morning. There's hardly any fat on you, either. You're just lankier than he is."

"Wiry," Robin agreed. "If I wasn't already spoken for..."

I looked up, eyes wide. When I saw the impish grin on her face, I knew she was playing with me. "Hah, hah! Don't you know better than to play with a young man's heart like that?"

We all laughed a bit at that. When we finished eating, Kenni stood and picked up one of the rifles. "I'm gonna take another pass around the area and make sure there's no one else there."

I grabbed my bow. "I'll go with you."

"No need. Rest for a bit. Maybe go through the house and see if there's anything else in here we can use."

"All right."

"Just keep your hands off my woman."

I smiled, finally feeling a bit more at ease. "What about her keeping her hands off of me?"

Kenni snorted and left the room.

CHAPTER 19
SHELTER

THE NIGHT PASSED WITHOUT INCIDENT. Still, I didn't get much sleep. Images of Mr. Roesch getting shot and me stabbing the faceless man in the throat kept me from getting any real rest. I finally gave up on any further chance of sleep when I noticed the room beginning to lighten with the coming dawn. Bella was snuggled up in front of me, and Cricket snored lightly at my feet. I got up, trying not to wake anyone else.

Mr. Roesch was still breathing. Beyond that, I couldn't tell anything more about how he was doing. I led the girls outside, and we all did our business in the backyard.

Wandering around outside the house, I checked on the horses and was ashamed to realize they hadn't had any water all night. I went to Tallulah, rubbing the bridge of her nose. "I'm sorry, girl. There's no water here. We'll get you some when we get back on the road."

She snorted into my palm, nuzzling it as if hoping for food. "Nope. No treats, either."

I started saddling up the horses so they would be ready when Kenni and Robin got up. I didn't figure it would be too long. Sure enough, Kenni walked in while I was cinching down the tack on Ford. Without a word, she grabbed the blankets for her and Robin's horses. Minutes later, Robin came out and joined us. "Looks like everyone's about ready to get on the road."

"If you think Mr. Roesch is strong enough for the trip."

"He seems to be stable enough. And we need to get him someplace safer than here."

"I like your suggestion yesterday on how to get Mark into a sling between horses," Kenni said. "You have an idea on how to build one?"

"I have some cordage in my bags, and I found some old blankets in the house that are pretty sturdy. If we cut poles about ten feet long and a few inches around, we can wrap the blankets around the poles and lash them between Tallulah and Ford."

Kenni nodded. "Sounds like a plan." She went to her horse and reached into one of her bags while I pulled my machete from Tallulah's gear.

We ducked under the hanging garage door and walked to the side of the house. There was a huge, spreading elm tree with long branches extending in all directions. I picked out one that was the right diameter about three feet above my head. Gauging the distance, I pulled my machete from its sheath and swung. I swung several times, flinging wood chips as I worked the branch.

Kenni shook her head as she stepped forward. "Hang on, Hercules. You're going to take forever like that."

"Well, I don't have an ax. And the machete will eventually get the job done."

She waved her hands at me, motioning me to step back, and took my place. She opened a small pouch and dropped a length of black-and-silver chain into her hand. She tossed the pouch at me, and I caught it absentmindedly, watching as she slung the chain around the branch. I noted the leather loops on either end of the chain as she grabbed them, stepped a bit to the side, and started pulling the chain back and forth. Sawdust drifted down as the narrow chain bit into the branch, and my jaw dropped as I saw how quickly it made its way through the wood.

"Holy crap, what is that thing?"

"Pocket chainsaw. You need to move, or this thing's going to fall on you."

I jumped aside as the branch began to splinter, the last half inch breaking under its own weight.

"Why don't you use the machete to clean the smaller branches off while I get another pole down?"

She had the second pole before I'd cleared half of the branches off of the first one, and we had the sling constructed and Mr. Roesch loaded into it within the hour. We slung him between Tallulah and Ford, with Robin riding the larger horse. Robin's mount was loaded with all the extra gear we'd gotten, both from our attackers and what little we'd found in the house, and Kenni led the little appaloosa ahead of us.

The ride back to Owen's trading post was fortunately uneventful. We took things especially slow, taking as much care as we could not to jostle Mr. Roesch too much. We got to the trading post half a day later, and Owen met us outside as we tied the horses in front of the water trough. "What in the bloody blue hell happened?"

"We found some of those horse thieves you mentioned," Kenni said.

"Mr. Roesch was shot." I was wearing my Captain Obvious cape.

Owen ran around to look at him. "Diana!" he shouted. "Get a room open. Hurry!" He looked around, as if checking to see of we'd been followed, then gestured. "Come on. Get him inside."

I liked the fact that he didn't hesitate. He helped us get the sling free from the horses and guided us as we carried Mr. Roesch, improvised stretcher and all, to where a thin woman with a rifle slung over her shoulder held a door open. It took a bit of grunting and maneuvering, but we managed to get him into the bed without dropping him.

Robin was immediately by his side, checking his pulse and his breathing. She pulled the bandage back and checked the poultice she'd applied to the wounds. "He's doing fine. Doesn't look like the ride did him any harm."

Owen's wife asked from the doorway, "What do you need? We have some medical supplies. Not a lot, but some."

"I need to replace the poultice, and I'm running low on comfrey and plantain. And if you have clean bandages, that would be a big help too."

"We have comfrey growing in a bed out back. Plantain grows wild in the woods, so I've never bothered cultivating it. I'll get the comfrey, and we can get the plantain later. And young man?"

It took me a second to realize that she was talking to me. "Uh, yes, ma'am?"

"If you go back to the front room, you'll find a door on the wall behind the big mirror. Go in there, and there's a big first aid kit mounted on the wall. There's a box full of antibacterial ointments and some sealed gauze. Bring them to your friend here."

"Yes, ma'am." I ran to find the kit.

The wall-mounted first aid kit was a treasure trove. I found the box of antibacterial ointment and sealed gauze. I also saw packets of burn gel and antiseptic wipes as well as a host of others labeled with words I couldn't even pronounce. I grabbed what I had been instructed to get, along with a few of the antiseptic wipes, and ran back to the room.

Robin actually smiled when she saw what I held. She looked at Owen. "Thank you so much."

The portly man shrugged. "Can't lose the ambassador for my grand trade-route plans, can I?"

His wife came in carrying a wad of leaves, and she and Robin began to confer on how to treat Mr. Roesch. Owen led Kenni and me out of the room. "He looks like he's in good hands. Now, tell me what happened."

As we walked back to his office behind the mirror, I let Kenni do most of the talking, only filling in gaps for parts of the story she hadn't experienced personally. He nodded when she was finished. "I'm really sorry y'all ran into so much trouble. I hope your friend pulls through all right."

"Thanks," I said. "We took the gear off the people who shot him. We can trade for whatever supplies we use up."

Owen smiled. "I won't turn it down. Then again, I wouldn't have turned you away, either."

Kenni spoke up. "That M-16 your wife carries... you need ammo for it as bad as you did for the nine millimeters?"

He arched an eyebrow. "Worse. Not that I'd tell anyone, but we only have two magazines and a few loose rounds for it."

"So would a few hundred rounds for both cover your inconvenience?"

He smiled. "I suppose it depends on how inconvenient you become. But don't worry about haggling just yet. Like I said, I'm not about to turn out a friend in trouble."

"Is that what we are? Friends?"

Shrugging, he turned and opened a drawer. He pulled out a dark-blue wine bottle and put it on the table. "I suppose it's too soon to go that far." He pulled some coffee cups out of another drawer. After blowing them out, he poured an amber liquid from the bottle into each of the cups. "So for now"—he raised his cup—"here's to future friendships."

We all tapped glasses, and Owen slugged his back in a single swallow. I sniffed it, found it to be a pleasant smell, and took a quick sip. I smiled at the sweet burning. "What is this?"

Owen grinned. "You like it? I made it myself. It's mead."

Kenni took a swallow and smiled too. "You made this?"

"Bees are out back."

"Bees?" That surprised me.

"You don't know what mead is, do you, son?"

"No, sir, I guess not."

"Honey wine. It's tricky to make, but smooth when you get it right."

I took another swallow and felt the warmth settle into my chest.

"More?" Owen raised the bottle and leaned forward.

"No, thanks. I guess I don't drink much."

"Don't worry about it. I probably drink *too* much." He filled his cup again. "Can't help it. I love this stuff."

His wife opened the door and peeked into the room. "Your friend's awake."

Kenni and I jumped to our feet and were down the hall in seconds.

⊬——⊬——⊬——⊬——⊬

Mr. Roesch wasn't sitting up or smiling. But at least he was coherent. He lay in the bed as Robin spoke to him, explaining some of what had happened. His eyes flitted to us as Kenni and I sat beside the bed.

Kenni took his hand. "How are you, Mark?"

"Been better." His voice was barely louder than a whisper and weak. It frightened me that he could sound so frail.

"I guess so. Well, at least you're still with us on this side of the veil."

He closed his eyes. "So far." He was quiet for a few seconds before opening his eyes once more. With what looked like a lot of effort, he turned his head slowly and focused on me.

"Looks like you're gonna get to make that trip without me after all."

"What?"

"You have to represent Rejas."

I shook my head. "I don't think so. If I've learned anything from you in the last week, it's that I'm not as ready as I thought I was."

"No, you aren't. But Kenni can go with you. She'll teach you what to look for. What to listen for. You have time to learn."

Kenni seemed as concerned as I was. "Mark, why don't you just rest tonight? We can talk more about it tomorrow."

"All right. But we both know I'm not going to be able to travel for a while. And I'm sure as hell not gonna be up for a two- or three-week ride across country." He turned his head back and closed his eyes again. Within seconds, his breathing was slow and even.

I stood there looking at him for a bit longer, the implications of his words spinning in my head. *Now he wants me to take over? After he's done so much to point out how much I don't know? Even Kenni doesn't want to do it.*

121

She shrugged. After another few seconds, she turned to Owen. "So can we bother you for another couple of rooms?"

"Sure." He led us from the room, and we walked back to the office. "If you don't mind me asking, what's he talking about?"

Kenni eyed me, for once waiting on my lead. "It's something they caught wind of in Rejas. It's not my place to talk about it."

Owen looked at me expectantly.

"Owen, I need to think about this. Can we talk about it in the morning?"

He laid a friendly hand on my shoulder. "Of course. I'll open some rooms for you."

CHAPTER 20
DECISIONS

I AWOKE EARLY AGAIN AND SLIPPED outside to check on the horses. I had a moment of panic when I found them missing. I feared someone had stolen them after all, but then decided it was more likely that Owen had a barn or stable in which they had been housed for the night. Starting with the dirt out front, I followed tracks to the back of the building and found there was, indeed, a stable out behind the hotel. And someone had taken care of the horses after I had retreated to my room to hide for the night. Since Robin had been busy with Mr. Roesch, I figured it had probably been Kenni. I felt guilty for a few seconds then thought better of it. I'd taken that duty every morning and every night for over a week. A night off seemed only fair.

Since the horses had plenty of food and water, I took Bella and Cricket to the edge of the tree line and turned them loose to hunt while I took care of my bladder. After relieving myself, I kicked dirt over my waste and walked to the back of the trading post. I'd only seen it from the front and the inside before then. The view from the stable showed me just how large the place had once been. It was three stories tall, and from the side, I could see about twenty rooms per story. Patched shingles and rotting wood indicated there had been some sort of structural damage that someone, presumably Owen and his wife, had patched up. There were also dozens of windows that had been boarded over, victims of more than a decade without replacement parts.

Behind the building was a large, thriving garden and what looked to be the handle to a well pump. A little effort with it confirmed the existence of cool, clean water under my feet. I took off my shirt and filled a bucket that I found hanging on the pump handle. With the bucket filled, I washed my face and splashed my armpits. It had been a long time since I'd had a chance to bathe, and it looked like washing up at a well was going to be as close as I'd get for the time being. I poured some of the water over my head, combing my fingers through the tangles.

The girls came bounding across the clearing. Only Cricket had anything in her mouth. When they got to me, I saw it was a squirrel.

"Slim pickings, eh, girls?"

Cricket laid the rodent at my feet, and the two of them looked up expectantly.

I knelt and praised them, rubbing them behind the ears. "You're good girls, aren't you? Good girls!" I picked up the squirrel and tossed it behind them. "All yours. I'll get my own breakfast."

They dove in, and I drew another bucket of water for them to drink from before I went back to the front of the hotel.

Kenni was sitting in a chair in the lobby when I walked in. "Good morning," I said. "You mind if I sit?"

She waved her hand. "Help yourself."

We sat in silence for a few minutes, neither of us broaching the topic I was sure was on both our minds. I broke first. "So what do you think about what Mr. Roesch said? You think we should go on without him?"

"I don't know." She paused a moment before she continued. "At first I was dead set against it."

"Not that I'm going to argue, but why?"

"Because I don't think you're ready to take it on, and I *can't* take it on."

I avoided looking at her while I absorbed her condemnation of my ability. I felt the same way, but it hurt a little to hear it come from someone else. After I swallowed my pride, I asked, "Why can't you do it?"

She furrowed her brow at that. "I notice you aren't asking why I don't think you can do it."

I shrugged. "I don't think I can do it either. I told him that yesterday. So why would I argue? But I don't know why you think *you* can't do it."

Kenni leaned back as she looked at me. "That one's simple. I'm not from Rejas."

"Yeah. I figured that was what you'd say."

We were interrupted by the sound of Owen shuffling into the room. He seemed surprised to see us for a moment. "Well, you folks are early risers. Would you like some tea? Maybe some chicory?"

"Tea sounds great. Thanks," Kenni said.

Owen smiled. "What about you, Mr. Zachary?"

"Whatever you're having will be fine."

He nodded and left the room for places unknown within the bowels of the hotel, leaving Kenni and me to continue our discussion.

"I'm not sure that you not being from Rejas really matters. The call was a general broadcast. They don't know who received it or who's answering it until we get there."

"But the idea is that they're looking for groups who have the technology necessary to capture the signal from an orbiting satellite. And while I love my neighbors in Jason Grove, we hardly fit that description. We're just over a hundred people and barely scraping by."

"But the message didn't specify how many people. And it didn't say anything about how you got the message. What if you were only half your number but one of you had the radio setup that would let you pick up the message? Wouldn't you say that qualifies?"

Kenni paused, contemplating that.

I pushed further. "What if I told you we have three of the ham radios in Rejas and could take one to your home?"

125

"You do?"

I smiled. "No. But just think about how that changes things. It's only a radio. But it changes your whole way of looking at the situation, doesn't it?"

"Zachary Dawcett, that's just mean!" But she grinned. "And I guess it does change the equation a bit."

"So you could do it then, couldn't you?"

"Not really, no. It's not just the matter of having the radio. They're going to want to begin rebuilding by connecting with large groups... groups with enough resources to have supported and maintained a luxury item like that radio over the last decade."

"I don't follow."

"Think about it like this. If you wanted to kick-start the rebuilding of a nation, would you want to get every starving individual showing up at your doorstep and asking for help? Or would you want larger groups who would need less from you and could actually offer help instead? Which one would contribute more toward the rebuilding effort?"

What she said made sense, but it just seemed so wrong. There had to be a better way. But I couldn't think of one. *And that's another reason I shouldn't be the one to do this.* Feeling frustrated, I stood. "I'll be right back. I'm going to check on Mr. Roesch."

He was asleep, but Robin saw me peek in and stepped outside to speak without disturbing him. "He slept most of the night, although we had a bit of an argument when he had to use the bathroom. He didn't want to use the makeshift bedpan I handed him at first."

"What happened?"

"I let him try to sit up." She grinned. "He quit arguing after that. He may be a strong man, but there are still limits, and he has to learn to accept that."

I looked into the room at his sleeping form. "How long will it be before he can ride?"

"Weeks. Even then, it will only be for short distances."

I sighed. He really wasn't going to be able to make this trip. And he had known that the previous night—otherwise, he wouldn't have told me to go on without him. "All right. Owen is making tea. Would you like some?"

"I need to stay with Mark. But if you could bring it to me, that would be wonderful." She smiled, and I could see that she hadn't gotten a lot of sleep.

"I'll do that."

Owen had a large pot of tea and several mugs on the table when I returned. He was sitting across from Kenni, and the two were chatting like they were old friends. They looked at me expectantly as I approached.

"Robin says he's doing a little better."

"That's good news!" Owen said with a smile.

I continued. "She also says he won't be riding much for at least a few weeks."

They got quiet, contemplating the implications of that simple statement while I poured two mugs of the tea. I raised them. "Robin asked for a cup."

Kenni scooted her chair back. "Wait. I'll go with you." She turned to Owen. "Sorry, Owen. Can we finish our conversation later?"

"Of course. Go take care of your friends. I'll put some breakfast together."

"Thanks. Put it on our tab."

Owen smiled. "I'll do that."

As we left the room, I told her, "That tab's probably gonna get pretty steep if we're staying here for weeks."

Kenni nodded. "Yep. But I don't think we're all going to be here that long."

"So you think we should split up like Mr. Roesch said?"

She didn't answer immediately, appearing to think a bit before committing herself. "The best I can say at the moment is that I'm no longer as opposed to it as I was last night."

I was going to ask her what had changed her mind, but we were at the door to Mr. Roesch's room, and as we rounded the corner, I could see that he was awake again.

"Morning, Kenni. Zachary." His voice was still weak, but I thought it seemed better than it had the night before.

"How are you feeling, Mark?" Kenni smiled. "You're looking better this morning."

"When you start at the bottom, there's really no place to go except up."

"I guess that's true."

I walked past Kenni and sat on the side of his bed. "Robin says you're going to be laid up for a while."

"She was just telling me when you two walked in." He took a deep breath as if it pained him before continuing. "So have you all discussed what I said last night?"

"We have." I said. "We haven't made any decisions yet, but we talked a little about it. We don't think I'm ready. Neither of us." I watched Kenni as I continued. "I think Kenni should represent us, but she says no."

When I looked back at Mr. Roesch, his eyes were closed, and I wondered for a second if he had drifted back to sleep. But he spoke without opening them. "Why not?"

"She says she can't represent Rejas because—"

"Not that." He opened his eyes. He turned his head, looking past me at his friend behind me. "Why don't you think he's ready?"

Kenni put a hand on my shoulder in what I could only assume was meant to be a gesture to soften the condemnation she was about to put into words. "I didn't think he was mature enough to recognize the responsibility of representing so many people. I didn't think he was mature enough to recognize his own shortcomings. And I didn't think he realized how much he still has to learn about negotiating on behalf of others—how to read people. I was afraid he was too naïve."

I stared at the bedsheets as she spoke. Kenni's words were hard to hear, knowing as I did that they came from someone Mr. Roesch so implicitly trusted. But I had to admit they were probably true.

When I looked up from the sheet, Mr. Roesch's eyes were still closed, but he was smiling.

"And everything you said there was in past tense."

"Yes."

"You don't still believe that?"

Those words caught my attention.

I felt her hand squeeze my shoulder. "Not all of it. He's still pretty naïve, and he still doesn't fully understand his role in negotiating for a town. But he does recognize the fact that he's not really ready and that he has a lot to learn still."

I turned around for a moment to look at her, dumbstruck, and she smiled down at me.

"What about you, Zachary?" Mr. Roesch said. "What do you think?"

"I still don't think I'm ready." I realized as the words left my mouth that this was exactly what he meant. I wasn't the same kid who had stolen out of town in the middle of the night, expecting to ride hundreds of miles and broker some deal that would make me the town hero. I knew enough to know just how little I really knew. I snorted as I repeated that little tongue twister in my head. "And that's what you're talking about, isn't it?"

He smiled faintly before laying his head back on the pillow. Eyes closed once more, he spoke. "Kenni, can you teach him along the way?"

"Not as well as you could. I'm no lawyer."

"Neither am I. Not anymore. But I get your meaning. You bring something else to the table, though."

I knew they were talking about that second sight they had mentioned. I wasn't sure I believed in it, but I respected them enough to not say so.

"Maybe. It won't do any good if he's not willing to listen, though."

I looked back up at her then. Even though she was speaking to Mr. Roesch, I found she was looking directly at me. "Are you?"

"What?"

"Willing to listen to what I say?"

I hesitated. I liked Kenni. I respected her. But I wasn't sure I could buy into the whole second-sight thing as the others had. I also didn't want to lie to her. So I hedged. "I'm not sure. I know you're talking about that thing you said. Talking with the dead. But I just don't know if I can believe it the way you do."

To my surprise, Kenni laughed. "You know, that sounds like the same argument my brother and I used to have about my mother's gift."

"He didn't believe in it either?"

"Oh no, he believed all right. It was me that didn't believe."

I didn't expect that. "You?"

"All I ask is that you listen and keep an open mind. Can you do that?"

The question was more than it appeared on the surface. She was asking if I was willing to let her teach me while we traveled to Oklahoma. If I said yes, I was agreeing to continue the journey and represent the people of Rejas. And by that point, I recognized it as a commitment, not the selfish impulse that I had started with.

But while my reasons had changed, I found my decision hadn't. "Yes, ma'am. I can."

We all spent the rest of the day planning for our split. Kenni and I were to leave the next morning, continuing the trip to the Burns Flat spaceport. As she had pointed out, she didn't have the legal background Mr. Roesch did, but she had been in the Marines. Since we were heading to a military base, her insight in that regard could be invaluable. So she would continue my education with the basics of military life. And of course, there was always the hoodoo stuff too.

Since Robin was the closest thing we had to a medic, she was going to stay with Mr. Roesch at Owen's to help him with his recovery. For his part, Owen agreed to do whatever was necessary to help. He pointed out that doing so was a good way to keep in the good graces of the people who might be able to aid him in his plans to become a hub in a budding trade route across eastern

Texas. Of course, the fact that Kenni gave him one of the AR-15s, as well as two hundred rounds of ammunition for it, certainly didn't hurt our cause, either.

I had trouble getting to sleep that night. My emotions were all over the place. One minute I was fearful of the responsibility I was taking on, and the next minute, I was thrilled and excited at the prospect of being trusted with such a huge undertaking. Then I felt guilty at allowing myself to be excited at the prospect, which came at the cost of Mr. Roesch's physical well-being. At some point, I finally fell into a deep and fitful sleep.

CHAPTER 21
MOVING ON

KENNI AND I LEFT WITHOUT much fanfare. Mr. Roesch gave a relatively brusque pep talk about how I needed to pay attention to Kenni, learn as much as I could, and not take anything I was told at face value. And there were some quiet tears shed between Robin and Kenni. I made myself scarce when those started, figuring it was time they needed together. A few hours after sunrise, we were back on the road—Kenni and I, Cricket and Bella, Shadowfax and Tallulah, and a lot more firepower than we'd had when we left Owen's the last time.

Kenni had insisted we each keep one of the AR-15s. She still had her pistol and had given me a pair of what she sometimes called "forty-fives" and other times referred to as "nineteen-elevens." It was all pretty confusing to me, but she said she would teach me about them on the road. "Until we get a chance to go over it all, though, you just stick to your bow. I've seen what you can do with it."

That first day on our own was a hectic ride with very little said between us. I wasn't sure about how Kenni felt, but I was on edge the entire time. We rode up Highway 59 again but kept a faster pace than the last time. We didn't strain the horses too much, but we didn't make any unnecessary side trips, either. And we didn't slow down until we were well north of Marshall. I could see the tension leave Kenni's shoulders as we left the last of the buildings behind us, and while she remained vigilant, I could tell she was as glad as I was to be away from the town that had almost cost us Mr. Roesch's life.

About an hour out of Marshall, she was considerably more relaxed and began to talk. Taking her cue from Mr. Roesch, I suppose, she began to work the conversation around to a lesson about what she called *man's untapped gifts.* "There have always been stories of people with special gifts. Some cultures thought they were inherently evil, some that they were gifts from the gods. Still others simply viewed them as magical powers. But there were always stories about them. Hell, we even built movie franchises around them."

That led to a two-hour discussion of the exploits of a boy wizard who attended a school for magic. I just shook my head at the insanity of it all. But at least the story had distracted her for a while, letting her unwind from the stress of traveling through Marshall.

Late that afternoon, we came to a long stretch of crumbled concrete where the highway had once been raised up on short columns, turning it into a low bridge of sorts. It had been designed to go over a low area that was evidently prone to flooding, but in the midst of summer, the only water we encountered was a shallow stream about a hundred feet wide.

The collapsed concrete gave testament to the fact that the stream hadn't always been so placid, though. The footing on the highway was so treacherous that Kenni led us off the road, electing to ride through the trees alongside it. We traveled that way for a half mile or so.

When we got to the actual stream, she halted. "Let's stop for a bit here. Let the horses cool off and drink."

"Sounds good to me." I swung my aching legs out of the saddle, stretching for a minute before leading Tallulah into the shallow water. Kenni did the same with Shadowfax. Even Bella and Cricket waded into the stream to cool off, lapping up the water as they did.

Kenni looked around at the tree line on either side of the water. "Have you seen any sign of anyone?"

"Not for the last couple of hours. Why?"

"I figure this might be a good place to give you your first lesson with your pistols."

I shrugged noncommittally. "All right." I wasn't sure how I felt about it. A part of me was honestly a bit frightened by the things. I'd never even fired my dad's pistols. With ammunition being so scarce, opportunities had been rare. And I was perfectly content with my knives and bow. But there was also a part of me that wanted to feel the power of the Old Days weapon in my hands. I had seen them fired. I had seen the damage they could do. And I wanted to control that power. It intrigued me and terrified me all at once.

Within minutes, she had me standing on the stream bank with the pistols lying on an Old Days plastic tarp she had laid out. I was a little disappointed. I'd expected her to hand me a pistol and point me toward a tree or something. But other than bringing them to the tarp, she hadn't let me touch them. "First, there are some rules. They're very serious, so pay attention. Rule number one is you always treat the pistol as if it's loaded and ready to fire. Got it?"

"Yes, ma'am."

"And cut out the *ma'am* crap. I'm still Kenni." Before I could reply, she went on. "Rule number two. You never, *ever* point it at anyone unless you're ready to shoot them. Until then, you point it at the ground or away from wherever there are people."

She looked at me, waiting for a reaction, so I nodded.

"Rule three. Keep your finger off the trigger until you're ready to fire. They don't fire by themselves, so keeping your finger off the trigger helps avoid accidents."

She raised her eyebrows, again checking to make sure I understood.

"Got it."

"Then the last rule is that you never fire unless you have a clear shot, you know that you're aiming at what you intend to hit, and there's nothing behind your target you don't want to shoot."

"Pretty much the same rules as for bow hunting," I said.

"All right. So I guess before we get going, do you have any questions?"

I thought about what I had been told so far. "You said my pistols are forty-fives?"

"Yes."

"But didn't you also call them nineteen-elevens?"

"The type of pistol is a nineteen-eleven. The ammunition they fire is forty-five caliber." She bent over and picked up one of my pistols. I noticed that, true to her rules, she kept the pistol pointed away from both of us as well as the horses. I missed what she did next, but there was a metallic sound, and part of the pistol came out of the grip and into her left hand. She handed me the piece that had come away from the rest of the pistol, and I held it delicately, uncertain about how dangerous it might be.

Kenni then pulled her own pistol from behind her back and repeated the process with it. She handed me the same piece from her own pistol. "See the difference in the size of the rounds in the magazines?"

I stared at her blankly. Turning the two pistol pieces over in my hands, I shrugged. "What am I looking at?"

Kenni blinked. "You really don't know anything about these, do you?"

"No."

"Okay, have a seat." She squatted cross-legged and waved her hand at a spot opposite her on the tarp. I sat down and watched as she took the pistol pieces from me again and began repeatedly pushing on one end of mine with her thumb. Each time she did, a bullet thudded to the tarp in front of her. She repeated the process with the piece from her pistol. When she finished, there were two small piles of ammunition in front of her.

She took one bullet from either pile and handed them to me. "See the difference in the size?"

I nodded.

"The big one is from your magazine. It's a forty-five caliber. The smaller one is from mine. It's a nine millimeter."

I remembered from school that there had been two ways of measuring things before D-day. One was called the metric system, and I remembered it being full of measurements with names like *millimeters* and *centimeters*. I didn't remember too much else about it except that we didn't use it.

And there was something called a "caliber" too?

"You look confused. What's wrong?"

"I guess I just need to know how much of this I need to remember. Do I need to learn more about the metric system?"

She laughed. "No. For now, you just need to remember that there are different sizes of ammunition and you can only use the ones that are designed for your pistol."

I sighed with relief, causing her to laugh yet again. Over the next half hour or so, she showed me the basics of how to load the ammunition into the magazine, which was the part that came out of the pistol's grip. She showed me how to shove the magazine into the pistol, how to eject it with the push of a button on the grip, and how to load a round into the barrel. She called that *chambering a round*.

She had to remind me a few times to keep my finger off the trigger and showed me how to lay it comfortably along the side of the trigger guard, but finally, I was relatively comfortable holding the heavy thing in my hand.

"Okay, take these." She handed me a couple of small wads of cloth. "Stick them in your ears, because things are about to get really loud."

She stuffed cloth in her own ears, and I followed suit.

"You ready?" Her voice was muffled, but I could still hear her. I nodded.

"Good. Now, aim at that tree. Don't fire yet. Just get it in your sights like I showed you."

I did, concentrating on getting the sight picture where I thought it should be.

Kenni came up beside me and adjusted my grip. "Now, take a deep breath, and squeeze the trigger slo—"

I nearly dropped the pistol when it fired. Between the sound and the unexpected kick, I was completely unprepared. Bella and Cricket both yipped and ran nearly twenty feet before turning to see what had caused the deafening noise. Wide eyed, I started to turn to Kenni, only catching myself at the last second, avoiding pointing the pistol at her by force of will.

Keeping the pistol pointed at the tree, I took my finger off the trigger and looked at her, my heart pounding in my chest with excitement and a bit of fear. She must have seen it in my face, because she laughed.

"All right. Let's try again."

CHAPTER 22
BAD WEATHER

WITH MARSHALL BEHIND US, KENNI was considerably more relaxed, and the first day past the town, we exchanged stories. She told me about her time as a Marine, describing her training and something called *boot camp*. I was surprised when she told me how short a time she had been in uniform.

"I was only in for about two years," she admitted as we rode. "I was a lance corporal, getting ready to move up to corporal, when the shit hit the fan."

She must have seen the look on my face because she chuckled. "Corporal is a rank. I was just getting started with a career in the Marines."

That surprised me. With the way Mr. Roesch had treated her, I'd assumed she had been some big important warrior in the Old Days.

"Mark is right. You really need to work on hiding your emotions better."

I felt my face warm, knowing as I did that blushing was yet another example of what they were talking about.

She laughed again. "You must be a terrible poker player."

"Yeah, I am."

We rode in silence for a short while before she asked, "Mark told me Rejas was attacked when you were a kid. What happened?"

"He didn't tell you?"

She snorted. "In case you haven't noticed, Mark isn't big on talking."

I smiled at the understatement. "I guess it really started on D-day." I told her the story of how my parents had gotten us out of Houston before the bombs fell and how they had come across the remains of an ambush and my dad had been captured. I described how we turned the tables on the thugs who had captured him, ambushing them and setting in motion a series of events that would play out over the next few years, culminating in Crazy Larry's attack on Rejas.

"He had tanks? Where'd he get tanks?"

"Some of the men we captured told us it took him more than a year to build his army from prisons and street gangs. He eventually found some people who were able to get him into a National Guard station."

"And they just turned over for him? No way."

I shrugged. "All I can tell you is what they told us after it was all over."

"And you defeated them with deer rifles and homemade explosives? Must not have been very modern tanks."

"Something called Abraham, I think."

Her eyebrow arched. "Abrams? Those things are monsters! They suck up an ungodly amount of fuel, but they're damn near impenetrable, with heavy armaments... they're freaking fortresses. How the hell did you defeat them?"

The story took more than an hour, and I intentionally dragged it out when I realized that as long as I was talking, she wasn't. So I managed to get out of a few hours of lessons.

When I wound up my story, she nodded. "That's amazing. You're lucky to be alive."

"I know."

"So why does it bother you? Sounds to me like you guys are freaking heroes. You should be proud of what you accomplished."

"I'm no hero," I couldn't help myself. It pissed me off when people said something like that to me. "My sister was a hero. Dad was a hero. Me? I was the kid that got himself kidnapped. I was the one who was too weak to fight back when Larry had me and too scared to run away when I got the chance. So people had to come and rescue me." My anger faded, replaced by shame and bitterness. "And a lot of them died. That's how much of a hero I am."

I swallowed and turned away as I knuckled the tears away.

"That's why you were so insistent on doing this, isn't it? You're trying to make up for what you see as a weakness."

I didn't answer. I couldn't. When I thought about it, I honestly didn't know whether or not it was true. Maybe what I thought of as wanting to make my own mark was really an attempt to make up for the lives lost when those people had come to rescue me.

"Zachary? You said you were ten years old when that happened. You can't blame yourself for any of that."

I couldn't look at her, fearing the look of sympathy that I knew would be there. Sympathy I didn't want. Sympathy I didn't feel I deserved.

I pulled Tallulah ahead, the knot in my chest making it difficult to breathe for the moment.

Neither of us mentioned the discussion again. Instead, Kenni began instructing me much as Mr. Roesch had, only she seemed even more determined. Over the next few days, she lectured me with a detailed knowledge of the Constitution of the United States. She carried with her a small book describing the Constitution and its amendments. She had me memorize the preamble, and each day as we rode, she taught me more about that document than I wanted to know. After only five days, I was begging for a break.

"Not a chance. If these people really are representatives of the government, then the Constitution is the key to the laws of the land. If you know the Constitution, you know the foundation of the government."

"But there's no way I'm going to be able to memorize that thing!" I pointed to the book she carried.

"Probably not. But you can learn what it means. Now, from the beginning, what's the significance of the first ten amendments to the Constitution?"

I sighed. "They establish a Bill of Rights to limit the power of government and protect individual rights."

"What's the meaning of the First Amendment?"

"It establishes that freedom of speech and religion are basic rights and that the government can't interfere with them."

"Good. And why is that significant?"

And so it went. Every day, she lectured me on the Constitution and the meaning of the various amendments. After a few days, when she felt I had a good grasp on that, she changed things up.

"On D-day, the president announced he was placing the country under martial law. That means the military is put in charge of taking care of things and parts of the Constitution are temporarily suspended."

"What? Then why did I spend all this time memorizing it? If it doesn't apply, then what's the use of learning it?"

"I never said it doesn't apply, only that portions of it are superseded. Now we're going to discuss something called *habeas corpus* and the Uniform Code of Military Justice. Since we're heading toward a military base, this may be especially important."

By the end of each day, I was ready to claw my eyes out. I enjoyed the brief period after each day's ride. Each evening, we made it a point to find an area well away from any populated town on the map, and Kenni continued my firearms training. I was getting used to the pistols, though I still wasn't comfortable with the rifle. But I was still happy for the break at the end of the day. At least while I was learning to shoot, I had wads of cloth in my ears, so there was no way for Kenni to lecture me anymore.

With my reassurance, the girls quickly learned to mostly ignore the noise the shooting made. Kenni commented on just how quickly that had happened. Apparently, it normally took several weeks to train a dog not to panic at the sound of gunfire. She attributed it to my supposed mystical gift with animals, and she talked to me in depth about it. She approached it from the viewpoint that it was somehow similar to the *sight* she claimed to have, and she wondered if I might be able to tap deeper into my elusive talent. I had come to accept the *possibility*, at least, that my ability with animals could be — much as I hated to use the word — a supernatural thing and that I was able to do something that others apparently couldn't. It was hard to deny the evidence of my own eyes, after all.

But Kenni wasn't content with that. She had me try to predict the future, guess what she wrote in the dirt when I couldn't see it, and even move a piece of thread with my mind. I felt like an idiot, but I had promised her I would try to keep an open mind. She had me try meditation, visualization, relaxation, and even a bout of hypnosis, which neither of us was very good at, but she was determined. I even awoke one night to find her whispering suggestions into my ear. And let me tell you, that about freaked me out.

After that, I began hanging my hammock again and sleeping in the trees. Before that night, I hadn't wanted to appear rude and give the impression that I didn't want to be around my only traveling companion. But after that incident, I reasoned that if I couldn't keep her from filling my head while I was awake, at least I could keep her from trying it while I slept.

The weather turned bad on us after a few days, and travel became a slow, wet, and miserable experience. Where we had been making twenty miles or more in a day, we were suddenly making roughly half that distance, and it quickly became evident that the trip was going to take longer than I had hoped.

Three days into the rain, Kenni and I huddled in front of a small fire beneath her tarp. It was the end of another wet and nasty day, and my nerves were definitely beginning to wear thin. The rain was bitter cold and kept the Red River to our north much too high for us to try and cross without a bridge. We'd been paralleling the river for the last two days, looking for a surviving bridge to get across it, but all the smaller ones we'd come across so far had long ago succumbed to decay and the current.

We had pitched the tarp at an angle over the fire pit, making an improvised lean-to, and the patter of the rain on the Old Days plastic was irritatingly loud. But I had to admit that it kept the majority of the wind and rain out much better than my oiled leather one would have. Kenni held the map while I held a small burning branch over it so we could see. Bella and Cricket huddled beside us, munching the remains of a raccoon Kenni had shot. It wasn't the tastiest meal we'd had on the road, but neither was it the worst. And the girls weren't picky.

Kenni pointed to an intersection on the map. "We should get to Highway 271 before noon tomorrow. With any luck, the bridge will still be crossable. It looks like it was a big enough highway that even if the bridge has some damage, chances are good it'll still be in good enough shape for us to get across on the horses. Once we're on the other side, we'll be in Oklahoma."

"And then how far to the spaceport?"

My hopes fell as she unfolded the map to show another section. She was silent for a few minutes as she tried to calculate the distance. "It depends a lot on which route we end up taking. We could stay on 271 and go up to 40. It's a longer route, but we would have the advantage of better roads for the most part. Of course, that also means we'll probably run into more people. And" — she pointed on the map — "it'll also send us through Oklahoma City."

"Is that necessarily a bad thing?"

"I don't know. It keeps us well north of the Dallas-Fort Worth region, so there isn't much chance of us hitting any fallout areas. Assuming Oklahoma City wasn't nuked too, then all we have to worry about is whether or not the people in there are friendly."

She traced another path on the map. "If we do a more direct path, we could take minor roads and cut across country in places. It's less distance, but it takes us closer to DFW, and the rougher terrain is more likely to slow us down." She shrugged. "It's probably a tossup as to which way is faster, but either way, it looks like we have at least another week before we get there."

"A week!"

"Assuming the weather clears up soon. And that we don't run into too much trouble." She grinned at the look on my face. "And you thought you were going to make this trip by yourself?"

That seemed like years ago. "So which way makes more sense to you?"

"I would stick to the better roads."

I noticed she didn't hesitate. "All right, then."

"Don't you want to know why?"

I shrugged. "Not really. If it's good enough for you, it's good enough for me."

She shook her head. "Zachary, you do realize you're supposed to take charge of this trip at some point, don't you? And that means you need to start making some decisions on your own."

"Yes. And I just did. I decided that since there are pros and cons to both routes, and I don't have any experience with either one or any opinion on which way I would prefer to go, then it makes sense to let you choose. It's called picking your battles."

Kenni laughed out loud. "All right. Let's try to get as much sleep as this miserable rain will allow. You sleeping down here, or are you pulling another Tarzan tonight?"

I shook my head. "I think I'll stay down here tonight. It wouldn't do to slip in the rain while I'm twenty feet up." I looked at her. "But you have to promise not to try any of that whispering-in-my-ear crap while I'm asleep."

"Fair enough. I'm too tired to try anything tonight, anyway."

So we rigged our tarps together over the wet ground and settled in for a gloomy night.

The rain had let up by morning, though the clouds remained a threatening reminder of how wretched the day could still turn. But the threat remained just that, and we were allowed to dry out a bit as we traveled.

The Highway 271 bridge was more accurately three bridges. One was for northbound traffic, the other for southbound. The third was an old railroad trestle. Or at least it had been at some point in years past. Most of the railroad bridge was gone. And the southbound side of the concrete bridge had a huge section missing near the shore. Lumber and tree trunks piled up underneath the base showed that at some point in the past, a flood had swept the trestle and a considerable amount of other debris into the concrete supports. It had been enough to collapse a good thirty feet or more of bridge.

The northbound side had taken some damage as well, but luckily for us, it was still good enough for a couple of people on horseback. So finally, after nearly three days of searching, we were able to cross into Oklahoma.

PART 2
OKLAHOMA

CHAPTER 23
ENTERING OKLAHOMA

OUR FIRST FEW DAYS IN Oklahoma were uneventful. The sky was still overcast and seemed to depress even the local wildlife. There weren't even any birds that ventured into the dreary gray skies. For some reason, I had expected the land to somehow look different, but the north side of the Red River looked just like the south side.

That changed by the middle of the second day when the terrain began to get hillier. At first I was happy about the variation in scenery. The new view was much more interesting than the usual flat land I was used to around Rejas. But I quickly realized it was simply one more thing that further slowed our travel.

With the soft, wet ground and the increasingly steep hills, our progress began to slow. I noticed also that as we wove our way up and down and through the hills, the roadway got worse and worse until there were many places where entire sections of road had been washed downhill. We were easily able to swing clear of those areas, but it was enough to make me temper my earlier excitement over a bit of topographical variance. By the fourth day, I had come to accept that the journey was simply going to take as long as it took, and I actually found myself going over some of the lessons Kenni and Mr. Roesch had drilled into me.

"Something wrong with Bella?" Kenni's question drew me out of my contemplation. I glanced up the road to see Cricket romping through the brush. Expecting to see Bella following her, I waited a few seconds before asking, "Where is she?"

Kenni pointed, and I turned in my saddle to find Bella lagging behind. That alone was unusual. But she kept glancing back as if there was something following us. I pulled out my binoculars, but the way was clear for as far as I could see. I scanned the trees on either side of the roadway but saw nothing there either.

"Bella. Come on, girl."

She trotted up to me, tail wagging again.

Kenni looked at me, and I shrugged. "She's acting like there's something back there, but I can't see anything."

Bella's odd behavior continued off and on throughout the day, making me more paranoid than I cared to admit. After a few hours, I rode up beside Kenni. "After we top the next hill, I think I'll double back and see if I can spot anything."

"If there really is someone back there, they'll hear Tallulah."

"I think so too. So I want you to lead her. I'll hit the trees and go back on foot."

Kenni shook her head. "Not a good idea. What if there's a group?"

"Then I should hear them before they hear me."

She hesitated. "I still don't like it."

"I'm not going to take any chances. But if there really is someone following us, we need to know."

"Fine. But get back as soon as you know something." She looked up at the sky. "Another hour and a half of daylight. I'm going to keep the pace slow. If you haven't caught back up in an hour, I'll start looking for a place to stay the night. It'll be on the downhill side of the road, near trees. You know what to look for."

"I'll find you."

"All right. Be careful. I know you don't like the rifle, but take your pistols with you. If something goes wrong, at least I'll be able to hear you shooting."

I nodded. Kenni had insisted I carry the pistols and extra magazines on me ever since she had started showing me how to shoot. I was still a little nervous with them but was comfortable enough that I wasn't afraid I was going to accidentally shoot myself. As we rode up the hill, I casually loosened the strap on my go-bag. I glanced down at Bella and Cricket. They had sensed I was preparing to dismount and were watching me expectantly.

Should I take them with me or try to get them to stay with Kenni? One look at them, and I knew there was no way they were going to stay behind.

"The girls will be going with me."

"I figured as much."

As soon as we topped the hill, I tossed my reins to Kenni, grabbed my gear, and ran for the trees. As I had expected, the girls were right on my heels. Once I made it inside the tree line, I stopped briefly and strung my bow. I checked all my gear, securing everything so I wouldn't lose it as I trotted through the brush. The holstered pistols were hard to get used to, but Kenni's insistence that I wear them at all times for the last few days had helped in that regard. As soon as I was satisfied, I looked at the two dogs waiting patiently for me.

Together, we moved quietly through the brush, backtracking along the road we had already traveled.

For half an hour, I carefully searched for any sign of someone following us. Light was fading, and I was about to give it up and turn back when the fur on Bella's back ridged up like a Mohawk and she started a low growl. A second later, Cricket was beside her, legs locked, attention riveted on the brush ahead. "Stay!" I hissed at them as I moved to put a tree between myself and whatever was in there.

I instantly transferred the four arrows I held in my bow hand to my right, nocking one and placing each of the others between my fingers, where I could quickly swing and nock them one at a time in rapid succession.

I took a calming breath, whispered to the girls, "Come," and stepped out from behind the tree. Bella was trembling, whining slightly as we moved forward.

We were halfway to the stand of brush when a large shape squealed, charging out of the foliage toward us. The girls launched forward, barking and snarling, and I let loose with two arrows before I even knew what I was looking at. My mind registered the shape of the wild hog as my third arrow found its mark. Panic began to set in as the thing kept coming at me even as I loosed my fourth arrow.

The hog was close enough that I could clearly see its tusks and the rage in its eyes just as the dogs hit it from behind. The feral beast spun to confront its attackers, and I dropped my bow and fumbled at my holster. My hand was shaking as I drew a pistol. I tried to aim, but the snarling, squealing, spinning mass of fur wouldn't hold still long enough for me to get a good shot. "Bella! Cricket! Hold!" But they were caught in a fighting rage with the hog, and they either wouldn't or couldn't disengage.

I was terrified that the hog was going to hurt one of them, but I didn't trust my aim with the pistol to hit the writhing pig without endangering the girls. Snarling my own fright and anger, I ran forward, pointing the pistol at the fight, watching for a clear shot.

I was barely ten feet away when I saw my chance. The hog spun toward me just as the girls jumped clear. With a shout of fear, I pulled the trigger.

And nothing happened.

I knew instantly what I had done, and I fumbled my thumb to release the safety, even as the hog fixated on me and charged. Squeezing again, I fired three times and jumped aside. The hog flew past as I backpedaled, scurrying out of its way until my heel caught on a branch. Everything went into slow motion. I had time to curse my clumsy feet even as I felt my arms flailing for balance. I saw the big porker slip as it tried to turn back toward me in midstride.

Panicked, I struggled to bring my pistol back on target even as I fell, swinging the sights back onto the pig not five feet away. I pulled the trigger once more as I landed on my butt. Fearing I would accidentally shoot myself or one of the girls, I yanked my finger off the trigger and scrambled to get back up before the thing got a chance to gore me or the dogs. Rising to one knee, I raised the pistol once more as the girls flew past me. "Bella, Cricket, no!"

I was frantic to keep them out of the line of fire. But as I looked on, I saw it was over. The hog had taken four arrows and four rounds from the pistol. One lucky shot had penetrated the porcine skull, and that had finally been enough to bring the big animal down. The hog lay quivering on the ground, spilling its life into the moist earth.

CHAPTER 24
PORK

KENNI CAME AT A GALLOP when she heard the gunshots, Tallulah still tied behind her. She arrived, rifle at the ready, while there was just enough light to see us. When she saw me dragging the big carcass onto the road, she shook her head. "You know, I would have been just as happy with rabbit again."

I was still shaking too much from exertion and adrenaline to find any humor in her joke. She must have sensed that, because she swung down out of the saddle and drew her knife. "No need to haul the whole thing. Let's dress him here and lighten the load."

I sat in the road and let her do the work while my nerves settled. After a bit, I managed to breathe without my chest shaking and remembered some of the breathing exercises my dad and Megan had taught me during my training. I concentrated on inhaling and exhaling, willing my trembling to stop with each breath until I felt I could speak without my voice breaking.

Finally, I looked up to see Kenni watching me as she tossed the pig's intestines aside. "You okay?"

I nodded. "Just shook up."

"He didn't get you, did he? Those tusks can be nasty."

"No. He got close, but I'm okay." With a start, I thought about the dogs. I hadn't checked to see if they had been hurt. I looked around and found them lying just behind me. "Bella, Cricket!" They came up to me, tails wagging, snouts covered in blood.

"I already checked them. They're fine." Kenni looked back at the hog. "He was a big one. It's a shame, really."

I looked up. "A shame?"

"Yeah. There's no way to preserve it while we're on the road." She tossed a few of the internal organs to the dogs and shoved the intestines and bladder aside. "And there's no way we can eat all of it before it goes bad. Just seems like such a waste."

"Well, you know, I guess I just wasn't thinking about that when the damn thing was charging at me."

She chuckled as she hacked the hindquarters off, wrapping them in her tarp before walking into the tall grass beside the road. I saw her kneel and wipe her blade and hands in the grass, cleaning them as well as she could before coming over to sit beside me. "We can roast some of the haunches and eat fresh meat tonight, and I can make a rack to smoke strips overnight. They should last a week or so. Scavengers will get the rest. I just hate wasting a kill."

She nudged me, and when I turned to her, she handed me a small bundle. "Here's a reminder."

I unwrapped the bundle to find four tusks, each one around four inches long. "Funny, when they were coming at me, they looked a lot bigger."

"Don't underestimate them. Those are plenty big enough to have torn you up pretty good. And they would have easily killed either one of your dogs."

I wrapped the bundle back up and shoved it into my pocket. We rested for a few minutes before she patted me on the shoulder. "Come on. It's been a fun evening and all that, but we really should get back to camp." She held up her still-sticky hands. "I need to get this blood washed off."

"Where?"

"I found a place next to a little river about a mile north of here. I was about to start setting up when I heard you shooting."

I took a deep breath. "All right."

She helped me get to my feet, and I struggled to hide my tremors from her as I climbed back into the saddle.

That was the first clear night we'd had in several days. The clouds had parted, and I lay in my hammock with a belly full of fresh pork, staring at the stars. The trees weren't nearly as dense as back home, but by that point, Kenni knew what I liked for my hammock. She had found a place near the river with some tall trees growing near the bank, and I had done my high-wire act, stringing the hammock and support lines as high as I felt safe climbing. The trees weren't quite as tall as I was used to in the Texas Big Thicket, but they were respectable and served to hold me a good twenty feet above the ground.

The curve of the river had the added benefit of giving us an unobstructed view of the eastern sky. Kenni slept below, and the girls had gotten used to her company. As far as they were concerned, she had long ago become part of the pack.

I thought about that. Before I left Rejas, I'd never met the woman, and my biggest worry had been whether or not I would ever find a girl who would like me for who I was. Just a few weeks later, I was traveling with her on a journey that had the potential to be the most important thing I would ever do in my life. I'd killed three people and learned to fire an Old Days pistol and, in fact, carried two of the priceless firearms on my person. I had also seen Mr. Roesch nearly killed by a total stranger just because that person wanted our horses.

I reflected on all the changes I'd been though in the last several days. It reminded me of a saying my older sister had: "Life is what happens when you aren't paying attention." If that was true, I needed to pay closer attention. I didn't know if I would survive much more life like that coming at me.

CHAPTER 25
WAR PARTY

WHEN THE SUN FINALLY MADE its appearance the following morning, I had cause to regret that unobstructed view of the eastern sky. The sun's fiery blaze was impossible to ignore as the bright orb made its appearance over the crest of the hill across the river. I raised my hand to block the blinding light and groaned as I felt every aching muscle in my body protest. Now that the immediate fight-or-flight situation was over, my back, legs, and shoulders were telling me in no uncertain terms that they objected to the abuse to which I had subjected them the day before.

I looked up at my support line and suddenly regretted having decided to sleep above the ground. It was a comfortable enough sleeping arrangement, but swinging from tree to tree to break the hammock back down promised to be a painful experience.

True to its promise, the morning did start with a multitude of aches and pains. But I managed to get my gear to the ground without breaking anything in my pack or my body. Kenni grinned as she saw me wincing.

"Looks like you're hurting pretty good this morning." She was working on stoking the previous night's fire.

"I wouldn't have thought I would ache like this. It's not like I wrestled the damned boar. I just shot it."

"Didn't you say you had to dodge it?"

"Yeah."

"And you fell on your ass."

"Don't remind me."

"And then you dragged it to the road. What was that—fifty yards?"

"I don't know," I said. "I didn't pay attention."

"And from what I saw, you were fighting an adrenaline rush the whole time, weren't you?"

"I guess."

She just shrugged. "The body demands its due."

I looked at her as she fed more wood to the coals. "That's it? That's the inspirational advice you have for me? The great words of wisdom? All you have for me is 'The body demands its due'?"

"Well, there's always the one my mama used to tell me." She made her voice old and wizened as she recited, "Things is what they is, child."

I picked up a twig and tossed it at her, and she laughed as I winced at the pain in my shoulder that simple action brought.

"That'll teach you!" she said.

I almost showed her the lonely finger but decided at the last second that I didn't quite know her well enough for that, so I settled for waving her off as I limped over to check on the horses. After making sure they were all right, I went back to the fire and pulled the map from my bag. "Any idea where we are?"

She shook her head. "All I know is we're north of some place called Daisy." Before I could ask, she said, "Remember the intersection yesterday afternoon? I saw a sign laying on the ground before we got to it. Said it was the exit for Daisy and Stringtown."

I found Daisy and checked our progress. I looked at how far we still had to go and sighed.

"I could have told you we still have a good distance. Until we hit Highway 40, there's no need to get excited."

Checking the distance between Daisy and Highway 40, I groaned. "That's gonna take a couple more days at least."

"And from there, it'll be about another week to the spaceport."

Kenni shredded some of the smoked pork strips and mixed them in a small pan with some eggs.

That caught my attention. We had run out of eggs several days ago. But Kenni had been after me to be more observant, so I looked around. I felt a small measure of triumph when I solved the mystery. "Duck eggs?"

Kenni smiled and nodded. "You hungry?"

It was the best breakfast we'd had in days. My full belly and the bright sunshine improved my mood considerably, and I was actually smiling as we got back on the road. But the mood didn't last. By noon, the heat had combined with the moisture-saturated ground to make the ride absolutely miserable. Bella and Cricket were filthy, their fur crusted in mud, paws all but invisible against the squishy dirt. To make matters worse, Bella seemed to be spooked again. She was skittish, snapping at Cricket when she tried to lure her into playing. She kept looking backward, checking the road behind us, just as she had the previous day, in a manner that made me think once more that someone might be following us.

"Kenni?" When she turned, I pointed to Bella.

Kenni looked down the road then shrugged. "I don't know. I would have thought it was the boar. Maybe not, though." She turned and continued riding.

"Wait." I prodded Tallulah up to ride beside her. "Shouldn't we check it out?"

"You did that yesterday. We lost two hours of travel time and didn't find anyone." She glanced over her shoulder then shook her head. "No. If someone is following us, they don't want us to know it. And they're good enough that we can't catch them. If it wasn't for Bella, we wouldn't even suspect anyone was there."

I thought about that and figured she was right. But like Bella, I was spooked. I kept turning suddenly in my saddle, hoping to catch a glimpse of movement. Each time, I only succeeded in making myself feel more foolish.

We were finally making headway again. The sun and heat were helping to dry out some of the soggy ground, and though the humidity made the air thick and had us dripping with sweat, we had nevertheless been able to step our pace back up to normal. Kenni was quizzing me on the reasons for the Electoral College when she abruptly pulled Shadowfax up and raised her hand for me to get quiet.

"Bella. Cricket. Sit!" I hissed. I peered ahead, northward, on the road, but saw nothing. Reining Tallulah up beside Kenni, I leaned over and whispered, "What do you see?"

"Nothing. Thought I heard something."

I strained to hear but got nothing except the sound of insects and birds. After a few seconds, I shook my head. "Are you sure?"

"No. But let's get off the road."

We rode into the trees beside the path of what had once been Highway 271 and waited in silence. After several minutes, Kenni sighed. "Maybe I was—"

The faint shout was unmistakable, and we looked at one another. We dismounted and tied the horses to a tree. I told the girls "Stay," and we crept carefully forward through the trees. Less than half a mile through the woods, we began to hear voices more distinctly, and I smelled cooking meat. I was about to mention it to Kenni when a flicker of movement ahead caught my attention, and I tapped her arm. With a barely perceptible jutting of my chin, I indicated that she should look to our right.

She took the hint and turned her head slowly. Just twenty feet or so beyond the scrub we were hiding behind, a tall man faced away from us. He wore a leather vest that left dark, muscular arms uncovered. Darker than I was, though not as dark as Kenni, the man had long black hair. His shoulders moved as he worked on something, and I wondered for a second what he was doing until the splash of water on leaves and the sudden smell of urine wafted our way.

I looked around, watching for any movement that might give away the position of anyone else, but I saw nothing. The sound of his stream eased, and with a shake and a hunch, the man finished his business and tucked himself back into his pants. He turned, and we froze until he was out of sight. When I felt safe, I gestured toward the direction he had gone and raised my eyebrows in a silent question. Kenni nodded, and we crawled slowly through the brush, watching for anyone else, every foot of the way. We reached a point where the sounds of several people resounded from a short distance ahead. I saw movement through the leaves and once more tapped Kenni's arm. I pointed to the right, and she nodded then pointed to my left. There were two of them. From our crawling position, all I could see were legs as the people walked a methodical patrol.

I silently slipped my quiver and gear bag off my shoulders and eased back to put a large hickory between the guards and me. Kenni watched as I pulled myself into the lower branches. Moving slowly so my movements wouldn't attract any attention, I climbed higher and higher until I could see their camp. I watched carefully, taking note of its layout and occupants.

It was in a clearing several yards ahead, and it looked like there were ten men and six women, plus the four men walking patrol just outside the clearing. I hugged the trunk of the hickory, so I didn't think anyone could see me as I watched. Many had dark skin like that of the man who had relieved himself in the woods, but about a third of them were white, and one was ebony black. One of the white men was very pale with bright red hair and a massive beard.

But the thing that immediately caught my attention was the fact that about half of them had painted faces. I saw one man walking in my direction across the clearing and got a good look at him. He had a band of green painted horizontally across his eyes. The green was trimmed in red, and above it, his forehead was painted blue with faint black streaks in it, and a black handprint covered his mouth.

I saw similar patterns on many of the others. Handprints were common, as were large patches of green across the eyes. Foreheads varied, but most were red or blue. Some had odd symbols and streaks in yellow or black.

Most had bows and arrows, though a few had pistols or rifles. There were also other firearms, crude-looking affairs that lacked the sleek and deadly look of the Old Days weapons. They were obviously recent manufactures, and the idea that someone was making firearms again was invigorating.

As I peered down over the camp, I overheard bits and pieces of various conversations. Some were in English, but others were completely foreign to me. When I thought I had seen enough, I waited until the guards were looking away before easing back down the tree to the ground. Kenni was waiting impatiently. She raised an eyebrow in query, and I just jerked my head back, indicating we should put some distance between us and the camp.

Several hundred yards into the woods, I turned to her excitedly. "You're not going to believe what's out there."

"A bunch of Indians?"

That took the wind out of my sails.

"I saw the guy's face when he was peeing in the bushes," she said. "If you hadn't turned all squirrel man on me, I could have warned you. This is Oklahoma after all."

I stared blankly. "What's that got to do with anything?"

"Oklahoma? Indian Territory? It's where a good portion of the Indians were relocated in the 1800s."

My confusion must have still shown because she shook her head in exasperation. "I thought you said you went to school! Didn't you ever hear of the Trail of Tears?"

"Let's just assume I didn't. It has something to do with there being a bunch of painted-up Indians in the clearing over there?"

"When the white men took the lands east of the Mississippi, they forced the natives there to relocate to what's now Oklahoma."

"They took their land?"

"Yep. Forced them to march thousands of miles to the west. Basically decimated the Indian population."

"Holy shit."

Kenni looked at me. "You know, I think that's the first time I've heard you cuss since I met you."

I closed my mouth.

"It's okay. It was a dark time in the country's history. But you should know about it. Remember it. Because this fairy-tale picture you seem to have built up in your head about the United States? You need to make sure you understand that while it might have been the best country in the world at one time, maybe even up until D-day, it also had its dark side. We had slavery, the Trail of Tears, the Civil War, presidential scandals, government corruption, and all sorts of nastiness that a lot of people didn't want to see."

Her expression had gotten grim by that point. "But if you don't acknowledge that these things happened, how do you know to stop them from happening again?"

CHAPTER 26
HUMMINGBIRD

FOR TWO MORE DAYS, WE slowed our pace, being extra cautious in our travels. Four times, we avoided more bands of Indians. We debated about it, wondering if we could simply walk up to them and see what they were up to. But the face paint decided us against it.

"I don't know what's going on," Kenni said. "But I only read about face paint being used for ceremonies, hunting, and war parties. I don't see any kind of ceremony going on, and these groups are all heading west, and they're too big to be simple hunting parties."

"But they aren't all Indians, either," I countered.

"How do you know?"

"Well... I saw white people and black people in the groups too."

"Did you know I'm a sixteenth Cherokee?"

That stopped me. "No, I didn't."

"So am I Indian?"

"I guess I don't know."

She nodded. "That's my point. These tribes have been living here in Oklahoma for nearly two hundred years. They've intermarried with other people in the area, and their children sometimes look whiter than you or blacker than me. And at least during my lifetime, most of the tribes were very inclusive about who could claim Indian ancestry. If you could prove your genealogy included Indian blood, you could claim membership in that tribe. For the most part, they were happy to have you too."

"Then if they're so inclusive, why can't we just go up to them and find out what's going on?"

"And what if it really is war paint?"

"So? They aren't at war with us."

"Think, Zachary! Think! First, how do you know they aren't at war with us? Second, how do *they* know they aren't at war with us? And third, who *are* they at war with?"

I tried to think about all the various possibilities as yet another conversation turned into a training session. Kenni had just dropped a lot of history in my lap as well as a series of thought problems. I spent the rest of the evening trying to unwind the tangle of possibilities. Even when we stopped for the night, I went to sleep thinking about the potential for unintended disaster. And that night was probably the first time I really began to appreciate just how complex the implications of our journey might be.

The next morning, I awoke to birds chirping and the sun shining through the trees to the east. I stretched and yawned.

"You always sleep in the trees?"

I froze at the voice that questioned me from just a few feet above my head and behind me... in the tree. Moving slowly, I craned my neck to find the source of the girl's voice. I sat up slowly to turn around carefully in my hammock and saw her. Perched on a branch was a slender, exotic-looking young girl. She was grinning from ear to ear as she watched me. But I didn't find anything to smile about. I didn't like the fact that she had managed to get into our camp, climb the tree, and wait for me to awaken. I didn't like that she had done it without waking me, Kenni, or the dogs. And I especially didn't like the fact that she was holding one of my pistols while she watched me.

"How did—"

"I'm quiet."

"But the dogs should have—"

"We've been following behind you for the last three days. I've been feeding them the whole time. When I got to your camp last night, we were good friends."

I looked at the pistol in her hands. "And that?"

She handed it to me. "I didn't want you to get startled and shoot me before we got a chance to talk."

There was a surreal element to our discussion, and it occurred to me that Kenni should have heard us talking by that point. I looked over the edge of my hammock and saw her aiming her rifle up at us.

"It's okay, Kenni. She's not causing any trouble."

The girl looked down and waved. "Could you please not aim that at me? My friends would probably get pretty upset if you were to put your finger on the trigger."

Kenni didn't flinch, but I actually rocked my hammock as I spun around, looking for her friends. I didn't spot anything until I saw Cricket staring up a tree. I followed her gaze. "She's not bluffing, Kenni. There's a guy with a rifle at your four o'clock, about ten feet up in a tree."

"There are two more." She stood on the branch, one hand braced lightly on the trunk for balance. "Look, guys, if we had wanted to do you any harm, we could have already done it. That's not what we're here for."

"Then what *are* you here for?" I asked.

"We're supposed to take any visitors into town. Bring you to see the elders."

I looked down at Kenni. "What do you think?"

She held her aim, evidently still thinking about it, and I began to get concerned. If she moved her finger less than an inch, it would begin a sequence of events that there would be no coming back from. I remembered what she had once said about never backing down from a fight just because the opponent was a woman. But this girl in the tree wasn't an opponent. She didn't intend us any harm. I didn't know how, but I was sure of it. I also remembered that Mr. Roesch had wanted me to take charge of this trip and to represent Rejas. And I suddenly had a moment of clarity.

The trip was my responsibility. It was my job to make sure everything went smoothly, and my actions were going to have repercussions that would affect not just my fate and Kenni's, but the fate of everyone in Rejas. They would affect Mr. Roesch, Robin, Owen, and the people Owen was expecting to set up trade with. There was an interconnectedness that would ripple outward from that point in time in more ways than I could possibly imagine.

And if that was the case, then I shouldn't be asking Kenni what she thought. It was my responsibility, not hers.

"Kenni, you and Mr. Roesch said this is on me. So put the rifle down. You wanted me to take the lead. I'm taking it."

She arched an eyebrow. Then she smiled. "It's about damn time." She lowered her weapon and looked up at the young woman in the tree above me. "We have a little pork left. You and your friends want some breakfast?"

There were four people — three men, and the woman who had perched in the tree above me. Most of them were closer to my age than Kenni's. One of the men was pale white with dark-red hair like the one I had noticed in the clearing the previous day, though this man was considerably younger and didn't have the enormous beard. Mentally, I labeled him "Red" for obvious reasons. The others were all darker skinned, though not as dark as Kenni.

The biggest of the other men was also the oldest. Broad and muscular, he towered half a head taller than everyone else in his group. I noticed while we were standing that unless I looked up at him, I would stare at a point just below his collarbone. He looked to be about Kenni's age and had a shaved head that was decorated with a tattoo on the right side behind his ear. It was a large, seven-pointed star surrounded by some kind of leaves in a wreath pattern.

The last man was so thin that, if not for his wiry musculature, I would have thought him to be starving.

We all sat around the morning fire, picking at the last of the ham as we stared uncomfortably at one another. After just a couple of minutes of this, I decided it was time to end the silence. "I'm Zach. Zachary Dawcett."

The four strangers looked up then at one another. The men just looked back down, but the young woman smiled. "I'm Wa—"

The red-haired man jerked his head and interrupted her in some other language. I wasn't sure what he said, but it sounded a bit like "*Walela? Doh yoost hadonay?*"

The woman's face froze for a second, and I saw a distinct flicker of anger before she forced her smile back on. "Excuse me?" She made it a question, as if waiting for my permission to address her companion.

"Ah. Sure."

Quick as a whip, she whirled on the man who had spoken to her and hissed back in the same language. It was so fast I couldn't tell where one word ended and the next began. "*Shaygah dinu? Onayluck gayhaste ayuh!*"

Red put his food aside and stood, glowering at her. "*Doh`gayhut?*"

"*Hahzo-uhee oo-noo-dashoo ayoo-gwahzaylee!*"

Anger flashed in his eyes, and while I didn't know what the two were saying, it was apparent that he didn't like what she was telling him. "*Gayest shkee eesh keeway shate yick!*"

He stepped forward, jaw clenched, and I saw the woman tense. But before Red had taken more than a single step, the big one with the tattooed head interrupted. His voice was calm and quiet, leaving absolutely no doubt about who was in charge. "*Zoh lay stee!*"

The redhead clenched his fists, looking from the woman to the man. Finally, he looked back at the woman. "*Skwee yah heewohnee.*" And he sat back down.

"Maybe I do talk too much," she replied. "But it's not *your* place to shut me up." She started to turn away from him then finished with, "And speak English when we're with these people. They haven't insulted us or tried to harm us in any way, and you're sitting there eating food they freely offered you. At least have the courtesy of not talking behind their backs!"

She turned back to me apologetically. "I'm sorry about that. Simon's new to the team. He's a little overly enthusiastic."

I filed his name away for future reference as I looked at Kenni, who took her hand off her pistol, shrugged, and went back to her breakfast. She made it clear that this conversation was on me.

"No harm done," I said.

"Now, as I was saying before I was interrupted"—she narrowed her eyes at Simon, who scowled and looked back at his food—"my name's Walela. And before you ask, it's Cherokee for hummingbird."

"Wally-la?"

"Wa-lay-la," she corrected.

I repeated it a couple of times.

She nodded. "Good enough."

"You say it's Cherokee. Is that what you were all speaking a minute ago?"

"Yes. You know you're in Oklahoma, right?"

"Well, yes."

She looked at me for a second, apparently appraising. "You're what—twenty? Twenty-one?"

"Twenty."

"So you're my age. You were what... eight or nine when the grid went down?"

"Eight."

"Where you're from, do you still have any schools?"

"Of course we do!"

She laughed. "No need to be insulted. There are plenty of places that are more worried about day-to-day existence. Some of them haven't had the time or opportunity for formal schooling."

"Yeah, there were a couple of years after the..." I remembered how she had referred to D-day. "After the grid went down, when the school wasn't organized yet. I think it was two years before we got it back up and going."

"Good. So did you have a history class? Did you ever learn about Oklahoma being Indian Territory?"

"Not really. My folks told me how the Indians here kept getting cheated by the settlers and got run off their land. And Kenni just gave me a little more detail on it a few days ago."

"Yes. And we were finally pushed into a few areas that the settlers didn't want. Oklahoma was the biggest of those areas. There were other large reservations in New Mexico and Arizona… smaller ones in a lot of other states. But Oklahoma was always referred to as the Indian Territories."

I was beginning to get the gist of her lecture, and I wasn't sure I liked where the conversation was going. "So you're telling me —"

"That the tribes of Oklahoma have declared themselves a sovereign nation. Once you're inside Oklahoma, you're in the OTA, the Oklahoma Tribal Alliance."

She watched my face as I absorbed what she was telling me. "And you said you're taking us to see your elders? I take it that's some sort of government you've set up?"

"Not me. But yeah, the elders are part of the local government. And yes, we're supposed to take any strangers in to see them."

"How soon?"

"There's an intertribal council in McAlester. It's about half a day's ride from here."

I must have looked nervous because Walela chuckled. "Don't look so glum, Zachary. We hardly ever scalp people anymore."

CHAPTER 27
MCALESTER

"CAN I ASK WHAT THE argument at breakfast was about?"

Kenni and I rode beside the Cherokee woman as we all headed up the road to McAlester. The dogs padded along beside the three of us while the other three from the scouting party rode behind us. They hadn't disarmed us, but their position was a not-so-subtle reminder that they were in charge... at least for the time being.

Walela considered my question for a moment, briefly glancing back at the redhead before she replied. "You ever hear the saying that the fiercest zealots are the converts?"

Before I could answer, Kenni said, "I served a tour in the Middle East. They told us that the fiercest jihadists were the converts. They were the ones searching for something to believe in and eager to prove the strength of their belief."

Walela and I both looked at her.

"What?" Kenni looked at us.

"What's a jihadist?" I finally asked.

Kenni sighed. "Never mind. What does that have to do with the argument?"

"Because it applies to Simon. Hell, it applies to a lot of people here. You have to remember that even though this is the center of the Indian Territories, less than ten percent of the people here were full-blooded Natives. There were a lot more who were mixed heritage. Look at me." She raised a dark arm in the sunlight. "Notice how I'm darker than the rest of the team?"

"Sure."

"It's because I'm part black, part Cherokee."

I thought of my conversation with Kenni. "Makes sense."

"Well, while everyone here is a member of the OTA, not everyone is full-blood Indian. Before Grid Down, most of the tribes accepted anyone who could prove the slightest percentage of Native blood. For most of us, it was more about preserving the culture than whose great, great, however-many-times-removed grandmother was an Indian princess. And since the Tribal Alliance took over, they accept anyone who will swear allegiance. It doesn't matter what color your skin is so long as you ally yourself with one of the tribes."

She bobbed her head back, indicating the three men following us. "But there are still some people who are so desperate to be accepted as Indian that they completely immerse themselves in the old ways and adopt them as if they still apply. Simon, with his red hair and pale skin, is determined to be more Indian than anyone else." She shrugged. "You see it a lot these days."

"Is that why some of the people we saw before were wearing face paint?"

"No. Face paint is only for certain occasions. Usually before or after a battle or a ceremony. If someone's painted their face these days, it means they're either a brave or they're participating in a special ceremony."

"A brave?"

"What you would call a soldier. Although calling one of us a soldier is a bit of an insult. That's one instance where we *have* all adopted the old ways. Basically, if you see a bunch of us painted up, it's a safe bet we're going into battle."

"And you all speak Cherokee?"

"All of us on this team do," Walela said. "It's why they put us together. Most of the teams are Cherokee, Choctaw, or Chickasaw. But there are also some—"

"Walela?" Tattoo Head had come up behind us.

"What, Keith?"

So Tattoo Head was Keith. Another name for the mental file.

"Simon might not be the most diplomatic person on the team, but he's right in pointing out that you're not the one to tell them anything." He looked at us apologetically. "Sorry, folks, but these are questions the elders either will or won't answer as they see fit." He looked pointedly at Walela. "It's not up to us."

Walela clapped her mouth shut. "Sorry, Keith."

I looked at Kenni, anticipating questions, but once again, she simply nodded and looked away.

"Did we just get you in some kind of trouble?" I asked when Keith dropped back.

"Not really. But Keith is in charge of the team." Walela hesitated then sighed. "And I suppose he's right. The council will decide what you need to know when we get to town. It's not really any big deal, but it's not my place to be telling you tribal business, either."

"I understand. And I'm sorry if I got you in trouble."

She shrugged, but the smile that I had become accustomed to seeing on her face was strained, and I couldn't help but feel a little guilt over that.

There was an Old Days city-limit sign at the edge of the town. It was metal with only a little rust on it. "Entering McAlester City Limits."

I looked around. "Not much of a town."

Walela snorted. "Town's still a couple of miles ahead."

She was right. Just a few miles ahead, the highway curved gently to the east, and as the town came into view, I wished I could take my earlier words back. "Holy crap."

Compared to Rejas, this was a bustling metropolis, bigger than any city or town I had ever seen. The roads were still torn up just like the ones in most other towns I had seen, though not as bad as the cross-country highways. But the sidewalks were smooth and solid. To be sure, they had been patched in many places, but as far as I was concerned, that was a point in their favor. They had been patched!

And the people—there were hundreds of them. As we rode through, I saw people walking, riding horseback, and even a few on bicycles. There were people milling about as far as the eye could see. One man even wore some sort of shoes with large wheels on the side that allowed him to weave in and out of foot traffic almost as fast as a person could run but with only a fraction of the effort.

The streets were lined with shops of all sorts. There were food vendors in carts rolling up and down the bumpy road, and Old Days glass-fronted restaurants that had been converted so that they could run without electricity. Most of the places sold foods of various sorts, but there were also signs advertising leather goods, alcohol, handmade paper, dry goods, and handmade furniture. There were a few signs advertising various services as well. I even saw one advertising "romantic companionship."

I must have looked like a wide-eyed child as I looked from one wonder to another, because Kenni nudged me. "Don't look the rube, kid. Remember what you represent."

I swallowed and nodded, but I suddenly felt very unequal to the task. "Kenni," I said sotto voce, "I really think you should take the lead on this."

"Sorry, Zach. You're already committed. You accepted the lead in front of our hosts. I'm the assistant now."

Walela rode up beside us. "Yeah, it's a bit much when you first see it, isn't it?"

"It's bigger than any place I've seen." Then I took what Kenni said to heart. I was supposed to be the representative of another population center. "I think it's probably a bit bigger than Rejas."

"Really? You have a town this big?"

"I'm not really sure. How many people do you have here?"

"I think they have close to ten thousand."

I nearly choked but managed to act nonchalant as I shifted the conversation. "So you aren't from here?"

"What?"

"You said *they*. That implies you're from someplace else."

"Touché. No, I'm from Tahlequah. It's the capital of the Cherokee nation. McAlester is the intertribal hub, the unofficial capital of the OTA." Walela stopped then shook her head. "And once again, I'm probably talking about things I shouldn't be talking about." She smiled at me. "Sorry, but can we hold the questions until you see the elders? It's not too far now."

"Sure. I'm sorry. I'm just curious."

"I understand. It's just that there are too many things going on…" She clapped her mouth shut and shook her head. "The council building is just up the road." With that, she pulled her horse ahead.

We waited outside with Simon, Walela, and the lanky guy whose name I still didn't know while Keith entered the building. Bella nudged my hand to remind me that I should be paying her more attention, and Cricket wallowed on her back as Walela rubbed her belly.

"You have a real friend there," I said.

Walela smiled. "She's hard to resist."

The girls both liked the young woman. They were more relaxed around her than I had ever seen them with anyone else. I didn't know if it was because she had been feeding them treats for days to win them over or if there was a more primal bond, but the fact that they accepted her as a pack member spoke volumes to me. She was a good person. She was a *worthy* person.

I looked around at the others. We definitely weren't being treated as captives. Our escort hadn't even bothered to disarm us, though they also left no doubt that they expected us to cooperate with their requests. It occurred to me to wonder what would happen if Kenni and I were to simply stand up and walk away.

But I also recalled how Owen's trading post had appeared vulnerable until we found out about his hidden observation room. With that in mind, I looked around. I didn't find anything—no mirrors, no peepholes, nothing that obviously pointed to us being watched. Nevertheless, I felt sure we were under observation. I shrugged it off as unimportant. We weren't there to cause trouble, and for the moment, there was no indication that we were in any danger.

To take my mind off of who might be watching us, I turned to Kenni. "What do you think of this place?"

"It's big. Bigger than any town I've seen since D-day. But in a way, it makes sense."

"What do you mean?"

She reached over me and grabbed one of my saddlebags. After untying the flap, she opened it and pulled out the map we'd been using. As she unfolded it, I noted with a pang of guilt that it was beginning to show some serious wear from the trip, and I wondered how the people at the Rejas Library were going to react to my misuse of their property.

Kenni pointed. "Here's McAlester. Before D-day, it was a pretty good-sized town. If the area on the map is any indication, it was at least twice as big as Rejas."

I looked then traced our route back to the only other large town I had seen since leaving. "It looks smaller than Marshall, though. And I sure don't recall Marshall having this big a community."

"True, but we didn't exactly take our time looking around, either. Plus, look at this." She pointed on the map. "Here's Marshall." She moved her finger north. "Here's McAlester." And she moved her finger once more. "And here is DFW."

I got it. "So you think the reason Marshall didn't have much of a population is because of fallout from the DFW strikes on D-day?"

"Prevailing winds are typically from the west. There's a lot of variance due to the Gulf winds, but it holds mostly true. I would guess that as long as, say"—she traced a finger to the west of McAlester—"Oklahoma City didn't take many direct hits, McAlester would have ended up with a much better time of it than Marshall did."

"Oklahoma City did get hit." I looked up as Simon spoke, his tone bitter. "My dad was there when it happened."

I was surprised that he would volunteer that information, but it seemed to require an obligatory, "I'm sorry."

He nodded. "Winds here are from the south to southeast. Has to do with the mountains." He looked like he was going to say more, but Keith came back out before he could.

"You can come in now."

Kenni folded the map and handed it to me. I put it in the saddlebag, and we gathered up our weapons and gear. It suddenly occurred to me that the girls might not be welcome inside. I caught Keith's attention. "What about my dogs?"

He considered. "They seemed to be well trained on the road. Are they?"

"Very."

"Then you can bring them in. But if they get out of line, I'll have to take them back outside."

"Fair enough."

With that, Kenni, the girls, and I followed Keith inside. Just inside the door, he pointed to a wall full of metal doors with keys in them. "You can stow your gear here. Put it in one of the lockers, and lock it in with the key. No one will bother it."

I looked at Kenni with a raised eyebrow. She shrugged. "You're the boss."

I sighed, thought about it for a split second, then stood and walked toward the lockers. I put my saddlebags inside and started to close the door when Keith stopped me.

"I need you to leave your weapons too. They're okay in town, but not in the council chamber."

That gave me pause, but I noticed Keith no longer carried his rifle or knife. I felt better seeing that the rule applied to everyone. I looked at Keith pointedly as I unbuckled my pistols. "No one else can get to them? You have no idea what they cost us." I was thinking about Mr. Roesch as I said it.

"You'll have the only key."

I put my pistols in the locker on a shelf. My rifle and bow leaned against the back wall, and I began stripping my blades from my belt, laying each one on the shelf beside the pistols. When I was finished, I felt more naked than I had in a long time.

Keith nodded. "I have to search you now. Please put your hands out to the side."

I did, and he patted me down, then repeated the process with Kenni.

"Thanks, guys." He handed us the keys to our lockers and led us through the next door.

CHAPTER 28
THE ELDERS

THERE WERE THREE WOMEN AND two men sitting at a long table in the council chambers. All of them had the same dark skin that Keith, Walela, and Lanky had, but theirs was wrinkled like the paper of the map I had stowed in the locker. One of the women smiled as we approached and waved us to a couple of chairs on the other side of the table. "Please have a seat. We appreciate you coming to see us."

We sat, and I smiled. "I didn't realize we had a choice in the matter."

"There are always choices. And there are always consequences. You've been on the road for quite some time, so I imagine you have already learned this basic life lesson, though, haven't you?"

Again thinking of Mr. Roesch, I nodded.

"So shall we begin?" the woman asked.

"Begin what?"

"Our conversation. We simply like to get to know the people who come into our lands. Who they are, why they are here. So who are you?"

Not entirely sure where this was going, I answered simply. "My name is Zachary Dawcett. And you are...?"

The old woman laughed. "You're an impertinent one, aren't you?"

"I apologize, ma'am. I mean no disrespect."

But she was waving my apology away even as I gave it. "Don't worry. This is all very informal. You intended no offense. No offense was taken."

She leaned back in her seat. "We represent a quorum of the elders currently residing in McAlester for the Oklahoma Tribal Alliance. Have your escorts made you aware of the OTA's existence?"

"Yes, ma'am."

"Good. Well, we" — she spread her hands to indicate her companions — "are representatives of the OTA's Intertribal Council. I am Andrea Walkingstick. I am the local representative for the Tsalagi. You call us Cherokee. I am the chairperson for this council. My fellow elders are Joseph Smallwood from the Choctaw Nation, Pamela Adams representing the Chickasaw Nation, Edna Berryhill from the Muscogee Nation, and Thomas Parker of the Seminole Nation."

I nodded at each one as they were introduced. "Thank you. As I said, I am Zachary Dawcett. My assistant is Kennesha Anderson." Despite Miss Walkingstick's assurances to the contrary, the whole proceeding struck me as pretty formal, so full names seemed appropriate.

She smiled. "Welcome, Zachary, Kennesha. What brings you to our town?"

I glanced at Kenni, hoping for a clue, but she stared straight ahead, not even looking my direction. I was on my own.

"I'm on a diplomatic mission, representing the people of Rejas, Texas," I said, hoping they would take the hint and leave it at that.

"Representing them to whom?" Thomas Parker asked.

I hesitated. "With all due respect, I'm afraid that's a private matter."

The elders all looked at one another before coming to some sort of unspoken agreement. Parker nodded, and Miss Walkingstick spoke. "Mr. Dawcett, we can appreciate that you don't know us, and the circumstances of your being here haven't been completely in your control. So I can understand your reluctance to be more forthcoming in your reasons. You don't know us or our purpose here, and I'm sure it has come as a shock to find that one of the former states of the US has declared itself to be a sovereign nation. So let me cut to the chase. Are you perhaps heading toward a certain spaceport near Burns Flat?"

My face must have given me away. The old woman smiled and shrugged. "You aren't the first. Word of their message came to us several weeks ago. Since that time, we've had six other groups before us who were answering the call. And that's just here at McAlester. We have similar councils set up in five other locations around the state. At our last communication, the others had all seen similar groups of pilgrims traveling through our lands. You can understand our concern."

I shook my head. "No, ma'am, I don't think I do. I would think that we should all be in favor of the government rebuilding the nation." I felt stupid even as the words left my mouth. "Unless... you were already working on establishing your own independent government. Yes, I can see where that would be of some concern to you."

Walkingstick shrugged. "Yes, there is that. There is also undeniable history to be considered. I'm sure you already know that there is a long line of treaties between the Indian Nations and the US government over the last few hundred years, nearly all of which they broke as soon as they became inconvenient." She smiled. "So yes, there's a bit of distrust involved." She looked at her fellow council members. "But there is also the fact that we sent our own representatives to Burns Flat when we received word of the satellite and its message."

The man representing the Choctaw Nation spoke while I struggled to recall his name. "You see, the Burns Flat facility falls within the boundaries of the Kiowa Apache Nation. We wanted to discuss their plans for the use of the spaceport. It did not go well. They are well armed and disinclined to discuss anything other than their own agenda. Four of our delegates were arrested and conscripted into a work detail."

That caught my attention. Were we also walking into a

situation from which we might not be allowed to leave? Or were we in danger of getting caught up between two political factions?

"I'm sorry for your difficulties, but if I might be perfectly honest, I'm not sure what they have to do with us. We aren't part of either of your groups."

She leaned forward, clasping her hands together. "That is precisely why we wanted to speak with you. Not necessarily you, but *any* groups coming through here. And if *I* may be perfectly honest, you aren't the first people we have spoken to, though you are probably the smallest group of pilgrims we've seen."

There was that word again. "Pilgrims?"

"It's what we've taken to calling those people who take the pilgrimage to Burns Flat."

Kenni snickered and spoke for the first time since we'd walked into the council chamber. "A little bit of a double meaning there too. Isn't there?"

Walkingstick only shrugged.

I stopped the detour in the conversation and brought us back to the discussion at hand. "To be fair, our party was larger when we started out." How long had it been since we had left Mr. Roesch and Robin back at the trading post?

Walkingstick saw my expression. She peered closely at me, and her face took on a sympathetic expression as she leaned back. "Yes. As I said, life lessons in this day and age are often quite difficult."

"Yes, ma'am, they are." Mr. Roesch had repeatedly stressed the need to analyze the situation and control my reactions. But it took every bit of self-control I could muster to remain calm when I saw Bella's ears twitch forward.

The old woman peered at me a short moment, and if it hadn't been for Bella's reaction, I wouldn't have thought anything of it. "You lost friends on the road here?"

Bella cocked her head to the side, and Cricket sat up and twitched her ears. It was the same reaction I had noticed when Kenni claimed to be using her sight.

"As I said, our group was larger when we started."

I glanced to my left to see if Kenni had noticed, but there was nothing in her demeanor indicating she had any idea that the leader of the tribal council had the same *sight* that she claimed. For that matter, I still didn't know whether or not I even believed in Kenni's supposed powers. All I knew was that before that moment, I had only seen my girls react in such a way to one other person, and that was Kenni.

Walkingstick's eyes narrowed. "Something wrong, Mr. Dawcett?"

I turned from Kenni to face the elder once again. "No, ma'am. I was just wondering where this conversation was going. Are you planning to let us go or imprison us?"

"Imprison you? Why on earth would we do that?"

"Maybe you would consider it one of those consequences you mentioned at the beginning of our conversation."

Her head inclined as she conceded the possibility. But rather than continue the path of our conversation, she turned to the old man to her right, and the two of them began to speak in low whispers.

I took advantage of her distraction and caught Kenni's attention. She looked at me quizzically as I whispered to her. "Do you get any kind of feeling about that woman?" I emphasized the word *feeling*, causing her to furrow her brows as she shook her head.

"No. I told you, I can't just turn it on and off like that."

"Well, try whatever you can because..." I noticed Keith was close enough that he might be able to overhear part of our conversation. It didn't look like he was paying attention, but I didn't want to take the chance.

"Because what?"

"Because the girls tell me she's like you."

Kenni glanced at the elders still talking among themselves. "How many of them?"

"Just Walkingstick as far as I can tell."

"Mr. Dawcett?"

I turned my attention back to the woman at the center of the table. "Yes, ma'am?"

She held out her hand. "Would you be so kind as to take my hand?"

I stared at her. "I beg your pardon?"

"If you would indulge an old woman, I would like to touch your hand."

I glanced at Kenni, who only shrugged. I reached across the table and took Ms. Walkingstick's hand in mine. As I did, Bella sat up and put her paws on my leg. I looked at her, noted that her tail was wagging, and hoped that was an indication that everything was all right. I looked back at our clasped hands then up into Walkingstick's eyes.

She was looking directly into my eyes, and she smiled. "You're a sensitive."

That threw me. She didn't say I *was* sensitive but rather that I was *a* sensitive.

"And a rather strong one, at that."

"But you"—she turned her attention to Kenni—"you are something more." Walkingstick released my hands and gestured for Kenni to reach across. As their hands touched, I saw the other council members look from Walkingstick to me and back again.

Walkingstick had closed her eyes, lips moving silently as she muttered to herself. I watched Kenni closely for any sign of pain or discomfort, but she sat impassively, watching the old woman across from her. After several seconds, Walkingstick released Kenni's hands and opened her eyes. She smiled. "The force is strong with you."

Kenni cocked her head to one side as if trying to determine whether the woman was serious or not. As I watched, Walkingstick winked. Kenni smiled, then laughed outright. "You did not just say that, did you? Seriously?"

Walkingstick shrugged. "I thought I needed to ease some of the tension in here."

The rest of the elders chuckled. I looked from one face to another, but why they all found that so funny was beyond me.

Walkingstick sobered after a moment and spoke again. "It's true, though. You have power within you."

Kenni nodded. "My mother had it. She called it the sight, and on her deathbed, she... did something to me. She passed it on to me." Kenni shrugged. "I've had it ever since that day."

"But no training."

"No. Before just this moment, I've never met anyone else who had it."

"Well, you're much stronger than I am, though you don't know how to use your strength."

"Not really. Sometimes I can pierce the veil, hear the voices of the dead. Sometimes they tell me things. And sometimes I just know things. I don't know how, but I do."

"But she didn't teach you how to use it?"

"She didn't have a chance. She died the day after she touched me."

"Our ancestors have always believed that there were people who have such abilities to varying degrees. For a few centuries, we adopted other beliefs and religions, and many of us lost the old ways. But the world has changed again, and many of us are returning to the old beliefs. And we have begun to discover that people with the gifts are with us again. Perhaps they were always here, but we didn't look up from our computers and phones long enough to see them. Maybe they were so busy trying to make a living in the old world that they didn't have time to think about the strange things happening around them. Or maybe they are returning to us because the technology of our old world interfered with them.

"Whatever the reason, we have begun to notice them again. They are still rare, but when we find them, they are cherished and encouraged to explore their gifts in whatever manner helps them. Some are simply sensitive enough to observe a bit of the world beyond the mundane but unlikely to ever actually affect it. Others are like Mr. Dawcett here" — she held an open palm in my direction — "in that they have a stronger medicine, perhaps an innate understanding of herbs and plants or an ability to tame horses no one thought could be tamed."

How could she tell that just by holding my hand?

"And then there are the truly rare ones. People with truly strong medicine such as you have." She smiled warmly at Kenni. "In the time since the grid went down, I have only heard of three others. Two of them are here in McAlester."

"You're one, aren't you?" I asked.

The old woman nodded her head modestly. "I am. There is also a young boy I am training. The third is a chiropractor who lives in Tahlequah, several days' ride north of here."

She turned her attention back to Kenni. "You are the fourth. And I believe you are likely the strongest of any of us by far."

———— ✂ ———— ✂ ———— ✂ ———— ✂ ———— ✂

The conversation wound up soon after Walkingstick's declaration to Kenni, and we were escorted to a hotel in the middle of town. Walela led us to our rooms. As she handed us our keys, she told us we were invited to dinner with the council. "It's a big honor. Elder Walkingstick said to tell you that you'll get the chance to meet..." She paused as if trying to remember. "Her padawan. I'm pretty sure that's what she said."

"I thought you spoke Cherokee," I said.

But Kenni just laughed. "It's not Cherokee. She means we'll meet her student."

Walela looked as puzzled as I felt, and for some reason, that made Kenni laugh even harder.

CHAPTER 29
DINNER

W E MET AT AN OLD open-air restaurant just down the road from our rooms. Walela told me it was the best place in town and that they had closed it off for the council's use that evening. The dinner started as an informal affair where people wandered about with little plates of appetizers, mixing, mingling, and conversing. I stayed near Kenni at first, and noticed quickly that much of the conversation was a barely veiled attempt to convince her to stay with them so they could help her to explore the medicine path.

It hadn't occurred to me until then that having Kenni stay was an option, but as I thought about it, I realized the town presented a unique opportunity for her. And as much as I didn't want her to stay, I also thought it would be unfair to try and influence her. Her *sight* was a huge part of her life, and if they thought they could help her learn more about it, who was I to stand in the way?

As part of the conversation, Walkingstick introduced us to her protégé, Chris O'Brien. Chris was almost as fair skinned as Simon, and his nose and ears were sunburned to the point that they were peeling. He said he was thirteen years old, and he seemed to be a happy kid, though he had an intensity about him that I had never before seen in someone his age. He bounced from happy to wistful in the blink of an eye, and his melancholy was out of place in someone so young.

He talked about how much he enjoyed fishing back home. "Dad used to take me out on Lake Eufaula. He had an old boat made out of thin metal, from before the grid went."

I grinned with him. "That must have been great. Is Eufaula a big lake?"

His smile faded. "It used to be. But the dam washed out a few years ago. The whole town of Whitefield got washed away."

"I'm sorry."

"Yeah. Nearly a hundred people drowned."

"That's how I heard about Chris," Walkingstick said. "He had been warning his parents about it for two days before it happened. He was frantic and went into great detail about what was going to happen."

The kid frowned. "No one would listen."

Kenni nodded. "I didn't use to believe my mother when she told me things like that, either. I didn't let myself see when she was trying to help me. I think it was easier for me to chalk such things up to coincidence than to believe there was something so far out of my simple world of books and school. If I couldn't see it or touch it myself, then I didn't believe in it."

"What changed you?"

And Kenni began telling him her story. I had already heard it, and this telling was meant more for the troubled boy than anyone else, so I wandered off and found a small corner in the shadows. I was munching on a mixture of stewed vegetables and chicken when Walkingstick walked over.

"Not one for mixing, are you?"

"No, ma'am. I hope you aren't offended."

"Not at all." She sat on the bench beside me.

I put my plate down, too self-conscious to eat in front of the old woman. Together, we watched the comings and goings of the crowd, and after a few moments of almost companionable silence, she finally spoke. "You have a difficult choice to make, young man."

"I do?"

"Despite the fact that you are younger and less experienced,

Kenni has made it very clear that you are the one in charge of your little expedition."

"Believe me, I tried to get her to take charge."

She chuckled. "Yes. She told me that as well. She said both she and your teacher had decided that you were better suited for it than you knew."

"I don't know about that. Mr. Roesch should have been the one leading this thing. I'm just supposed to be his assistant."

"The fact that you feel that way tells me they're likely correct." She patted me on the leg. "One of the things we forgot in the Old Days was that politics and diplomacy were duties. They were supposed to be done in the service of our neighbors. The system began to fall apart when the rich and powerful found ways to make the political system profitable."

That didn't seem to require any response, so I kept quiet.

After a moment, she spoke again. "So the dilemma falls to you."

I gathered my thoughts, suddenly aware that she was addressing me not as a guest at a party, but rather as the representative I claimed to be. I struggled to act accordingly. "And what dilemma would that be?"

"You've stumbled into a situation where two groups wish to ally themselves with you and your people. Unfortunately, those two groups are currently enemies, so choosing one will put you at odds with the other."

I sighed. "I've been worried about that."

"I can assure you that dealing with the OTA will be more to your advantage than allying with the military men at Burns Flat."

"That may be true," I conceded. "But I won't know for sure until I meet with them and hear what they have to say, will I?"

She chuckled again. "Yes, I think Kenni is right. You are well adapted for this path."

"It sure doesn't feel that way."

"Which proves my point."

The old woman didn't try to influence me after that. And I realized, as we ate, that her letting me choose my own way actually *had* influenced me, leaving me with a more favorable opinion of the people who shared their dinner with us despite the fact that we had told them we were going to meet with people who were their enemies.

Did she do that on purpose? Did she decide to show us the hand of friendship in order to influence our opinions?

Once more, the twists and turns of diplomacy confused me. *But you* wanted *this, remember? You wanted to make your mark.*

Careful what you wish for.

CHAPTER 30
PADAWAN

TWO DAYS LATER, WE WERE back on the road, albeit with a larger party. Keith, Walela, Simon, and John—the man I had called Lanky—had been assigned to escort us to Burns Flat. It turned out that John was their medic. Each member of their team had a specialty as well as combat training, and they were going to be our escorts to the spaceport. They had brought us in, so they were charged with seeing us to our destination. Also, their presence would keep other teams from detaining us again as we journeyed west to the spaceport.

We were also well supplied. The elders had given us plenty of food and water as well as maps of the route to take to Burns Flat, marked with suggested waypoints for camping. Each waypoint had fresh water for the horses and was far enough off the main roads that it was unlikely anyone would stumble across it by accident.

Once word had gotten out that Kenni was in favor with the elders, Keith had struck up an unlikely friendship with her. He had quite an interest in the paranormal, and with the elders' proclamation that Kenni had "strong medicine," he spent as much time as he could quizzing her.

"Is there one particular spirit that comes to you, or are there many?" he asked. "I've heard stories from the old ones that spirits don't speak directly to you but only show you pictures in your head that you have to interpret. Is that true?"

He asked question after question as if the days of stoic silence had been a forced façade, and now that he had been released to treat us as potential allies, he wanted to make up for lost time.

I, on the other hand, found myself in the constant company of Walela. She had an infectious smile, and I found myself watching her even when she wasn't with me. I accepted that I was attracted to her but figured it was unlikely that she could feel the same way about me. I was nothing more than an interesting distraction from the boredom of her regular patrols.

Our second night on the road, I hung my hammock tent in the trees above the camp. I felt the eyes of the others below watching me, but I did my best to ignore them as I swung from one tree to the other, stringing my lines and hanging my gear.

When I finished, I swung into the hammock and looked over the side to see all eyes on me. Keith nodded approvingly. Simon and John were doing their best to look unimpressed. Walela smiled in that way she had, and for some reason, that was all that mattered.

"Zachary?"

Her voice came from behind and above. Groggy, it took me a moment to realize that she had to be in the tree with me. My eyes snapped open. By the pale light of a waning crescent moon, I saw her balanced on a limb just above my lower support line.

"Shhh…" she warned, "don't wake the others."

I kept my voice low. "What are you doing up here?"

Instead of answering my question, she asked, "Is that thing strong enough to hold both of us?"

Heart pounding, I said, "Yes."

She reached up and grasped the upper support line and stepped onto the hammock line. Balanced precariously, she walked lightly across the rope and into the actual hammock. When she reached sturdier footing, she let go of the upper line and dropped to lie beside me. "This is nice."

"Ah. Yeah, it is." Why was it that anytime I was around a

woman in an intimate setting, my vocabulary dropped to that of a caveman?

Walela just smiled and snuggled closer. "I can see why you like it up here."

"Yeah. It's safer."

She arched an eyebrow. "Safer?"

"Sure. I mean, if someone comes across the camp, they don't usually think to look up."

She just nodded.

Idiot! Are you trying to make her think you're brain damaged?

"I was talking about the view. I love seeing the stars like this. It's almost like you're in the sky with them." She casually took my arm and draped it around her shoulders. Then, before I could think of a witty response, she closed her eyes. "Good night, Zach."

I blinked at the abrupt end of the conversation. "Good night."

Within minutes, her breathing slowed, and her body relaxed as she fell asleep. At some point, she turned to her side and draped an arm across my chest.

I smiled, and despite the conviction that I would never be able to sleep with her lying against me, I drifted off a short time after her.

There were catcalls and hoots in the morning when Walela swung down from the hammock before me, but it all seemed to be in good fun. Even the normally surly Simon snickered at her. Initially, I was embarrassed, but I chose to use the moment as a training exercise. Kenni and Mr. Roesch had told me that I needed to learn to hide my feelings, so I practiced keeping my expression neutral as I broke down my gear.

My tactic seemed to throw the group after a bit, especially when I kept quiet through breakfast. They all seemed a bit self-conscious when we mounted up and resumed our westward journey. When I did finally speak, I noticed that all eyes went to me. I would have to remember that particular strategy. "Kenni?"

I wasn't sure, but she seemed to have a bit of a twinkle in her eye as she looked at me. "Yes?"

"At the council meeting, you and the others were talking about some things I never heard of. Something about a force and a padawan?"

She and Keith laughed, which told me it must be an Old Days reference. They were the only ones in our group who were old enough to really remember those times. For the next few hours, the two of them took turns regaling us with the exploits of the Skywalker family, who really seemed to be pretty messed up. The father so crazy that he destroyed the adopted world of his daughter, who was coincidentally rescued by, and made out with, someone who turned out to be her brother. The father later caught up with the son and cut off his hand in a sword fight. But later on, the son returned the favor and cut off his father's hand. Then, the father was mortally wounded while rescuing his son minutes later, and died in the son's arms.

Like I said — messed up.

But eventually, the story ended, and I sighed as Kenni pulled the little book out of her pocket.

"Okay, enough play time," she said. "Let's start with the Fourth Amendment. What does it say?"

I took a deep breath and began. "The Fourth Amendment protects the people against illegal searches and arrest."

"And what does that mean?"

I almost groaned but caught myself. *Hide your feelings.* So I kept my thoughts to myself and recited the lessons as I had learned them. And that time, I paid attention rather than simply reciting what she'd had me memorize. Finally, I felt as if I was truly beginning to grasp the meaning behind all the words.

When Keith called on us to stop, I was surprised to find the sun was setting. Kenni and I had kept our discussion going for hours, and for the first time, I thought of it as a discussion rather than a lesson.

Kenni grinned at me. "You have done well, my padawan."

I snorted.

CHAPTER 31
LET'S TRY THAT AGAIN

HEARD HER THAT NIGHT AS she climbed the tree. Now that she knew the hammock would support us both, she didn't bother announcing herself. She simply climbed up and shinnied onto the hammock without a word.

Unsure of what to say, I lay there in silence as she snuggled up against me. After a few moments, she asked, "What was all that stuff you and Kenni were talking about today?"

"It's the Constitution. It's the basis of the laws that ran the US before D-day."

"D-day? You mean Grid Down?"

"Yeah, sorry. We call it D-day."

"So why do you study it?"

"What? Oh. The Constitution. Mr. Roesch and Kenni figure that if I'm going to be negotia—"

Her lips interrupted mine with a clumsy kiss. Admittedly, I had thought about kissing her. I had been attracted to her ever since the morning I'd awakened to find her perched on the limb above me, holding my pistol. And I'd had trouble thinking about anything else during the ride since then. Having the object of your daydreams climb into your bed and curl up next to you for the night tended to do that to a guy.

But the possibility that something might come of my little fantasy actually froze me. Funny, but in all those daydreams, I had been so suave. There was even one scenario in which the two of us managed to get away from the rest of the group and sneak off for a private tryst that made me blush just thinking about it. But at that moment, with her lips pressing against mine and my heart pounding in my chest, I just froze.

And she definitely noticed. She pulled back, looking at me with a puzzled smile. Pursing her lips, she sat up, moving carefully in the hammock. "I'm sorry. I thought..." She looked away, and it occurred to me that she was just as embarrassed as I was. "Maybe I should go back down to the campsite." She shifted toward the end of the hammock.

"No!" I almost shouted, and suddenly, I was in a competition to see which of us could be most embarrassed. Lowering my voice, I said, "No, please don't go. You just surprised me."

She turned back toward me, but the crescent moon chose that moment to slide behind a cloud, so I couldn't tell anything from her expression.

"Look," I said, "I'm not exactly a big ladies' man back home. I guess I'm pretty clumsy when it comes to girls."

She stayed quiet. In my imagination, that was her trying to decide whether or not I was worth her time, and I very much wanted the verdict to come out in my favor. I was terrified that if she left my hammock, I was never going to get a second chance. And I desperately wanted one.

"Walela, I'm sorry. I'm an idiot when it comes to women. I guess I've got issues. But I definitely like you. You're all I've been able to think of, and if you leave right now, I'm afraid I'll have blown my chance with you." I reached out for her hand. "What can I do to make it up to you?"

The cloud cleared the moon, and I could somewhat see her face. She was smiling. "I guess I did sorta rush into that, didn't I?"

I shrugged. "I don't know. Like I said, I don't really have a lot of experience to compare it to."

Her shoulders relaxed. "Sorry. I guess I just assumed you did. You just seemed to have it all together, so I thought you were..."

After a short pause, I prompted, "Thought I was what?"

"I guess I thought you were more... experienced. Is that the right word?"

I chuckled, thinking back to my comical aborted attempt to *un-um* with Donna back home. "No. Afraid not. The truth is that other than a bit of steamy kissing and groping, I've never actually been with a woman."

"Never?" She sounded surprised, and I felt my cheeks warm as I blushed. But my embarrassment abated when she relaxed and lay back down beside me.

"No. I came awfully close a while back, but it didn't work out."

"What happened?"

So I told her the story of the night Donna and I had first seen the satellite, and as she giggled at my clumsy exploits, I felt both of us relax. When I reached the end of my sad little tale, she was snuggled securely back under my arm. Patting my chest lightly, she laughed again. "Poor Zachary."

"You have no idea." I was relieved that we were comfortable with each other again. "What about you?"

"What? You mean did I ever drop my pants and get left high and dry?" She giggled.

"No, I mean do you have any embarrassing story like that to tell?"

I felt the subtle stiffening of her body, and I knew I had touched on a sensitive subject. "No. I fumbled my way through losing my virginity the way I figure most girls do. There was a boy back home who I just knew was the love of my life. He swore undying devotion to me, and I was convinced we were going to spend the rest of our lives together. After we'd been seeing each other a little while, he took me to a secluded place in a nearby lake where we went skinny dipping. One thing led to another, and before I knew what was going on, I was on my back with him on top of me."

She stopped, and I wasn't sure if I should say anything more. Before I could decide, she continued.

"The next day two other boys asked me to go to the lake with them. Turns out the love of my life had bragged to anyone who would listen that I was a sure thing. So I found him the next evening and kicked him in the nuts so hard that he puked all over the street."

I felt moisture on my chest, and I realized she was crying. Desperate to break her mood, I quipped, "So I guess you were all kinds of popular after that, weren't you?"

She chuckled then sniffed. "I'm sorry."

"Don't worry about it. You have every right to be upset. The guy was a jerk."

"Yeah, he was. But I meant I'm sorry about jumping on you earlier. It was kinda pathetic. But you seem like a decent guy, and I really like you."

"I like you too. A lot. Like I said, you just caught me by surprise." Heart thumping in my chest, I lifted her chin with my finger and leaned in slowly. Our lips met, and there was no clumsy rush and bumping of teeth. It was slow and tender, and I pulled away to look in her eyes. "It's definitely not that I didn't want to."

Grinning impishly, she pulled my head back down. "Let's try that again."

I sighed, trying to sound exasperated. "All right. If you insist."

CHAPTER 32
TREASURE HUNT

THE NEXT DAY WAS A bright and sunny scorcher, hot enough by midday that we were dripping and miserable. Simon, with his pale skin, was bright red and looked like he was about ready to fall off his horse.

"Okay," Keith said. "You guys have any objection to us getting out of the heat?"

"Not in the least." I wiped the sweat from my eyes for what seemed to be the hundredth time.

Tongues lolling, even Bella and Cricket looked ready to drop. We all gathered around Keith as he scanned his map. Finally, he nodded toward the north. "Looks like there's a little stream a couple of miles that way." He folded the map. "How about we go cool off?"

Needless to say, there were no objections to the idea.

The stream was shaded by a thick copse of willow and water oaks, and the water was cool and welcoming. I soaked a towel in the stream and draped it over my head, reveling in the cool, clean water.

"Keith?" John's voice called from the opposite bank.

The bald man looked up.

John pointed past the bank, into a small thicket. "Looks like we have an old ranch house."

Everyone waded across the stream to peer over the grassy bank.

Just as John had said, the remains of a big, ranch-style home were nearly hidden in the undergrowth. The windows were long gone, but the home appeared to be in relatively good shape otherwise.

John smiled at Keith. "Got your tools?"

Keith patted a pocket on his vest. "Always."

The two of them trotted toward the structure, leaving Kenni and me looking at one another. "You have any idea what's going on?"

She shook her head.

"They're treasure hunting," Walela said from behind us.

"In there?" My voice must have betrayed my disbelief because she laughed.

"Sorry," I said, "but they don't really expect to find anything of any value in there, do they?"

She waded across the stream, heading toward the house. "Keith used to be a locksmith. He likes to see if places like this have safes in them. And if they do, he tries to crack them."

"Crack them? You mean he can break into a safe?" The concept was new to me. Safes were Old Days things, almost arcane in their security. I'd read old stories about thieves who could crack safes, but they always had power tools and special equipment. I'd never known anyone who could actually do it.

"Usually. He's pretty good, and we've gotten some really good stuff in the past." She was walking up the bank toward the house. Kenni and I followed. "You coming, Simon?" Walela called back.

He waved us on. "Not this time. Think I'll stay here with the horses and cool off in the water."

I hurried to catch up.

"What kind of stuff do you usually get?" Kenni asked Walela.

"Depends on the kind of safe. A place like this... ranch house out off the main roads, good distance from any town... I wouldn't be surprised if there's a gun safe." She pushed her way through what had probably once been a neatly trimmed hedge in front of the home but was now wild and unruly undergrowth that blocked much of the entryway. I ducked as she let go of a limb and it whipped back at me.

She continued, completely unfazed by the attacking shrubbery. "Could have pistols, rifles, ammunition..."

Kenni and I followed her into the open doorway, our damp feet leaving prints on the rotting wood of the old floor.

"Keith?" she called out.

"Back here."

We followed John's voice to find him watching Keith as the bigger man knelt in a dark closet. Keith held the release lever of the floor safe while slowly spinning the dial on the combination lock. His eyes were closed, and he seemed to be holding tension on the lever, concentrating on the feel of it as he turned the dial. He cocked his head to the side, stopped turning the dial, then squinted into the darkness of the floor.

He looked at the rest of us gathered in the doorway. "You guys mind not blocking my light?"

I saw that our shadows threw the inside of the closet into pitch darkness.

"I thought you worked it with your eyes closed," John quipped.

"I can feel the tumblers catch without looking. I still gotta read the numbers, though."

"Sorry." Walela stepped back. Kenni and I followed suit, moving to either side of the door frame.

Keith looked down once more, this time grunting as he read the number and pulled a small screwdriver from his vest pocket. I thought he was going to use it on the dial somehow, but he turned to the wall inside the closet and scratched the number "22" into the moldy sheetrock.

John looked up at Walela and smiled. "Fifteen minutes?"

Walela eased forward, making sure her shadow didn't block the light that fell on Keith, who was once more feeling the handle as he spun the dial. She seemed to concentrate a moment then shook her head. "Ten."

The two of them shook hands as I wondered at the odd exchange.

"Go," John said.

"Are you guys betting on—" I began.

She held up her hand in an imperious gesture that shut me up. I noticed she was counting under her breath.

I was pretty sure they were betting on how long it was going to take Keith to crack the safe, but I had no idea what the stakes were. As I watched, Keith shook his head. He drew three boxes on the wall and scratched an "X" through the first one. He spun the dial, pulled lightly on the handle, and began slowly turning the dial once more.

A moment later he nodded to himself and drew another set of boxes on the wall, writing "43" in the middle box. He spun the dial, pulled lightly on the handle, and began turning again.

I looked back at Walela, who was still counting quietly, and she held two fingers up.

Eight fingers later, she cursed. Keith had two numbers in the three boxes, but the third one seemed to be giving him trouble.

John grinned up at Walela. "I win?"

"If he gets it in the next five min—"

The mechanical sound of Keith yanking the handle down interrupted her. She closed her eyes with a pained expression. "Yes. You win."

Keith smiled at his accomplishment. "I still got it." He lifted the small square door and looked into the hole in the floor. Reaching inside, he pulled a stack of papers out, tossing them carelessly into the room. He reached in again and pulled out a small stack of green paper with a white band around the middle. Kenni's eyebrows rose, and she whistled.

"Need some toilet paper?" Keith chuckled and tossed the bundle to her.

She sighed and ran her thumb across the end of a stack of ten-dollar bills. Keith tossed similar stacks at Walela, John, and me and threw one more into the middle of the room.

I looked at the bundle in my hand. The white band had yellow borders and the notation of "$1,000" stamped on it.

"Holy crap," Kenni said. "How many are there?"

"Just the five there."

"Five thousand dollars? In a floor safe?" Kenni stared at the bundle in her hands. "Who does that?"

"Well, nobody anymore. Back before the bombs, though, lots of folks out here didn't trust banks." He reached into the dark cavity once more, this time withdrawing a small pouch made of a dark, velvety material. He pulled open the drawstring and whistled.

"What?" John sounded eager. "What did we get?"

Keith tossed the bag to John. "A third is mine."

John opened the bag and poured a tangle of jewelry into his other hand. "Score!"

With a groan, Keith stood in the closet, holding hands to his back as he stretched. "How long?" he asked Walela.

"About ten and a half minutes from when I started counting. You already had just figured out the first number at that point."

"Figure another two minutes for that, so twelve or thirteen minutes?"

She shrugged, and Keith laughed at her. "You lost?"

She nodded as Keith began to lead the way out of the room. "I thought since you already had the first number, you'd be able to pop it faster."

"The first one's always easiest. Don't judge by that."

Kenni, John, and I followed them, and I listened to their conversation.

"So what was the bet?" I asked.

Keith turned back as if he had just noticed the rest of us following. "They bet on how long it'll take me to pop a safe. I always keep a third of what we get. After all, I'm the talent." He grinned. "Whoever bets the closest to how long it takes me, without me going over their time, wins another third. The rest of the team splits the last third."

"So you do this a lot?"

He shrugged. "Not as much lately. We have to find a place with a safe that hasn't already been ransacked." He turned around as we walked outside, raising his hands in a way that indicated the house we had just exited. "A place like this."

He turned back and continued to the stream. "But places like this are getting harder and harder to find unless you get off the beaten path."

"So how do you split the jewels? I mean, you say you split it by thirds, but who decides on what each piece is worth?"

"We take it to one of the larger towns and trade it for supplies. It's actually the supplies that we split."

I had to admit it sounded like a fair deal and a good way to supplement their gear. I wondered if he could teach me.

CHAPTER 33
TROUBLE

WELL RESTED, WATER CONTAINERS REFILLED, and with everyone cooled off, we got back on the road in a much better mood. We'd lost more than an hour, but it was during the hottest point of the day, and we could make it up in the evening.

Walela rode beside me, listening intently to the discussion between Kenni and me. Keith rode point while Simon and John rode behind us. Kenni was talking about some of the loopholes in the Constitution that people had taken advantage of, like how women hadn't been allowed to vote because the wording had only mentioned men. That led to some pretty strong language from Walela, and I chuckled at the distraction.

We'd been at it for a few hours and were just getting into the way politicians had twisted the definition of the word *man* when Kenni went silent in midsentence.

"What—"

She held up a finger.

In front of us, Keith wheeled his horse around. "Get in the trees!"

I'd heard the sound often enough during my evening practice sessions to recognize gunfire. But what we heard wasn't simply someone doing a bit of target practice. The initial few pops of distant gunplay turned into a long volley that I assumed must have been hundreds of guns firing at once.

Keith pulled his rifle from its carry case beneath his leg and checked to make sure it was ready to fire. He turned to the rest of his team. "Simon, you're with me. Walela, John, get them to the next waypoint. Wait for us there."

"Wait a minute," Kenni protested. "You're not about to go and do anything stupid, are you?"

Keith shook his head. "No. Our job is to make sure you get to Burns Flat. But we also need to see what's going on and make sure it doesn't interfere with our trip."

Kenni nodded. "All right. Be careful."

Keith said, "Simon?"

The redhead looked nervous as he brought his horse up beside Keith, but he didn't hesitate. The rifle he held didn't have the sleek, streamlined look of Keith's Old Days weapon. It was obviously one of the less sophisticated, post–D-day firearms out of McAlester.

"We should see you at the next waypoint before midnight." Keith reined his horse toward the sounds of gunfire to the northeast.

"Wait."

He and Simon turned back at my call.

"Simon, are you any good with that thing?" I pointed to his rifle.

He looked at me as if I'd insulted him. "Good enough."

I drew my AR-15 from its pouch under my leg. Walking Tallulah over beside him, I handed it to him. "I want this back in the morning."

Simon licked his lips as he looked at the rifle. Then he pushed it back. "I can't."

"Look, I'm all right with the pistols. Not great, but all right. But I haven't had much time to learn to use the rifle, and I'm a lot better with the bow."

He looked like he didn't believe me. I called over my shoulder, "Kenni, am I any good with the bow?"

She chuckled. "He's the best I've ever seen. Get him to show you when you get back."

Simon nodded his thanks. "I'll give it back in the morning."

"I know you will. Here." I untied a pouch from my bundle and looped the strap around his saddle horn. "Two extra magazines plus about a hundred rounds of loose ammo."

"Thanks." He and Keith turned and rode into the forest.

Kenni pulled up beside me. "Why'd you do that?"

I shrugged. "Simon still holds a bit of a grudge from when Walela embarrassed him in front of us. I figure this should make him feel a bit more favorably toward us. And if he gets himself killed trying to shoot that crappy thing he was carrying, we'd be down one person. Worst-case scenario, we lose a rifle." Looking directly at her, daring her to challenge me over risking the rifle, I finished with, "Better than losing a person."

But Kenni just grunted. "You're turning into quite the diplomat, aren't you?"

"Between Mr. Roesch and you, how could I help it?"

From ahead, Walela called, "Come on, you two. We need to get going."

We left the sounds of gunfire behind, eventually arriving at the waypoint just a bit after sunset. John, who was normally so withdrawn, was suddenly snapping orders at the rest of us. "No fire tonight. Water the horses, and be ready to mount up and leave at a second's notice. Until Keith and Simon get back, we stay ready to fight or run."

That the man was nervous was evident. That he was qualified to be in charge was less so. Kenni and I looked at one another. I raised an eyebrow. She shrugged. Not having any better ideas, I figured there was no reason to argue with him. Not yet, anyway.

So we did as he said. I didn't bother stringing up my hammock, figuring it wouldn't do any good anyway. If we were going to have to bug out, I needed to be able to mount up and make a run for it, and if we were going to have to fight, I had to be mobile. I couldn't very well do either from twenty feet up in the trees.

We took care of the horses first then munched on some of the corn cakes the elders had sent with us. Washing down the dry, grainy lumps with water from the creek, we sat in silence, staring at one another. As dusk turned to full darkness, we waited.

After several minutes of sitting quietly and staring at the trees, Kenni cleared her throat. "We should set up watches, two awake and two asleep."

John looked as if he was going to protest, but I cut him off. "Sounds like a good idea. You want to draw straws?"

"No need. I'll take first watch. John, you have any binoculars?"

He nodded.

"You mind watching with me?"

Another nod. I made note of how smoothly Kenni had taken charge of things. In a matter of seconds, John had gone from giving orders to following them. I was glad to see he wasn't going to make an issue of who was supposed to be in charge.

"How long?" I asked.

Kenni looked at John. "Three hours sound good?"

He nodded again.

"All right. Three hours and we'll wake you."

Walela tossed a bedroll on the ground, spreading it wide enough for both of us to fit on. She laid her rifle on the ground beside her and tossed a saddlebag at one end to rest her head on. I watched as Kenni and John moved a bit away from us in opposite directions.

"You just going to stand there?" Walela asked.

I felt a little self-conscious as I arranged my gear within easy reach. We had kissed and groped in the hammock the last few nights, but the flimsy barrier of the hammock's material had managed to give some semblance of privacy. It wasn't as if no one knew what was going on, but we hadn't made any big deal of our growing relationship.

Lying down beside her in the open made more of a statement. We were fully clothed, but it still seemed more intimate — especially when Walela pulled me up to snuggle behind her. But after a few minutes, I realized that she seemed perfectly at ease with the situation. And if she was okay with it, who was I to worry?

With that realization, I drifted off to sleep.

CHAPTER 34
WALTER'S STORY

SOMETHING IN CRICKET'S MOVEMENT ALERTED me, and I was reaching for my pistol before I came fully awake. Peering through the darkness, I tapped Walela as I saw a shape coming out of the brush.

My breathing began to settle back to normal as I recognized Kenni's voice. "Shhh. There's someone coming this way," she whispered. "Get ready to go."

I nodded, and Kenni faded back into the brush. Quickly and silently, I got to my feet and strung my bow in the dark. After setting it back down, I felt for my pistol belt in the darkness and slung it around my waist. I heard Walela gathering her things behind me.

Less than a minute later, we had all our gear together beside the horses. John slipped up beside me. "Go ahead and saddle up. They're still a couple of minutes out. If you're ready to go, then there's no problem if we have to leave in a hurry."

"Is it Keith and Simon?"

"Not sure. I thought I recognized Simon's white ass reflecting what little moonlight we have, but it could have been another pale skin. If it's Keith and Simon, though, they brought company. I saw five riders. So like I said, be ready."

I threw my saddle over Tallulah and cinched it down in record time. We were all mounted and waiting in the scrub when a faint nickering announced new arrivals from the north. I nocked an arrow and peered through the darkness.

A hushed voice called through the trees, *"Waziya awgha?"*

John stepped away from us and answered in the same language. *"Dayzeedo agwadooley!"*

"Dammit, John." The familiar voice was no longer quiet. "Don't you know my voice by now?" Keith stepped out of the brush across the clearing. He was followed by Simon and three other figures. John was right. Simon's pale skin made him terribly visible as he rode toward me.

With a faint smile, Simon handed me the rifle I'd loaned him. "Thanks. It came in handy."

"Glad you had it, then." I slid the bundle back into place under my leg, and he handed me the pouch of ammo. It felt a bit lighter than when I'd handed it to him.

Kenni reined Shadowfax up beside Keith. "I take it there was trouble?"

Keith nodded then waved the three newcomers up. They were dressed like Keith and his group — buckskin clad, bare chested, and armed. One of the men had a bloody bandage on his left forearm. Keith indicated the bandaged man. "This is Walter Sixkiller. He was leading a team toward Burns Flat when they ran into a little trouble."

Walter nodded greeting.

"What we heard sounded like more than just a little trouble," Kenni said.

"Yeah, it was," Walter said. "Listen, can we take a break? I'm beat."

John asked Keith, "Are we all right to stay here tonight?"

"We should be." He looked around at us. "You guys didn't make camp?"

"Didn't know if we were going to see you or someone else coming in. Figured it made more sense to be ready to run if we needed to."

"Smart. But we can rest now. Let's get some sleep, and we'll figure out what we're going to do in the morning."

We all picketed our horses again, this time with the knowledge that we were definitely planning to stay through the rest of the night. Twenty minutes later, we were all relaxing in the small clearing and passing around jerky, cornbread, and water skins.

The other two members of Walter's team were quiet. He introduced them as David and Carl. Then he started his story without any preamble.

"We found a group of six pilgrims coming down Highway 75 toward Tulsa. They would have headed straight into the fallout zone if we hadn't stopped them. Said they were coming in from Iola, Kansas. Same story as the others."

"Message from the satellite?" I asked.

"Yeah. We took them to meet with the elders in Ponca City. They got the proposal to consider allying with the OTA, and we escorted them down through the dead zones between Tulsa and Oklahoma City."

He took a bite of cornbread and followed it with a swig from his water skin before he continued. "We were coming up on Norman yesterday when we ran across a dozen soldiers in uniform. Told us we were trespassing on federal land and ordered us to lay down our weapons. Jerry started cussing them, told them it was OTA land." Walter shook his head. "He started waving his rifle around, and one of the soldiers must have thought he was going to fire. Next thing I knew, everyone was shooting. Jerry died right there. We scrambled, protected the pilgrims until we could get them into the trees, but we were outgunned."

Walter fell silent, and it was obvious to all of us that he was distraught and exhausted. But Walela prompted him again. "What happened to the pilgrims?"

"Soldiers took 'em. They yelled out for us to release our prisoners, like we'd been holding them against their will." He laughed, and it was a dry, bitter thing to hear. "Hell, they were as scared of those soldiers as we were. But after a few minutes of us all taking potshots at each other, the soldiers opened up with full auto into the trees. There were branches and splinters flying all over the place. I imagine they didn't think they were going to hurt anyone, but one of the pilgrims got hit by a long splinter. It got him in the face right next to his eye, and he was screaming... thrashing around on the ground with this two-inch-long toothpick sticking out from under his skin...

"I yelled out at those sons of bitches that they had hurt someone, and they stopped shooting. They said it was our fault that an innocent had been hurt... that if we had released them when we were told to, none of this would have happened. Then they told us to send them out again."

He looked at the ground and sighed. "So I did. God help me, they were terrified. They thought the soldiers were going to shoot them, but I knew we couldn't protect them if those bastards opened up for real. I figured they had a better chance with the soldiers than with us. I tried to explain that to them, but I don't know if they really believed me."

"But you were right, weren't you?" Keith said. "I saw them with the soldiers."

"Yeah. They had a medic, I guess, because one of them took the guy who was hurt and started working on him. The others called out for us to surrender, and when we didn't, they opened up on us again. I thought we were gonna die right there until you guys showed up." He raised his canteen in salute.

Keith chuckled. "Lucky for us, they didn't realize there were only two of us."

Simon chimed in, "And it helped that we were shooting from behind them. They were caught between us. Didn't really have a chance." He chuckled. "You shoulda seen them run."

"It's not funny, Simon." Keith didn't sound angry, but neither did he seem willing to let anyone's spirits rise. "Have any of the rest of you ever heard of them out this far from Burns Flat? I know I haven't."

They all shook their heads.

"So something's changed."

"Maybe they're looking for something." Kenni said. "Walter? You said they told you it was federal land. Where were you?"

"We were just coming in on the north side of Norman. And I

can guess what they were doing. There were a bunch of old army trucks in the parking lot around the building they were at. I'd be willing to bet it was an old National Guard base or something. They were probably hunting for supplies."

"So because it was an old base, they probably figure they had more claim to it than anyone else."

Walter shrugged. "I guess. So we were just in the wrong place at the wrong time."

Keith nodded in the dim moonlight. "That would be my guess."

"Wow. Lucky us."

The conversation dropped off at that point, and Keith suggested we all get some rest. With the events of the evening, we decided it was smarter to keep watch as Kenni had suggested.

"We probably should have been doing that all along," Keith said. "But before today, we never had any trouble like this."

Everyone got quiet for a few seconds before Walter spoke again. "This is a bad situation that's just gotten a lot worse." I was surprised when he looked directly at me. "Keith tells me you're heading for Burns Flat."

"Yes."

"Even after what you just heard?"

I took a deep breath, thinking. Finally, I said, "Yeah. I hope this was just a case of a few hotheads getting carried away. I can't believe they really represent the attitude of the US military. The sooner we get to Burns Flat, the sooner we can find out what's really going on."

He turned to Keith. "And you?"

"The elders told us to escort them. That's what we'll do."

"You know something's not right."

"But I don't know what it is. And my duty is to the elders." Keith's eyes narrowed as he looked at Walter. "But you're free of your duty now. Your pilgrims are gone."

"I was thinking the same thing."

"So what are you going to do?" Keith asked.

Walter looked at the other two members of his team. They all nodded at one another in some unspoken agreement before he turned back to Keith. "Tomorrow morning, we'll split up. We'll head to the major towns and meet with as many elders as we can—spread the word about what happened. Then it's up to them to decide what to do."

CHAPTER 35
CASINO

WE RODE IN HARD, SHORT sprints the next day. I couldn't speak for everyone, but there was a determination on my mind, and everyone else seemed to share my mood. We elected to gamble a bit, traveling in the long clearings of the once-upon-a-time Highway 35, sacrificing cover for speed. We would race across a clearing, slowing when we reached a tree line as we waited for the dogs to catch up to us. As much as I hated to admit it, Bella and Cricket were slowing us down, but I wasn't willing to leave them behind.

The trees gradually disappeared, making way for a large open plain only occasionally spotted with small clumps of small trees and scrub. Keith pulled up at an intersection, and we all stopped while he checked his map. He folded it and looked up. "There are a few waypoints to choose from. One of them is just a few miles ahead on Highway 9 here." He pointed to the left.

Kenni looked up at the sun. "It's barely noon. You really want to stop now?"

"The next one is a hard ride west. Almost another twenty miles. It'll be rough on the horses." He looked at the girls, tongues lolling as they dropped to the ground while we spoke. It was obvious that they were exhausted. "And I don't think your dogs will make it much farther."

"Who says we have to stop at a waypoint?" I asked. "If we make it, fine. If not, we find a place and make camp for the night."

Keith nodded. "All right. But we should stop at the waypoint up ahead long enough to water the animals. We're working them pretty hard."

We slowed for a bit to let the dogs and horses cool off as we neared the waypoint on Keith's map. It turned out to be a huge old abandoned building standing in the middle of a large clearing. Hundreds of rusting automobile carcasses decorated the field around it, giving testament to the fact that at least part of the clearing had once been a parking lot.

Judging from the remains, it looked like the building had once covered an area as big as the old Eagle Stadium back in Rejas. As Keith led us toward the back of the monolith, I asked, "What was this place?"

"Old gambling casino and hotel." He pointed to a section of wall that had caved in. Several of the cars lay on their sides. One was upside down. "Tornado took a piece of it out about six years ago."

"Where are we going?"

Keith pointed to a windmill in the clearing back behind the casino. There was a large, rusted metal trough at its base.

"We maintain the pump on the windmill. That's why it's marked as a waypoint. We can water the horses and rest here for a little bit."

"On behalf of my chapped hindquarters," Kenni said, "I thank you."

I was worried about slowing everyone down. While we were moving at a leisurely pace, the dogs weren't any trouble. But now that everyone was in a hurry...

I looked at Tallulah while we all rested on the ground around the watering trough. "Kenni?"

"What?"

"You think you can carry some of the supplies I have in my saddlebags?"

She cocked her head, clearly wondering what I had in mind. "I don't see why not. Why?"

"I have an idea." I pulled the larger set of leather bags off of Tallulah's back and began rearranging the gear in it, shifting much of it to some of the smaller bags, dumping what wouldn't fit onto the ground. Suddenly excited, I pointed to the pile on the ground. "If you can find someplace for this, I think I can help with our pace."

Before anyone could say anything, I slung the saddlebags over my shoulder and trotted toward the parking lot. I knelt at the back of the first car I came to and pulled out one of my smaller belt knives.

"What are you doing?" Walela asked from behind me.

"You have a knife?" I asked.

"Of course."

"I need a dozen of these license plates. Maybe more." I removed the one I had been working on and stuffed it into one of the saddlebags.

She looked at me a second before shrugging and moving to another vehicle. Within minutes, we had unscrewed several license plates. I placed each one in a saddlebag in such a way that they spread the bags to their maximum width and supported the bottom. When she brought me the last plate, I had the bottom of each bag lined three plates thick, with more lining the sides.

Satisfied with what I had so far, I began trying the handles on cars. "I need to get into one of these," I said, pulling ineffectively on another locked door.

"You need the glass?"

"No, why?"

Rather than answer, she bent, picked up a large chunk of concrete, and smashed the window. Reaching inside, she pulled the door handle and popped the car open. She waved her hand in invitation, her smirk telling me she thought I was silly for not thinking of breaking in the way she had. In retrospect, I had to agree.

Not taking the time to worry about it, I bent over the seat and began slicing the upholstery and padding from it.

"How much do you need?" Walela asked.

"Both front seats. All the padding and the cloth covering on the seats."

She nodded. "Are you making a carrier for the dogs?"

"Yeah."

"And this is to line the inside?"

"Yes."

"Then can I suggest something?" She pointed out the cloth I was cutting out of the seat. "That stuff is so old and sun dried it's almost useless."

I felt the material, and she was right. It practically crumbled in my hands.

She pointed to another car. "Some of the fancier cars used to have leather seats. The leather will probably be in better shape."

I went to peek into the window of the car she'd pointed out. Sure enough, the covering for the seats in that one were leather. Following her lead, I picked up a chunk of concrete and smashed it through the window. A few minutes later, I had two large saddlebags with reinforced bottoms. The bottoms and sides were lined with padding from the seats then covered in leather. I had my carriers.

"Think they'll work?" Walela asked.

"I hope so." We walked back to the others.

———— ✳ ✳ ✳ ✳ ✳ ————

The carriers worked. The girls weren't entirely happy about being in them, but I was able to convince them to stay in while we rode. We were able to push the horses a bit more, and while Bella and Cricket whined at what had to be an uncomfortable ride for them, they eventually lay down and rested as we rode. Of course, carrying them was a tradeoff. Bella weighed just over fifty pounds, and Cricket weighed about forty, so Tallulah was carrying nearly an extra hundred pounds. It had to be hard on her, but some of that extra weight was offset by the absence of the gear Kenni had taken.

So while we couldn't move at full speed, we *were* able to travel considerably faster than we had during the first part of the day. We kept a hard enough pace that Tallulah began to pant. I looked at the sky, noticing dusk was still a few hours off.

"How much farther to the waypoint?" I called.

Keith pointed. "See where the trail peaks at the top of that next hill?"

We had left the main road nearly half an hour back, and the trail ahead was barely visible. Still, there was enough of an opening to show the relatively straight path and where it kissed the sky about a quarter of a mile ahead.

"Yeah."

"There's an old log cabin just past it. It's near Lake Chickasha and has a stable and a well, and we try to keep it stocked with a little food."

"Good. I think Tallulah's about had it."

Keith nodded. "I think we've all had it."

I couldn't argue with that.

We were just approaching the top of the hill when we heard the familiar sound of gunfire coming from the direction we were headed in.

Keith whipped out his map. "John, same drill as yesterday. Get them to—" He began tracing his finger on the map.

"No," I interrupted him. "Not this time."

Keith looked at me as if I was nothing more than a minor irritant. "Look, Zach—"

I interrupted again. "We're not staying behind. If it's the same group that Walter talked about, then you need the numbers."

More gunfire sounded.

"Kenni and I aren't a couple of innocent little children you need to protect. We came on this trip knowing it could get rough. And I won't lie—it has been. But we agreed to see it through long before we ever met you."

Keith started to open his mouth, and I went on before he could speak.

"Look, we can either sit here and argue about who does what, or we can get moving and stop whatever's going on ahead."

As if to punctuate my words, more gunfire sounded. Keith still looked like he was going to argue.

"Come on, Keith," I said over the sound of the latest barrage. "You really can't stop us, can you?"

He pursed his lips and cursed. "All right. But we're not going in guns blazing, either. We need to see what's going on. If we have to get involved, we figure out how to get an advantage before we do anything. Got it?"

"Got it." Looking around, I could see everyone else was in agreement.

Keith looked at me. "And if you get yourself shot, you'd better hope it kills you. Otherwise, I'll probably be pissed enough to finish the job."

I just nodded, and we moved out.

CHAPTER 36
AMBUSH

WE HAD GOTTEN AS CLOSE as we were comfortable with for the moment. There was still plenty of distance we needed to cover, but riding closer could expose us to a stray glance into the trees.

I was playing squirrel man, as Kenni liked to call it, peering through my binoculars from the top of one of the big oak trees. I saw six men in uniform in front of a ramshackle log cabin.

When we arrived, two of them in front were arguing about something while four others took occasional pot shots into the window of the cabin. Six other people sat on the ground, huddled behind a wagon loaded with boxes, crates, and all sorts of bags and sacks. From our vantage in the underbrush, I could see one of them wore a bandage over one eye.

I shimmied back down the tree to report what I had seen.

"The guy with the eye patch must be the wounded pilgrim Walter's team was escorting," Simon said.

Kenni chimed in. "If that's the case, it means there's not just six soldiers. Walter said there were a dozen."

"The rest must be around back. And that means they outnumber us two to one." Keith looked at me. "You sure you're up for this?"

Walking over to Tallulah, I grabbed my bow and quiver. "We already had that discussion." I planted one end of the bow against my boot and quickly strung it. "We're hitting them from behind, and whoever is in that cabin is still shooting too. They'll be caught between us." I slung my quiver across my shoulder. "We need to split up so we can cover the people in back. I'll take that since it looks like the tree line in back is closer to the cabin."

"What?"

I lifted the bow. "My range is less than yours."

"Seriously? You're planning to use that?"

"Trust him," Kenni said. "He's better with it than most people are with rifles."

Keith sighed, and I could see he didn't fully believe her. But neither did he have time to argue. "Fine. You, Simon, and Walela take the back. The rest of us will cover the front."

"Simon, you want to use my rifle again?"

"Hell yeah! It's a lot more accurate than my scatter gun."

I gestured with my chin to where the rifle was still strapped to Tallulah. "Help yourself."

Keith looked up at the angle of the sun. "I'll give you about five minutes to get into position, and we're going to start screaming for them to surrender."

"Think they will?" John asked.

"We can always hope." But his tone showed he didn't think it likely.

"One request?" I said.

"What?"

"Can we try to keep them alive? I still plan to meet with their superiors. Turning over live prisoners would probably go a lot further than leaving a bunch of bodies."

Keith grimaced. "No promises, but I'll try."

"That's all I can ask for." I called the girls. "Bella, Cricket. Hush." I watched to make sure they got the command. Seeing that they had it, I nodded. "Come." Together, we turned to run through the trees to the back of the cabin.

Simon, Walela, and I moved back into the trees and began to circle around. Simon slipped into the lead, surprisingly quiet and agile in the underbrush. We'd barely gone halfway around before Simon froze, signaling us to wait. Looking back, he held up two fingers, then pointed to the underbrush ahead and to the left. He held up his hand, indicating we should hold still, and began to raise his rifle.

I eased up and tapped him on the shoulder. Signaling him to wait, I slipped past him and pulled out my belt knife. My dad had made it for me. It had an eight-inch blade, and the handle was aged hickory burl with a brass guard and pommel. I breathed deep and slow through my mouth to keep from being heard as I got right behind them and raised my hand. I slammed the pommel into the back of the rearmost man's head and had the blade at the second man's throat before the first one hit the ground.

"Don't move, and don't say anything," I whispered. "The blade's wicked sharp, and I'm afraid the slightest move would leave you bleeding in the bushes. Understand?"

Wide-eyed, the man barely nodded. I heard light rustling behind me and glanced back to see Simon and Walela coming up on us.

"Good. Now, real slow, I want you to pass your rifle back to my friend on your left. No. No need to look. Just hold it by the barrel and hand it back."

The man did so, and Walela grabbed it.

"Good. Now hold still while my other friend gets your pistol."

Even though we hadn't rehearsed it, Simon and Walela knew how to take prompts, and Simon slipped the man's pistol from its holster. That told him there were at least three of us, and I hoped that realization would be enough to keep him from trying anything.

"All right, now, I need you to put your hands behind your back. We don't intend to kill you unless you make us, but we also have to make sure you aren't going to cause any trouble. You understand?"

He nodded once more and put his hands behind him as if waiting for us to tie him up. As soon as his hands were behind him, I whipped the pommel of the knife into his head, letting his unconscious form drop to the ground.

"Grab their weapons and let's go. I don't know how much time we have before Keith starts things going."

Walela hefted the man's rifle. "Better than mine. I think I'll just keep it." She pulled a length of leather cord from a pouch and tossed it to Simon. Together, the two of them hastily tied our captives' hands and feet.

Running as quietly as we could, we slipped into position in back, where four more soldiers were still taking pot shots at the cabin. With all the gunfire, I wasn't too terribly worried that they were going to hear us. The three of us quickly spread out to give us maximum coverage of the unsuspecting soldiers facing the cabin. They were joking with one another, laughing as they fired their weapons.

I slipped closer, just to the edge of the tree line. I judged the distance to be a bit over twenty yards and felt confident of my aim. I drew four arrows, nocked one, and held the other three in my draw hand as I waited for Keith to start things rolling. The men fired another volley into the cabin, laughing once more as they did, and I wondered where they had gotten so much ammunition that they could afford to waste it that way. I didn't have time to think about it much, though, before I heard Keith call from the front.

"You men shooting into the cabin. We have you surrounded. Drop your weapons and surrender!"

His yell was immediately followed by a volley of gunfire as the soldiers made it perfectly clear that they had no intention of surrendering. The men in back shouted to one another and started to move up to help their buddies. I shouted to keep them in place.

"Stay right where you are! You've got your own problems to deal with. Drop your weapons and—"

I didn't get to finish my sentence as they spun and began shooting. I ducked behind a tree as Simon and Walela opened up. When I peeked back around the tree, one of the men was lying on the ground, grabbing his leg. The other three were running toward the trees. They were in profile to me, and I stepped out and let loose a couple of arrows, taking two of the men in the right shoulder. At that range, it was actually an easy shot, and I eased up on the draw so the arrows would be less likely to go through the shoulder and into the chest.

The last soldier dropped as someone fired from inside the cabin.

The two with arrows in their arms screamed and dropped their rifles. With another arrow nocked, I scanned the men and found the one who had been shot in the leg fumbling for his pistol. I leveled on him and yelled, "Drop it! I don't want to kill you, but if you make me, I'm not going to lose any sleep over it."

Bella and Cricket were at my sides, hackles raised, teeth bared. I could only imagine how fierce they appeared to him. He looked from me to the dogs then to Simon and Walela as they emerged from the brush. He tossed the pistol away and raised his hands. Keith yelled from the front, "You guys all right?"

"Under control," Walela replied.

It had been less than a minute since he had called out for the men to drop their weapons. None of us were hurt, and the soldiers had two dead, six wounded, and four incapacitated.

CHAPTER 37
AFTERMATH

THE AFTERMATH OF THE FIGHT was much less organized than the fight itself had been. We had twelve captives to watch, six pilgrims to tend, an unknown number of people inside the cabin to check on, and a pile of newly captured weapons to sort through. And there were only six of us.

That didn't slow Keith down in the slightest. "Kenni—you, John, and Simon keep an eye on the soldiers. Anyone tries anything, shoot them. Walela, see if the pilgrims are all right. Zach, come with me to check on the folks in the cab…" His voice trailed off as the cabin door opened and four people came out.

"Never mind." He began walking toward them. "Everyone all right?"

One of them—probably the group leader—spoke up. "Thanks to you guys." The woman was hardly taller than a child. But her expression was anything but childlike as she approached Keith. She stopped a few feet from him. "Thanks for saving our asses."

Keith nodded. "Seemed like the thing to do. I'm Keith Wilson."

"Tara Blackwood." She looked at me expectantly.

"I'm Zachary Dawcett." I stuck my hand out.

Tara seemed to hesitate a moment then reached out and clasped my hand. She looked at Keith. "You brought a pilgrim into a fight?"

"How did you know I was—"

"Shaking hands is a white thing. Most people from around here already know that, Indian or not."

I dropped my hand. "Sorry. I didn't mean to offend."

She laughed. "Don't sweat it, kid. No offense at all. I've just gotten out of the habit."

"He's a little stubborn," Keith told her. "And to be perfectly honest, we needed the help."

"Well, I'm glad you didn't stop to argue. We were damn near out of ammo. Another few minutes, and those sons of bitches probably could have walked through the front door and we wouldn't have been able to do shit about it. Hell, if I was a man, I'd have whipped my pecker out just so I could at least piss on 'em when they busted in."

Her language surprised me, and from the look on Keith's face, it caught him unawares as well. I found myself smiling, and I honestly didn't know if it was from the hastily covered look of shock on Keith's face or the fact that Tara seemed so unfazed by the effect she had.

As she answered Keith's questions, I realized she was just one of those people who cussed like a sailor and didn't think twice about it. I had a friend back home who was like that. Ed claimed it was more honest than trying to watch what you said so you didn't hurt anyone's feelings. Personally, I always thought he just liked to see if he could shock anyone. I wasn't sure if the same applied to Tara, but anyone with delicate sensibilities was going to have a hard time around her.

She and her team had had the bad luck to simply be in the wrong place at the wrong time. They were riding through the ruins of the little town of Tuttle when the soldiers met them on the road.

"Bunch of ass clowns who thought they could force us to surrender our weapons!" She intentionally raised her voice while looking past Keith, staring at the line of uniformed men tied up in the grass. I got the distinct impression that she was hoping one of them would try to argue, but they didn't even look our way. Seeing she wasn't going to get a rise out of them, she turned her attention back to us. "I told them to kiss my ass, and for some reason, they didn't like that idea." Her account included a lot of wild shooting and wilder riding and ended with them holing up in the waypoint cabin until we heard the gunfire.

As the two of them talked, I realized she was speaking exclusively to Keith. I figured that as a pilgrim, I wasn't really important enough to warrant attention, at least in her eyes, so I decided to go see if I could help elsewhere.

When I turned to leave, Tara stopped me. "Hey, kid."

I turned back at Tara's call.

"You said your name was Zachary, right?"

"Yes, ma'am."

"I saw you out there, and I want to thank you. Not everyone would have jumped into a fight that wasn't theirs. You did good."

I shrugged, a little embarrassed at her words. "No problem." I left Tara and Keith to their conversation.

Walking to where Kenni, John, and Simon watched over the prisoners, I noted the blood still seeping from the leg of the man Walela had shot. He was lying on the ground, eyes closed, with a light sheen of sweat on his face. The patch on his chest showed his name was Odom. I stopped to kneel beside him, noting how pale he looked. I reached out to feel his forehead, and his eyes snapped open.

"Get the hell away from me."

I pulled my hand back. "You're not looking so good."

"That tends to happen when you get shot. You the son of a bitch who did it?"

"No." I pointed to the two with arrows in their arms. "I used the bow."

He scowled and closed his eyes again.

"Come on. Where's your first aid kit? We need to patch you up."

"Screw you."

I shook my head, stood, and walked over to Kenni. "Which one of them is in charge?"

She pointed. "Him."

Together, we walked to the man she indicated.

"You're in charge of these men?" I asked him.

He looked at me briefly. Then, as if completely uninterested in me, he turned away again.

Kenni kicked his foot. "Look, Sergeant," she said, "all I see are privates, PFCs, and corporals. You're the only one with more than two stripes on his shoulder, so we're going to proceed under the assumption that you're top in this outfit."

He continued to ignore us.

"I don't believe this," I said to Kenni. "He's got a man bleeding to death, and all I want to do is give their first aid kits to them." I looked back at the silent man. "Do you *want* your man to die?"

"Let us go, and we'll take care of ourselves."

"Well, that sure as hell isn't going to happen."

"You have no right to detain members of the United States Army!"

I thought about that. I had to be careful how I addressed that claim.

"United States Army? So you're telling me that you're out here acting on behalf of the US government?"

"I am. And you've just stepped in a big pile of shit, raising arms against us the way you have. You killed two of my men!"

"Men who were just performing their duty, right?"

He looked at me warily, probably realizing I was leading him. "We were ordered to collect supplies."

"And were you ordered to take private property from US citizens? Tell me something" — I looked at his name tag — "Sergeant Collins. Did they swear you in when you joined the Army?"

"What?"

"When you joined the Army, didn't you have to take some kind of oath or something?" I knew perfectly well that he had. Kenni had told me about it long ago. "Kenni, how did that oath go again?"

She drew herself up. "I do solemnly swear that I will support and defend the Constitution of the United States against all enemies, foreign and domestic; that I will bear true faith and allegiance to the same; and that I will obey the orders of the president of the United States and the orders of the officers appointed over me, according to regulations and the Uniform Code of Military Justice, so help me God."

I turned back to Collins. "Is that the oath you took?"

"Yes. And before you even go down this road, you should know that martial law has been declared, so the regular articles of the Constitution don't apply."

"That may be true. I'll even grant you that it usually gives the military the right to suspend some of the articles of the Constitution as well as..." I turned to Kenni. "What was that again? Habeas corpus?"

She nodded, the slightest of grins on her face.

"Do you know what habeas corpus is? No? Well honestly, neither did I until recently. But it turns out that the concept of habeas corpus means a person can't be held without a valid, legal reason. Martial law allows you to suspend that right so you can take someone into custody without having to go through the normal legal channels. What it *doesn't* allow is for you to serve as judge, jury, and executioner in the field. When you find people in violation of the law, you have to bring them in to stand trial. Granted, it would be a court-martial, but they're still accorded the right to a trial."

Collins blinked. After a moment of silence in which I could have sworn I heard gears turning in his head, he swallowed. "I was acting under orders."

"Look, Collins, we can debate the legality of your orders and whether or not you should have done what you did all day long. But the fact of the matter is that you initiated an armed assault on US citizens, who successfully defended themselves. As a result, you and your men were defeated and are being detained. During the course of the fight that you and your people started, two of your men were killed and several more were wounded." I let my voice rise. "Now, one of those wounded is lying over there bleeding to death, and I am doing my best to get you to help me to get him the aid he needs! So where the hell are your first aid supplies?"

There was a mixture of anger and confusion in the man's eyes, but finally he nodded at the wagon.

"I don't have time to search through the whole wagon. More importantly, the man bleeding on the ground doesn't have time. Come with me, and show me where it is."

I kept a close eye on him as he led the way, half expecting him to have a hidden weapon in or under the wagon. But he simply reached for a green canvas bag.

"Wait a minute."

He stopped, and I reached past him, pulling the bag off the wagon. Stepping back from him, I unlaced the bindings and glanced inside. A quick scan showed an abundance of white bandages and various jars with writing on them.

I said, "Good. Now let's get you back."

As we walked the short distance, he asked, "You're really going to patch my man up?"

"Not me, but we have someone who's a kind of medic."

He simply nodded. "Thanks."

As we got back, I saw Kenni lower her rifle and realized that she had been covering us, watching for trouble the same way I'd been. I tossed the bag to John, our medic. "John, would you see what you can do for the guy on the end? Wouldn't want him to bleed to death."

He grunted, but he took the bag down to the bleeding soldier and knelt beside the man.

Collins asked, "So are you the one in charge?"

"Me?" I chuckled. "No."

He looked confused. "But you're the one who's been giving orders."

"No. I'm the only one who cares enough to try and keep your man from dying. The others just don't give a damn."

His lips drew into a tight line. "So why do you care?"

"Because I'm heading to Burns Flat. And one of the things I

need to find out is whether or not your orders really came from there."

"Why does that matter?"

"It'll let me know what kind of people are asking for help rebuilding the country."

CHAPTER 38
HELPING THE WOUNDED

WALELA HAD TAKEN THE PILGRIMS farther away from the soldiers and was tending to them. When I went to check on her, and the pilgrims of course, she saw me and smiled. For some reason, that lifted my spirits like nothing else could.

"How is everybody doing?"

"Pretty good. They all seem to be in pretty good health." She patted the shoulder of one of the men as she stood. "We'll be right back."

Walking past me, she tugged my sleeve. Together, we left the group behind us. Once out of earshot, she told me the bad news. "The guy with the bandage on his eye is Rick Bradford. Whoever patched him up did a pretty piss poor job of it. He said they held him down, yanked the splinter out, and wrapped him with a bandage. I took a look, and I think it's infected. The area all around the eye is swollen, and there's pus oozing out from the corner of his eye. I'm afraid that if we don't get the infection under control, he might lose the eye."

I had to force myself not to look back at the man while we were talking. "You really think it's that bad?"

"I don't know. But I knew a kid back home who had something similar happen. The infection got into the eye, followed the optic nerve into the brain, and killed him. I'm not saying this is that bad, but I'd feel better if John could take a look. He's better at the medical stuff than I am."

I nodded. "He's working on the guy with the leg wound. I'll go get him."

"Thanks." Then, before I could move, she pulled my face to her and planted a tender kiss on me.

I was still standing there like an idiot when I realized she was already walking away. My mind thoroughly muddled for the moment, I licked my lips, savoring the phantom sensation of Walela's kiss, and headed back to where John was finishing up the soldier's leg.

"You nearly done?" I asked.

"Yeah. Bullet went completely through. Doesn't look like it hit any major veins or arteries, so I made a poultice from some crushed comfrey and black pepper. It should stop the bleeding, but he's not going to be able to ride anytime soon."

"Thanks. Think you could look at one of the pilgrims? Walela thinks he has an infection in his eye."

"Sure." John gathered up the first aid gear and followed me. He knelt beside the man with the wrapped-up eye. "Hey, what's your name?"

"Rick Bradford."

"Hi, Rick. I'm John, and I'll be your medic today. Can I get you any refreshments?"

The man grinned at the joke, and though I could tell he was still in a bit of pain, John's manner had obviously put him more at ease.

"Sure, Doc. You got a shot of whiskey in your bag of tricks there?"

John began unwrapping the bandage. "Sorry. Nothing nearly that good." He pulled the bandage off and lightly touched around the infected wound. "However, I do have a little something for this wound."

"Guess that'll have to do."

"Zachary, would you start mixing a poultice with some of the lavender and yarrow in those two pouches?" He pointed. "There's a small wooden bowl in my bag."

The cut itself didn't look too bad, but the inflamed, red tinge looked painful. I found the bowl in his bag, as instructed, as well as the pouches he indicated.

"What can I do?" Walela asked.

"Look around for some plantain, would you? As much as you can get."

She nodded and immediately began searching the ground.

"You don't keep it in your bag?" I asked.

"Nah. The stuff's so common this time of year that I don't bother. Works better when it's fresh, anyway."

He pulled some white cloth from his bag and unrolled it carefully in his lap. "Hand me the bowl."

I did, and I watched as he poured the contents into the middle of the cloth just as Walela returned with a handful of small, broad leaves with sharply defined veins. "This enough?"

He nodded, taking some of them and handing more to me. "Crush them up. Just roll them between your hands like this."

He demonstrated, rolling them vigorously between his hands before laying them on the cloth. "That's good enough," he said, holding his hand out for my leaves.

He took mine, then Walela's, adding them to the poultice he was making. Carefully folding the inner cloth away from the outer, he made a pouch of the herbs, which he then rolled into another cloth. When he finished, he had a long strip of white bandage with the poultice in the center. "Zachary, I need you to take the rest of the cloth out of my lap, but be careful to only touch the bottom cloth. The ones in the middle are still clean. Fold them in half, then roll them up tight and put them back in my bag."

When I finished, John was smearing a syrupy liquid on Rick's wound. "Okay, Mr. Bradford. I need you to close your eye and keep it closed. I'm going to smear this over your eyelid, and it's going to be sticky. You're going to want to open your eye, but I want you to fight the impulse, okay?"

"Sure."

The smell from the syrup surprised me. "Is that honey?"

John continued to gently slather the golden syrup around the eye as he spoke. "Yep. Honey fights the infection while the herbs in the poultice heal the actual wound."

"You're kidding!" I'd never heard of such a thing.

But John just shook his head. "Nope. It's been used since ancient times. Long before you white folks crossed the ocean." He grinned as he smeared a thin layer on the wound and then on the eyelid. I noticed he made sure to get it all around where the eyelid was weeping pus. "Good. Just hold still for a minute while we finish up this poultice."

He turned to Walela. "My hands are sticky. I need you to pour just a little bit of that honey over the herbs. We want it to just barely seep through the cloth."

I watched as she followed John's instructions.

"Your turn, Zachary. Walela and I both have sticky hands, so you get to tie the poultice in place." He held the small package of honey and herbs over Rick's eye while I tied it with a clean bandage. After minimal fumbling on my part, the whole contrivance was in position.

"Excellent. Now, Rick, remember what I said about opening your eye. It should be easier to ignore with the patch over it, but I still want you to be aware of it, okay?"

Rick nodded. "Sure. Thanks."

"No problem. We'll change the dressing and refresh the poultice in the morning. We'll need to make sure the infection is healing properly, but I think you'll be all right as long as we keep on top of it."

The cabin wasn't big enough to house all of us, so we split into groups. Walela and John took the pilgrims inside while the rest of us set up outside. As the sunlight began to fade, we split into two groups of four in order to effectively watch the camp and the prisoners through the night. Fortunately, nothing happened that warranted any action. The worst thing was having to work out bathroom breaks for them.

The next morning, we got everyone on the road with little trouble. We put Rick Bradford in the wagon along with Corporal Odom. The other wounded were still able to ride their horses, and there wasn't a lot of room in the back of the wagon anyway. Keith and Tara had checked through the crates and found rifles, pistols, ammunition, Old Days medicines, and jars of home-canned food. There were also boxes of books and magazines as well as several hand tools.

"Where'd they get all this?" Keith wondered aloud.

I watched from Tallulah's back as Kenni hefted a jar of pickled eggs.

"Same place they were trying to get Tara's rifles." She looked accusingly at the sergeant, who was tied to his saddle. "They took whatever they wanted from whoever had it. They're raiders. Only difference in them and the groups we've dealt with before is that they're wearing uniforms now."

The thought that those men had been stealing food and supplies in the name of martial law made my stomach churn. "Well, let's get them back to Burns Flat and find out whether or not their superiors condone this." I spun Tallulah around and rode to the front of the line.

Kenni caught up to me shortly. "You know, you did really well back there yesterday."

"You've seen me shoot before."

"Not that. I mean when you were talking to Collins. You remembered the constitutional issues and the little bit of the UCMJ I taught you. It's reassuring to know I haven't been wasting my breath."

I grinned a bit at that.

CHAPTER 39
BURNS FLAT

KEITH LED US INTO BURNS Flat without any further incident. From the waypoint where we had captured Collins and his men, it was less than a two-day journey even with the additional people and wagon. When we trotted into town, I wasn't sure who was more interested in whom. The people there seemed to outnumber even the population we'd seen in McAlester, and they all watched us pass with keen interest. The streets were crowded, and there were campsites all around the outskirts of town. I mentioned that to Walela, and she shook her head.

"It's not that there are more people here. I was here about three months ago, and it looked the same. I was told there were about five thousand people here. It looks like more because the town isn't big enough to house that many. That's why you see so many campsites."

"If the town can't house so many people, then why are they all here?"

"It's a blockade," Kenni said. "They're trying to keep supplies from getting in."

Walela nodded. "It's not foolproof. They still get teams in and out on occasion, but we do our best to stop them."

I kept my mouth shut. The information put a whole new light on why the soldiers were raiding the surrounding towns. It also made their antagonistic aggression more understandable.

"So where is the spaceport from here?"

"You're still going in?"

"It's the reason we came."

Keith pulled up beside me. "If you're sure you're going to do this, then we need to take your firearms before we let you in."

"Now, hold on a minute! What gives you the right to take our weapons? You do that, and you're no better than these guys." I jutted my chin at Collins and his men.

"We'll hold them for you until you come back out. They're still yours. But we can't let you take them inside the fence. If you do, the soldiers will confiscate them, and we'll have that many more weapons pointing at us."

"He's got a point," Kenni said, "and they haven't done us wrong so far." To show what she thought of the matter, Kenni dismounted and pulled her rifle from where it hung from her saddle.

Shaking my head, I dismounted to follow her lead. "What happened to me being in charge?"

She stopped what she was doing and looked at me. She pulled back the arm holding the rifle she was about to hand to Keith. "Sorry. You're right." Looking at Keith, she asked, "Do you mind if we speak in private for a minute?"

He looked surprised but shrugged. "No, just stay close. And don't try to go to the fence with your weapons. You're liable to get both sides worked up."

She guided me a short distance away from the others before saying, "You're right. I shouldn't have ignored what you were saying. Did you want to do something different?"

Surprised that she appeared to have taken me seriously, I stammered. "No, no. I was just... I don't know. I guess I was just grumbling."

Kenni looked at me then at the fence down the road. "Zachary, this is possibly the last time I'm going to be able to speak openly to you before we go inside that fence, and we don't know what we're going to run into once we're in there. We've come a long way, both in distance and in what we've learned, and it's time for us both to fully commit to our roles in this thing."

She gripped my shoulder, making sure I was looking at her. "You're ready for this. You showed me that when you ran rings around Collins the other day. You might not be up to Mark's level, but you've learned about all I have to teach you. The days of you wishing I would take on the task of representative need to be behind you, because I can honestly say that I don't think I could do any better than what you've shown me you're capable of doing. So as of this second, I'm committing to my role as your assistant. Anytime we're in public, I'm your aide. I'll answer any question you have, and I'll perform any task you need done to the absolute best of my ability. I won't lecture you. I won't question you. And I sure as hell won't contradict you again." She squeezed my shoulder then dropped her hand. "You're the lead on this. Understand?"

I swallowed at the sudden weight of the responsibility she was laying on my shoulders. "Aw, crap."

She grinned. "Don't worry. You're ready."

Taking a deep breath, I nodded. "All right. Let's give Keith our weapons and see about getting on the other side of that fence."

CHAPTER 40
TURNING THE TABLES

KEITH, WALELA, AND I LED the way toward the gate to the spaceport. Kenni followed, driving the newly emptied wagon with Corporal Odom lying in back. The supplies had been confiscated by the OTA in town, but I'd convinced them to let me take the wagon back in. Collins and his men trailed behind the wagon, all of their horses tied in a train behind it, their wrists tied to their saddle horns. We wound our way through the milling throng of bystanders and up to the barricade, about a hundred yards away from the gate.

"This is as far as we go," Keith stopped about halfway between the blockade line and the guards on the other side of the fence. "No need tempting fate."

I started to offer my hand then recalled Tara's words and simply nodded. "Thanks. For everything."

"Good luck."

"How long do you think you'll be?" Walela asked.

"I wish I knew." I nodded to the gate. "We don't really know what to expect in there. Could be a few days—could be a few weeks."

She was silent, appearing to think about that. Finally, she said, "Then I'll give you two weeks. If I don't hear from you by noon, two weeks from today, then I'm coming in after you."

"Oh, you are?"

"Yeah," she said. "We have unfinished business, you and me."

My pulse quickened at the implication. "We do, eh?"

"Unless you're not interested?"

"Oh, I'm interested. I'm definitely inter — "

"All right you two." Kenni snorted as she drove the wagon alongside us. Our prisoners trailed behind it, horses tethered to the back. "Take that up later. Right now, we have business to take care of."

I sighed. "You mind watching the girls for me?"

Walela looked down at Bella and Cricket. "Of course not." She looked back up with a huge smile.

"What?" I asked.

"If you're leaving them with me, at least I know you plan on coming back."

As first the wagon, then the soldiers rode past, Walela smiled, "Wish I could kiss you right now."

Heart thumping, I asked, "What's stopping you?"

"You're about to go inside that fence. You think people in there aren't watching you right now? How well would your talks go if they immediately assume you're romantically involved with one of us?"

"I guess that's true."

"So I'll see you in two weeks."

"Or less."

"I hope so." She winked and turned her horse back toward the blockade. "Bella, Cricket," she called. "Come."

They looked from me to Walela. "Go on," I told them. Cricket trotted after her, but Bella looked at me and whined. "Go to Walela."

With a final whine to let me know she wasn't sure about the situation, Bella turned to follow Walela and Cricket. I watched them for a few seconds before turning Tallulah and galloping up to the head of the line. Drawing up beside the wagon, I spoke to Kenni without turning my head. "You ready for this?"

"Hell if I know. Seeing how Collins and his men were acting, I have to admit I'm a little nervous about what we might be getting ourselves into."

"I know what you mean."

But neither of us slowed, and when we were a stone's throw out, one of the three guards shouted for us to stop. "That's far enough. State your name and your purpose for being here."

Before I could speak, Collins shouted from behind us, "I'm Sergeant William Collins. My men and I were illegally attacked and have been taken prisoner. I have wounded men out here."

With a sinking feeling in my gut, I saw my control of the situation dissolving as the guards at the gate raised their weapons. I should have gagged the man, but I hadn't thought that far ahead. I considered dumping him off his horse, but at that point, I figured the damage was already done. The only thing I could think of to do was to comply with the guards as they yelled for us to raise our hands, not make any sudden moves, and all kinds of other cliché orders.

I raised my hands and yelled. "My name is Zachary Dawcett. My aide and I are here in answer to your satellite broadcast. Collins and his men were captured while they were attacking a group of civilians. We took them prisoner and brought them back here to determine whether their actions are sanctioned by the same people who sent out that broadcast. What we find out will help us determine whether or not our people decide to ally ourselves with you."

Kenni set the brake on the wagon and raised her hands as well. Looking over at me, she smiled nervously. "It would have been nice to let me know you were planning to challenge them right off the bat."

"Planning?" I shook my head. "I hate to disappoint you, but I'm making this up as we go."

"Damn. I was afraid you were going to say something like that. I think I'd rather you *had* planned it. At least then I could pretend you knew what you were doing."

"I couldn't very well let Collins make an accusation like that and not counter it somehow, could I?"

We watched as two of the guards walked toward us. They had their rifles lowered, but the guard at the gate didn't. I made sure my hands stayed completely visible and still.

One of the guards, a huge white man whose head seemed to attach directly to his shoulders without virtue of a neck, leaned back to look up at me. "Please turn over your weapons. Slowly."

"We're unarmed."

I expected him to challenge my words, but he simply nodded. "Please dismount. We'll need to search you and your horse."

I dropped to the ground and stood still as he patted me down thoroughly while his partner, a much smaller man who reeked as if he hadn't bathed in days, checked through Tallulah's pouches and packs. When they finished with me, they repeated the action with Kenni.

Once satisfied, Neckless walked back to see Collins and his men. I heard Collins tell him, "Corporal, cut me and my men loose. I'm not going back inside like this."

"Yes, Sergeant."

I remained facing forward as I heard the movement behind us. Seconds later, Collins rode up beside me. From where I still stood on the ground, I looked up to see him staring at me from the back of his horse.

"Now, what am I gonna do with you?" he asked.

"You're going to escort us inside to meet with whoever we're supposed to see about an alliance, just like the broadcast suggested. And you're going to do it with the same courtesy and respect that we showed you and your men."

Collins dropped to the ground beside me. He moved to within inches of my face, and in his gravelly voice said, "You shot at me and my men. As I recall it, you actually put arrows into three of them, and from what I understand, you pistol-whipped two more."

"Technically, it wasn't pistol-whipping them. I used my knife. And I figured it was a bit more merciful than killing them."

"You think you're being smart?" he snarled. "I don't think you really understand how much things just changed. I'm not your prisoner anymore, kid. You're *my* prisoner." He reached up very deliberately and wrapped his hand in my shirt. "You *belong* to me."

I casually reached up and grabbed his hand, digging my thumb into a pressure point as I'd been taught. I saw the pain in his eyes as the nerve cluster sent its message of agony to his brain, and he drew his face back. He tried to pull back the hand that he had laced into the material of my shirt, but I held on, digging deeper.

"I don't belong to you, Collins. I'm the designated representative of the Sabine River Trading Coalition. I've been sent here to speak on behalf of our more than twenty thousand members in response to an invitation that was broadcast via satellite. Now, I seriously doubt it was you that issued that invitation, was it? That means my invitation came from someone inside that gate. And I'm willing to bet it's someone quite a bit higher up the food chain than a sergeant."

I saw the determination in his eyes as Collins balled up his other fist and began to move it. Knowing he was about to take a swing at me, I inverted the wrist I held and shoved him away from me. He staggered only a little before stepping right back in front of me, fists balled tightly, rage in his eyes.

"Do you really want to do something stupid in front of all these witnesses?"

He stopped and looked at his men, Kenni, and the guards.

I jerked a thumb over my shoulder, and he looked past us all to where I knew the OTA crowd was watching our every move.

"Now, Sergeant Collins, as far as anyone back there can see, all that's happened so far is that you have gotten off your horse and gotten in my face. My body has blocked everything else. But if you lose your temper and try to take that punch you seem to want to take, then you're liable to make an already tense situation a lot worse."

Stepping forward again, he once more put his face within inches of mine. "You think you won something here?"

"I think I've made my point. At least I hope I have. Now, I'm sure you think you're going to have time to get at me once we're inside the gates, but you have to remember... I'm here by invitation to discuss business that your superiors seem to regard as relatively important. I don't think you want to interfere with that business, do you?"

He stared for a moment, and I didn't know if I had pushed him too far. He might go ahead and punch me. If he did, should I fight back, or would it be better to let him pound me a little and get himself in trouble? I hadn't been kidding when I'd given him my analysis of the situation. I really was pretty confident that he answered to some higher-ranking officer. So if he were to be seen abusing an invited representative, it was possible that it would cause serious problems for the man.

On the other hand, if I fought back, I could be the one seen as causing trouble. Not to mention the fact that it might get me killed.

But Collins surprised me. He grinned. "Damn, kid. You got some serious balls on you. I like that." With that odd declaration, he remounted his horse and looked back down at me. "Mount up, kid. If I'm not your prisoner, and you're not mine, we might as well ride in together."

I climbed into Tallulah's saddle and nodded to Kenni to get back in the wagon. Once Collins saw we were ready, he assumed lead of our little procession. He said to the guards, "Let us in, Corporal. It appears these people have business with the colonel."

As we trotted toward the gates, Collins leaned slightly toward me, and in a voice low enough that there was no danger of anyone else hearing him, he told me, "This isn't over by a long shot, kid."

I had no doubt. He didn't strike me as the type to let a perceived loss of face go unanswered. I'd be hearing from him again. Soon.

Despite what he'd said about riding together, Collins pulled ahead, entering the gate at the head of the line. That suited me just fine. It allowed me to drop back to ride beside Kenni on the wagon.

Without turning her head, she asked me, "What did he say to you just then?"

"Pretty much told me to watch my back."

"Figured it was something like that. Guy like that doesn't like to lose."

"Any advice?"

"Sounds like he already gave it. Watch your back."

We rode through the gate to see a line of uniformed men and women watching. Kenni stiffened.

"What is it?"

"Marines." She was watching a group of men and women in uniform as they sat at wooden tables, stripping down rifles and cleaning them. Their uniforms were a bit darker than almost all the others around us, and their caps looked different, though I couldn't put my finger on why. And unlike the gawkers, they barely looked up as we went past.

I looked back at Kenni, who had an almost wistful expression on her face.

"You miss it?"

She took a deep breath and turned away. "I miss parts of it. I miss the idea of belonging to something... more."

"More than what?"

"Just more. Something bigger than me. Bigger than any individual." She looked at them once then turned back to me. "I never thought I would see those uniforms again. Seeing them there, acting just like I remember... yeah, I miss it."

PART 3
ON BASE

CHAPTER 41
ALCATRAZ

OLLINS RODE STRAIGHT TO A group of soldiers who, judging by the way they greeted him, knew and respected the man. Many of them grinned at him as he insulted them, and when he dismounted, he slapped many of them on the back in obvious camaraderie.

I dismounted, and he turned at the reminder of my presence. The smile left his face. "Draker, take these two to holding until we can have medical take a look at them. They've spent a lot of time with the hostiles, and we need to make sure they haven't been infected with any diseases."

"Will do, Sergeant."

Hostiles? I almost laughed.

"And get someone to take a look at my wounded."

One of the men had been searching the wounded. He approached Collins. "Sergeant? Where's Dillon?"

Collins looked genuinely sad. "I'm sorry, Jim. We were ambushed while we were gathering supplies. We lost Dillon. Him and Parks, both."

The man looked like he'd been punched in the gut.

Collins grabbed his shoulder. "Jim? You have to put it behind you for now. We have a job to do."

Jim nodded.

"Now, go get Doc, and have him take a look at our wounded, Corporal."

Jim's "Yes, Sergeant" was barely audible as he turned away. When he was out of earshot, Collins turned to me. "See that man? That's Jim Thompson. You might want to keep your eyes peeled for him. One of the men your people killed was his brother. No telling what he might do when he finds out."

Several eyes turned my way as I noted Collins didn't bother keeping his voice low that time.

Great. I wonder just how long it is before I get a visit from Corporal Thompson?

Collins raised an eyebrow in an "I told you so" manner and smiled.

Yeah, this is not *going to end well.*

"What? Did you think word wasn't going to get out? You guys should have killed all of us then." He spread his hands, indicating the area around us. "This is a combat zone, and every one of us has to depend on the person next to him. We're family."

I saw subtle nods from many of the men. Collins stepped forward, once more trying to intimidate me. I had to admit it was a bit more effective with all of his men standing around us. "You don't screw with one of us without it affecting the rest of us."

Whatever further tactics he was going to use were interrupted as another man came running up to him. "Sergeant Collins? The colonel wants to see you immediately."

Collins nodded to the new man. "I'm on my way, Private."

Turning back to the men surrounding us, Collins pointed one of the men out. "Andrews, you and Reeves get these two over to Alcatraz. I'll see what's up with the colonel."

Two men stepped forward and swung their rifles from their backs into their hands. It was a subtle but effective threat. One of them stepped in front of us. "Follow me."

The other soldier followed behind us as the first one led us to a nearby building. They weren't overtly hostile or rough, but there wasn't a word or a smile shared between them, either. They were two professionals performing a task, and nothing more.

Alcatraz turned out to be an unused office building, where they separated us and locked us into rooms with guards posted outside. Looking around my accommodations, I figured things could have been a lot worse. I had a chair, a desk, a cot... but the thing that took my breath away was the lighting. It was the first electrical lighting I had seen in years, and I had to admit it was impressive as hell to think that they had electricity.

Other than that though, the office was empty. Empty desk, empty chair, empty cot. I rectified that particular oversight by filling the chair with my butt and putting my feet up on the desk as I looked around my accommodations. No windows or decorations broke the monotony of those dusty white walls, but I figured we wouldn't be there more than an hour or two.

I figured wrong. Locked away from the sun, held under artificial light, I had no way to know exactly how much time passed. But my stomach was making some serious noises when the door to my room opened and a uniformed man I hadn't seen before brought in a tray with a pitcher of water, slices of bread and meat, and a hard yellow cheese.

He seemed surprised when I thanked him for the food, and he said, "I'll be back to pick up the tray in half an hour."

"What about bathroom breaks?"

"Excuse me?"

"I haven't been out of this room in several hours. I'm starting to feel the urge already, and once I finish this" — I waved my hand at the tray — "I'm really going to need to go. I don't know about you, but I'm not wild about the idea of having to mess up the floor."

The man looked like he had swallowed something particularly distasteful, but he thought it over for a moment. "I'll make arrangements to have you and your friend escorted to the latrine when we pick up your trays."

"Thank you."

He left without further comment, and I set to taming the beast that growled in my stomach. The meat was tasty, as was the bread. But the cheese was hard and rubbery compared to the creamy goat cheese I was used to, and it had a sharp, bitter taste. I nibbled a bit of it but ultimately left most of it on the plate, deciding it was an acquired taste. I washed down the last bits of bread and meat with the water.

Almost as soon as I set the cup down, my bladder reminded me of a basic tenet of the digestive system—if you put something in, something else is bound to come out. By the time the man came to take the tray, I was so far past uncomfortable I was practically dancing when the door opened.

"Please tell me you're here to take me to the restroom. If not, I suggest you turn your back, because the dam's about to burst."

The man nodded. "Yes, sir. If you'll follow me?"

"Follow you? If you don't hurry, I'm liable to run you down."

I could have sworn the man almost smiled as he led me outside. A woman in uniform waited outside with Kenni, who looked relieved when she saw me.

"You all right?"

"As long as we get to the bathroom in time. Otherwise, I'm going to be really embarrassed."

"Sir, ma'am? I'm sorry, but Sergeant Collins says we're not supposed to let you talk to each other."

That put a damper on things, but I was too preoccupied with my bladder to argue. The four of us walked down a couple of hallways to stop before a pair of doors, and I nearly knocked the poor guy over while quickstepping for a toilet. With a huge sigh of relief, I felt the pressure on my bladder subside. I noted that the same electric lights illuminated the inside of the bathroom—or latrine, as the soldier had called it. There was a steady drip, drip, drip from a sink on the wall behind me that served to keep my bladder flowing for the next several seconds.

Finally, I finished my business, laced up my pants, and turned to leave. That was when the door opened, and I knew just how bad my stay was going to get. Part of me had expected it, but I had hoped against hope that I was just being paranoid.

No such luck. I recognized the first man to come through the door as Jim Thompson, the man whose brother we had killed. He was accompanied by two others, who stepped to either side of him.

The look on his face told me there was nothing I could say to stop him. He was in no mood to talk. He simply strode forward and swung at me.

He evidently expected me to stand there while he pounded me, for there was no finesse to the strike. It was a wild haymaker that would have laid me out if it had landed. The man was a soldier and had likely seen combat. The clumsiness of his attack must therefore have been due to the fact that he didn't expect me to know how to fight back.

His mistake. I stepped inside the wide punch, dropped my hips, and drove my knuckles into the inside of his knee hard enough to collapse the leg. He stumbled to one knee, and I kicked him in the solar plexus hard enough to drive the wind from him. I stepped back as his companions rushed forward.

I had sparred multiple opponents in training many times, so I knew what to expect. At least I *thought* I knew what to expect. When multiple opponents attacked, there was usually a lull of a split second or more as they checked one another to see if both were ready. I had learned to watch for that lull and then shift toward whichever of them moved first.

These two had never learned that they were supposed to coordinate. They just rushed in like wild horses, slamming into me and driving me against the back wall. I leaned forward to keep my head from striking it, and when I hit, I used my legs to push off the tile wall, shoving against it with all my strength.

I got about three feet off the wall when the two men yanked me back, smashing me once more into the tiles. Changing tactics, I drove my foot into the instep of the man on my right and yanked my arm up, but it was like moving against a tree branch. I yanked my arm again, and as soon as I had him working against that, I kicked my heel up into his groin.

My right arm was suddenly free, but Jim had regained his feet and was barreling toward me. I slammed my fist down on the back of the skull of the man whose testicles I had just smashed, judged the distance right as Jim rushed forward, and kicked up at him as I braced against the wall behind me.

As I did, the man on my left yanked down on my arm, and my kick flailed well off target. Jim's shoulder slammed into my chest, and it was suddenly impossible to breathe. He followed his body slam with a flurry of punches I couldn't avoid. One hit me on the cheek, and my head flew back. A hollow thunk resounded inside my skull, and I briefly saw flashes of light just before everything went mercifully black.

CHAPTER 42
A NASTY FALL

I AWOKE LYING ON A COLD, hard surface. There was a buzzing in my ears, and it took me a while to realize it was the unfamiliar electric lights I had noticed before. I assumed I was on a floor since I didn't hear the dripping of the faucet in the latrine. Just trying to open my eyes sent daggers of agony through my skull, but after a few mental rebukes to my unwilling body, I finally managed to open my right eye. The left refused to cooperate.

I groaned as I tried to raise a hand to touch the uncooperative eye. Even moving my hand hurt. Forcing myself to ignore the pain, I got my hand up to my head and gingerly touched my closed left eye. It was very obviously swollen, and the eyelid was stuck closed with a matted, sticky mess. I could only assume it was partially dried blood.

"Good! You're awake."

I recognized Collins's voice without moving my head. It was disgustingly cheerful.

"I honestly wasn't sure if you were going to wake up or not. That was a pretty nasty fall you took."

So that was the story he was going with? I tried to laugh, but my ribs hurt too much. The laugh sounded like crying even to my own ears. I ended with a choking cough that hurt me to my core. I tried to sit up.

"Careful there." He moved into range of my one open eye. "We wouldn't want you to hurt yourself any more than you already have." He raised his boot, set it on my shoulder, and shoved me back down to the floor, not that it took much effort. He looked down at me as he grinned maliciously. "Just stay right there. Rest a little bit, and I'll have the doc come by and take a look at you." He lifted his boot and walked past me out of my sight. "Now, you be careful, and keep still. I'll have some more of my boys check in on you after the doc looks you over." I heard him open the door. "So don't go causing any trouble, and don't get too loud. Wouldn't want your friend down the hall to hear you and get the wrong idea. She might misunderstand and do something stupid trying to help you. Then we'd have two people hurt, and you wouldn't want that, would you?"

My blood ran cold at the implied threat as I heard the door close. I lay there for a short while, trying to assess my aches and pains. After a bit, I managed to roll to my hands and knees and crawl to the desk. Using it, I was able to get to my feet, and I shuffled to the chair and fell into it. Just the effort of that little excursion had my hands shaking and my head pounding. In a few minutes, when I no longer felt like I was about to throw up, I brought shaking hands to my closed left eye. I tenderly felt around the swollen tissue and managed to peel the lid back, sacrificing more than a few eyelashes as I did so.

The door opened as I finished, and two more soldiers entered. One held a rifle, and the other carried a pouch of some sort. They seemed surprised to find me at the desk but said nothing about it. The soldier with the rifle took up a position just inside the door, obviously guarding it.

The one with the pouch unsnapped it and approached me. "I'm Private Taylor. I understand you took a pretty bad fall."

I snorted, but he ignored my sarcastic and witty reply.

"Why don't you let me take a look at that eye? We'll see what we can do to get you fixed up."

The lights stayed on all the time, so the passage of time was a bit muddled while I was in that room. I got tired and slept three times. I didn't know how long I slept, but various guards had brought me seven meals and taken me to the restroom after each one of them. I was wary during the *latrine breaks*, as they called them, but no one offered any further trouble.

I was determined I wouldn't remain helpless any longer than I had to, so when I felt like I could do it without throwing up, I began working on my stretches and light calisthenics. With nothing else to do, I quickly lost myself in the routine. Eat, latrine, return, stretch, calisthenics, rest. Repeat as necessary.

I was pretty sure it was the third day after my beating in the latrine when they interrupted my routine. It must have been midday, since the last meal they had brought me was scrambled eggs and some kind of meat-and-potato hash, the third breakfast I'd had since waking up. Many things had changed since D-day, but for some reason, there were certain foods people still associated with the first meal of the day. Scrambled eggs definitely fell into that category.

I'd already been through the normal eat-latrine-return part of my morning routine and was stretching my legs when the typical perfunctory knock at the door told me someone was about to come in. The knock wasn't really a request to enter since no one ever waited for me to answer. It was simply the procedure they had adopted before opening the door.

I sprang to my feet, pleased that my muscles hardly protested at all. I was recovering quickly. When the door opened, a guard stepped in with a meal and a folded uniform. "After your meal, if you would like to change into some fresh clothes, we'll get you ready to meet with the colonel." He put the bundle on the desk. "I'll return to escort you in a few minutes."

"The colonel? Is he the one running this prison?"

"Sir? This isn't a prison."

"Really? So if I were to tell you that I want to walk out that door right now, would you let me?"

"No, sir. I'm afraid I'm not authorized to do that."

"And are you authorized to stop me?"

"Yes, sir, I am."

"Then can you please tell me how that's not being imprisoned?"

The man clapped his jaw shut. "The colonel will answer your questions when you see him."

He closed the door before I could say anything more.

I ate mechanically, staring at the folded uniform, contemplating the thought of changing clothes before meeting this "colonel," whoever he was. The clothes I was wearing were worn, but I was at home in them. My pants were comfortable deerskin, soft and durable. My shirt was a light, hand-woven fabric sewn into a simple, loose tunic. My belt was empty, bereft of its normal knives, but it held the shirt in place.

Sure, maybe the tunic was travel worn and sweat stained. I looked down and noted there were drops of blood on it too. But the thought of changing clothes rankled me, especially since it appeared that it was to make some sort of impression on the man who was responsible for holding me against my will for the last few days. No—I decided I wasn't going to change to please someone who had so far done nothing to show that he had anything but contempt for me. It wasn't up to me to make a good impression. It was up to *him* to repair the bad one his people had made on me.

That decided, I felt better. I put my empty plate on the folded uniform and sat on the desk, breathing and meditating, doing whatever I could think of to calm myself. I had learned to do that before sparring matches at home, and I had a feeling that this meeting was going to turn into a sparring match of a kind I'd never before been a part of. I just hoped I was up to the task.

The knock announced my guard's return. He seemed nonplussed to see that I hadn't changed clothes. "I'm sorry, sir. Would you like more time to get ready?"

I stood. "I'm ready now."

The guard pointed once more to the uniform. "Wouldn't you like to change into something cleaner?"

I looked at my travel-worn clothing and shook my head. "No." I looked back up at him. "I'm good with what I'm wearing."

He looked as if he wanted to argue but evidently thought better of it and nodded. "Yes, sir. If you'd follow me." He turned and led me out of the office.

Kenni was outside with her own guard. She winced as she saw me. "You look like hell."

"Thanks. I feel as good as I look." I noticed she was also dressed in her travel clothes. "Did they offer you a uniform?"

"No talking, please," Kenni's guard said.

"Yes." Kenni ignored the guard. "It was an Army uniform—"

"Ma'am! I have to insist that you stop talking."

Once more, Kenni ignored her guard. "And I'm not in the Army."

I found the way she phrased her answer interesting. She'd said she wasn't in the Army. But she'd neglected to mention that she'd been a Marine. I didn't know why, but I was smart enough not to mention it if she didn't.

I turned to her apoplectic guard. "Will you please stop interrupting my aide?"

"My orders are—"

"Your orders are idiotic. And if you had any sense yourself, you would realize that. Either we're prisoners or we aren't. Since I've been told repeatedly that we *aren't* prisoners, I have to assume that you regard us as free, although I'm not sure that your definition and mine are quite the same. However, if I'm free, then you have absolutely no call to interfere with our basic rights."

The guard stood there, frozen, jaw open at my outburst. But I wasn't finished.

"You know, now that I think about it, for a group that claims to represent the United States, you don't seem to be doing a very good job of it."

She closed her mouth, and to keep her from saying anything else, I jumped back in. *Keep your opponent off balance. Take control of the situation.*

"Look, I realize you think you're just following orders. I also understand that a lot of your actions are due to ignorance, but that simply means that you should stop trying to keep *us* quiet and maybe try to follow your own advice. So please, close your mouth, and take us to this colonel of yours so we can get some of the answers we're after. It's been one hell of a trip to get here, and I'd like to see if it's all been a waste of time."

When I turned back to Kenni, she was grinning. "Yep. You're definitely ready."

CHAPTER 43
EVEREST

A MAN IN UNIFORM STOOD FROM his seat behind a desk as I walked in. "Good afternoon. I'm Lieutenant Colonel Nathan Everest." He stuck his hand out for us to shake. I was immediately reminded of Tara's words about that being a white man thing. But I shook the proffered hand.

"I'm Zachary Dawcett."

I looked around the room as Kenni shook his hand. I heard her introduce herself as I noted the two uniformed guards in the back of the room.

"It's a pleasure. Please have a seat."

Colonel Everest's manner was friendly enough, but it was also a bit brusque, and I immediately got the impression that he was someone used to getting what he wanted. I would have to be careful around him.

I sat in the chair he indicated. "Lieutenant Colonel, eh? Last time I was held prisoner by a man in a military uniform, he was wearing general's stars." I pointed to the oak-leaf insignia on his chest.

I could see I'd caught him off guard. In one sentence, I'd told him so much, yet so little.

He opened his mouth as if to speak then stopped himself. "While that sounds like an intriguing story, I think it's going to have to wait for a later time. For now, let me start by assuring you that you're not being held prisoner." His smile actually looked genuine, and I wondered if he really was the monster I had expected.

"It's funny. We keep hearing that. Yet the truth of the matter is that we've been held against our will, and we haven't been allowed to leave our rooms. Whatever you choose to call it, in my book, that's imprisonment."

He sighed. "I can tell our conversation is going to get complicated. Let me offer you some refreshment." He signaled over my shoulder as we sat, and the man who had escorted us into his office walked around with a tray of cups. The aroma was pleasant enough. Kenni actually smiled a bit.

"Real coffee?" Her voice was hopeful and reserved as if she was afraid it might not be real.

Everest nodded. "Kona Blend. We still have a few nuclear subs that were out of range when the country was attacked. As I understand it, they're instrumental to the government's plans for getting the electrical grid back up."

I sniffed the fragrant steam wafting up from my cup while I thought about what he'd said. I knew next to nothing about nuclear submarines. I'd read a bit about them in the library, and I recalled that some of the old-timers had speculated that a submarine deep under the ocean could have been immune to the effects of the EMP that had decimated the grid. Such a sub would basically a self-contained town, full of the wonders of Old Days technology and powered by the amazing and terrifying power of a nuclear reactor. Everest's words seemed to confirm the conjecture.

Beside me, Kenni let out a sigh of contentment.

Everest chuckled. "I guess it's been a while since you've been able to enjoy a cup of coffee?"

"Yes, sir, it has."

"And you, Mr. Dawcett?"

"I've never had it."

His eyebrows went up at that. "Never?"

"No, sir. I was eight years old on D-day. I was twelve before things around home began to stabilize enough that we could concern ourselves with much beyond just staying alive."

"I'm sorry. I hadn't realized you were so young."

"No apology necessary."

He took another sip of his coffee, and I sipped mine cautiously. The brew was bitter and had a bit of a charred-wood taste. But I had to admit that the smell was wonderful.

My reaction must have shown, because Everest chuckled at me. "I'm sorry. I vaguely recall feeling the same way about coffee once. Of course, that was many, many years ago. Probably longer than you've been alive. Would you prefer some tea?"

"Yes, please," I said, embarrassed.

"Oh, please. Don't worry about it." He signaled again. "Private? Would you please bring a cup of tea for Mr. Dawcett?"

"Yes, sir."

"So while we're waiting, shall we begin? I understand there was a misunderstanding on your way here. Specifically, trouble with some of my men."

I spread my hands. "Yes, sir, there was. And I'm glad you brought it up."

"Of course. And I hope the incident doesn't color your opinion of what we're trying to accomplish here."

"Oh, I can assure you it absolutely will."

He blinked. "I beg your pardon?"

I leaned forward. "We're here because we received a request from your satellite—an invitation to come here and discuss your plans for reconstruction." I pointed to my still-swollen and blackened eye. "This was the reception I received."

"Yes, and I can assure—"

I didn't give him a chance to finish. "In a military setting, the actions of the men under your command are ultimately your responsibility. That means they were either acting on your orders or disobeying them. How you handle the situation will tell me which one it is, and that will most definitely color my opinion of what you're trying to accomplish."

The smile left the colonel's face as I spoke, and he looked at me with considerably less joviality than he had initially. "It sounds to me as if you're trying to tell me how to command my soldiers."

"No, sir. Not at all. I'm simply letting you know that while I'm here I plan to observe your command and that my recommendations to the people I represent will be influenced by everything I witness."

We were interrupted as the private entered with the tea Everest had requested for me. He placed it in front of me and left without a word. I sipped it and raised my cup to the colonel. "Thank you, Colonel. This is more what I'm used to."

"You're welcome." Steepling his hands on the desk, the man pursed his lips and watched me as I sipped the tea. "And you should be happy to know I've already conducted an internal investigation into the behavior of some of my people. Whether you know it or not, your arrival here triggered an incident that exposed some unsanctioned actions some of my people have been conducting."

"You mean Sergeant Collins?"

"I do."

"So you didn't condone his attacks outside?"

He was silent, brow furrowed, as he stared at me. "It seems there may be more to our discussion than I expected."

He looked past me. "Please ask Captain Mallory to join me here immediately."

I heard a "Yes, sir!" behind me, and someone—I assumed one of the two guards—left the office. Colonel Everest picked up a fountain pen and a piece of paper, scribbling a few words down. I wasn't entirely sure what was happening, and I went over the last moment of our conversation. For some reason, my question seemed to have thrown him. But he had indicated that he already knew about Collins, so I wasn't sure how anything I said could have surprised him.

Everest cleared his throat. "I expect the captain will be here in a few minutes. While we wait, I'd be very interested in the story you touched on earlier. You were held by a general? Of the US Army?"

"That's what he claimed."

The colonel's eyes narrowed slightly as he looked at me, and I could tell he was trying to determine whether or not I was telling the truth. "And what was the general's name?"

"He said he was General Larry Troutman."

"I've never heard of anyone by that name."

"I don't imagine you would. He's been dead a few years now."

He smiled. "And I suppose you killed him?"

"Of course not. I was ten years old at the time. My sister killed him."

To his credit, the man didn't lose his cool. Instead, he simply sat back in his chair and laughed. "This should be interesting. So a man in uniform walks into your town and claims to be a general of the US Army, and your sister kills him?"

"There was a bit more to it than that. For instance, he didn't just walk into town. He rolled into town with six Abrams tanks at the head of an army of three thousand soldiers."

Once again, Everest was interested. "Six Abrams?"

I nodded. "As well as several Humvees."

He leaned forward eagerly. "I don't suppose you still have them? The tanks, I mean. There aren't many left, and as you can imagine, our manufacturing capabilities are rather limited these days."

I was about to tell him that we had destroyed them but decided it might be better to let him think we had at least some of them in our possession. I compromised, remembering something Kenni had told me many days prior. "We destroyed three of them when we defeated Troutman and his men. The others haven't moved in years. They use up an ungodly amount of fuel."

"They do indeed. How did you defeat this man and his army?"

"With considerable loss of life, Colonel."

He looked interested, but we were interrupted by a knock on the door.

"Come."

I turned in my chair as another man entered. He was in the same camouflage uniform everyone else at the base seemed to wear. The difference was the rank insignia on his chest. The man paused when he saw Kenni and me, but Colonel Everest waved him in.

"Pull up a chair, Frank. I want you here for this." He nodded to the two guards. "You can leave us now."

Once the guards closed the door, Everest relaxed a bit, as did the captain. As the other man settled into his chair, Everest turned back to me. "I know this might seem a little confusing at first, but I need to ask you a few questions. Is that all right?"

After hesitating only a second, I nodded.

"All right. First, I need to give you a little background." He sat back and appeared to think for a second before saying more. "You told me you received the satellite message, so you already know what we're trying to accomplish here. What you probably don't realize is that the satellite message itself took three years to implement. We've been working around the clock, in what has turned out to be relatively hostile territory, for nearly three years — scouting locations, scrounging or making parts, finding and transporting educated technicians, building the satellite itself, and getting it launched. The satellite and its broadcast were the culmination of a major project that started long ago.

"That means many of my men and I have been out here, away from our friends and loved ones, for years. During that time, certain factions have arisen among the men. The fact that we're months away from any immediate support structure has encouraged some of them to push the boundaries of our situation."

"Push the boundaries? Is that what you —"

At the same time, Captain Mallory spoke. "Nate, I don't think this is the time to go into this!"

"Please, I'm not making excuses. Let me finish." He looked over at Mallory. "The captain and I, as well as all the other officers and many of the enlisted men, strongly believe in what we're trying to accomplish. We believe in what our country used to stand for, and we are more than willing to make these sacrifices if it means we have a chance to bring it back from the brink.

"But there's also a significant portion of the enlisted men who feel we've taken advantage of them. They resent the situation, and we have reason to believe they're planning to either desert or, even worse, sabotage our efforts here. We think Collins is one of the ringleaders."

"And you can't do anything about it? I'm sorry, Colonel, but that doesn't inspire much confidence in your cause."

I expected to see some anger when I made the comment, but he simply nodded. "I imagine that's true. But without proof, there's nothing we can do. What kind of message would it send if I punished men based on suspicions alone? If I really want to reinstate the United States, then I have to operate within the confines of her laws."

What he said made sense, and as much as I hated to admit it, I had to agree with him.

Colonel Everest pointed to my eye. "Initially, I hoped your beating would let me enforce a bit of discipline on the men who actually attacked you, though I'm willing to bet Collins wasn't one of them, was he?"

I shook my head.

"I didn't think so. He's been too smart to do anything I could use against him. But you said something that leads me to believe we might have a bit more on him than that."

"What?"

"Collins regularly leads his men out on supply runs. His orders are to scavenge abandoned military facilities within a few weeks' ride, finding goods and supplies to add to our stores here on base. He's been doing this for more than a year and has been pretty good about bringing supplies in." Everest leaned forward. "I got word a few days ago that he had brought someone else in and they'd been in a skirmish—that he'd lost some men, and others, including you, were wounded and were being tended by our medic."

"And you believed that?"

"Not at first. But I sent one of my men in to check on you, and he confirmed that you were pretty beat up. At that point, it didn't matter who did it. You needed a few days to heal." He shrugged. "As soon as I got word you were well enough, I asked to see you."

He leaned forward, and his gaze grew intent. "But now you say he's been attacking people while he's outside the base?"

"Yes."

"Can you prove it?"

I smiled. "We caught him and his men in the act."

He raised an eyebrow at that. "You caught him?"

"Yes, sir."

Kenni interjected. "Sorry, but I don't think that's going to help."

"Why not?" I asked.

"Because I believe these two officers are looking for grounds for a court-martial, and we can't prove anything."

"But we were there."

"Not when it started. We showed up after the fight had already begun. We can't prove, or even testify as to who started it."

"But we know they killed one of Walter's men the day before."

"No, we don't. We just have Walter's word on that."

Mallory narrowed his eyes at Kenni. "You seem to know quite a bit about what we're looking for. Why do I get the feeling that you're a bit more than just an aide?"

Kenni swallowed then reached into her pocket. With her closed fist on the colonel's desk, she slowly turned her hand and opened it as if reluctant to reveal what she held.

"May I?" Mallory reached for the coin. Kenni nodded, handing it over without comment.

I had never seen a coin like that one. I watched as the captain turned it over in his hands, and from my time working on the forges with my dad and Mr. Roesch, I immediately recognized the metal as bronze. But the detail of the decoration was much finer than anything we were able to make these days. It must have been an Old Days coin. On one side was an image of a winged angel bearing a sword. He stood, long blade raised over another body, and I couldn't tell whether he had slain the person or was protecting him. The words on the coin proclaimed him to be St. Michael, and though I wasn't religious, I vaguely recalled that he was supposed to be some sort of warrior angel—the strong right hand of God, or some such.

When Mallory turned the coin over, I saw an eagle perched atop a globe. An anchor ran through the globe, and the words "United States Marine Corps" encircled the emblem. My mouth went dry. Kenni had just shown them that she was a Marine.

Captain Mallory handed the coin to Colonel Everest. The colonel's eyes went from the coin to Kenni. "Where did you get a challenge coin?"

"It's mine." She sighed then sat up straighter in her seat. "Lance Corporal Kennesha Anderson, MP."

Everest nodded. "That would explain your familiarity with court-martial requirements."

"Sorry," I interrupted. "What's MP?"

Kenni looked at me. "Military police."

My jaw dropped. That was how she had known so much about the law and the code of military justice. It had once been her job.

"Then you know what we need in a witness." Everest handed the coin back to Kenni.

"Yes, sir. And I'm afraid we don't fit the bill except for Zachary being able to testify about what happened to him personally. And as I understand it, you're not after the muscle. You want the head. You want something so egregious that you can nail Collins dead to rights."

I took a deep breath, thinking it through. I quickly realized she was right. We hadn't actually witnessed them starting anything. But I knew who had.

"The pilgrims."

Kenni nodded slowly. "Maybe. If they're still around."

The two officers exchanged a look before Everest asked me, "Do you mind filling us in? What are pilgrims?"

"It's what the OTA has started calling those of us who are answering your satellite broadcast," I told him. "They consider us to be making a pilgrimage. When we jumped Collins and his men, they had a group of pilgrims they were holding as prisoners."

"Prisoners? And where are they now?"

"One of them was wounded when they were taken. We brought them with us to Burns Flat to see their healers, and then they were going to head back to Kansas. Said they didn't want anything to do with you after what they'd been through with Collins."

Everest looked at Mallory. "See why I wanted you here? As soon as he mentioned Collins attacking people outside, I thought this might just be the opportunity we've been looking for."

"It could be." Mallory turned to me. "Maybe you should give us your whole story. We'll try not to interrupt you anymore. And when you're through, we'll see if we have something we can work with."

So Kenni and I spent several minutes telling the two men what had happened from the time we entered Oklahoma forward. When we finally wound down to my telling of Collins's subtle threat when I woke up on the floor, I spread my hands. "That's about it."

Everest and Mallory were silent for several seconds, evidently thinking through the various ramifications of what Kenni and I had just told them. Finally, Everest spoke. "First, I have to apologize for what happened to you when you got here. I know that's hardly enough, but it's all I can offer for now."

I nodded.

"I suppose the first thing I can do is find you better accommodations than an abandoned office." He called for the guards. "There are several empty houses in officer country. Find one, and escort Mr. Dawcett there immediately."

I blinked. "Wait. Now?"

"Yes, Mr. Dawcett. If you don't mind, I have things I need to discuss with Captain Mallory and Corporal Anderson."

My heart dropped. I wasn't sure what his keeping Kenni meant, but I had a suspicion it wasn't going to be good. I looked at Kenni, and her expression showed that she had similar feelings.

"Colonel," I said. "You are aware that Kenni hasn't been part of the US military in twelve years? She is now my aide, and your interference with that function could jeopardize any negotiations between us."

"Mr. Dawcett, I'm afraid it isn't quite so cut and dried. You see, the nation has been functioning under a state of martial law ever since we were attacked. As such, any military personnel can be drafted back into service as needed." He pointed at Kenni. "Corporal Anderson, Captain Mallory, and I have more business to discuss." His face had grown more reserved and more determined. "Now, if you would accompany Private Lange to your quarters, the rest of us need to get to work on some important matters."

I hesitated.

"Something else, Mr. Dawcett?"

"Yes, Colonel. I had some personal items in my gear when I came through the gates. I haven't seen any of that gear since I've been here."

The colonel cursed. "I'll see what I can do, Mr. Dawcett. But to be perfectly honest, I have my doubts that we'll be able to find your belongings."

"Of course. That's why I'd like to make sure there won't be any problem with my going to and from the town. I'll need to replace much of my gear, including clothing."

"Mr. Dawcett, you know we can supply you with more clothing. I have to confess, I was surprised when you rejected our offer to begin with."

"With all due respect, Colonel, what I was offered was a military uniform. I'm not in the military."

"Son, wearing the uniform doesn't obligate you to serve." He raised his hand as I started to reply. "But since I have repeatedly told you that you aren't here as a prisoner, I can't very well confine you to the base if you want to go into the town."

"Thank you, Colonel."

"We aren't responsible for your safety while you are in town, and you will be subject to being searched each time you come in the gates. You won't be allowed to bring any firearms onto the base. Other than that, I have no objection."

"What about blades?"

"I'm sorry?"

"I had knives that I left hidden before we came on base. You said no firearms. Do you object to my carrying knives?"

He thought about it. "Considering the fact that my men carry firearms, I suppose the least I can do is let you carry knives."

"Thank you."

"Have a good evening, Mr. Dawcett." He stood pointedly, and I knew the discussion was over for the time being.

CHAPTER 44
SERGEANT ANDERSON

MY NEW QUARTERS, ACTUALLY A small house, were similar to my old home in Rejas with one relatively huge difference: the house, like everything else at the spaceport, had electricity. I vaguely remembered electric lights from my childhood, as well as televisions, computers, and hundreds of other minor electronic wonders. This was nothing like the world of wonders I recalled, but there were lights that came on at the touch of a switch. That was wonder enough.

As I explored the house, I noticed water in the toilet bowl. Clean water. *No way!* But to my utter fascination, I found that the house did, indeed, have running water in the bathroom. The toilet really flushed at the push of a lever just as I remembered from my childhood. Looking up from the miracle of swirling water in the toilet bowl, I caught sight of myself in the bathroom mirror. *Well, are you a mess or what?* Left eye black and swollen, cheek bruised to match, and my hair standing out in every which direction. I noted with some amusement just how long my hair had gotten. Yeah, I was definitely a mess.

In the mirror, the reflection of a stall caught my attention. I turned around and drew back the curtain. Staring for a moment at the knobs in the shower, I wondered if I dared get my hopes up. After a few seconds, I turned the one marked with an H and stuck my hand in the stream that magically sprayed from above. I was disappointed to find it was cold.

"I guess that was too much to hope for," I muttered. But I hadn't had the chance to really get clean since I'd come through the gates, and as my reflection attested, I was in dire need of it. Figuring it was no worse than bathing in a cold stream, I stripped my dirty clothes off, braced myself against the cold water, and stuck my arm into the stream. After a few seconds, I eased more of my body in until only a few seconds later I was immersed in the bracing shower.

A block of soap sat in a recess in the wall, and I grabbed it to wash away the grime caked on my skin. And as I did, a miracle happened. The water warmed. Evidently, it just needed a few minutes to warm up. Seconds later, I was hissing, hopping back to get my tender bits out of the water as it went from cold, to warm, to scalding, all in a matter of seconds. Biting back a scream, I scrambled to turn the faucet marked with the C, assuming the addition of cold water to the hot would level the temperature out. I honestly didn't remember showering when I was a kid, but I recalled washing my hands, and I assumed the shower faucet worked the same way.

Sure enough, a bit of tweaking soon had me moaning in delight as sinfully pleasant, warm water sluiced down my skin. After several minutes of simply reveling in the ecstasy of a hot shower, I grabbed the soap again and began to scrub.

I didn't notice how long I stayed in that shower, but my fingers were soft and wrinkled when I finally decided it was time to get out. The mirror was covered in steam, and I wiped it away with the towel hanging on a hook by the door. I then dried myself with the towel and pulled my fingers through my wet hair, trying unsuccessfully to untangle the knots in it. Finally giving it up as a lost cause, I rubbed my hair briskly with the towel to dry it as much as I could then left it for the air to dry. I would have to figure out what to do with it later.

I picked up my clothes from the pile on the floor, and while the buckskin of the pants was still fine, a look and quick sniff of my dingy shirt made me wish I had accepted that change of clothes before we went to see Colonel Everest.

I took it to the shower and scrubbed it with some of the soap and hot water. After wringing it out, I hung it over the curtain rod and slipped on my pants to explore the rest of the house. There was nothing else unusual. The whole place consisted of a small kitchen, a front den with a couch and a few chairs, the magical bathroom, and a single bedroom, which held a bed, a dresser with a mirror, a bookshelf with a few old books, and a painting of a dog lying in the sun. I looked at the bed. The hot shower had me feeling relaxed, and the bed looked so inviting. Even though it was early afternoon, the clean linens and soft mattress were irresistible, and with a groan of contentment, I lay back and closed my eyes.

When I awoke, my hair was dry, and the sun was noticeably dimmer through the bedroom window. Giving up on getting my hair presentable, I tore a strip of cloth from the edge of the towel and tied the mess back out of my face. I decided I would have to ask someone for some scissors to cut it with later — or, at the very least, a comb to keep it halfway neat. I wandered through the house again and noticed the door in back. Through it, I had access to a tiny fenced-in backyard, and I actually had a nice view of the sun setting behind the trees in the distance.

I was still back there an hour later, watching the stars and thinking about what the next day might bring, when I heard the knock at the front door. I trotted through the tiny house to find Kenni smiling wearily on the porch.

"Hi, Zachary."

I stepped back. "Come in. You all right?"

She stepped through the door and took her cap off. That was when I noticed her clothes. She was wearing the same uniform most of the others had been in. I sighed. "So they drafted you?"

"They did. It's part of the plan to get Collins."

"What? How is drafting you going to do that?"

"Well, for one thing" — she pointed to the insignia on her chest — "they jump promoted me. I'm now a staff sergeant."

I began to see. "Same rank as Collins?"

"Actually, one rank superior to him." She walked across the room and sat on a couch. "Back in my day, it was unheard of to get jump promoted by more than one extra rank. But now?" She blew out a deep breath. "Between the lack of reliable communications between military outposts and their struggle to find any kind of experienced personnel, the colonel's been given a lot of autonomy in what he does to keep this base going. Since he's technically operating out of a remote location and is out of touch with his command structure, he's in a relatively unique position. It's a bit like old submarine commanders during long-term missions. Like them, he's been given a lot of leeway."

She plucked at the rank insignia on her chest, looking at it and shaking her head. "So while it's still contingent on later confirmation, for all intents and purposes, I'm now Staff Sergeant Kennesha Anderson." She let go of her uniform and smoothed it back down. "And like I said, it's part of his idea to take Collins down." Looking down, she patted the cushion. "A lot nicer than the little offices we were held in."

"Yeah, it is." Determined not to let the conversation get sidetracked, I continued my questions. "So how does you being promoted above Collins help bring him down?"

"There are only two squads of Marines on base."

"How many is that?"

"Each of the squads here is fifteen men. This is mostly an Army operation. As far as Everest and Mallory know, Collins and his little following are all Army. None of the Marines appear to be involved. Part of my job is going to be to confirm that. And since I'll now be the ranking Marine, I'll be able to make sure Everest has a reliable force on his side if things get ugly."

"You think that might happen?"

She shrugged. "Not likely. At least, not as long as things are done properly."

But I saw something in her eyes. "So what's bothering you?"

She looked down and sighed. "I've got one of my feelings about it."

I wasn't sure what to say. I still didn't have the same level of belief in Kenni's abilities as Robin and Mr. Roesch had, but their conviction gave enough credence that I couldn't simply dismiss her words out of hand. "About the promotion?"

"No. About the whole plan. Like we're not seeing the whole picture. It's weird. I know it's my mom sending me the message, but it doesn't make sense."

"What? You can't... I don't know, hear her?"

"It doesn't work like that. It's not really like a voice. At least, not hers. But it's like she sent someone else's message and signed it herself."

This was still new territory for me, so I wasn't sure how to follow what she said. I knew I didn't want to give her the impression that I doubted her, though. "So ah... can you read the note?"

She smiled. "That was just an analogy. It's not really a note. It's a song. Not even that. More like the impression of a song. But I know that Mama sent it to me."

"A song? Okay, what's the song?"

"I don't know. I just know that she's trying to get me to listen to a Christmas carol."

I was dumbfounded. Kenni's dead mother was trying to send her a Christmas carol. And I was supposed to take that seriously?

Her reply was sharp. "Yes. We're supposed to take it seriously."

A chill ran up my spine. "Okay. So you think there's something wrong with Everest's plan. Any ideas—impressions of what it could be? Do you think Everest and Mallory are lying?"

"No... maybe..." She shrugged. "I don't know."

"You think maybe Collins is the good guy in all this? 'Cause I have to say, I'm pretty set on him being the bad guy, what with him having his goons pound my face and all."

She chuckled. "No, I don't think he's the good guy, either. And I don't even feel like Everest is lying. But there's something... off about all this."

I was silent, waiting for her to go on, but when several seconds passed and she didn't, I felt like I had to fill the silence. "So what should we do?"

"For now, we go on with their plan. But we make sure we keep our eyes open."

CHAPTER 45
UMM

KENNI AND I WERE ALLOWED to go into town the next morning. For the purposes of our visit, Kenni wore the travel clothes she had worn into the base rather than her new uniform. Several people were waiting for us as we crossed the no-man's land between the spaceport and the town of Burns Flat. One figure elbowed her way to the front of the crowd, and I couldn't help but smile.

There was no big emotional reunion as we greeted each other. We were still in public, still unsure of our relationship. But I couldn't deny the feeling I had when I saw her up close.

Bella and Cricket, on the other hand, weren't worried in the least about being discreet. They ran up to me, tails wagging so hard that their butts wobbled from side to side, and they whined in pleasure as they vied for my attention. I knelt to pet them, and Bella reared up onto her back legs and pushed me back onto the road, where I fell, laughing, under their onslaught.

"Okay, girls. I missed you too." I rubbed bellies and scratched ears for several seconds before getting back to my feet.

I was still bent over, petting them, when Walela asked me, "Think you'll ever want to say hello to me?"

I chuckled and looked up at her. "Just wait until we're out of sight of the gates."

She smiled briefly before her expression went from smiling,

to frowning, and then to furious. "What the hell happened?" She reached up and touched my black eye.

I pulled back, wincing a bit at her touch. "Collins had some of his goons pay me a visit. Don't worry — it's being taken care of. As a matter of fact, that's part of the reason we're here. We need to see if the other pilgrims are still here."

"What?"

"We need witnesses against Collins for a court-martial."

"Well, hell, I'll testify. So will Keith or Simon or any of the rest of us."

Aware that there were still possible eyes watching us from the spaceport, I took her elbow and guided her away from the base, putting our backs to any long-range surveillance as I continued our conversation. "That won't work. None of you actually saw him or his men start any trouble. We arrived after things had already blown up. We really need the pilgrims."

Walela shook her head. "I'm pretty sure they left yesterday. We can check with the healer, though. It's this way."

She led us between some buildings and down a street to a building with a simple hand-painted sign that proclaimed "Medicine."

I started to open the door, but Walela pulled my arm, holding me back. Kenni arched her eyebrow. "Something wrong?"

"No, I just need to ask Zach something."

Kenni stared for a second before rolling her eyes.

"What? What's wrong?" I looked from Kenni to Walela. Kenni just shook her head, and Walela looked like a kid caught with her hand in the cookie jar. "What'd I miss?"

Kenni sighed. "I'll check inside." She looked pointedly at Walela. "Try not to break him. We have to be back at the base by sunset."

Suddenly, I felt like *I* was the one with my hand in the cookie jar as I understood what Kenni was implying. But Walela wasn't quite finished with Kenni. "When you get through here, you might check with Keith and see if he has any suggestions. Ask for him at the Blue Star Hotel. It's two streets north and four to the east from here."

"I'll do that. As a matter of fact, I might be busy for a few hours. Think you can keep each other entertained for a while?"

Walela grinned. "We'll find something to do." With that, she dragged me down the street by the hand.

"Hey!" Kenni shouted from behind us. "Bella, Cricket, come!"

I had forgotten the girls until then. I looked at Kenni.

"Don't you think you two need a little privacy for a while?"

I probably blushed. I knew my face got warmer than the heat of the day could account for. Bella and Cricket looked from Kenni to me as if to ask what I wanted them to do.

"It's okay," I told them. "Go to Kenni."

Kenni coaxed them again. "Come on, girls."

With my approval, they joined her as Walela tugged on my hand.

"Wait. Where are we going?"

"I have a room up the road." She looked at me very deliberately. "I told you we had unfinished business."

I swallowed, trying to play it cool... hoping she was thinking what I thought she was thinking. Fearing that saying anything more about it might cause her to change her mind, I kept my mouth shut and let her pull me down the road.

Her room was a tiny single bedroom with a bathroom and a closet. There were two cushioned chairs around a small, round table, and a bed. Her pack lay in one corner, and various bits of clothing were scattered around the room. I had just enough time to take it in before Walela closed the door behind me and pulled me into a kiss that made my head spin. I sighed into her mouth and felt her lips move into a smile.

"I feel the same way." She kissed me once more, and I found myself being maneuvered around the room and suddenly felt the bed against the back of my knees. She pushed, I fell onto my back, and my dark and exotic beauty straddled me as she leaned in again.

Her kisses—our kisses—grew longer, deeper, more urgent, and

I no longer had any doubt about what she was thinking. Gasping breath and subtle moans echoed faintly off the walls of the little room. My hands went under her shirt, feeling the bare skin of her back as she ground against me. Her hair fell across my face, a dark curtain that blocked the light as it draped our kiss. I smelled some kind of flowers from whatever soap she used on her hair.

It occurred to me that I was taking a passive role in this, and I decided it was time to let her know I was as eager as she seemed to be. I let my hands roam up her back and felt the tiny hooks on her bra. I'd heard friends back home brag about unsnapping bras with a single hand. "Like snapping your fingers," they'd said.

They lied. I tried twice before I growled, and Walela giggled. She sat up on me, reached behind herself, and grinned as she performed the arcane magic necessary to undo the snaps. Then she reached into one sleeve of her shirt, pulled the straps out over her arm, and removed the entire bra through the opposite sleeve.

"I don't know whether to be impressed at your mystical abilities or disappointed that you didn't have to take your shirt off to do that."

She dropped the garment on the floor and cocked her head slightly. "Of those two thoughts, you really don't know which one should have priority?"

I tugged gently on her shirt, trying to coax her back down to me. "Yes, I do. I just didn't want to seem like someone with only one thing on his mind."

"Trust me." She leaned forward, her hair once more draping my face. "Your having only one thing on your mind is *exactly* what I was going for."

A fine sheen of sweat coated both of us as we lay beside one another on the bed. I plucked at the little hummingbird necklace that hung on a leather thong between her breasts.

"You told me your name meant hummingbird, didn't you?"

"Yes. The necklace was a gift from my mother when I was little. She used to tell me this story, an old Cherokee legend that her mother told her. According to the story, in ancient times, men and animals all spoke the same language, so they could all communicate with each other. At that time, there was only one tobacco plant in the whole world, and it was stolen by geese."

I laughed. "Geese?"

She laughed and hit me. "Hey! It's a legend. Be respectful!"

"All right, all right."

"Tobacco was a sacred plant. It was considered big medicine, and the geese were fearsome warriors. No matter what man or animal went to take the tobacco plant back, they were always defeated. Finally, the hummingbird volunteered to go, and all the others laughed, telling him he was too small and inconsequential. But Hummingbird flew so fast that the geese never saw him. He used his beak to snip off some small branches with seeds and brought them back so quickly that the geese never even knew he had been there."

She looked at the wooden fetish. "Now it's supposed to represent playfulness and joy, as well as speed and endurance." She sighed. "My mom had a rough life. She wanted better for me. So she gave me this crazy name and taught me the stories, hoping it would bring me better luck."

"Where is she now?"

Walela frowned. "Dad was away on a business trip when the EMP took out the grid. We never found out what happened to him. Mom didn't take it well. She had some friends who got her into drugs, and she killed herself with meth less than a year afterward."

"Meth?"

"Used to be pretty popular in the drug crowd. The chemicals used to make it aren't available now like they were back then. My grandmother told me about it when she thought I was old enough."

"So your grandmother raised you?"

"Yes." She rolled onto my chest, and I was momentarily distracted by the feel of her bare breasts against me.

"So what about you? What's Zachary Dawcett's sad story?"

I shrugged. "About like everyone else's. Everything was normal until someone cut off the electricity. Then life got crazy for a while, and now I'm here with you. All in all, I'd say I got off pretty lucky."

"Oh no you don't! You don't get to pull the defining moments of my life out like that and then just shrug. This is the part where we share."

"All right." I thought about it. There was definitely a defining moment for me. And though I didn't often like to talk about it, if we were going for an honest relationship, she deserved to hear it. "About two years after D-day, a lunatic rolled into our town with a bunch of tanks and soldiers."

I told her about Crazy Larry and how he cut through the town of Rejas, killing hundreds of people because my dad had beaten him on D-day. I told her how he had kidnapped me and used me to force my dad to come after him and how dozens more had been hurt or killed.

"Please tell me they killed that son of a bitch."

I smiled. "They did. He had a gun to my head but took it away to shoot my dad. As soon as he moved the pistol away from me, my sister put a crossbow bolt through his eye."

"Good!"

I chuckled at the ferocity of her response, and our talk turned to lighter topics.

A loud banging on the door interrupted our post-*um* conversation. Keith's deep voice boomed. "Hey, if you two are finished in there, we need to make some plans. Get dressed already!"

Walela sighed. "I guess it's time to get back to the rest of the world." She got out of bed. "Just a minute," she yelled.

I watched her naked body as she began gathering her clothes from where they had been tossed around the room. Slipping her pants on, she finally noticed that I wasn't moving. "I'm opening the door in about sixty seconds. You can either be dressed or not."

"So the show's over?"

With a giggle, she picked up my shirt and threw it at me. "Yes,

285

it most definitely is." She stepped close and kissed me fiercely enough that I groaned with renewed lust. I tried to pull her back down to the bed, but she shook her head. "But only for the moment. Now, get dressed."

I was pulling my boots on when she opened the door. Keith, Simon, John, and Kenni stood outside with knowing smirks on their faces.

"Yeah, yeah," Walela said. "Come on in." She turned her back on the group and came to sit beside me on the bed.

Bella and Cricket bounded in first, jumping up and landing on the bed. Cricket sniffed around at the sheets before cocking her head to the side as she looked at me accusingly.

"What?" I asked her, rubbing her head.

Keith came in next. He sniffed, shook his head, then walked across the room and opened the window. I blushed at the realization that the room smelled of sex. But other than that, no one made any comment on it.

"Kenni told us you took a beating." Simon pointed to my eye. "Doesn't look too bad."

I shrugged. "It's getting better."

"You should have seen him a few days ago," Kenni said as she walked in. She tossed a wrapped package on the bed next to me. "I think I got the sizes about right."

I unwrapped the bundle to find a couple of simple tunics and a pair of buckskin pants.

"That was the reason you gave Everest for coming into town, remember?"

"Yeah. I just got distracted."

Everyone laughed as I looked at the new clothes. They weren't anything fancy by any means, but they were serviceable. And it looked like everything was adjustable with drawstrings and laces, so it would most likely all fit with little trouble.

"Thanks," I said as Kenni settled into one of the two chairs in the room.

Keith took the other chair while Simon and John settled on the floor and leaned against the wall.

"So while you two were up here making like rabbits," Kenni said, "the rest of us were working on a few ideas."

I tried not to blush again.

Walela said, "And?"

"First of all, the Iola pilgrims are gone. The healers said they left two days ago. They couldn't wait to get back home and said they didn't want anything to do with the spaceport."

"Can't say as I blame them," Simon said. "Why would anyone trust the government people after all the crap they've pulled?"

Keith looked at Kenni and me. "That's a valid point. I mean, you've seen what they did to Tara's team and the Iola folks. You two sure you still even want to keep up your talks with them?"

Kenni raised an eyebrow at me, letting me know she was still willing to defer to me on the matter. I thought about it for a few seconds. We had gone through so much just to get here. And while Collins had made about as bad an impression of the military as could be made, if Colonel Everest could be trusted, then maybe all the bad blood between the US military and the OTA could be set aside. Maybe there could be a more peaceful resolution to the standoff between them.

Maybe.

"Yeah. We've got to give Everest a chance to straighten up his mess. I can't speak for Kenni, but I get the impression that he really wants to clean house. I've come too far to turn around over something that might not even be a true representation of what they're trying to do."

"For what it's worth, I think that's a good call." Kenni walked to the window, looking out over the street below. "I think the colonel's in danger of losing control of things in there. I'm not saying I fully trust him, but he seems to want to clean house. Unfortunately, I don't think Collins is playing by the same rule book. And if Collins has his way, everyone inside that gate who follows him is going to come outside the gate determined to take anything they want by whatever means they have at their disposal."

"Let 'em come," Simon sneered.

Kenni turned and shook her head. "You haven't seen all they have at their disposal. There are mortars, cannons, grenades, automatic weapons... they could wipe this town out without ever leaving their base."

Simon's eyes widened. "They have all that? Why haven't they used it?"

"I don't think Colonel Everest wants a war. He seems sincere in wanting to build up the country again, but I think he knows it has to be voluntary."

"What the hell does that mean?"

"It means he understands that all the weapons in the world won't do them any good when their goal is rebuilding. They need people to *want* to join with them, or at the very least to leave them alone while they rebuild on their own. You can't force a population to help rebuild the country they're going to live in. Not when it's supposed to be free."

I could hear the noises of the town outside—the shouts and yells of street vendors and their customers, the laughter and arguments of passersby. From the sounds out there, you would never know the whole town was ready to explode into violence if the wrong thing was said or done at the spaceport.

Kenni turned back, asking the group, "Do you have a library in Burns Flat?"

Keith shrugged. "I don't have any idea. I don't think so, though. It's a pretty small town."

John spoke from where he sat on the floor. "There's one at the high school."

Kenni pursed her lips then shook her head. "I doubt a school library is going to have what we need."

I watched her, knowing her well enough to understand she had a plan brewing. "So what do we need?"

"Law books. Specifically, military law. I don't think we'll find anything on that in a high school."

"But you might find it in the law offices in a small military town," Walela said.

We all looked at her. She shrugged. "Can I help it that you guys don't know the town as well as I do? There are three small law offices here in Burns Flat. Maybe they have what you're looking for."

Kenni nodded. "Let's hope so. Can you show me?"

"Sure. Which one do you want to see first?"

"Whichever one's biggest," I said. "It would be more likely to have books in it, wouldn't it?"

"Sounds like as good a reason as any," Kenni agreed.

Walela hopped off the bed. "Let's go, then."

CHAPTER 46
HAMMER HANSON

A T FIRST I THOUGHT WALELA had brought us to the wrong place. The building was a tiny affair, about the size of an old convenience store. Before I could ask, she said, "Yes, this is the biggest one. The other two are run-down trailers."

The glass front door had long ago been shattered, making me wonder, not for the first time, why Old Days people had ever made doors from such a fragile material. There were letters missing from the wall, but enough was left for me to tell that "Hammer Hanson" had once been a divorce attorney and private investigator. The front room showed the typical damage you would expect from having been exposed to the elements. But the wooden doors to either side of the reception area were still closed, giving me hope that whatever lay behind them was in better shape. Kenni, Keith, and John went to the door on the right. Walela, Simon, and I went left.

Turning the knob simply told us that the door we'd chosen was locked. Looking behind me, I could see that the others had been luckier. "Why don't we see what they find first?" I said. "No need busting our humps breaking into a locked room if we don't have to."

The room they had entered was a small meeting room of some kind. It contained a long table and eight chairs. The chairs were scattered around the room, not neatly shoved up to the table, and

I wondered if people had been sitting in there when that initial high-altitude nuke had shown up like a second sun in the sky twelve years earlier.

Bookshelves lined the walls, and everyone immediately started for them. "We're looking for anything about military law or the Uniform Code of Military Justice," Kenni called out.

I was skimming through the titles when John called out, "*The Handbook of International Law and Military Operations.*" He started to pull it off the shelf but suddenly jumped back, dropping the book and screeching like a frightened child. Everyone stepped toward him to see what was wrong. Cricket barked and jumped at the shelves, joined a second later by Bella.

I got the immediate impression that they weren't alarmed at anything, but that they were hunting. Kenni and Keith had drawn pistols, but John held up a hand to stop them. "It's all right. Just a mouse."

"Damn, John," Simon joked. "You scream like a little girl."

We all started laughing.

"Hey, everybody has something that freaks them out. For me it's little creepy crawlies," John said. But he smiled along with the rest of us... until he picked the book back up. With a much more mature curse, he tossed it onto the conference table where a puff of white, shredded paper scattered across the wood. He gingerly reached out and lifted the front cover to reveal a literal rat's nest of torn paper and mouse feces. "Damn it."

"Keep looking," Kenni said. "They can't all be that bad."

"Here's something," Keith called out. "*Manual for Courts-Martial, United States*, 2014 Edition." He pulled it off the shelf, and I noticed he only used two fingers. This one was in better shape, though the edges were chewed in places.

Kenni took the book, running her hand reverently over the cover. "Good. This will be a big help. Anything else?"

Walela laid another book on the table with a triumphant "Hah!"

I looked at the big volume. Embossed on the leather cover were the words "Uniform Code of Military Justice." Kenni opened the front cover, and though the paper was a bit brittle, the book was otherwise undamaged. She looked at me with a huge smile. "Perfect."

There was nothing else in there that Kenni deemed of any worth to us. "Was there anything in the other room?"

I shrugged. "The door was locked. I figured there wasn't any point busting down a door if we didn't need too."

"Locked door?" Keith smiled. "Did you forget about me? I love locked doors."

I honestly *had* forgotten about his penchant for picking locks, having only seen him in action the one time. But he rubbed his hands together and pulled a small roll of picks out of a vest pocket.

Within seconds, he had the door open, and we walked into a private office. There were more books on a shelf on the back wall but none that would help us. Keith worked on a locked drawer at the desk, taking even less time than he had on the door. He whistled. "Now, this is interesting."

We all gathered around him, peeking at the contents of the drawer.

"What is that?" I asked. "Some kind of safe?"

"Yep. It's a hidden fire safe."

The lock on that one took Keith a little longer, as it had a round hole where the key went. But after a few minutes, he popped the lid up. "Well, wasn't this guy just a model of good behavior?" He pulled out a bottle of amber-colored liquid. "An old friend I haven't seen in years. Ladies and gentlemen, I'd like to introduce you to my old friend Jack." He put the bottle on the desk and reached into the drawer once more. "And it looks like Jack has some friends." He pulled out a couple of Old Days cameras and several glossy pictures of naked men and women in the act of— well, of *umm*ing their brains out.

"Holy crap!" I was immediately embarrassed. "Sorry, guys, but I've never seen anything like that."

Everyone in the room began laughing. Everyone except Walela. She simply turned on her heel and left the room.

"Wait. What did I say?" But I immediately realized *exactly* what I'd said. "No! I didn't mean it like that!"

Walela kept walking, leaving me with the distinct taste of chewed shoe leather in my mouth. I caught up to her outside, everyone else following me. I could only assume they wanted to see how much more I could mess things up. "Walela, wait!" I begged. To my immense relief, she stopped. "Look, you already know I'm terrible with the whole relationship thing. You know I didn't mean..." I wasn't sure how to finish my sentence.

"I know. It's just that we're just getting started on our relationship." Mercifully, she gave me an awkward smile. "We'll figure it out as we go."

"If you two are finished with your little crisis, Zach and I have to get back to the base." Kenni's smile took the sting out of her words.

"Now?" Walela whipped her head around. "I thought you didn't have to be back until sunset."

Kenni pursed her lips as if unsure what to say, and I realized that she hadn't told any of them she'd been drafted back into service.

"My fault," I jumped in. "I told them that if the pilgrims weren't here, we would probably be back earlier. I didn't want to get off on the wrong foot now that things are finally starting to settle down with Colonel Everest."

"It's okay, Zachary." Kenni stopped me. "I want everything out in the open."

She looked at Keith. "Part of us getting Collins..." She hesitated then seemed to start over. "During our discussions with Colonel Everest, in order to get them to trust us, I had to let them know I was a Marine."

Keith cursed.

Simon, John, and Walela just looked at him.

"What's the big deal?" Walela asked. "It was twelve years ago."

Keith shook his head. "The president declared a state of martial law when we were attacked. I imagine their stance is that we're still under that, right?"

Kenni shrugged. "We didn't get into all the details. Either way, it doesn't really matter. I was only three years into my stint when the shit hit the fan. I was just about to test for corporal when the country fell apart. That means they can reactivate me to complete the eight years I originally signed up for."

Simon and Walela joined Keith with some pretty colorful language. John, as usual, stayed silent, waiting for Kenni to finish talking.

"To soften the blow, Colonel Everest jump promoted me. Skipped me past corporal and up to staff sergeant as a sort of a bonus."

Walela shrugged. "So?"

"So now I outrank Collins. That pretty much makes me immune to anything he can legally do to me. It also means I outrank every enlisted person on the base. I only answer to the officers."

Simon grinned. "Nice."

But Kenni shook her head. "Not necessarily."

"Why not?"

"Look at it this way. There are men and women there who've served twice as long as I did, and now I'm going to outrank them? How do you think they're going to feel about that? Am I going to be able to gain their respect? And I have to wonder why the colonel would do it in the first place. Is he trying to make me feel indebted to him? With officers, you never know what's really going on."

She stood. "But for now, I've been drafted back into the Marine Corps. I've sworn an oath, and I intend to abide by it. That means I have orders I have to follow." She shrugged. "And for now, my orders happen to coincide with what we're all trying to accomplish here — to build a case against Collins and try to stabilize relations between the base at the spaceport and the OTA."

"And what happens when your orders conflict with your relationship with the OTA?" John asked.

"My goal is to make sure that doesn't happen." Kenni looked at me. "You ready?"

"Sure." I turned to Walela then realized we had an audience.

They watched us intently, smiles growing on their faces. "You guys mind giving us a minute? We'll catch up."

There was laughter all around.

"Make it fast," Kenni said as they all turned and headed back up the street the way we had come.

"So now that I have—"

Walela silenced me with a kiss. When her lips left mine, I was having trouble remembering what I was about to say.

"What?" she asked.

"I was..."

"You were what?" Her eyes crinkled at the corners as she smiled.

"Apologizing for putting my foot in my mouth? Like I sai—"

Another kiss. Another smile.

I got the message. "All right. I'll shut up."

She smiled, and that time there was no more of the awkwardness from before—only contentment. "Come on," she said. "We'd better go before they start harassing us again."

CHAPTER 47
MCMAP

"WHAT NOW?" I ASKED KENNI as we walked back through the gates. I noted several eyes following us. Many of them appeared indifferent, and a few actually raised their chins in greeting, surprising me until I realized they were the Marines, and word had likely gotten out that Kenni was one of them. But there were also more than a few surly looks thrown our way, and I knew Collins still held sway with many of the enlisted men and women.

She stopped and looked at me with an appraising eye. "You told me you've trained to fight."

I was suddenly very wary. "Yeah..."

"You any good? I've seen you with the bow, and I've seen you with a few wrist locks, but are you really any good?"

"Kenni, what are you getting at?"

"You see the group of Marines playing cards just over my left shoulder?"

I glanced past her and noted the four men. One of them appeared to be watching us, so I cut my eyes away.

"I see them. I think they're watching us too."

"Probably. I imagine scuttlebutt about my promotion has started to make the rounds. And I'm sure our meetings with Colonel Everest have been noticed too."

"So what do you want me to do?"

"If you think you're up for it, it might be a good idea for you to make some friends with them."

"And you want me to—what? Start a fight with them?"

"Nothing quite that dramatic. Just let them test you."

I still didn't get it. "I have no idea what you mean, but I'll follow your lead."

"Good." She turned and led me to the group of Marines. "Semper fi, Marines."

The four of them stood slowly from the card table. One of them inclined his head slowly. "Semper fi. Heard a rumor there might be a new sergeant coming in." He raised an eyebrow. "Any idea if it's true?"

Kenni nodded. "You know, I think I heard the same rumor. Right now, I'm on special assignment for Colonel Everest. We'll see what happens after that." She stuck her hand out. "Staff Sergeant Kennesha Anderson. Call me Kenni when we're in civvies."

The man clasped her hand. "Corporal John Hardy. This is Lance Corporal Matt Larson, and PFCs Simmons and Roberts."

Kenni shook all their hands then introduced me. "This is Zachary Dawcett. He's here because of the satellite signal."

Then it was my hand that made the rounds.

"I assume you men heard he had a bit of trouble with one of Collins's people."

"Yeah. Pretty shitty, if you ask me."

"Well, Zachary says he's had quite a bit of self-defense training. The way things are out there, most people have, right?"

Nods all around.

"You guys still training with MCMAP?"

"No better way to go."

"Would you mind checking him out? Ease him into it. See whether I can let him loose or if I need to keep an eye on him."

Everyone smiled at that, and I went along with it.

Corporal Hardy nodded. "We can do that. Ring's behind Marine Central."

"Behind what?" I asked.

"It's our barracks. Since there aren't that many Marines here, we only need one building."

"Well, why aren't there many Marines here?"

Kenni replied before anyone else could say anything. "Because it only takes a few Marines to do the job."

"What job?"

"Any job. Am I right, Corporal?"

"Oorah, Sergeant."

I had no idea what "oorah" meant, but his grin told me that he and Kenni were bonding on some level that I wasn't privy to.

Kenni turned to me. "Go with them. They'll keep an eye on you and see if you're as good as you think you are."

"Where are you going?"

"I'm going to report back to Colonel Everest." She raised the two books we'd brought back. "Then I have some homework to do. I'll see you back at your quarters shortly after sunset." She turned to Hardy. "Can you make sure he gets to his quarters by sunset? The colonel put him up in officers' country."

"Can do, Sergeant."

And with that, Kenni left me to the tender mercies of four hulking Marines who had basically just been given instructions to put me through my paces in the sparring ring.

"So you've had some training?"

"Yes, sir."

He chuckled. "I'm just a corporal. No *sirs* here."

I winced. Kenni had warned me about that. "Sorry. It's just the way I was raised."

"Yeah, I had an uncle like that." He waved me into the ring.

Calling it a ring was being pretty generous. There were four wooden posts someone had driven into the ground in what appeared to be about a twenty-by-twenty-foot square. Ropes were strung around the posts, and I had to duck between them to enter the enclosed area. Long strips of cloth hung from the rope in various places, and I wondered what they were for.

"Let's see what we have to work with." Hardy picked up some of the cloth strips and began wrapping his knuckles, and I understood.

I grabbed some and began copying him. The cloth I grabbed was stained and stiff from dried blood, and I realized that this wasn't going to be a light-touch bout. I calmed my beating heart and looked to see how Hardy wrapped his hands. He left his fingers free, so I did the same. Open fingers usually meant grappling would be allowed—not my strongest suit. And considering he looked to be about twice my weight, I wasn't eager to go to the ground with him. I determined to do whatever I could to keep our match upright.

The big man checked to see that I had wrapped my knuckles properly and, after a minor adjustment, guided me to the center of the ring.

"So exactly what kind of style is mic-map?"

He smiled. "MCMAP is an acronym. It stands for Marine Corps Martial Arts Program, and it's a mix of a lot of different styles." He settled onto the balls of his feet. "You ready?"

I nodded. Hardy slid closer, the only indication that we were starting our match. I tried to remain relaxed, giving nothing away in my posture as he moved closer. There were only so many attacks he could use with his stance, and it looked to me as if the man wanted to shoot in to take me to the ground.

Sure enough, he lunged forward, reaching for my legs in an attempt to take them out from under me. I shifted back a few inches, raised my center of gravity, and as he came close, I slammed down on his shoulders, shoving him to the grass in a heap.

I danced back out of reach while he rolled to his feet.

"Why didn't you follow up?" he asked.

"You were down."

"But I'm not alone." As he said it, one of the other Marines slammed into me from behind. I hit the ground with enough force to drive the breath from my lungs. I rolled to my knees, attempting to turtle up beneath the weight of the second Marine, but he moved with me, yanking my arm out and rolling me onto my back. Using the arm as leverage, he spun onto his own back then threw one leg over my chest and the other across my throat as he wrenched my elbow across his thigh in a vicious armbar.

I tapped frantically on the thigh across my throat, and he immediately released me. I got to my feet and grinned. "So it's like that?"

Hardy smiled back. "Sarge said to test you. Plus, I heard you got your ass handed to you by three dogface Army dicks. Figured you would know better than to assume only one attacker by now."

"Fair enough." I backed to one corner of the ring where I could see both opponents. "Again?"

The second time, there was no pretense. Both of them moved forward. I looked around to make sure the other two weren't circling around behind me. Then I set myself opposite the two others in the ring with me, the three of us at the points of a triangle. I let my gaze unfocus.

It was something my dad had taught me many years ago. "It's absolutely impossible for two attackers to move in perfect synchronization. One will always move first. Make *him* your target."

Sure enough, my peripheral vision caught a slight shift as Hardy stepped. Ignoring the fact that his partner — was it Simmons or Roberts? — also started to move a second later, I leapt at Hardy. That served the purpose of putting me inside his attack and outside of his partner's. In short, I wasn't where either of them expected me to be, and before they could adjust, I had thrown Hardy off balance and into his partner. The two of them bounced off one another, and I slipped out of the ring. Hardy looked around and found me waving at him from outside the ring.

"You think you beat us?"

"You're busy untangling yourselves, and I'm gone. My intent isn't to beat you. It's to keep myself from getting pounded again."

"Fair enough. Let's try it again." He waved the other two into the ring.

"Seriously?" I said. But inside, I was ready to laugh. I'd been sparring multiple opponents for years and had long ago learned that it was often easier to spar three or four than it was to spar two. Past two, a person's opponents usually got in one another's way.

Sure enough, as soon as I signaled I was ready, Hardy jumped forward. I knew he would be watching for me to leap in again, so I moved the opposite direction, surprising one of the other men before he even knew things had started. He swung a fist at me, but I had planned for it, brushed and trapped the wrist, and used his momentum to pull him into his buddies.

Once more, I ran past them and was out of the ring before they had untangled themselves.

I could tell from Hardy's expression that he didn't know whether to be frustrated or amused. "Okay," he said, "you've shown you know how to get out of a situation. But that doesn't tell me if you know how to fight."

"But you're the one that turned this from a sparring match into a self-defense demonstration."

"Okay," he said. "So what's the difference?"

"In a sparring match, two people test their techniques against one another. With a self-defense demo, you force me to show how I would save my hide in a more serious situation. Since we all know I don't have a snowball's chance in hell of actually fighting against all four of you, I decided I wouldn't."

Hardy grinned. "Discretion is the better part of valor, eh?"

"More like 'Run, run, run away. Live to fight another day.'"

"Okay, then. Let's check your technique." He signaled for everyone else to leave the ring. Once they were out, I stepped in. And then the real workout began.

A few hours and several bruises later, he called it quits. "Come on, Mr. Dawcett. We need to get you back to your quarters."

"Hey. If I can't call you *sir*, you don't get to call me *mister*. Just Zach."

"All right. Zach it is."

I wiped the sweat from my eyes and began unwrapping the cloth from my knuckles. "So how'd I do?"

"You did great. Your hands and feet are really good. Nice

technique and outstanding speed. As a matter of fact, you have some parrying techniques I'd like you to show me in more detail a little later if you don't mind sharing them."

"Sure." I figured he was talking about the trapping techniques that were pretty much second nature to me.

"You need to work on your ground techniques," he continued, "but you already knew that, didn't you?"

"Yeah. It's never been a big strength. It's why I work so hard to stay on my feet."

"And that's something else. The most important thing is that you know better than to just start swinging. You keep your head. You have enough sense to know when to fight and when to get the hell outta Dodge. There's been plenty of times when I wished some of my buddies knew that."

"So I did all right, then."

He slapped me on the back, and I nearly staggered under the force of the big man's blow. "You did all right. Now, let's get you back to your quarters before I get in bad with the new sergeant. We'll see you here again tomorrow."

CHAPTER 48
MAMA'S TALKING

A s soon as I got back, I stripped and spent another glorious half hour in that miraculous hot shower. I would have been in longer, but the water eventually began to cool, and I didn't want to risk having the memory of a perfect shower spoiled by a bad ending. I dried myself off and stood in front of the steamed-over mirror, wiping it with my towel then brushing my hair as I walked nude from the bathroom to the bedroom.

I jumped when I saw Kenni sitting on the couch in the front room. "Holy crap! You scared me." Suddenly realizing that I didn't have a stitch on, I turned modestly away and reached for the towel I'd left on the bathroom counter.

Kenni laughed, but I noticed immediately how tired she sounded.

I wrapped the towel around my waist. "You all right?"

"Yeah. Got a headache from all the reading, and I'm not sleeping too well." She straightened her back in an effort to look more energetic, but she didn't fool me. "I'm all right. Go get dressed, and we'll catch up."

Back in the bedroom, I shook out my extra clothes. I called out as I dressed, "Why aren't you sleeping? They working you that hard?"

"No. Mama's still bugging me."

"Christmas carols?"

"Yeah."

"And you still don't know what it means?"

"No. And it's getting pretty frustrating."

I was pulling my shirt down as I joined her in the den.

"So how did your training with Hardy go?" she asked.

"All right. I think I'll be sore for a while."

"Did you guys end up on good terms?"

"I think so. Why?"

"Because we need allies while we're here. And not just with the officers. We need some enlisted men and women we can count on. If I'm going to be leading them, I have to keep them at arm's length. I can't be their friend and also command them."

"So you sent me instead."

She nodded.

"Sneaky."

"Not really. Just being practical. We don't know how all this is going to play out. Whether I have to stay or not, I can't give someone an order and expect them to immediately obey it if they look at me as a buddy. But you can keep your finger on their pulse, so to speak. You can pal around with them, let me know who I can trust and who I can't."

I wasn't sure I liked my role. It felt too much like deception. And though I had only just met Hardy and the others, they seemed like genuinely likeable people. "And what did you do while I was earning new bruises?"

"Reported in to Colonel Everest and asked for some time to go over my findings with Captain Mallory. Had to work out some of the technical issues, like what sort of court-martial we'll be going for. Stuff like that."

"There's more than one kind?"

She nodded wearily. "Three, actually. We had to figure out what charges will have the best chance of sticking and compare that to what resources we have available. I can't really talk too much about it with you since you're a witness. But in general terms, I can tell you that each kind of court-martial requires a certain number of officers on the jury, and we have a limited number here.

"There's also the matter of us not having direct witnesses to him or his men killing Walt's man, so trying him for murder would be a waste of time."

"What do you mean? We know he killed him."

She shook her head. "No, we don't. All we know is that Walt said he did. Did you see it happen? I didn't. Neither did Keith or anyone else we asked."

"So he's going to get away with it?" The idea galled me, but I could see she was right.

"Well, we can't prove murder, but we do have witnesses to some of his other offenses. Tara and her people can testify about his group's attack on them. You and I both heard him imply that you were responsible for the deaths of his men, which led to your beating."

"So that's all we can go after him for?"

She shrugged. "All I can say is that a murder trial is off the table. In a way, that's a good thing. With the state of affairs in the military, and the extenuating circumstances caused by the destruction of the country's communications grid, Colonel Everest has been given quite a bit of autonomy, especially when it comes to maintaining discipline over his men. But a murder trial is outside even his reach. It would require a general court-martial with a military judge and — if I recall correctly — five officers for the jury panel, plus counsels for the defense and prosecution. Also, you have to offer the accused the option of a one-third enlisted jury. The enlisted men wouldn't be a problem, but the officers… there simply aren't that many here. That means Everest would have to send back to home base for the extra personnel. Shuffling messages back and forth to make the arrangements, getting the proper personnel out here for a trial — it would likely take months.

"Instead, we go with the lesser charges of assault, theft, and destruction of private property. This lets us address the charges in a special court-martial. It requires fewer officers and lets us bring him to trial immediately."

"You do know a lot about this."

"While I was an MP, I was called up on a few trials. One was a domestic disturbance that escalated into murder. I believe in being thorough, so I learned all I could." She smiled, but I couldn't help noticing just how weary she looked. "Of course, the books we found today helped too. I've been going through them with Captain Mallory all afternoon."

"Not Everest?"

"No. The colonel will have to serve as the judge advocate for the trial, so he can't take part in the actual investigation or planning of the case."

Kenni stood. "And I have another meeting in a little while. I just wanted to let you know that I might not be able to see you for a few days. Things are going to start getting pretty tense around here starting tomorrow. It's going to be my first day showing my new rank on the base. There will also be some discussions about going against Collins, and we don't know what the fallout from that might be, so you need to be careful. That's why I wanted to make sure things went well with you today. "

"Sure."

"You stay near Hardy or whoever you think you can trust. Carry your blades with you. Until we get this business with Collins settled, we're not going to be able to figure out what we're really dealing with."

CHAPTER 49
ESCALATION

OVER THE NEXT FEW DAYS, I managed to stay out of trouble. What time I spent on base, I spent with Hardy and the other Marines, making fast friends both in and out of the sparring ring. I learned how things had changed since D-day around the world, even within the military. Each evening, Kenni would drop by, and I would tell her what I was learning about these men and women. Usually, she already knew what I would have to say. But on occasion, I was able to surprise her.

"Did you know that no one in the Marines has any living relatives?" I said.

"What?"

I could see by her expression that this was news to her. "Hardy says it's a requirement for joining now. It started shortly after D-day."

She was silent for a few seconds. "Now that you mention it, Everest and Mallory did ask about my family before they promoted me. Did they tell you why?"

"Yes. They're some kind of elite fighting force."

"We always were." Her voice held a note of pride.

"Not like now. Seems they pride themselves on being absolutely ruthless in battle. You know that motto you guys always throw around? That 'semper fi' thing?"

"Yes."

"Hardy told me it means 'always faithful.'"

"I know that."

"But I think it means something different now than what it used to. For them, it means they're always faithful to the ones they lost, and every battle they fight is a chance to show it. They go into every fight almost hoping to die."

Kenni shook her head. "You probably misunderstood."

"I don't think so. There's another saying I've heard them use when it comes to fighting."

"What?"

"'Nothing to lose.' It's why they're so hard-nosed. Between the fact that they don't have anyone left to live for and the idea that they can bring honor to those who've already died, they don't really seem concerned with whether or not they make it back from a battle. They're friendly enough, but deep down, these guys are a little bit scary."

That discussion made her withdraw a bit, and she left soon after. For the first time since putting the uniform back on, she seemed ill at ease in it.

Other than my time with the Marines and Kenni, I spent most of my days away from the base. Specifically, I spent as much time as I could with Walela, and it became clearer with every passing day that our relationship was more than a passing infatuation. At least, for me it was. Neither of us was using the L word, though. Any time I even thought of that, I felt a mild panic in my chest. But that tightness became even worse at the thought of not seeing her again. And as if that wasn't enough to think about, a new worry intruded on the third day.

I left the base as I had the last few mornings, but even before I reached the blockade on the street, I could tell something was different. For one thing, the crowd seemed larger. And there was something different about their mood. It was surly — menacing. And sprinkled here and there within the crowd were several people with painted faces. Walela had told me that anyone painted up like that was considered a brave, and I remembered her warning from the first day I'd met her. *If you see a bunch of us painted up, it's a safe bet we're going into battle.*

While no one said anything to me directly, there were several in the crowd who watched with open hostility as I approached. Surprisingly, Walela and the girls were waiting for me at the front of the crowd. Other than that first day, she had made a point of keeping out of sight when we met so that no one from the base would notice I was meeting anyone in particular. It was possible I was just being paranoid, but I had no intention of letting any of Collins's people know about my relationship with her.

"What's going on?" I asked as I pushed my way through the crowd.

She turned to walk beside me. We didn't kiss or hold hands or in any other way show our feelings for one another. Both of us were terribly aware that we were still within sight of the gate. But as she fell in beside me, she spoke without turning her head.

"People started trickling in last night. They brought word that a gathering of elders has been called to discuss what Collins and his men have done."

We rounded the corner of the next street, putting the first building between the base and us. It was a boundary of sorts, marking the point at which we were able to show affection for one another. For the last few days, we had stopped for a kiss at that point. But that day, we had serious business to worry about. My lessons had finally become second nature, and I tried to think through the implications of what she had told me before I said anything.

"Walt?" I asked.

She nodded. "Remember they said they would spread word to some of the elders in nearby towns? Sounds like the elders have decided to take action."

"Please tell me they aren't calling for a fight." My heart thumped. "I know what a fight against these kinds of weapons can cost. We lost over a thousand people when we fought Crazy Larry."

"All I know is people are starting to filter in from all over, and the word is that some of the elders will begin arriving tomorrow. Walkingstick is coming from McAlester." The thought of the frail old woman making the trip took me aback.

Then the rest of what she had said sank in. "She's coming here? They're meeting here?"

Walela nodded. "They're convening a special council."

"But why here?"

"Do I look like an elder?"

"Sorry."

We walked the rest of the way to her room in silence as I tried to think through the possible scenarios. No matter what I came up with, none of it boded well.

⊢—⊬——⊬——⊬——⊬—⊬

When I arrived back at the spaceport that evening, the guard at the gate stopped me. "Mr. Dawcett? Colonel Everest has requested that you see him as soon as you get back."

I looked at the single chevron on his chest. "Thank you, Private." I was getting pretty good at identifying ranks.

As I walked to Everest's offices, I noted several people watching me. Their expressions looked a lot like those I'd seen in the crowd at the blockade line. The exception was the small group of Marines I passed. Hardy had made sure they looked out for me, and a camaraderie had begun to form between us. There were thirty Marines on base, and while I didn't know all of them personally yet, they all knew me by sight.

I exchanged nods with them and felt more comfortable as I passed, heading into the command building. The corporal at the front desk evidently recognized me. The name tag on his shirt read "Tibbik," and as soon as I walked through the door, he stood. "Please follow me, Mr. Dawcett. Colonel Everest asked that I bring you in immediately."

"Lead the way, Corporal." I followed him down the hall until he stopped and knocked on Everest's door.

Everest's voice called, "Come."

310

Corporal Tibbik opened the door and waved me inside. "Have a seat, Mr. Dawcett."

From his seat, the colonel waved me to one of the empty guest chairs.

"What can I do for you, Colonel?"

"Mr. Dawcett, I've gotten reports of a noticeable increase in the number of hostiles in the town of Burns Flat." He pulled out a few sheets of the fine-pulp paper that almost looked like Old Days paper, holding them up for me to see. "As a matter of fact, according to our observations from the tower, there are an estimated seventy-five campsites around the base that weren't there just two days ago, and there's been an influx of caravans, which have been arriving at an alarming rate throughout the day today. Can you confirm that?"

"Hostiles? No, Colonel. I didn't see any hostiles when I was in town this morning. Maybe if you told me what they look like—"

He slammed the papers down on his desk. "Don't you play games with me, Dawcett!"

I'd only met the man a few days earlier, but until that moment, I'd never seen him lose his temper. I needed to tread carefully.

"Colonel, if you're talking about the *citizens* who've been coming into town, they are no more hostile to you than some of your men have been to them. As a matter of fact, I could argue that they're *less* hostile than some of your men."

The anger in his eyes flared, then faded, replaced with a defeated weariness. He knew I was right. "Okay." He rubbed his eyes, took a deep breath, and started over. "Can you confirm whether or not there has been a marked influx of *citizens* coming into Burns Flat?"

I hesitated, not knowing how much I should tell him. I wasn't one of his soldiers, and I didn't work for him. I didn't owe the man anything. On the other hand, the same was true for the OTA. I had to remain neutral. And the best way to do that was to be honest.

"Yes, there are more people there. And more are on the way."

"Why? What's happened?"

"You remember when we told you about the group of pilgrims that Collins and his men took from their escort?"

Everest nodded.

"Once that happened, the team that had been escorting them split and rode to several of the nearest towns to spread word to their elders. That was just over a week ago, and it seems some of those elders are coming here for a special council meeting."

"Why?"

I shrugged. "They didn't tell *me*. But I can think of several possibilities. Can't you?"

Everest sat back in his chair. He looked tired and defeated. "This Collins situation is getting worse by the day."

I kept my mouth shut while he thought. He apparently came to some sort of decision after only a few seconds. "Tibbik!"

His sudden shout startled me. The rapid footsteps down the hall told me the man was running, but he rounded the door frame calmly. "Yes, sir?"

"Ask Captain Mallory to join us right away."

"Yes, sir." The footsteps retreated back down the hall as quickly as they had come.

Everest turned back to me. "Mr. Dawcett, I think it's probably safest if you stop your trips into the town until we get this all sorted out."

"Are we back to this?"

"Back to what?" His tone left little doubt that he was getting tired of arguing with me, but that wasn't going to stop me.

"Am I a prisoner again?"

"You were never..." He sighed.

"Colonel, I know it wasn't your intention to make me a prisoner. I know that I'm on your base and that you can detain me without reason. And I know that Collins has put you in a bad situation. "

"But?"

"But the truth is that I've been safer away from your men than with them. If you really think you're keeping me safe, you might want to consider that."

He was silent for a moment and finally shook his head. "This is really starting to piss me off."

The door opened again, and Captain Mallory entered. "You wanted to see me, Colonel?"

"Come on in." Everest sounded defeated.

Mallory walked across the room and stopped before the colonel's desk. He didn't sit. "What can I do for you?"

"Without giving me any details, how close are you to having your case against Collins?"

"It depends on how tight we need the case."

"We have a situation in town—we need to bring him into custody right away. That means we need to bring charges. Are you ready to do that?"

"How soon did you want to bring him in?" Mallory asked.

"Now."

I swallowed.

Mallory hesitated. "I'll make it happen, sir."

Everest waved his hand. "It's just us, Frank. Don't *sir* me. I just need you to know that if we're not careful, this could blow up in our faces. I want us to be actively working on the problem when the spotlight hits us. The further along we are, the better we're going to look to the hosti—" He looked at me. "To the citizens in town."

Captain Mallory said, "All right. You really want us to bring Collins in now?"

"Yes. Have our new sergeant send a squad of Marines, and put that son of a bitch in the brig."

"Yes, sir."

"Warn her that this is liable to get ugly before we're through."

"We've already discussed it. She's well aware."

After Mallory left, Everest turned back to me. "Is there anything else I need to know?"

"Just that I'm not one of your men. I'm trying not to choose sides in this."

He stared at me for a moment, sighed, and nodded. "I appreciate your honesty."

CHAPTER 50
JIMBO

LEFT MY QUARTERS THE NEXT morning, heading out for my regular outing to the town. The quad was quieter than usual, and several of the soldiers looked sullenly at me as I walked past, but I wasn't too worried. As long as I was out in the open, no one was going to try anything.

A man carrying a load of lumber crossed in front of me, and as he did, several of the long boards slipped, barely missing me. "Sorry, sir." He bent over, trying to balance the boards slung across his shoulder while attempting to pick up those that he'd dropped.

I reached for the boards on the ground. "Here, let me give you a hand."

Two other soldiers were nearby and trotted over to help. "Need a hand?" one of them asked with a smile.

I glanced at him as he approached. My smile died on my face as I recognized the man. It was my old buddy Jim Thompson from the bathroom skirmish.

"Hi." He shoved me around the corner and into the arms of two other men waiting in the shadows. They began to drag me farther behind the building, while the second man who had come over with him calmly helped the first pick up the rest of the boards, and they walked away.

I'd been set up. As soon as I realized that, I attacked. They weren't going to catch me against a wall again. I kicked back behind the feet of the man on my right, forcing him to stumble. While he struggled to regain his balance, I jerked my arm free and slammed an open palm into his groin and squeezed. He froze in agony, and I shot my elbow up into his nose. He cried out, putting a hand to each injury as he stumbled away.

Jim saw it happening and rushed at me, fist balling up as he came. But my right side was free at that point. I ducked, spun in front of the man holding my left arm, drove knuckles into his inner thigh, and jerked him around. With him between me and Jim, I stood up, driving my elbow into his chin as I rose. His hand on my left arm went slack, and I grabbed the lapel of his shirt and shoved.

He was stunned, but only for a second. As he fell against the rushing Jim Thompson, his eyes refocused, and the two of them attacked.

I was ready for them. Jim was a bit faster. He jumped at me, leading with another haymaker. The fist grazed my ear as I slipped outside, parried the punch, and shoved him past me before he realized I wasn't going to engage him.

His buddy realized it too, but not until it was too late. He tried to throw a jab, but I slammed my palm into his shoulder, jamming the punch and robbing it of any power. It still connected, but only on my shoulder and with a fraction of its original power. At the same time, I kicked behind me, landing a solid boot on Jim's hip as he turned back to me.

Jim fell away from us, and I turned back to the attacker in my hands. I stepped closer, slamming an elbow at his nose again as I shuffled directly in front of him. He screamed, spraying blood from his mangled nose. While his eyes were unfocused, I reached around his neck with both hands and yanked his head down even as I raised my knee. His nose turned into a crimson fountain, and he went limp.

I turned to find Jim back on his feet. He rushed at me, trying to knock me to the ground. I slipped aside and kicked hard.

He staggered, and I grabbed his shoulder as he passed. I

yanked his arm up and drove a fist into his ribs with everything I had.

Once. Twice. Three times.

On the third punch, I heard a rib break, and he screamed.

I let go, and he fell to his knees. Panting, I started to leave him there. But he reached for his waist, and it suddenly occurred to me that he had his sidearm. For a second, I considered drawing one of my blades, but Jim was barely able to move. Snarling, I kicked him in the face, and he fell to the ground.

I looked around. The first man was moaning, clutching his groin, and blowing bloody snot all down his front. Jim and the other man were out cold. My hands and legs trembled from the fight-or-flight adrenaline rush as I fumbled at Jim's belt, withdrew his pistol, and shoved it into my belt. I disarmed the other two men and stumbled out of the shadows.

Emerging back into the sunlight, I scanned the soldiers going about their various duties. No one seemed to be paying me much attention, so I headed to Marine Central. Lance Corporal Larson looked up and smiled as I walked in.

"Hey, Zach. What's up?"

"Had a little trouble." I laid the pistols on his desk. "The guys that jumped me in the bathroom wanted a rematch."

He stood, grabbing a rifle that was leaning against the wall. "Corporal Hardy!" he shouted back into the bunkroom. "We have a situation!"

Hardy came running, saw me, saw Larson arming himself, and narrowed his eyes. "What's going on?"

"Your Army buddies jumped me again."

"You all right?" Hardy asked.

"Yeah. Just a little shaken up."

"They all right?"

"Not really. I messed two of them up pretty good. The other one was still conscious when I left."

He shouted, "Richmond!"

A big Marine I had barely met poked his head in almost immediately.

"Grab your rifle, and come with us."

Richmond nodded. "Oorah, Corporal."

Hardy waved me toward the door. "Lead the way."

We walked at a brisk pace across the quad. "I was afraid something like this might happen," Hardy said. "Locking Collins up has pissed off some of his followers. This place is turning into a powder keg."

We arrived back where I'd left my attackers in the narrow alley between the woodshop and the old hanger. The man who'd been conscious was gone, but the other two were still where I'd left them. Jim was struggling to get up, and Hardy ran up to grab the man by his collar. "Heya, Jimbo. Didn't I tell you this was a bad idea?" He yanked Jim upright with a savage jerk. Jim groaned in pain. "Didn't I tell you that if I caught you messing with my friend again, I was gonna take it out of your hide?"

"Be careful," I said. "I think I broke a rib or two. He'll probably need some time with the medic."

Hardy grinned evilly. "Who? Jimbo here? Not him." He let go of the collar and slapped the man on the back—hard.

Jim groaned and tried to bend over to cover his ribs, but Hardy grabbed his collar and yanked him back upright.

"No. Jimbo is tough!" He slapped him again, hard enough that the wounded man fell to his knees, moaning at the pain the jostling caused him. Hardy grabbed his collar again and yanked "Jimbo" into a sitting position. He knelt in front of him.

"Yeah. So tough that he has to bring his buddies to jump someone because he can't handle a fair fight." Hardy reached out and very deliberately tapped Jim's ribs. "Course, from the looks of things, I guess you should have brought more than just the two, shouldn't you?"

Without looking away from the man's eyes, Hardy called over his shoulder. "Richmond!"

"Yes, Corporal?"

"Send word to Sergeant Anderson that we have two more visitors coming to Alcatraz."

"Will do."

"Larson, wake up Sleeping Beauty there, and get him on his feet." Hardy hauled Jim back to a standing position. "You said there was a third one?"

"Yeah. He was still conscious when I left him. He should be easy enough to find, though."

"This ought to be good. What'd you do to him?"

"Just look for a man who walks like he doesn't want to be a man anymore."

Hardy chuckled.

"He's also wearing a long streak of red from his nose to his belt."

Hardy laughed again. "Not bad, kid. Not bad."

For the next few hours, I was questioned first by Kenni, followed by a second session with Captain Mallory. Colonel Everest stuck his head into Mallory's office to make sure I was all right. But once he'd ascertained that, he left, saying he didn't want to risk anything that would jeopardize the upcoming court-martial.

Mallory seemed concerned that I couldn't identify the man who had initially dropped the boards in front of me, or the other man who had helped him clean them up. "You do understand they were in on it too, don't you?"

"Yes, but I didn't know it at the time. By the time I realized what was going on, I had more important things on my mind."

"Yeah, I guess you did. Although, based on Hardy's report" — he lifted the page on his desk — "it seems you managed to take care of things quite well. Doc says all three of them have broken noses, and Corporal Thompson has at least two broken ribs."

"He was going for his pistol."

Mallory pursed his lips. "Can I ask you something? I don't mean to sound like I'm demeaning you, but I have to ask... how is it you did all this damage to three soldiers when just a week ago those same men beat the absolute crap out of you in the latrine?"

I shrugged. "I've trained how to fight since I was a kid. But all the training in the world doesn't do you any good when something happens to throw off your reactions. It can be something tiny, like slipping in a puddle. When they jumped me in the latrine, one of them pulled me off balance at a critical point. That caused one thing to lead to another, and I got my ass kicked." I paused before continuing. "This time, things went my way."

Mallory nodded. "Back before the war, I learned about an old German military strategist named Helmuth von Moltke. There's a famous quote attributed to him that says something like 'No battle plan survives first contact with the enemy.' Do you know the saying?"

"Not exactly, but it sounds a lot like something my dad used to tell me, only he said it was from some famous Old Days fighter. He said 'Everybody has a plan until they get punched in the mouth.'"

"Tyson." Mallory chuckled. "It was Mike Tyson. So you know what I'm getting at."

"Yes, sir. Dad always told me that the outcome of any conflict is a combination of training, planning, perseverance, and luck."

"Your dad sounds like a smart man."

"Thanks. I think so too."

"So now the question is, do you want to press charges?"

"What do you mean?" I asked.

"We can handle this one a few different ways. Since you basically pounded the hell out of these idiots, and you aren't really injured, you could drop the matter. Of course, if that doesn't appeal to you, we have some other options. We could try to convince them to accept a plea deal. We could impose Article Fifteen nonjudicial punishment. Or we could go all out and prefer charges for another court-martial."

"Like you're doing with Collins?"

"Not quite. This one would probably be a summary court-martial, a much simpler affair than what we're having to go through with Collins."

"But it would mean another court case."

"It would." Mallory sat there watching me.

"No. I'd rather not do that. I don't want to slow down the case against Collins. What's that Article Fifteen thing?"

"It lets us bypass a trial and give them a minor punishment such as restriction to barracks and extra duties for a few weeks. Basically a slap on the wrist, but it could serve to keep them out of our hair for a bit."

I thought about it for a minute before shaking my head. "I don't know. What do you recommend?"

"If it were me, I'd try to get them to take a plea deal. Tell them we'll bring them up on aggravated assault charges and threaten them with a year in the brig, reduction in rank, and corporal punishment. Offer to drop it to two weeks in the brig with hard labor in exchange for a confession and a written guarantee that they'll keep away from you. We throw in the threat of bringing back the heavier charges if they so much as sneeze in your direction again."

"And if they don't go for the deal?"

"Then we can still go with the Article Fifteen punishment and assign some of your Marine friends to keep an eye on them."

I nodded. "That's fine. I'm not too worried about them coming after me again. I think Corporal Thompson probably realizes the first time he caught me in the latrine wasn't typical of how things will usually go with me."

"Let's hope so." Captain Mallory pulled out a sheet of that crisp, clean paper and began writing on it. "All right, Mr. Dawcett. We'll get going on the plea deal, and I'll send you word of whether or not they accept it."

"And I can leave?"

"You can. I'll let you know what happens."

I stood. "Thank you, Captain."

Mallory stopped writing and stood. "I'm just sorry this happened. Not as sorry as Thompson and his boys, but still sorry."

CHAPTER 51
MEETING REQUEST

WHEN I FINALLY GOT INTO town, the throng at the blockade line was even larger, and their mood was darker. Walela met me at the back of the crowd, walking beside me as we spoke. "Why are you so late?"

I took a few minutes to tell her about the attempted mugging, making light of it before distracting her with questions about the growing crowd.

"Advance riders got here just after daybreak. Walkingstick should be here in an hour or so. There's another party coming in from Ponca City. They should be in later this afternoon. No word yet from anywhere else."

I sighed. Everest was right. It was starting to look like things might get ugly.

We walked to the edge of town, taking Bella and Cricket for a romp in the fields to the east. Neither Walela nor I had a lot to say. We were content to just be together for the time being. She had a small leather ball she had taught Bella to fetch, and we spent quite a bit of time keeping them entertained with it. At some point, Cricket started barking and moved from play mode to hunting. Seconds later, she and Bella were chasing a small, furry rodent around the field.

Walela and I laughed as we watched them until we noticed the line of horses in the distance. The smile left her face as she looked at me. "Play time's over."

The knock at Walela's door came within half an hour after the party from McAlester arrived in town. She opened the door to find Keith on the other side.

"Figured I'd find you here." He was looking at me when he said it, so I wasn't surprised when he followed it with an invitation. "Elder Walkingstick is asking for you."

I kissed Walela. "Watch the girls?"

"Don't I always?" Her smile was wistful.

I touched her cheek, suddenly aware of how much it bothered me to have to leave her and how much I was coming to resent the duties and circumstances keeping us apart. And that told me just how badly I had fallen for her. There was a moment of clarity, and I finally accepted that I was in love with her.

Well, crap.

I turned to Keith. "Lead the way."

He surprised me when we went down to the ground floor then went to another room in the same hotel. He chuckled at my expression. "Not a lot of places to stay with all the new people in town. The entire ground floor has been reserved for the elders. Hell, they had to throw a couple of people out in order to get it."

A burly man with full face paint stood outside the door. Keith said something to him in Cherokee, and the man nodded and opened the door. Keith waved me in.

"You're not coming?"

He shook his head. "The invitation was for you."

"Please, Mr. Dawcett. I've had several rough days on the road, and I'm quite tired."

I recognized the old seer's voice and stepped inside. Someone closed the door behind me.

Andrea Walkingstick sat at a small desk near the window. She was scribbling notes on some rough paper and didn't look up as she spoke. "Thank you for coming, Mr. Dawcett."

"Yes, ma'am. What can I do for you?"

She continued writing for a moment more before finally turning to face me. She waved to the extra chair. "Please have a seat."

She waited until I did so before she continued. "I understand that you were witness to some of the problems we had with soldiers from the spaceport and that you actually helped our people during one of the fights. I would like to thank you for that."

"You're welcome. It was the right thing to do."

She simply nodded. "I also understand that you've been staying with the soldiers on the base and that you're working with some of them to try to bring those responsible to justice. What can you tell me about that?"

I spent the next several minutes telling her about Colonel Everest and Captain Mallory and how they were trying to determine the best course of action to maintain the peace while still working within the law.

"Do you believe them to be honorable men?"

I hesitated, remembering Kenni's reservations. "I don't know them well enough to say that. What I can say is that they appear to be following the best course of action with the resources available to them."

She cocked her head. "That's quite an equivocation."

"I'm sorry. I just see the word *honorable* as an opinion. They seem to believe in what they're trying to do. But I think that speaks more to their sense of duty than their personal code of honor."

"Why, Mr. Dawcett. You've turned into quite the diplomat!"

"Thank you. I think."

She chuckled. "When do you go back to the base?"

"I go back every afternoon. There are things I have to do there as well."

"Such as?"

I shook my head. "Miss Walkingstick, I had a conversation with Colonel Everest last night. I won't go into all the details, but I had to make sure that I stressed to him at the end that I'm not ready to choose sides between the soldiers and the OTA. My job at this point is that of an observer. I'm here to help my people decide whether or not it's in our best interest to ally ourselves with the soldiers here in their attempt to rebuild the United States. I don't work for him. But I also don't work for you. I won't be used by either of you against the other."

"Even after all you've seen?"

"It's funny how many people ask me that. Yes, even after everything I've seen. Because the problems I've seen so far have all been caused by a relatively small group of people who don't seem to want the colonel to succeed. How the involved parties react to the situation will tell me a lot about them."

"And who do you see as the involved parties?"

"Colonel Everest and his group, Sergeant Collins and his group, and the OTA."

She raised an eyebrow. "You're being awfully blunt."

"I'm being honest."

"So are you judging us?"

"No, ma'am. I'm trying to remain as neutral as I can, and I want to let everyone know it up front."

She pursed her lips, thinking, before she asked, "Would it violate your personal code of conduct to convey a message from me to Colonel Everest?"

"No, ma'am."

"Would you ask him if I could meet with him at his earliest convenience? I'd like to discuss the best way to defuse the growing tension between our people."

"Yes, ma'am. I'll do it right away."

Colonel Everest met with Elder Walkingstick and another elder who arrived later that afternoon from Ponca City. I escorted them onto the base and to his office but wasn't allowed into the meeting itself. A few hours later, a private knocked on my door to let me know that Colonel Everest would like to see me again.

When I arrived, the elders were gone. He waved me to my usual chair.

"I had a good talk with these... elders you brought here." He looked at a sheet of paper. "Walkingstick and Black Horse. It's my understanding that you know them?"

"I know Miss Walkingstick. Never met Black Horse before this afternoon."

He seemed to be weighing my words. This wasn't the same man I had dealt with before. He looked at me as if evaluating an enemy. I could only guess at why that might be.

"They want to be present during the trial. Them and a small group of elders."

I nodded. As far as I was concerned, it was his decision and didn't require any input from me. But the colonel didn't follow up with anything more. He just looked at me in that same manner.

"Was there something else, Colonel? I don't imagine you called me here just to tell me that."

"Walkingstick spoke highly of you."

I didn't know what I was supposed to say to that.

"I have to confess, her affection for you makes me wonder about your professed neutrality in this whole affair."

Keeping my face neutral, I asked, "How so?"

"Looks to me like you've already got some kind of alliance with these people. You're pretty chummy with them at the very least."

"Funny, I have some of them telling me that I'm getting too chummy with you. Colonel, I told Walkingstick the same thing I told you. I'm not choosing sides. I'm here to see what's best for the people I represent. That's all."

"Then why are you helping us with Collins at all? Seems to be a matter between our people and theirs. Other than the fact that you were involved in that last skirmish where you people captured him and his men, you really don't have anything to do with this mess."

I took a deep breath, thinking about how to explain it better. "We had a neighbor back home who lost his wife in the fight with Crazy Larry. I think I told you about Crazy Larry, didn't I?"

He nodded.

"So after his wife died, it was just him and two kids a little younger than me. He started boozing—a lot—and he turned out to be a pretty mean drunk. Eventually, he took to beating his kids. It finally got to the point that some of his neighbors had to go over and explain to him that they were more than willing to let him drink himself into an early grave if he wanted, but if he laid hands on his kids again, there were plenty of other families who would be willing to take them in."

"Okay. I'll bite. What happened?"

I shook my head. "What happened isn't the point. The point is that the people of Rejas saw a problem affecting innocent people. They saw a problem and stepped in. As a community, we let him know that what he did to himself was fine. But we wouldn't allow him to hurt innocents. That's the kind of action my people value."

"And Collins was the drunk, out hurting innocents."

I nodded.

"You already know I don't condone what he did out there."

"But what are you going to do about it? That's what shows me what kind of community you want to build."

He sat there, face relaxing, and I got the impression that my words had somewhat mollified him.

After a moment of silence I cleared my throat. "Is that all you wanted, Colonel?"

"I suppose so. I just wanted to look you in the eyes and make sure I'm not being made a fool of."

"Colonel, I've been honest with you in everything I've said. I'm not your enemy."

"But you're not my friend, either, are you?"

"Not yet. Maybe in the future. But I can tell you that I don't believe you're a bad person."

"I guess that's all we can hope for," he said. "At least for now."

"For now," I agreed. "Is that all, Colonel?"

He nodded, and I stood to leave. Just as I reached the door, he asked a final question.

"Mr. Dawcett, what happened to the neighbor? Did he stop drinking?"

"No, sir. He got drunk again shortly after his neighbors

confronted him. Decided nobody was going to tell him how to raise his kids. So he beat his oldest with an empty bottle. Beat him to death. When he realized what he'd done, he put a bullet in his own brainpan. One of the neighbors took in his youngest."

CHAPTER 52
COURT-MARTIAL

THE COURT-MARTIAL BEGAN THE FOLLOWING day. I was surprised to find that there were few soldiers from the base observing, but once I thought about it, I realized that the spaceport was a working base and the men on it likely had little free time. But there was a relatively constant influx and outflow of servicemen and servicewomen in the back of the courtroom as they came on or off duty. The more permanent observers sat closer to the front. That group included an entire row of OTA elders and their bodyguards.

The trial started out mostly as I'd expected, with Collins and his men claiming that they had been under orders to gather supplies from military bases, that they had been on one of those old bases when they had been attacked by a group of hostiles, and that they had only fired back in self-defense.

It seemed to confuse a few of the men that they weren't being questioned about the incident in which they had killed one of the OTA scouts. Mallory kept having to bring them back to the incident in which Tara and her crew were trapped in the waypoint cabin. But after two days of testimony, including mine and that of all the OTA scouts involved in the battle, the trial began to wind down.

It ultimately turned against them when Captain Mallory called Corporal Thompson to testify. Both eyes blackened, nose bandaged, and walking stiffly as he took the stand, Jimbo looked absolutely miserable.

"Corporal, are you all right?" Mallory asked him.

"Yes, sir."

"Are you sure? It looks like you've got some pretty severe damage there. Did you sustain that during the battle?"

"No, sir. I wasn't in the squad involved in that firefight."

"No?" Mallory went back to his table and picked up some notes. "I'm sorry. I must have mixed up my notes. Where did you sustain your injuries?"

Jim hesitated. "I got into a fight."

Mallory raised an eyebrow at that as if surprised. "That must have been one hell of a fight."

"Yes, sir." Thompson glanced in my direction as he answered. "It was."

"But you weren't involved in the altercation in question?"

"No, sir."

"But I have a Corporal Thompson listed as a member of the squad involved in the firefight."

"That was my brother, sir."

"I see. But you are aware of the battle in question?"

"Yes, sir," Thompson said.

"Oh, good. And how do you know about it?"

"I talked to Sergeant Collins about it. I wanted to know what happened to my brother."

"And what, exactly, did he tell you?"

"Sir?"

"Well, was the sergeant happy with the way things went?"

"No, sir. Of course not."

"Really?" Mallory said. "How can you be sure?"

"With all due respect, sir, we lost men that day. Good men."

"That's right. I'm sorry." Mallory looked up from the paper in his hand. "Your brother was one of the two men who died in the battle, wasn't he?"

"Yes, sir."

"And you're sure?"

Corporal Thompson hesitated as if unsure he'd heard correctly. "That my brother is dead?"

"Oh, no. I assume you saw the body when it was brought in. But are you sure about how he died?"

"Yes, sir. Sarge told me how it happened."

"Couldn't he have been mistaken?"

"Not likely, sir."

"Maybe he lied to you?"

"No, sir!" Thompson said. "The sergeant wouldn't lie."

"You're certain of that?"

"Yes, sir."

"Well, what about you? Maybe you heard him wrong. Maybe you missed some detail. For that matter, how do we know you're not lying to the court?"

Thompson was getting upset. "No, sir. I had him give me every detail of what happened when my brother was killed. I heard him just fine, and I don't lie!"

"All right, Corporal." Mallory held his hands up. "I apologize. No need to get upset. I'm just trying to get to the bottom of all this." He pulled another page to the top of the stack he held in his hands. "So, Corporal, you said that you spoke with Sergeant Collins about the firefight in which your brother was killed. Would you please share what you were told?"

"That Dillon was shot when a group of hostiles attacked them from behind."

"And what was Dillon doing when he was shot?"

"He was gathering supplies."

"Where?"

The corporal shrugged. "Sarge didn't say."

Mallory looked up from his papers. "Have you ever been on a supply run?"

"Yes, sir."

"So you're aware of the restrictions placed on such runs?"

"Yes, sir. Any old government facilities, such as old military or National Guard bases, are fair game. So are abandoned buildings far enough away from population centers that they're unlikely to be useful for civilians."

"And civilians?"

Thompson hesitated.

"Corporal?"

"Civilians are off limits," Thompson said.

"And are you aware of the earlier testimony alleging Sergeant Collins and his men not only ignored this order but intentionally confronted civilians and ordered them to surrender their weapons and their supplies?"

"They wouldn't do—"

"Furthermore, are you aware of the claims that when those civilians refused to do so, Sergeant Collins ordered that their goods be taken by force, which resulted in the firefight in which your brother was killed?"

"That's not true!"

At the same time, Collins's counselor stood up. "Objection! Captain Mallory is trying to get the witness to engage in hearsay while the man being charged with the crimes is sitting right here!"

Mallory turned to Everest. "Colonel, this line of questioning isn't to judge the veracity of Sergeant Collins's statements but to determine whether or not Corporal Thompson believes what Sergeant Collins told him. I'll wind it up very quickly here."

Everest nodded. "Very well, Captain. See that you do."

Mallory turned back to Thompson. "Repeating the question, are you aware that multiple witnesses claim Sergeant Collins ordered his men to open fire on civilians, in direct violation of orders indicating that they were not to engage civilians?"

"No, sir!"

"You're not aware of that testimony?"

"Yes, sir. I mean, yes I am aware of the testimony, but I don't believe it to be true."

"We'll set aside for the moment that it's not your place to determine whether or not the testimony is true. I'm curious as to why you don't believe it. Is that not what you were told?"

"No, sir!"

"It's not what Sergeant Collins told you?"

"No, sir."

"What did he tell you?"

"That they were on a supply run when they were attacked."

"At the cabin Near Lake Chickasha?" Mallory asked.

"Yes, sir."

"And who killed your brother?"

"One of the attackers."

"From inside the cabin or outside?"

Corporal Thompson shrugged. "Sergeant said it was hard to tell. They were surrounded."

"That's right. They were attacked from behind."

"Yes, sir."

"Outside the cabin."

"Yes, sir."

"So why didn't they take cover inside the cabin?" Mallory asked.

"They couldn't. There was enemy fire coming from inside."

"From inside the cabin?"

"Yes..." From the look on his face, I guessed that was the first time he had actually thought about the scenario. And I could tell by that look that he finally understood. He pressed his lips together.

"So your brother was part of a squad who found themselves caught between a group of civilians behind them, outside the cabin, and a group of civilians inside the cabin as well. Is that correct?"

"I'm sorry, sir. I wasn't there."

"But you said that you were told what occurred by Sergeant Collins. You also said that Sergeant Collins wouldn't lie."

Thompson stared straight ahead.

"Yet the only way this incident could have happened would be if your brother was part of a squad who was attacking a group who were already inside the cabin... a group of *civilians*."

"But they chased them to the cabin! It's not like they lived there."

"And in order to chase them there, they must have engaged them somewhere else. Either way, Sergeant Collins and his squad must have engaged civilians before they were attacked from behind by the second group outside that cabin."

Collins's defender was on his feet again. "Objection! Leading the witness."

Everest nodded to Captain Mallory. "Wind it up, Captain."

"Corporal Thompson, I simply have one question. In light of all that we have just covered and all the evidence presented to support the scenario, do you still believe Sergeant Collins's testimony that his squad was attacked by a group of unprovoked civilians on the day that your brother was killed?"

Thompson looked from Mallory to where Collins sat, stoic and silent. He looked back at Mallory.

"Well, Corporal?"

Still, Thompson remained silent.

Mallory turned to Colonel Everest. "Colonel, could you instruct the witness to answer the question?"

"Corporal Thompson, you will answer the question, and I will remind you that you are under oath."

Thompson looked directly at Captain Mallory. "No, sir."

"No, sir *what*?"

"No, sir, I don't believe the squad could have been attacked outside the cabin the way it was described to me."

The trial wound up quickly after that. Both sides closed their arguments, leaving Colonel Everest and the panel of jurors to determine the fate of Collins and his men. It took less than two hours.

When we were all seated again, Everest rendered their findings. "This court finds the defendant, Sergeant Anthony Collins, guilty of four specifications of assault, one specification of theft, and one specification of misuse of government property. You are hereby sentenced to an immediate reduction in rank of one pay grade and fifteen lashes to be administered in a public flogging at sunrise tomorrow morning, to be followed by two-weeks' incarceration.

"This concludes these proceedings. I hereby declare this court to be adjourned."

Colonel Everest banged a knob of wood on the desk, and there was considerable stirring in the room. I heard whispers that sounded like people were concerned about the punishment. But I didn't understand it. A week in prison and fifteen lashes didn't sound like much of a punishment. Still, judging from the responses around me, there was clearly something about the sentence that I didn't understand.

Collins, hands cuffed in front of him, kept his face expressionless as two Marines led him from the room.

CHAPTER 53
CORPORAL PUNISHMENT

T HE BUGLE CALL OF REVEILLE pulled me from a restless sleep of worries and bad dreams. As poorly as I had slept though, I was fairly sure that Sergeant Collins—Corporal Collins now—had slept much worse. I almost felt sorry for him but then remembered the deaths he was responsible for.

After splashing cold water in my face, dressing, and eating some of the rations in my pack, I stepped outside to join the rest of the base. I had no idea where to go but quickly found a steady stream of people moving across the grounds toward the airstrip. It wasn't the regimented marching that I had seen so often when various squads moved as one in drill formation. This was loose, organic—a migration of sorts.

I fell in with them, following the general flow until I was one of more than three hundred people who surrounded an open area with a single, large, vertical post in its center. On the far side of the clearing, Colonel Everest, Captain Mallory, and the other officers sat on benches. Elders Walkingstick, Black Horse, and two others I didn't know joined them. A small contingent of braves in full face paint stood to the side of the benches, guarding the elders.

There was a low murmuring as the crowd gathered, and I was soon hemmed in by people on all sides as the last soldiers arrived. After only a few minutes, the murmur slowly ceased, and heads began to turn. I looked behind me to see what had attracted everyone's attention but was pretty sure I already knew.

Sure enough, a detail of Marines, led by Kenni, no less, marched in two lines toward us. Between the lines marched Collins, shirtless and staring straight ahead.

The crowd parted before them without a word being said. The Marine escort stopped at the edge of the clearing, but Kenni continued forward, marching without pause to stand before the post. She inspected the post, grabbing two eyebolts set in its side and pulling on them as though testing to make sure they were set properly.

She turned and nodded. Two more Marines walked to the post, carrying an Old Days blue plastic chest between them. The color was faded, and a corner was broken out. Something was written in white on it, but age had faded it so badly that all I could make out was the last part of the word—"loo."

The Marines put the chest on the ground, reached inside, and pulled out two sets of handcuffs. They hooked them through the eyebolts and stepped back. When they were done, Kenni once more inspected them. She nodded to the Marines who had affixed them, and they stepped aside.

Two more Marines brought Collins forward and manacled him in place. It was all done without a sound from the audience. The silence was a bit eerie.

After a final inspection, Kenni nodded once more to the men who had handcuffed Collins to the post, and they stepped back. They stood at attention around the perimeter of the clearing with all the other Marines except Kenni and Corporal Hardy. I could hear Kenni's boots on the ground as she marched to the officer section and came to attention before them.

She saluted. "Staff Sergeant Kennesha Anderson, reporting prisoner secured and awaiting punishment."

Colonel Everest stood and returned her salute. "Thank you, Sergeant." He reached forward and handed her a piece of paper. "Please carry out the sentence."

"Yes, sir." I watched as Kenni marched back to the center of the clearing, glanced at the paper, and then addressed Corporal Hardy. "Detail, take your position!"

Hardy marched to take a spot approximately ten feet behind Collins. Kenni turned to those of us in the crowd and opened the paper.

She began to read. "In accordance with the sentence legally handed down by court-martial, the prisoner you see before you has been demoted in rank by one pay grade and will receive corporal punishment in the form of fifteen lashes in a public forum. Let all present bear witness to this punishment."

She turned and walked to the blue plastic chest. Leaning over, she took off the lid and picked up the cooler. She carried it to Corporal Hardy, and I watched as he reached inside. My chest tightened as I saw him withdraw a coiled leather whip. After she put the plastic cooler back down, she addressed him directly.

"Punishment detail! On my count!" She paused only a second before shouting, "One!"

Hardy slashed his arm forward, and I jumped at the sound of the cracking whip.

"Two!" Once more, the whip cracked. That time, Collins moaned.

"Three!" *Crack!* Raised red welts were easily visible on his back at that point, and I saw small streams of blood beginning to flow.

"Four!" *Crack!*

"Five!" *Crack!*

"Six!" *Crack!*

"Seven!" *Crack!* There was no mistaking Collins's cry of pain, and it looked as if he was struggling to keep his legs from buckling.

"Eight!" *Crack!*

"Nine!" *Crack!* His legs did collapse then, but he pushed back up again.

"Ten!" *Crack!* He fell again, held up only by the manacles on his wrists.

I could see Kenni hesitate then swallow.

"Eleven!" *Crack!*

A low muttering began to move through the crowd as the

remaining lashes were administered to the hanging prisoner. By the end of the punishment, his back was crisscrossed with bleeding streaks of shredded skin, and he hung weakly from his shackles as two Marines stepped forward and released him, lowering him gently to his knees.

I watched, both fascinated and sickened, as the medic checked him over. He nodded curtly, and the Marines holding Collins up bent, speaking too quietly for anyone else to hear. Collins nodded, and they helped him to his feet, careful not to touch his back as he stood swaying between them.

Kenni pulled herself to attention, turned, and marched back to stand before the officers. She saluted and waited while Colonel Everest stood and returned her salute before handing her another piece of paper. She took it, pivoted on her heel, and once more marched to the edge of the clearing to address the gathering.

Kenni unfolded the paper and read again. "Let it be witnessed that the corporal punishment portion of the sentence has been executed. The prisoner will be incarcerated for a period of two weeks. During this time, he will be overseen by medical personnel while his wounds heal. At the end of this time, he will resume his duties in the capacity of his newly reduced rank with no further repercussions from anyone at this facility."

She paused, looking sternly out over the crowd. "This case is hereby ended. You are all dismissed."

CHAPTER 54
MISGIVINGS

I WANDERED THE BASE FOR A while after the flogging, eventually finding myself at the stables. The sound and smell of the horses was comforting, and I sought out Tallulah. She was in a stall toward the back, and I spent some time making sure she was being taken care of, happy to see that she seemed well groomed and well rested. I stayed with her for a short while before heading back to my quarters.

I'd considered finding Hardy for a workout, but only for a second. I knew he was following orders and that Collins had done more than enough to earn his punishment. But watching a man get whipped until his back was shredded was something that would haunt me for the rest of my life. I imagined it would be worse for the man who'd actually wielded the whip.

I went to my little house in officers' country and just sat in a stupor for a while. Finally, needing to do something, I went to the tiny backyard and began to work out. I started with stretches then did some basic forms from memory. Soon, I moved into freestyle forms. I imagined various opponents attacking, and I threw strikes, kicks, blocks, and parries at my imaginary foes until I lost track of time.

The sting of perspiration in my eyes brought me back to myself. The sun was high overhead, my clothing dripped with sweat, and my stomach growled to let me know I had neglected it too long. It had been several hours since I had started.

I went inside to clean up. Once more, the magic of the shower calmed my nerves as it relaxed my muscles. When I was finished, I washed my clothes in the shower and hung them to dry. I changed into my spare clothes and pulled some travel rations out of my pack. The idea of sitting in the mess hall with the troops just didn't appeal to me. So I munched on jerky and trail mix.

I thought of how I would normally share a bit of the jerked meat with Bella and Cricket and wondered how they were, which led me to wonder about Mr. Roesch and Robin and then about Owen and his wife. Yeah, I was starting to get homesick. It was time to finish up — time to determine whether an alliance with these people was worth all the trouble we had been through.

I was a little startled to realize that I wasn't thinking in terms of getting the United States back on its feet. Public floggings weren't part of the story I had always told myself about the old country. It was ironic that after traveling hundreds of miles to meet with a group of people who claimed to be working to restore the country of my dreams, it finally occurred to me to wonder if such a restoration was even possible.

My gloomy thoughts were interrupted by a knock. When I opened the door, I saw Kenni's face, looking as haunted as I felt.

"You all right?" I asked.

She sighed, walked past me into the den, and collapsed into the couch. "Hell if I know. I just officiated at a public flogging." She leaned forward and put her head into her hands.

I took a seat in the chair opposite her, unsure of what to do or say. I hated the utter helplessness I felt. "Can I get you some water?"

She looked up with a forced smile. "Sure. I'd appreciate that."

I walked into the kitchen and filled a glass from the magical spigot in the sink, noting for a second how quickly I was getting used to having running water. I took the glass to her. "You know he got off easy, don't you?"

She swallowed the water in her mouth and nodded. "I know.

I know he ordered his squad to steal food and supplies from civilians that could indirectly lead to the deaths of the people who were counting on those supplies. I know he ordered his men to attack anyone he saw that had anything he thought they might be able to use here on base. I even know he killed Walt's man."

"Or at least, one of his men did," I said.

"No. He did it himself."

"He told you? Were there any witnesses?" I started to get excited. If we could bring more evidence...

But Kenni shook her head. "No. No witnesses. He didn't actually say anything." She tapped her temple. "But I *saw* into him. He did it. Not that any of his men are going to testify. And my word isn't going to be much in the way of evidence." She stared into her half-empty glass of water. "Besides, I also got the weird feeling that he didn't do it out of malice. He thought he was doing the right thing."

"So he's nuts?"

She shrugged. "He doesn't think so."

I was silent for a few seconds, gathering my thoughts. "You know, I've been thinking about this all day."

"I'd be surprised if you weren't."

"Yeah, I guess so. But you know what? As harsh as that flogging seemed at the time, I can't forget that Collins is responsible for at least one death. When you take that into consideration, he got off easy. Still..."

She waited a minute for me to continue. When I didn't, she prodded. "Still what?"

"There's still something about the idea of a public flogging that doesn't seem right."

She shrugged. "It's probably the fact that it was public."

"What do you mean?"

"This wasn't just a matter of punishment. If that was the case, we could have done it in private. The effect would have been the same as far as Collins is concerned. But Everest made sure it was public."

"Okay. Why does that make it different?"

"Because it means this wasn't *just* a punishment."

I thought about that then nodded. "It was a warning to the rest of the men."

"Yep. And anytime you have to use fear and intimidation to maintain your command, trouble isn't far behind."

"So you think Everest is in trouble with the troops?"

She shrugged. "I don't really know. I've only been back in uniform for a few days, and most of that has been spent working with Mallory on preparations for the trial. Now that it's mostly behind us, I'll be able to get a better feel for what's going on with the base. So far, all I have a feel for is the two squads of Marines I'm in charge of. But there are nearly two hundred soldiers here too. Army, not Marines."

"Don't you outrank them?"

"Sure. But that really doesn't mean a lot. Especially when Everest and Mallory seem to be setting the Marine contingent up as some kind of enforcement group. They're pitting the Marines and Army troops against each other."

"What?"

She shrugged, "It's not overt. Yet. And Collins is the one that triggered it by gathering a group that cared more about what he said than their commanding officers. But you noticed that it was all Marines who conducted this morning's punishment detail, didn't you?"

"Yeah. But I figured it's because Everest knows he can trust you and the other Marines. And then with your rank, I just figured that accounted for it."

"That's what they said. But do you remember who gave me the extra rank? And why?"

I thought about that. "They wanted to bring Collins to justice."

"Again, that's what they said." She shook her head and rubbed her face. "Maybe I'm just too tired. Too paranoid. But it almost seems like everything was orchestrated not just to get Collins but also to put a power base in place for Everest."

"Well, wouldn't you want to make sure your men weren't going to go out and start a war or something with the people you were trying to get to help you? I mean, it's a pretty big stretch to think that Collins was the good guy in all this."

"No. I don't think he was a good guy. That's not what I'm saying. I just think a lot of this has been manipulated to... oh, hell. I'm not sure what I'm saying. It just feels... you know how I told you that the Old Days politicians used to manipulate things to keep themselves in power? It feels sort of like that. Like we're being played somehow."

I didn't know what to say to that. I thought it through, wondering if Kenni was just being paranoid. Was she being used? Were *we* being used?

She interrupted my thoughts.

"Sorry, Zach. I didn't come over here to dump my worries on you. I wanted to let you know that Everest says now that this is all behind us, he can meet with you tomorrow to discuss plans to help with getting the country back on its feet. He'd like to meet with you at midmorning."

"Are you going to be there?"

"No. I'm going to be pretty busy. As a matter of fact, I might not get to see you for a few days."

"What's up?"

"I need to start getting my feet wet with my squads tomorrow. The court-martial is over, and I have to get into the day to day."

"You're not really going to stay here as a Marine, are you? What about Mr. Roesch and Robin?"

She looked pained at that. "I swore an oath. I have to fulfill it."

That caught me off guard. I somehow thought that she was just playing whatever role she had to play in order to get us past the current crisis. In my mind, once Collins and his men were taken care of, she would take off the uniform and go back to helping me. I had never considered that she would actually stay with the military. I stared at her, not knowing what to say.

She rubbed her face. "Sorry, Zach. I don't want to get into all that tonight. I just wanted to let you know that you have a meeting with the colonel tomorrow."

"Sure. Thanks."

She considered for a moment. "And you need to watch yourself. Spend what time you can with Hardy's group, or even go into town and see Keith and that girl of yours." She smiled for a second before getting serious again. "But you need to watch yourself around the Army squads until we see what the fallout from Collins's punishment is going to be."

"Thanks. I'll be careful."

"Good." She stood. "I have one more meeting tonight before I can get some shut-eye."

She looked exhausted. "Still having trouble sleeping?"

She shrugged. "Merry freakin' Christmas, right?"

"I think you're a bit early for that."

"Tell it to Mama."

I walked her to the door. As she touched the knob, she turned once more to me. "If I can, I'll come see you again tomorrow. But don't count on seeing me until you see me."

"All right. Don't worry about me. I'll find out what Everest has to say."

"Just don't let him pressure you." She opened the door but turned back to me again before stepping out. "You're ready for this. You have the knowledge, the background, and the common sense. Don't let him push you around."

"Funny, out of all the times you've told me how you think I'm ready, this is the first time I think you might be right."

Kenni grinned. "You have no idea how much I've wanted to hear you say something like that. That tells me that now you also have confidence. And that's a powerful weapon when you're negotiating." She squeezed my shoulder and left.

CHAPTER 55
VISITORS

I WASN'T SURE WHAT WOKE ME up, but my heart was suddenly pounding as I stared into the inky blackness of the room. Was it a dream? A noise? A memory? My imagination? A slight creak from the next room told me it was definitely not my imagination. Slowly, silently, I reached down to the floor beside my bed and picked up the knife I kept there. I sat up, doing my best to remain silent, but the rustle of the sheets seemed deafening to my ears as I slipped out of bed.

Another noise from deeper in the house told me someone was moving in the kitchen.

Placing each foot quietly and firmly on the floor, I tiptoed to my door and rested my ear against it. I thought I could hear whispers, but it was impossible to be sure. I turned the doorknob so slowly that I wasn't sure it was moving at times. I must have taken a full ten seconds to turn it. But I didn't want to make any noise. When the knob wouldn't turn any farther, I pulled softly, and the door opened a crack. I peeked out. The house was still dark. Staring patiently, I watched for any sign of an intruder. After a few seconds, I thought I saw a slight movement in the kitchen doorway, but it was so dark that I didn't know if it was real or if my eyes were playing tricks on me.

I pulled the door open wide enough to slide through, and I slipped quickly and quietly across the room, clad only in my underwear. Hugging the wall, I approached the doorway into the kitchen. A whispered hiss and a boot dragging on the floor confirmed there was someone in there.

I clenched my eyes closed tight and reached around the door frame, flipping up the switch I knew was there. Voices shouted in surprise, and I flipped the light back off. I jumped through the door, and by the faint moonlight coming in through the kitchen window, I saw three people standing with their hands to their eyes. I leaped forward before they could finish blinking the stars from their eyes and slammed the pommel of my knife against the skull of the first one. He dropped with a grunt, but his body shoved me back as it rebounded off the stove. I heard a rattle and reached forward. My hand fumbled for only a second before I found the handle of a pan I'd left on the stove, and I swung it into the next person's head.

The pan clanged loudly, and another person fell. I was ready for it that time, and as the second body slumped toward me, I stepped over him and grabbed the third person. I slid my hand up to where I could feel his throat and moved my blade up against the back of my hand then slid it up to touch his throat.

"Don't make me slit your throat," I warned, and the man froze. "Good. Now, I'm going to turn the light on. Don't do anything stupid."

I maneuvered him over to the light switch and flipped it up. I turned the man slowly, careful to keep my blade at his throat, and blinked in surprise when I saw his face. Standing before me was Collins, eyes wide as he leaned heavily on the kitchen counter.

"Collins? What the hell? How did...?" I didn't know where to start. The man was supposed to be in the brig. And from the looks of him, he wasn't really in any shape to stand let alone attack me in my quarters.

"You mind if I sit down?"

The man looked as if he was about to fall over anyway. I pulled the knife back and looked him over. Not seeing any weapon, I waved him into the den. "Sit on the couch. I'm going to check out your buddies."

He stepped slowly through the doorway, and I heard him shuffle to the couch. In the meantime, I searched his two companions. Each of them carried a pistol and a knife. I took them all then put the pan in the sink and turned on the faucet. As it began to fill, I popped the magazine from one of the pistols and removed the round from the chamber as Kenni had taught me. I put the ammunition and the two knives in a cabinet and laid the empty pistol on the counter. By then, the pan was full. I shut off the water and tossed the contents of the pan on the two men on the floor.

They jumped as the water woke them, and their eyes narrowed as they saw me holding the pistol. "Come on. Let's get you into the next room with Collins." I waved them to their feet.

I took the chair opposite the couch, sitting right where I'd been when I was talking with Kenni earlier in the evening. But this time I held a pistol aimed at the floor in front of the men seated across from me. Collins leaned forward, and I realized that it had to be hell on the man to lean back on anything.

"So?" I prodded. "Did you come here to rough me up? Threaten me? Kill me?"

Collins shook his head. "I actually planned to scare you a little, but I mostly wanted to give you some information."

"You planned to scare me?"

He chuckled quietly. "Didn't work out as well as I had hoped."

His honesty surprised me. It also made me more inclined to listen to him. "You remember last time you and your men went up against me and mine? You didn't do so well then, either, did you?"

The man nodded. "You caught us by surprise. I was hoping to return the favor." I narrowed my eyes, but he continued. "I didn't think you knew what you were doing. Gotta admit, it looks like I might have been wrong."

"Yeah. You think because a person's not in the military, he hasn't had to fight all his life? You really don't have a clue as to what it's been like out there, do you? We've had to fight just to survive out there. It might not be as bad now, but there was a time after D-day when we fought off one attack after another for a couple of years. We lost friends, family..." I took a deep, calming breath. "And I've trained to fight nearly every day since then so I would be able to protect the ones that were left."

Collins snorted. "You think you're the only ones who've had it rough? I lost my wife when the bombs hit DC. I lost a son in the aftermath." His eyes darkened in anger. "I have another son serving somewhere at sea right now, and I don't know when or *if* I'll ever see him again. You don't have any idea of what all has happened around the world to ensure that you people even had the *chance* to survive! Did it never occur to you to wonder why the attacks on the United States were never followed up by an invasion?"

"Of course it did. It was one of a million other questions we asked each other. It was right up there with 'Who attacked us?' —'How many of our friends and loved ones across the country survived the bombs?' —'Will we ever see any of them again?' — 'Who's going to die in the next wave of raiders?'"

I leaned forward to meet his angry glare. "But one of my all-time favorites was, 'Why hasn't anyone come to help us yet?'" Taking another breath, I leaned back. "Eventually, we realized that there wasn't going to be any beneficial government coming over the hill to pass out food and supplies. No one was going to be bringing aid. We couldn't count on the government or the military. So we learned to take care of ourselves. And you know what? I think we've done pretty well without you."

Collins shook his head. "But you wouldn't have." He turned to his companions. "Wait outside the back door for me."

They left without question. After we heard the door close, Collins turned back to me. "You know how the EMP worked?"

I nodded. "We've been taught about it in school ever since it happened."

He looked surprised at that but continued. "So you know it was line of sight? That it wiped out the electrical grid for the entire continent, right?"

I nodded again.

"Did it never occur to you to wonder why none of our enemies came over here and just wiped up? There were countries all over the world that were out of range. They should have been unaffected, right? Without communications and power, we wouldn't have stood a chance."

I imagined how much fighting must have taken place around the globe. Colonel Everest had said that we'd had subs that survived. They must have gone through hell defending us.

"The submarines?" I asked.

Collins took a deep breath. "Kid, I really believe you and I got off on the wrong foot. I misjudged you. I don't expect you to understand what you walked into here, but I don't blame you for it, either."

"I don't care." I was as blunt as I could manage. "You killed at least one person, an innocent civilian. You stole food and supplies that people need to survive, and that could have caused even more deaths. I don't care how you try to justify it—I *do* blame you for that."

"So we're not going to be best buddies," he said. "I get that."

"Not very damn likely. So tell me whatever it is you wanted to say, and get the hell out of here."

"All right." He stood. "You're going to meet with Everest soon, aren't you?"

I nodded.

"Ever notice the gun safe in the colonel's office?"

I nodded again.

"Ever wonder why he would need a gun safe on a military base where everyone carries their firearms in the open?"

"Not really."

"He brought that safe with him from the coast. It took six of us to load it on the wagon. Damn thing's heavy as hell. But he brought it all the way from the west coast. Across the Rockies. By wagon."

Collins started walking slowly, obviously in pain. "Makes you wonder what's in it, doesn't it?"

I followed him into the kitchen. "So what's in it?"

He picked up the pistol from the counter. "Can I get the magazine back?"

"In the cabinet two doors over."

He opened the cabinet and withdrew the magazine and the knives. "Thanks."

"What's in the safe?" I repeated.

"There's been a rumor for years about something called Operation Silent Night. Supposedly, that's what saved the country."

"Saved it? Have you looked around lately?"

He shrugged. "As bad as it is, things could have been a lot worse. Silent Night is in that safe. One of my men saw it. Just a title on a folder, but it let me know it's real."

Collins held out his hand. "Can I give my men their sidearms back? It'll save us a lot of explanations in the morning."

I popped the magazine out of the pistol in my hand, then cleared the chamber. I handed it to him.

"Thanks. You mind getting the door? I kinda have my hands full."

Stepping past him, I opened the back door. The two goons who had accompanied him waited outside. Collins handed them the weapons and nodded to me. "I think I'm gonna go get my back looked at. Maybe get some rest. Good luck with your talks."

I shook my head and closed the door. Shutting off the kitchen light, I watched as the two big men helped Collins walk slowly back toward the brig.

Operation Silent Night. I recalled Kenni's words. *Merry freakin' Christmas.*

CHAPTER 56
DECISIONS

THE GUARD WALKED AWAY FROM me, lost in his thoughts as he patrolled the fence line, oblivious to me as I crouched in the brush. When I judged him to be far enough away, I ran to the fence. As quietly as I could, I scaled the ten feet of chain link and threw my blanket over the top. My pounding heart told me to simply jump and run, but I knew that would cause the fence to rattle. I forced myself to be methodical as I climbed over and down, pulling the blanket with me.

As soon as I was safely on the ground, I darted to the brush on the other side, finding a spot and crouching before the next perimeter guard came into sight. A few minutes after he was past, I was running into the town of Burns Flat.

⸻ ⸻ ⸻ ⸻ ⸻

"You're sure it was an Armatech brand?" Keith asked.

"That's what it said on the door."

"Okay, about how big?"

I thought about it. "About up to my chin."

"Big one. All right, how wide?"

"Maybe three feet?"

"Are you asking me or telling me?"

"Sorry," I said. "About three feet wide—not quite as deep."

Keith nodded, thinking.

After a moment of nothing else from him, I grew impatient. "So do you think you can do it?"

He said, "Yeah, I think so. How long do we have to get ready?"

"I was hoping we could go now."

He stared at me for a second, studying my face. "You're serious, aren't you?"

"Yes, sir. I have to meet with him in the morning, and I'd like to know for sure."

Keith took a deep breath. "All right. Let me gather up what we're going to need."

Sneaking back into the base was just as easy as sneaking out had been. Getting into Everest's office was a bit trickier, but we managed to find an open window in another office and entered the building through it. From there, it was simple enough to move down the hall to Everest's office, and Keith's lock picks got us in the door almost as fast as if he'd had a key.

We crossed the room to stand before Everest's gun safe. I feared it would be too dark for Keith to work then remembered the sight of him kneeling in the closet of the abandoned house, eyes closed as he concentrated on the feel of the locking mechanism.

"Fifteen minutes?" I grinned at him.

By the dim light that came through the window, I barely saw his return grin. "Let's hope. Go keep an ear on that door. Let me know if you hear anyone coming."

I scrambled to do as he said.

A few minutes later, I heard a click, and a sudden light appeared behind me. I spun around in alarm to see Keith reading the dial by the tiny flame of a small lighter. Heart returning to normal, I turned my attention back to listening at the door.

"Please come in, Mr. Dawcett." Everest waved me to the chair across from his desk. It was the same seat I'd had the first day we met. I glanced around the office, noting but not dwelling on the massive gun safe in the corner.

"Thank you, Colonel." I put my travel bag on the floor beside me and sat.

"That's new." He pointed to my bag.

I hesitated, unsure of how to phrase my decision. I finally settled on blunt. "I'm leaving."

He blinked. "Excuse me?"

"I find myself in a situation that makes it impossible for me to negotiate any longer in good faith."

"After all you've been through to get here?" His expression changed, and his eyes narrowed. "I'll be damned. It was you."

I tried to keep my expression neutral. "*What* was me?"

"I thought maybe one of Collins's men or even one of the Indians. I never really considered you." Everest sighed. "I check that safe every morning. I'm sure you noticed when you broke in that there are quite a few reports in it. I conduct a lot of the day-to-day business for the base with papers in there."

He knew. I'd known there was a chance but hadn't really considered it that much of a risk. But there was no need hiding it anymore. "It was me. I'd hoped the fact that there were so many would keep you from noticing one missing file."

"Not *that* file."

I just nodded.

Everest drummed his fingers on his desk. "This puts us in a bad predicament. What did you do with it?"

I reached into my bag and pulled out the folder. I slid it across his desk.

"Well, that makes things a bit better." He took the folder and thumbed through it, presumably to make sure I hadn't taken anything out of it. After nodding, he put it down and looked back at me. "So now what do I do with you? You realize that what you've done is considered a treasonous act, don't you?"

"I realize that you may see it that way."

"It's not a matter of how I see it. The United States is still under martial law. You stole top-secret government documents.

That's treason, plain and simple." He shook his head. "Guards!" he yelled.

I heard boots running up the hallway.

"Colonel, as it is, I was willing to just walk away. If you try to push this treason thing, you're essentially committing an act of war."

Private Tibbik opened the door. "Yes, sir?"

Everest held up a hand. "Tibbik, do you have a security detail out there?"

"Yes, sir."

"Post them outside my door until I call for them."

"Yes, sir. Will that be all?"

"For now," Everest said.

Tibbik closed the door, and Everest nodded to me. "All right. This should be good. Who am I committing an act of war against?"

"The Sabine River Trading Coalition."

Everest shook his head. "Sorry, you're going to have to do better than that."

"Why? We both represent groups that are trying to rebuild. We both have significant forces behind us—"

"You're not seriously trying to put your little trading coalition on an equal footing with the United States of America, are you?"

"No, I'm not. I'm putting us on equal footing with the people you represent, who are currently *claiming* to represent the United States of America."

That stopped him. His brow furrowed as he chewed my words. "So you think I'm another Crazy Larry?"

"No, Colonel. We called him that because he really was crazy. I don't think you're crazy at all. I simply think you're working for a group of people who are claiming to represent a nation that no longer exists. I'm sure that you're here in good faith, sent by people who *you* believe have the authority to send you. But as my dad used to tell me, just because you believe something's true doesn't necessarily make it so."

Everest sighed. "Sorry, son. I honestly like you. But I don't have time to try and show you how many ways you're wrong. I have a base to run and a nation to rebuild. And I can't have you running around to the public, spreading stories about a top-secret operation that you should never have found out about. So as much as I might not want to do it, I'm afraid I'm going to have to hold you until we can figure out what to do about this." He looked past me at the door and took a breath as if to shout again.

"Just one more minute." I reached into my bag again and pulled out what I hoped was my ace in the hole. "You are aware that the EMP did leave some small electronics untouched, aren't you?"

"Yes." His tone was cautious.

"I had an old music player when I was younger. It had survived the pulse, just a random item that happened to be in the right place to get just the right amount of shielding. It ran on batteries for a few years before I dropped it."

"What—"

I pressed the button on top and handed Everest the Old Days camera we had found in Hammer Hanson's fire safe. "If you look at the screen on back, you can scroll through the last several pictures."

He did, sighing as he saw the pictures of the pages of Operation Silent Night. "So you broke into my safe, stole the folder, took pictures of the documents, and now you're giving me back the folder and the pictures?"

"Not quite. If you look in the side of the camera, you'll see that the memory card is missing."

He lifted the cover on the side of the camera. "So you have copies of the pictures."

"Yes, sir."

"And what good are they? Without a computer and some way to distribute copies, a memory card does no one any good."

"I already told you about my music player. You have a working camera in your hands. Do you really think I would give it to you if it was the only one? For that matter, do you really think no one is going to find a working home computer and printer? For all I know, there are already several in existence."

Everest slammed his hand down on his desk. "Dammit, kid! Why are you doing this?"

"Because despite the fact that you've had these files for all this time, you don't seem to really understand what they mean."

"*I* don't understand? I spent five years fighting my way across Europe, fighting to destroy one of the last nuclear-missile silos, because a nation that had been our ally before D-day was planning to launch against us. Our ally! After D-day, the world turned into a very nasty place."

"After D-day? Or after Silent Night? Isn't it possible that from that other country's perspective, they were retaliating against a nation that had willingly plunged the entire world into chaos and killed millions of people in the process?"

"If we hadn't, every hostile nation in the world would have rolled in here and taken over. There were hard decisions that had to be made, or the United States would have ceased to exist!"

"With all due respect, Colonel, I think the United States ceased to exist on D-day. Silent Night was just the body thrashing around, not realizing it was already dead. All we can do now is try to rebuild something from what's left. And whatever it may be, it will never be the same nation that it was."

He leaned back in his chair, shoulders slumped. "You're forcing my hand. You realize that, don't you?"

"No, sir, I'm not. I've already told you I'm willing to walk away."

"But I can't let you. Whether you believe in them or not, I have to take my orders from higher up the chain of command. It's not up to me to decide whether or not you can walk."

I didn't try to stop him when he called the guards that time. Two Marines came in, men I recognized from our sparring sessions, Richmond and Sanders.

"Take Mr. Dawcett into custody. Treat him as a VIP, but he is to be held until I get orders from higher up."

"Yes, sir."

It was a different room that time, but it looked just like the office they had put me in when I first arrived at the base. Same white walls. Same empty desk. Same empty chair. Same empty cot.

"Home sweet home," I muttered as Richmond motioned me inside.

"Sir?"

"Nothing. Would you do me a favor, though, and let Sergeant Anderson know where I am?"

He looked up and down the hall to make sure no one was within earshot. "Sanders already sent word."

"Thanks."

He nodded. "I don't know what's going on here, but I hope it gets straightened out, Zach. I always enjoyed sparring with you."

"I'm afraid those days may be over," I said sadly.

"I hope not. I'm not looking forward to things going back to the way they were before you and the sarge got here."

I just sighed, and Richmond closed the door behind me.

CHAPTER 57
BREAKOUT

I T WAS SEVERAL HOURS BEFORE the door opened again. I was lying on the cot, expecting Kenni, but Hardy walked in, looking grim. I sat up and swung my legs over the edge of the cot. "Where's Kenni?"

Hardy turned and closed the door behind him. "Sergeant Anderson has been relieved of duty."

"What?"

"Colonel Everest accused her of helping you to do something, but he won't say what it was. All he'll say is that you've committed treason and that she must have known about it. I just got through locking her up next door to you." He pointed to the wall.

"But she didn't know anything about it! It was a spur-of-the-moment thing, and the only other person who knew about it..." But I'd told Everest that someone else knew. Of course he would suspect Kenni. I put my head in my hands. "Oh, hell."

When I looked up, Hardy was staring at me. "Are you telling me it's true? Treason? What the hell did you do, Zach?"

"I found out something I wasn't supposed to, and Everest is calling it treason. From his perspective, it may be. From mine, it's not."

"Just for finding something out?" Hardy shook his head. "I can't see him doing that. The colonel's a hard man, but he wouldn't do something like that."

"Well, I sorta broke into his safe to do it."

"You what?"

"I had to know if it was true."

"You broke into his safe?"

I nodded. "It was the only way to know for sure."

"To know what?"

I hesitated. "Everest says it's top secret. You sure you want to know? He might lock you up too."

Hardy pursed his lips, considering. "Tell me."

"You ever heard of Operation Silent Night?"

"Sure. It's like an urban legend. Some sort of top-secret operation that saved the world." His eyebrows shot up. "So is this where you tell me it's not an urban legend?"

I nodded.

"You know what it was?"

"Yes."

"And that's why he locked you up?"

"Yes."

"That doesn't make sense," Hardy said.

"It's not pretty. The United States doesn't necessarily come out looking..." I wasn't sure how to put it. "The US government did something terrible. They thought they were saving the country, and maybe they were. But it was still a terrible thing to do."

Hardy walked to the desk chair and sat. "Spill."

"All right. It was a contingency plan in case of something like D-day. Evidently, the government had known that the country was vulnerable to a massive EMP strike for several years, but no one had done much about it. Politicians kept kicking the can down the road because it would cost too much to harden the grid. Instead, they came up with a plan.

"They knew that an EMP attack would basically cripple the nation, so in order to keep any other nation from invading us, they developed Silent Night. In the event that the unthinkable ever happened, and the United States fell to an EMP, they would launch their own missiles from submarines around the world.

"It was a fail-safe that guaranteed that if the US was plunged into the Stone Age, no other nation would have an advantage over them. So within hours of the strikes against the US, three select submarines launched missiles that they detonated in a series of high-altitude explosions that guaranteed the entire world suffered the same fate."

"Bullshit. No one would be that crazy."

"Why not? For decades, the world was kept from nuclear war by a policy of mutually assured destruction. This was just a variation."

Hardy was agitated, chewing his lip as he thought. "You found this in Everest's safe?"

"Yes. And more. There were estimates on what kind of casualties to expect, more estimates that were written after Silent Night was implemented, estimates on how long it should take to rebuild afterward. Plans on how to begin reconstruction and how to keep the populace complacent while using them as labor to rebuild the infrastructure."

I spread my hands. "This base? Your mission? It's all part of the playbook. The details might vary, but the plan is the same."

"And you confronted him with this? What the hell did you expect him to —"

"I didn't say a word to him. Not at first. I just said I wanted to leave. I even talked to him about it. Told him all I wanted was to go home. I didn't want anything to do with any of it. But he locked me up instead. Said he had to get orders on what to do with me."

"Well, I don't think he's waiting. Now that you and Sarge are locked up, he jumped me up to sergeant, and I'm supposed to be putting together a firing squad."

My heart was suddenly trying to pound its way out of my chest. "Firing squad?"

"He says if you manage to agitate the hostiles in town, we could have a bloodbath on our hands. Says it's for the greater good."

"So he's going to execute me?"

"You and the sarge, both."

"But that's..." *What — crazy? Murder?* A tiny little voice in the back of my mind reminded me that Everest had labeled my actions as treason against the United States. Death by firing squad was probably completely justified in his mind. And if Hardy fell into line, Kenni and I didn't have a chance.

"But he went through all kinds of trouble to make sure Collins got a fair trial, and execution wasn't even on the table. Now he's going to execute us without any trial at all? That doesn't make sense."

"It does for treason!" He was clearly worked up.

"No, it doesn't! Think about this for a second. When we were figuring out how to handle Collins, one of the reasons he wasn't brought up on charges for killing that civilian was that Everest didn't have the authority to try a murder case without sending back home for more officers. If he didn't have enough rank to try a murder case, how can he suddenly have the authority to execute someone for treason without any trial at all?"

"I don't know. Because it's treason?"

"You don't really believe that, do you?"

He pursed his lips and shook his head. "I don't know what to believe right now. You know, I had hoped you would tell me this was all just some kind of misunderstanding."

"I think it is. Just not the one you were hoping for."

He sat silently for several seconds, staring my direction without really looking at me. Eventually he shook his head and stood. "I'm gonna go see what Sergeant Anderson has to say."

"Can I see her?"

"I'll see what I can do."

"Thanks."

Hardy shook his head. "This is some seriously screwed-up shit you stirred up."

"I know. But think back to all the other things you know about me. Did I ever do anything that was crooked?"

"Not until you told me you broke into that safe."

I had no rebuttal for that, and he closed the door behind him.

I received seven meals and three more bathroom breaks before I heard from Hardy again, so I knew it was more than a full day later. The door opened, and he stepped inside. Kenni was right behind him.

"So I hear you found my Christmas carol," she said.

"Yeah. See where it got us?"

Hardy looked from Kenni to me. "What are you two talking about?"

But Kenni shook her head. "You wouldn't believe me if I told you."

"Whatever. Look, I have a window of about five minutes before another guard comes around. Let's get this over with."

"Get what over with?" I asked.

"We're leaving," Kenni said. "We're supposed to leave the same way you got out with Keith."

"How do you know about that?"

She tapped her head. "Walkingstick told me. At least, I'm pretty sure it was her. Do you know a way out?"

"Sure, if we can get out of this building without being seen."

Hardy started ushering us both toward the door. "That's what I've been saying. But now we're down to four minutes." He walked us to the door and stopped. "This is where I stop. Sarge, it's been a real pleasure."

"Same here. But I'm not your sergeant anymore." And to my utter shock, she punched him in the face.

Hardy staggered back a bit, shook his head, and smiled as his nose began to bleed. He handed her his keys. "Thanks."

Kenni smiled back. "Go lay down and wait for someone to find you."

"Will do. Have a good life, Sarge."

"Just Kenni now. You're the sergeant."

Hardy nodded and lay down on the floor as Kenni dragged me out of the room. She locked the door behind us. "Which way?"

I was surprised to find that it was completely dark as we slipped out of Alcatraz. Being locked inside that white room had robbed me of my sense of time once more. But I was thankful for the darkness as we moved within the inky blackness between buildings. As we slipped behind the woodshop, I spotted a tarp-covered pallet. I pulled off the tarp and wrapped it around me.

Kenni looked at me like I was crazy. "What the hell are you doing?"

"We're going to need it." I trotted away before she could ask more.

It took only a couple of minutes to reach the clearing across from where I'd scaled the fence. I watched as the guard walked past, then I pointed. "See that spot of weeds on the other side of the fence?"

"Yes."

I began folding the tarp as I spoke. "It's right on the edge of a little depression. After the guard turns that corner, we scale the fence and run for those weeds. Once there, we wait for the guard to make another pass, and then we run for town."

Kenni shook her head. "What about the razor wire at the top?"

I held up the folded tarp, and she grinned.

A whistle sounded behind us. It was quickly followed by shouts and the sound of boots as people began running. The guard ran toward Alcatraz.

"Let's go!"

I sprinted for the fence, hearing the sound of Kenni's boots behind me. "Hold this," I whispered, handing her the tarp. I scaled the fence to within a foot of the top and held one hand back down. She handed me the tarp, and I slung it over the razor wire. Thirty seconds later, the two of us were sprinting toward town.

CHAPTER 58
REPERCUSSIONS

EITH, JOHN, SIMON, AND WALELA, as well as Bella and Cricket, were waiting for us at the edge of town. I smiled at the sight of Walela's worried face but wondered aloud at the team's presence.

"Miss Walkingstick said you might need some help." She handed me the weapons I had left with them weeks before. Keith handed Kenni her gear at the same time.

It felt good to strap on my pistols once more and even better to have my knives, bow, and quiver. And even though I knew how she was going to answer, I felt obligated to ask, "How did she know we were even coming?"

Kenni shook her head as she strapped on her own weapons. "You still don't believe? Even after everything you've seen?"

I didn't know what to say. There was really no other explanation, but I still fought the idea that Kenni had some kind of power. That was probably because they wanted to paint me with the same brush, though with admittedly lighter strokes.

"Sorry. I guess I'm still having trouble with it. So what now?"

"You're supposed to come with us to meet with the elders," Keith said.

The team led us to the same hotel and same room where I had previously met Walkingstick. It was hard to believe that had been just two days before. She and two other elders greeted Kenni and me as we entered. I recognized Black Horse as he nodded at me, but the third was a younger man I hadn't met—younger than the other two elders, anyway, though still considerably older than any of the rest of us.

"It's good to see you made it here all right," Walkingstick said.

"Thank you," Kenni replied. "I'm glad you heard me."

The old woman said, "I told you that you were stronger than you knew."

I shook my head, and Walkingstick chuckled. "And still you have trouble believing?"

"I don't mean to be disrespectful. It's still just—"

The younger man sitting beside her interrupted. "Can we stop all this mysticism crap already? We don't have time to pussyfoot around." He turned to me. "She's psychic, your friend's psychic. It took me a while to get used to it, but there we are. I suggest you catch up to the rest of us. Right now, if Miss Walkingstick tells me a fight is coming, then I prepare for a fight."

That caught me by surprise. "A fight?"

"What did you think was going to happen when you broke out of their prison and sought shelter with us?"

I hadn't considered that, but he was right. "Then we have to go."

"Too late, son. It's already in motion."

I looked from him to Walkingstick. The old woman nodded. "As unsubtle as Mr. Nashoba may be, he is correct. We will have fighting here no matter what you choose to do. And it will happen very soon."

I felt like crap. I'd brought a fight right to their door simply because I hadn't thought through all the ramifications of my actions. "I'm sorry." The words were pitifully inadequate. Bella must have felt my agitation, because she nudged up against my leg, and I absentmindedly reached down to scratch her.

Walkingstick held up her hand. "Don't worry. It was going to happen soon anyway. But I do need to ask what your intentions are now that you're free."

"You mean as far as an alliance goes?"

"Yes."

I shook my head. "There's not going to be any alliance."

"Because they imprisoned you?" Walkingstick asked.

"No. At least, not directly. They imprisoned us because I broke into the colonel's safe and learned about an Old Days top-secret operation."

"Yes. Silent Night. Keith showed me what the two of you found in the colonel's safe. My eyes aren't good enough to read the documents on such a small screen, but he read it to me. It was chilling."

"That was why I broke off talks with Everest," I said. "I told him I couldn't recommend an alliance with a group that would condone such an act. I also have come to believe that the United States, as it was before D-day, is now long since gone. Whatever comes next will depend on what we build. And I can't see any good coming from building on the foundation of Silent Night."

Walkingstick nodded once. "You've shown considerable wisdom. I'm sure your Mr. Roesch will be proud." She spread her hands. "And what about us? I once told you that an alliance with the OTA might be to your advantage. At that time, you said you couldn't know that until you met the soldiers at the base. How do you feel about it now?"

That caught me by surprise. I couldn't believe she was trying to pressure me into an alliance when they claimed a battle was brewing. I was about to say as much when I noticed Bella's ears twitch forward. I looked at Cricket and saw her doing the same. The girls stared at Walkingstick then back at Kenni. And again, I realized there was more going on than what I could see.

So I calmed myself, thinking it through rationally, and I realized that, even though I had brought a fight to their door and had accepted their help in escaping, I still hadn't declared an alliance. It also occurred to me that without an alliance, they were under no obligation to protect us at all. Not that I thought they would, but they would be completely within their rights to turn Kenni and me over to Everest at his first challenge.

I had been using them, taking advantage of the kindness they had shown at every opportunity. It was time to acknowledge that. "Under the circumstances, I'd be foolish to pass up the opportunity to work with the people who have helped me at every chance. I will definitely be recommending an alliance with the OTA."

All three elders nodded as if some official ceremony had just taken place. "Good. We look forward to settling the terms of the alliance at a later date. For now, let's take care of the business at hand."

— ✶ — ✶ — ✶ — ✶ — ✶ —

Mr. Nashoba had turned out to be in charge of defense, and he began issuing orders even as we all walked out of the hotel. "We meet them in the clearing in front of the old granary. I want teams all around in the shadows and inside every building and on every roof that has line of sight to the area. No one fires unless the soldiers fire first, or I give the order." He shouted orders to hundreds of men and women, all of whom sported face paint similar to what we had seen before, though I'd never seen them in such numbers. Some lined the road leading into town, while others ran to hide in and behind various buildings, ready to jump into battle if necessary.

He would issue orders to one group of runners, who would nod and leave only to be immediately replaced by more. They had obviously been working on this plan for a while, for his orders came without hesitation. Nashoba's only stumble came when Walkingstick announced that she was going to meet Everest in the clearing. He protested until she stopped him with a negligent wave of her hand.

"It's what has to happen. I've seen it."

Nashoba rolled his eyes. "Well, that's just freaking wonderful." But he didn't argue any more, confirming his belief in Walkingstick's professed abilities. "Braves! Extra eyes out for Elder Walkingstick! We do nothing that might endanger her while she negotiates."

We didn't have long to wait. Half an hour later, runners from the picket line reported that soldiers were mounting up inside the base. Hearing that report caused me a pang of guilt as I thought about Tallulah still held in her stall on the other side of that fence. There had been no way to get her during our rushed escape.

Seeing there was nothing we could do, Kenni and I tried to keep out of the way, and eventually all the preparations had been made. All we had left to do was wait. I was struck by the silence. There were hundreds of people lining the streets, eerie with their painted faces. But they were so quiet I could hear the crackling of the campfires two blocks away and the guttering of nearby torches as the flames wafted in the predawn breeze.

And then I heard the faint clanking of the gate nearly a quarter of a mile away as it opened and a line of soldiers began filing out of the base. Many of them, too, held torches as they wound slowly down the road toward us.

"You two need to get out of sight." Walela's whisper startled me as her hand touched my shoulder. Turning, I was startled to see her wearing war paint like everyone else, though I smiled a bit at the hummingbird symbol on her forehead. Then I realized just how well I could see her. The sky was beginning to redden with the first hints of the rising sun, and if I could see her, then soon it would be easy enough to see my face as well. Walela and Keith started pulling Kenni and me toward a nearby building.

"No." I shook her off. "I'm not leaving Walkingstick out here to take the heat for me."

Keith grabbed my shoulder in a huge hand. I had known he was big, but that was the first time he'd used his size against me. It was intimidating, to say the least. "If the soldiers see you out there, it could start the very fight she's trying to avoid. Let's do what we can to help her, not make things worse."

And though it galled me to sit back while someone else took on Everest, Keith was right. Still, I wasn't going to be out of reach, hidden away in some building, either. "Fine. I'll wait in the shadows at the back of the crowd back here. No one will know I'm here, and I'll mind my manners, but I'm not going to go hide, safe and sound, while she faces the soldiers."

"But my orders—"

"Are not *my* orders. Who told you to get me out of here? Nashoba?"

"Yes. He told me to carry you if necessary."

"Well, Nashoba doesn't give me orders. Just tell him you tried and Kenni used her voodoo on you. Tell him anything you want, but I'm not going any farther than the back of this crowd."

I moved into the crowd, as promised, and Kenni followed.

"You okay with this?" I whispered to her.

"I'm your assistant, remember? You give the orders, and I follow your lead."

"That's not what I asked." I turned to look at her. "Are you okay with me potentially putting us in danger?"

She grinned. "You're being prudent in staying out of sight, and responsible in staying where you can move in if needed. So yes, I'm okay with it. I wouldn't have it any other way."

I felt Walela's fingers intertwine with mine at my side. Bella and Cricket sat beside me, panting as they leaned reassuringly against my legs. Looking around, I saw the familiar stances of the rest of the team, and I felt better having my friends around me. I reflected on that thought, but they *were* my friends. They had shown it repeatedly in their actions, and I wondered how I had ever considered an alliance with Everest when the honor and integrity of these people had been so obvious from the first day I had met them.

Together, we watched as the line of soldiers poured through the gate.

There were both mounted and foot soldiers, and all were dressed differently than I had ever seen them during the time I'd been at the base. All wore helmets and bulky jackets. Every single one of them carried a rifle and had various pouches strapped to their uniforms. They looked more formidable than I had ever seen them up to that point, and there were so many of them that the back of the line was still filing out of the gate when the leaders halted before Walkingstick, who had planted herself firmly in the middle of the street.

Everest dismounted and approached her. "Miss Walkingstick, isn't it?"

"Yes, Colonel. To what do I owe the pleasure?"

He looked at the hundreds of stoic faces all around them and chuckled. "Pleasure? Somehow, I don't think either of us considers this a pleasure."

"Yet here we are. You with your army and me with mine. I hope we can keep things at least civil if not pleasant."

"Agreed. And if you would be so kind as to turn over to us the prison escapees that are no doubt hiding here, we can all go back to our daily business with no... *unpleasantness*."

"Prison escapees? But I thought your base was in the business of launching satellites. You mean it's a prison?"

Everest sighed. "Madam Walkingstick, I have no doubt that you mean well. But I don't have time for games. You will turn Zachary Dawcett and Kennesha Anderson over to me immediately, or I'll have to order my men to search this town door by door and remove them by force."

"That would be unpleasant indeed."

"I thought you would see it that way."

"Yes. Because the minute you issue that order, you will force my people to retaliate in response to your blatant aggression against the Oklahoma Tribal Alliance."

He looked around at the silent warriors lining the streets. "That would be unfortunate. Especially since I see nothing but hunting rifles, pistols, and bows."

"Yes. That *is* all you see."

"Look, you can play all the word games you want. None of it will alter the fact that we have superior firepower and body armor. I don't think your bows and arrows are going to have much effect. Now, you *will* turn over my prisoners, or I will order my men to dismount and begin searching the town."

"Silent Night."

Everest closed his eyes. I saw his shoulders rise and lower with a sigh I couldn't hear. I heard him tell the old woman, "I'd hoped he was bluffing. But he really had another copy?"

"He did."

"And you have it?"

"Not any longer. It's already been sent by courier to a safe place."

"Damn it!" Their conversation had been relatively quiet up to that point, so his exclamation seemed extraordinarily loud by comparison.

He whipped a pistol out and pointed it at Walkingstick. Rifles, pistols, and bows came up all around them as both soldiers and braves readied for a fight.

"Hold!" Nashoba's voice cut through the night as he stepped forward. He walked up to the colonel, his own pistol drawn. "Colonel, I will give you ten seconds to lower your weapon or I will shoot you where you stand."

Everest ignored him. "Dawcett!" he shouted. "Dawcett! I know you're nearby. I was going to give you thirty seconds, but this man says we only have ten. Show yourself, and this doesn't have to get any worse."

"Ten!" Nashoba shouted, pistol aimed at Everest's head. Soldiers aimed at Nashoba, and braves aimed at soldiers. The conflict had quickly reached a flash point.

"Come on, Dawcett! None of us wants this!"

"Nine!"

Memories of Crazy Larry pointing a pistol at my head jumped to mind, and without thinking, I stepped forward. "I'm here!" I was *not* going to have another group of people fight my battles for me while I stood by and did nothing. I was *not* the same helpless child I had been. That was *not* going to happen again.

"Eight!"

Kenni, Keith and the others flanked me as I stepped out of the crowd. "Lower your pistol, Colonel. This is getting out of hand."

"Seven!"

He pulled his pistol away from Walkingstick, focusing on me as I moved toward him. "Zachary Dawcett, I charge you with espionage and dissemination of classified information to a foreign body. This is a treasonous act punishable by death." Suddenly, the pistol was pointed at me. "Sorry, son."

Kenni yanked me aside while Keith shoved, and the morning was filled with the sounds of gunfire.

CHAPTER 59
WAR PAINT

THE BODY ARMOR EVEREST HAD mentioned proved to be his salvation. When the shooting started, I saw him take at least three hits before his men gathered around him. Then he and his soldiers scattered, breaking into squads as they attempted to overrun various buildings. Kenni and Walela were pulling at me while John and Simon tugged at Keith's limp form lying on the street beside me.

Blood began to pool beneath him as I realized that he had taken the bullet meant for me. I shrugged off the hands tugging at me. "Stop it! Let's get Keith into a building."

I didn't give them a chance to argue. I grabbed the big man's legs, while John and Simon each took an arm. A pair of soldiers rode at us, but before they got closer than thirty feet, Bella and Cricket charged, growling and barking as they snapped at the lead horse, causing it to rear. The rider struggled to bring his mount under control as his companion swerved to avoid a collision. Kenni and Walela swung their rifles to bear, each firing and knocking the riders off their horses. I had no idea if the men were all right, and I honestly was more concerned with the horses as the dogs continued snapping at them.

"Bella, Cricket, come!" I yelled as we carried Keith through the crowd and around the corner. The girls abandoned their harrying of the now riderless horses and ran back to me. Just as they joined us, painted faces waved us into the doorway of an old brick building. The sign on the wall said it had once been an air-conditioning repair shop, and I recalled my parents telling me about conditioned air and how cold it could be, even on the warmest summer day.

"On the counter over there." One of the new people pointed, and with his help, we managed to get Keith on a high counter with an Old Days computer on it. John took over from there, checking Keith's pulse and making sure he was still breathing. He had a hole in his left shoulder, just below the collarbone, and I recalled how I had noticed on the first day I'd met him that my head came to about that point. Everest had really been trying to kill me.

"Bullet's still inside him," John said. "I'm just gonna patch him up for now. We'll worry about getting the slug out later, assuming there is a later for us."

That cemented everything for me. The colonel might have been loyal to his beliefs, and in his mind, he was probably doing what he thought was right. But his beliefs weren't mine. And I wasn't about to let him kill me or my friends because of them.

I took Walela's hand. "Help John take care of Keith."

I realized I had dropped my rifle in the street when I'd picked up Keith's legs, so I reached over my shoulder to pull my bow. I turned, and I had my arm raised when Walela punched me in the ribs. It was hard enough to hurt, but not enough to do damage.

"What th—"

"Don't you ever try to keep me out of a fight. Especially one that you're about to jump into."

"That's not what I meant." Though I knew in my heart that it was. "Keith needs—"

"Keith needs a medic. John's the team medic, not me. And I am not about to sit back and watch while the man I love goes off to battle."

We both realized what she said at the same time. "You love me?"

She punched me again. "Screw you! This isn't the time or the place. We have things to do." She pulled out a small wooden container and unscrewed the lid. Inside were partitions with several colors of face paint that she dipped her fingers into. "This will keep any of our people from mistaking you for one of the soldiers."

"There's no time."

"It'll take less than two minutes. I'm not going to get all fancy, but it won't do any of us any good if you get shot. Right now, the soldiers are looking for you, and most of my people don't know you. This takes care of both problems."

"Somebody paint Kenni's face," she called out to no one in particular, and I saw one of the others from the building pull out a similar wooden container.

Walela smeared a white base on me, reciting as she did. "This is for the brothers and sisters who will lose their lives today."

She painted green around my eyes. "This is for endurance and vision."

Dipping a finger in the blue, she began drawing a quick series of lines on my forehead. "Blue is for wisdom and confidence. The shape of opposing arrows shows you are at war."

She coated the palm of her hand with black. She pressed it over my mouth, spread fingers marking my left cheek. "Black is the color of strength and victory. The shape of the hand represents the victories you've already brought us. It shows that you've proven yourself in battle and can be trusted not to falter in a fight."

Then she put red on her lips and kissed me on the other cheek. "Red is for energy and strength in battle." She closed the lid on her paints.

"What's the lip print mean?"

"It means that any other woman that has any ideas about you will have me to deal with."

I smiled. When I turned, Kenni was nearly unrecognizable, painted, just as I was, with various colors and symbols.

"We ready?" I asked.

"Not yet." Walela dipped her finger in the blue and approached Kenni. Drawing quickly, she did something to Kenni's face. When she stepped back, the braves in the room appeared surprised.

"What did you do?" Kenni asked. She turned to me. "What did she do?"

I cocked my head and shrugged. "Put something like a diamond inside a diamond, with a dot in the center, on your forehead."

"What's it mean?"

"It tells everyone that this person is able to bridge the gap between our world and the spirit world," Walela said. "It marks you as a shaman."

"Well, shit."

"It's what you are."

Kenni sighed. "I guess." She turned to me. "So what's the plan?"

I finished pulling my bow. I planted one end against my foot, bending and stringing it in a well-practiced motion. "Find Everest. Capture or kill him. Stop the fighting."

Kenni snorted. "Sounds simple enough. Any idea how we're going to do all that?"

"Not a clue." I turned to John. "Take care of Keith." He just nodded. He was already pouring herbs from his pouch, and I knew he would do what he could.

I bent over Bella and Cricket. "I can't be worrying about you in the street." I led them by their collars to the counter where John was working on Keith. Holding up an open palm, I gave the accompanying command. "Stay."

They sat.

I laid my left hand on John, who looked up at me briefly as I closed my right hand into a fist. "Guard."

They dropped their heads, and I could feel that they knew I was leaving them and that they weren't happy about it. But they would obey. I almost told them they were good girls, but I knew they would take that as an excuse to come to me, so I turned without another word.

The immediate barrage of gunfire in the street outside had faded. It sounded like there were several smaller fights going on in all directions. I went to the door and peeked out just as a small team of braves ran past across the street. I darted out after them, uncaring of who might follow me. I knew they would, but I would just as soon everyone had stayed behind. I didn't want the weight of worrying about who was going to be injured or killed on my behalf. I had grown up with that burden. It had branded me since I was ten years old. And my goal was to end this fighting as soon as possible to minimize any further karmic debt.

I caught up with the team I had seen. "Behind you," I whispered, and one of them spun, pointing a rifle at me.

"Who are you?"

"Zachary Dawcett. The one the soldiers are looking for."

"Well, this is a fine pile of dog shit you dumped us in."

"He has a habit of doing that," Simon said from behind me. I turned and saw the grin on his face. "On the up side, he usually lets me use his toys while we dig our way out." He held out my rifle. "You left it in the street."

It seemed pretty telling that I had dropped my rifle but managed to hang onto my bow. "Keep it. I'm not that good with it anyway."

Simon nodded then looked at the other man. "See what I mean?"

"Do you know if Walkingstick and Nashoba are all right?" I asked as Kenni, Walela, and two other braves from the conditioned-air shop came up behind us.

"Nashoba was injured but was still able to get Elder Walkingstick to safety," the brave before me said. "They were supposed to be heading for the old Technology Center about six blocks away."

"What about Colonel Everest?"

"The soldier that started this mess? He and a bunch of other soldiers got into the granary and are holding everyone else off with those damned machine guns of theirs."

"He can't do that for long," Kenni said. "They'll run out of ammunition pretty quickly."

"But a lot of people could die before that happens," I said. "What about the rest of the soldiers?"

"There's half a dozen pockets where they've overrun the

people we had in buildings." The unknown brave pointed up the road. "We're heading for one right now—a group of about twenty soldiers holed up in the old discount store around the corner. We got word that they're pretty hardcore. Act like they don't care whether they live or die."

Kenni and I looked at each other.

"We've got orders to flush them out," he said.

"You got a plan?" I asked.

"A couple. If they surrender, we take them prisoner. If they don't..." He shrugged, indicating that we should already know how the sentence ended.

Kenni shook her head. "That would cost too many lives. Especially if it's who we think it might be."

"You got a better idea?"

She nodded. "Maybe. Lead us there, and let me see if they'll still listen to me."

"Listen to you?"

"She used to be their boss," I told him. "It's worth a try, isn't it?"

"Guess it can't hurt." He cocked his head up the street. "Let's go."

CHAPTER 60
THE SHIP OF THESEUS

T HE OLD STONEWORK BUILDING WAS good cover for the soldiers. It was bulletproof and had very small windows though at least one on every wall. Whoever had chosen the location knew what they were doing.

We peeked from behind the corner of a pizza parlor across the street.

"You think it's them?" I asked Kenni.

She shrugged. "Let's find out." Motioning to the braves all around, she yelled, "Hold your fire! I need to talk to them."

They looked at her as if she was crazy until the ones closest saw the mark on her forehead. Word spread, and they fell silent. Kenni turned back to the building across the street.

"You inside! You have anything to lose?"

There was no reply.

Shaking her head, Kenni began stripping off her weapons.

"What are you doing?" I asked.

"I have to see who I'm talking to. And they're not going to listen to me until they can talk to me face to face." She grabbed the bottom of her shirt and brought it up to begin wiping the paint off her face. "Speaking of which, if they can't see my face, it sort of defeats the purpose."

Walela handed her a rag. I didn't know where she'd been

keeping it, but it made sense that someone wearing face paint would have something to wipe it off with.

Kenni wiped the last of the paint off before handing the rag back to Walela. "Thanks."

"So take your pistol at least," I said.

Again, she shook her head. "I need them to see me as one of them. That means no fear. Nothing to lose."

"And what if it's not Marines?"

She took a deep breath. "This might be a really short negotiation." She hesitated. "If something does happen to me, I need you to get back to Robin and—"

"Oh, would you just shut up! Don't you go and get all sentimental on me, all right? Just do the damn job, and let's finish this without anyone else getting killed."

Kenni grinned and nodded. "All right." Standing, she yelled at the building, "I'm Sergeant Kennesha Anderson." She rounded the corner, hands held out to her sides. "I'm unarmed. Send someone out to talk." Walking toward the building, she yelled again. "In the building! Send someone out to talk!"

"Give us a minute!"

"Dammit, Marine! You will send someone out here this fucking instant, or I will plant a boot so far up your ass you'll be flossing your teeth with my laces! Do you hear me?"

I pulled my head back at that. I'd never heard Kenni speak like that even when she was on base. But it worked. There was the sound of something large sliding across the floor, and the front door opened. A hand holding a white rag stuck out, followed a second later by a man in uniform. He walked out to meet Kenni.

They met roughly halfway between the two buildings and spoke briefly, too low for us to hear from where we were. After a moment, the two of them shook hands, turned, and walked back toward their respective sides.

We waited expectantly. When Kenni was with us again, she said, "It's them. I was pretty sure I recognized Hardy's voice when he yelled out. He's talking to the rest of the men, but I think they're coming out."

One of the braves around us asked, "How are we going to know?"

"I gave him three minutes to decide. Told him if they didn't come out by then, we would assume they had decided to make their stand and die here."

"You know they don't care about dying," I said.

"That could be changing."

"What do you—" I was interrupted by a shout from the building.

"We want to talk to Zach Dawcett."

I went cold. "What the hell?"

Kenni smiled. "I think it's good news."

"Why would you think that?"

"I might have hinted to them that you had the ear of the elders here and that you might be able to negotiate amnesty for them."

"What? You know I can't promise them that."

"I said you can negotiate it for them. Not that you could grant it."

I sighed, set my weapons down as Kenni had, and walked out with my hands to my sides. They opened the door and waved me inside. I looked at the familiar faces around me. I'd expected grim, battle-weary soldiers ready to surrender to superior odds. What I found was grinning men and women who had been friends.

"Hey, Zach!" Simmons laughed. "Got something on your face, man."

"Pipe down, Simmons," Hardy barked, but his expression was more humorous than angry. "But holy shit, Zach. He's right. That face paint is something else. Gone full-blown native, have you?"

I smiled back. "You know that alliance Everest was after? I threw in with the OTA instead."

"That's what I hear. It's also why I wanted to talk to you."

"Yeah. I know what Kenni told you. And I'll do my best. But you need to know up front that I can't make any promises. I don't know how the elders are going to react to me trying to get amnesty for soldiers that were just fighting against them."

"Even if we help you beat Everest?"

That stopped me. "Well, I imagine that would sure help your case. But I have to ask, why would you do that? You're Marines. You took an oath."

He nodded. "Yes, we did. But you made some pretty good points in the brig when you told me that you didn't believe that the United States existed anymore. It reminded me of a thought exercise I once read—a theological argument called 'the ship of Theseus.'"

"What?"

"It's a paradoxical thing. If you have a wooden ship and, as it wears, you replace the worn parts until none of the original wood still exists on the ship, is it still the same ship?"

"What does that have—"

Hardy held up his hand. "And what if, when you replaced all the wood from that ship, you saved all the old pieces, and used them to build another ship? Is *that* ship the same ship that it was?"

I blinked. "I don't know."

He smiled. "No one knows. It's a paradox. There's no right or wrong answer. Depending on how you look at it, either one is right. Ultimately, you just have to choose."

"I still don't get it."

"A country isn't made up of politicians—it's made up of people. Now, the way I see it, we have two groups. Both groups consist of people from the old nation. Neither group really *is* the old nation. So do I want the new ship built out of old wood, or the old ship made of new wood?"

"So is the OTA the new ship or the old ship?"

He shrugged. "Doesn't matter. As long as we choose with our eyes wide open, it's *our* ship. We've talked about it, and we all agree."

That surprised me. I looked around. "All of you feel this way?"

Every one of them nodded.

"We do," Hardy said. "When they train us as Marines, they teach us that we're the baddest SOBs out there. They pound it into us that the best way to honor our fallen is to take as many of the enemy out as we can. They teach us that we have nothing to lose because we've already lost everything but our lives. They make us believe that there's nothing scarier to face than someone who's already lost everything they value."

He shrugged. "I don't know that I still believe that. I think maybe having something worth fighting for might be a better motivator. We want that—something we believe in—something worth fighting for. So if the OTA will have us, we'd rather be on their ship than Everest's."

I stuck out my hand. "I can't guarantee that the OTA will take you in, but if they don't, you and your squad are welcome to come back with me to Texas. Either way, you all have a home."

We shook hands, sealing the deal.

"Good enough for me," Hardy said. "So here's my idea..."

CHAPTER 61
HARDY'S PLAN

STANDING WELL BACK IN THE darkness of the abandoned building across the street, I watched the soldiers in the granary parking area, checking their positions through the binoculars Nashoba had loaned me. Shooting in the immediate vicinity was nearly nonexistent, as everyone there had taken cover, and no one presented enough of a target to waste precious ammunition on.

There was gunfire from other places nearby, letting us all know that some smaller battles still went on. But everyone seemed to know that our position was where the main fight was. It was ironic that so many people gathered here, armed with firearms, bows, and arrows, yet no one on either side fired a shot. I looked around at the men and women crowded inside the building. There were easily more than fifty people, with another twenty or thirty taking cover behind whatever old, rusted, heavy equipment and crates they could find in the yard. And I knew there were three other buildings lined up beside us that were just as full of people ready to attack.

In the granary work yard, I saw movement behind what Kenni had called a bulldozer. "I see four guards manning the gate and three pairs behind cover scattered along the fence."

"Another pair near the far west corner of the yard," Nashoba said.

I looked. "Got 'em."

I passed the binoculars back. "What about inside?"

A man with an odd combination of a full beard and face paint spoke from my other side. Nashoba had introduced him as Adams. He was in charge of the braves surrounding the granary. "Near as we can tell, it looks like there are almost a hundred in the main building. And the paired guards you see along the fence? Well, there's four more pairs on each side of the yard, and we can't really tell how many more scattered around behind the old equipment and crates out there. It's more than enough to keep us from rushing them from any direction. Between them and the others manning the windows from inside the main building, there's no way we can take them without losing hundreds of people."

He pointed to the bodies in the street. "We've lost too many as it is."

"I'm sorry, Mr. Adams," I said, "but we're probably about to lose more."

"Well, it sure as hell better be worth it. And those Marines of yours better come through, 'cause I'm not throwing people's lives away for nothing."

"They'll come through." Kenni was calm as Walela stood before her, reapplying the face paint she'd taken off earlier.

"Even if they do, we don't know if it'll work. And even if it works, they're going to be facing damn near impossible odds."

Kenni nodded, prompting Walela to fuss at her to be still as she reapplied the shaman's symbol to her face. "They're trained to take on impossible odds. It's up to us to make sure they don't have to face them for very long."

"Don't worry. We'll take care of our end."

Nashoba tapped Adams on the shoulder with his good hand. His left arm was strapped tightly to his chest, blood oozing through the bandages. "It'll be fine, Adams. Just do like we discussed."

Adams drew his lips into a thin line, and we all fell silent for a few minutes, waiting.

Sudden shooting to the east told us the wait was over. People made way as Nashoba pushed through to the next window and raised the binoculars. "Here they come."

I shouldered through the crowding braves to stand beside Nashoba again, watching a line of mounted Marines galloping headlong up the street.

"Everyone knows not to actually hit them, right?" Kenni asked.

Nashoba nodded. "How many times do you want me to reassure you? Besides" – he jerked his chin toward the Marines – "it was Hardy's damned idea in the first place."

Nevertheless, one of the Marines slumped in his saddle as he rode past our building. It looked as if he'd been hit. At the front of the line, Hardy screamed at the granary for them to open the gate, and the guards scrambled to do so.

Three Marines fell from their saddles just as they got inside, and they lay still on the ground. Four more dropped a little farther in. Hardy and his remaining men left them all where they fell and hastily dismounted to take cover behind whatever crates or equipment they could find.

"I thought we weren't really shooting at them!" I hissed at Nashoba as I watched the Marines vanish behind the heavy bay door.

"We weren't." He snapped the binoculars back up to look at the battlefield. "Ah!"

"What?" I peered through the window again. It was hard to be sure at that distance, but it looked like one of the men had moved. As I watched, he rolled to his feet. As planned, he had a black handprint over his mouth and cheek, marking him as an ally. All the Marines had coated one hand with black greasepaint to mark themselves so we could tell friend from foe. And as they went into action, I was glad to see how well it had worked. That Marine and the two others who had fallen from their horses near the gate mowed through their targets before anyone knew what was happening. They gathered up the guards' weapons, opened the gate, and waved us in.

Nashoba signaled the braves, and Adams screamed at them, "Let's go!"

The parking lot erupted into a battlefield as Hardy and his men turned on the soldiers inside.

We all sprinted for the gate. Guards scattered around the parking lot began shooting again at this new assault, and braves fell in the street around me. I checked to my right to see Walela firing her rifle as she ran. Looking left, I saw Simon doing the same. Even Nashoba raised a pistol in his good hand, firing whenever he had a clear shot. Bow bouncing on my back, a pistol in either hand, I ran on, a single drop in a rushing wave of yelling, screaming men and women.

We ran at full speed, desperate to make it to the gate before they managed to close it again. But the battle in the parking area ensured that no one had time to think about the gate. Within the fence, the yard around the building turned into chaos as the soldiers were caught between the stealthy Marines among them and the OTA braves storming the parking lot.

Two men ahead of me fell to the ground, and I jumped over them to see a soldier with a terrified expression raising his rifle. Remembering that their rifles were automatic, I fired both pistols three times in a panic, hitting him in the chest each time. I knew he had body armor, but Kenni had told me that the impact of several rounds from a .45 should still knock someone down even through ballistic armor. I was glad to see she was right.

I dove into him, wrenched his rifle away, and shoved him into his partner. The second soldier then tried to bring his weapon to bear on me, so I fired three more times at point-blank range, knocking him to the ground.

The first one wasn't done with me yet, though, and while I had taken his rifle from him, he still had a knife. He slashed at me and I ducked back, feeling the burn that told me he had cut me. I fired three more shots.

He fell back, and I kicked him in the face. He hit the ground hard. Another brave grabbed his rifle, and we ran on. I looked around for Walela, but I had lost sight of anyone I knew as the crowd of braves washed through the gate, flooding through the yard.

I joined them as we ran for the building, shooting at anyone without face paint. The crowd around me knew the plan. At that point, we knew we had won. It was inevitable. We just needed to convince Everest's men of that fact. We weren't foolish enough to think that was going to be an easy task. Ahead of me, a door to the main building opened, and I heard the sudden, deafening roar of machine guns. People closest to the doorway began to scream and fall. I dove to the side even as it struck me that those doorways were choke points that Everest's men would easily be able to defend with only a few people. And they were doing just that. Anytime anyone broke cover to try and get closer, a barrage of bullets cut them down.

Three men in military uniforms came running up from behind me, yelling and firing as they zigged and zagged across the yard. I nearly fired at them, stopping when I saw the black handprints on their faces. Just before they reached the door, two of them swerved to either side while the third lobbed something inside and zigged once more to the side of the door. "Fire in the hole!"

He jumped over the nearest crate just as the grenade he'd tossed exploded. The Marine stood, and I recognized his face.

"Hardy?"

He looked at me. "Zachary?" Grinning, he ran to me and slapped my shoulder. "Hell of a party you folks throw."

Two other Marines I knew, Simmons and Richmond, joined him. They were also smiling maniacally.

I just stared at them in disbelief as I repeated. "Hardy?"

"Yeah?"

"You're crazy. You know that, right? All of you."

"Oorah! Wanna go end this thing?"

I checked my pistols and changed the magazines, felt to make sure my blades and bow were still where they were supposed to be, and nodded. "You bet. But you're still crazy."

Together, we led a new line of braves through the bloody mess in the doorway.

CHAPTER 62
ENDINGS

I FOLLOWED HARDY THROUGH THE DOORWAY into hell. The door opened into what had initially been a narrow hallway. His grenade had cleared the confined area, painting what walls still stood with red and granting us access to adjacent offices without the necessity of doors. I saw a boot lying on the floor, noting only in passing that there was still a foot laced into it. I refused to let myself dwell on it, afraid I would get sick.

Hardy led the way, ducking into a small stairwell to the right. I ran after him, as did several more braves. Others poured into the main floor of the building, screaming and firing at nearly anything that moved. We burst into a room on the second floor, expecting resistance, but there was nothing inside but a large opening in the wall that looked out over the main floor.

The big Marine hurried over to the window, ducking low as he got close to it. "Must have been a loading manager's office or something."

I knelt beside him, looking down over the battle just below us. There were bodies all over the floor, and as we watched, three more braves rushed across the concrete floor only to have two of them cut down from above. The third one made it to one of the huge, ramped pits in the floor where other braves fired up at the enemy.

"They're on the catwalk up there." Hardy pointed. The catwalk ran across the entire opposite wall, and there were dozens of soldiers firing down at the men trapped in the pits as well as at anyone foolish enough to enter the open floor below them. "And judging from the way your people in those pits are shooting, it's a safe bet there are others directly above us."

I saw several people in the pit shooting somewhere up above us and realized Simmons was right. Looking across to the other side of the loading floor, it appeared that the opposite side was a mirror image of ours.

Hardy jutted his chin toward the chaos below us. "They've set up a kill zone. And as long as they hold that high ground, they're damn near invulnerable."

I looked down as another group of braves rushed across the floor. Two of the five made it through to the pits that time. "We're making a mess of this, aren't we?"

He laughed wryly. "Yeah, ain't it great?"

I looked at him unbelievingly. *Yep. Crazy.* "So how do we end it?"

"Gonna be hard to do from below." He peered back through the window. "We need to find a way up to the catwalks."

"Can't you toss some grenades up there or something?"

"Only had the one."

"Well, that's disappointing."

He chuckled as he craned his neck at an awkward angle, trying to see directly above us. Shaking his head, he cursed. "Can't see shit from in here. But it looks like the only ways up are covered."

He was right. Based on the two stairways we could see, so many people had tried for them that there were bodies blocking the way at that point. I looked up.

"What's that?" I pointed to a metal beam that spanned all the way across the loading floor.

"Loading crane. If it was working, we could move it across the warehouse, but without power..." He shrugged.

"Without power, it's just a platform higher than the catwalks. Right?"

He slapped me on the back. "If we can get up there, yeah."

I turned to the braves still with us in the room. "We're going to need volunteers. People who can climb and who have good balance."

Every one of them raised a hand.

"Any of you ever fired an M4 or an M16?" Hardy asked.

Only two kept their hands up.

"Okay" — he pointed at one of them — "you're with me." He pointed at the other. "And you're with Zach, here. Now, here's what we're going to do."

We split into three groups. I led group one back downstairs, followed by Hardy and his group. Richmond and Simmons stayed with the third group. Hardy called them Team Charlie even though none of them was named Charlie. We slipped out of the hallway into the warehouse. But rather than running out into the kill zone as so many others had done, I led my group left, hugging the wall and taking cover behind the huge racks of equipment. Hardy took his group to the right.

When I reached the corner, I found the huge brace that formed one side of the platform for the loading crane. Making sure to keep on the far side of the beam, I grabbed either side of it and began climbing.

It was nothing at all like climbing trees to hang my hammock. The metal of the beams was ragged and rusting, and most of all, it was straight up. There were no perpendicular branches to help me rest a hand or foot on. The climb was pure grip and pressure, and I was shaking by the time I made it to the top. I wriggled onto the top rail and slid forward on my belly. If I was seen up there before I had more people with me, I'd be as good as dead.

Someone tapped my foot, and I looked back. A painted face motioned for me to slide forward, and I did, making room for more people who came up behind me. A minute later, there was another tap, and I slid forward again. I moved slowly with each tap, banking on the idea that the soldiers on the catwalk were paying attention to the kill zone below them, not to the framework ten feet above them.

Another tap on my foot, and I slid forward again. Looking ahead, I could see Hardy approaching from the opposite side. When we met in the middle, I drew a blade in either hand.

I saw the knife in his hand as he mouthed at me, "Ready?"

I looked across the gap. We were about ten feet above and six feet out from the catwalk above the office we'd been in. Below that was three stories of nothing... a long fall to the concrete if I missed. I took a deep, nervous breath before nodding at him.

Hardy sat up, jumped to his feet, and leapt into the midst of the soldiers below us. The rest of us were right behind him. The soldier in front of me turned slightly toward Hardy just as I hit him from above, driving a knife into his neck, twisting it, and turning to the next soldier just as the brave who had been tapping my foot on the beam above rammed his own knife into the gap between the ballistic plates in the man's body armor. Hardy had shown us that while the body armor they wore was designed to stop most bullets from penetrating, it was — ironically enough — still vulnerable to blade attacks. And since we didn't want to draw immediate attention to our attack, we elected to lead with knives until we came under fire from the catwalk across from us, gathering as many machine guns as possible as we went.

So we waded into our opponents with as much stealth and speed as possible, trying our best to take them before they realized what was happening. Each soldier we dropped added yet another rifle to our number, and within thirty seconds, we had decimated the majority of the soldiers on our catwalk.

The sudden, deafening chatter of machine-gun fire announced the end of our stealth attack, and three braves behind Hardy screamed and fell.

"Quiet time's over, boys!" the Marine yelled as he swung his rifle around.

I slammed my own knives back into their sheaths and drew my pistols. All around me, braves did the same, dropping any attempt at a silent attack and drawing whatever firearms they had on them. And as we had been instructed, we all dropped to our knees, allowing us to see that anyone still standing was an enemy. The cacophony of gunfire all around me made me wish I'd remembered to plug my ears as Kenni had shown me.

Past Hardy, I saw a man in uniform standing, aiming his rifle at one of the braves. Hardy jumped up, putting himself between that brave and his attacker, using his body armor to shield the both of them from the hail of machine-gun fire. The enemy soldier quickly went down under a hail of bullets as several of us concentrated our fire on one of the few standing targets in our area. Body armor or not, the concussive force of multiple sustained hits dropped him.

That applied to Hardy too, though. I saw the agony on his face as the bullets slammed into his chest. But he was still alive. He pushed himself off the brave whose life he had just saved, leaning his back against a handrail. His hands shook as he grasped at straps on his armor. I crawled over to him.

"Help me get this off," he gasped.

His hands seemed clumsy as they fumbled at the snaps, so I unclasped the armor and helped him out of the oversized vest. He hissed as I pulled it off, and I saw jagged, bloody shards protruding from the inside of the armor. There were corresponding jagged holes in his shirt, each one surrounded by spreading crimson.

"Yeah, that's what I thought. Plates shattered." His breathing was short and filled with pain.

"How bad is it?" I asked.

"Not great, but I'll live." He winced. "Course, I'm not really sure that's such a good thing, the way I feel right now." But he grinned as he said it. "Come on, Zach. Let's finish this."

He took a deep breath, braced himself, and leaned forward. "Grab a rifle, Zach. As bad as taking this catwalk was, it's about to get worse."

A brave beside me handed me one of our recently acquired rifles, and I turned it toward the opposite wall.

"Charlie team!" Hardy yelled at the top of his lungs. "Fire!"

From below us, in the office where we had first come up

with our crazy plan, the third group began shooting through the window at the catwalk across from us. And from below, the braves trapped in the loading pits saw what was happening and turned their own weapons on the catwalk.

The line on the catwalk across from us fell apart as their previously dominant position abruptly came under fire from all sides. Braves all around me screamed and whooped, and the warehouse became a veritable shooting gallery. There was no cover for us up on the catwalk. But neither was there cover for our targets. It was just a matter of which side could take out the other quickest, and we had help from below.

But it was bloody. I aimed and fired short bursts, ignoring the screams of pain around me. Occasionally, out of the corner of my eye, I would see a body fall from the catwalk to the concrete below. I ignored those as well. I only had time to concentrate on shooting as many of the enemy as possible, all the while waiting for the searing pain that would likely end my life.

Then it was over. I sighted along the barrel, and there were no more targets shooting at us. The few who were still alive had thrown down their weapons and surrendered.

It took my mind a few seconds to accept the idea that it was over. And I was still alive. I pumped my fist into the air, joining the victory cries of the braves around me. "We did it! Hardy, we did…"

But Hardy was gone. Had he already climbed down from the catwalk? Was he already organizing cleanup squads?

I wanted to believe it. But I knew better. My memory kept playing back something I had barely seen—a body falling from the catwalk to the concrete below. I ran for the staircase.

It had been a quick but ferociously bloody fight, and cleanup was a somber business. Of the twenty Marines that Hardy had led through the gates, only six survived. Hardy wasn't one of them.

Just as I had feared, I found his body on the loading floor three stories beneath the catwalk. He'd been shot twice in the chest and once in the throat.

"Severed his spinal column." Kenni startled me. I hadn't heard her as she knelt beside me. "He didn't suffer."

"I hope not."

"It's not a guess," she said with a sad smile. "He wants you to make good on your word. Take care of his men. Give them a place to call home."

I just nodded. I wasn't going to doubt her ever again. "Can you find his men and have them come take care of him? He deserves..." But I didn't know what he deserved. How did Marines honor their own?

But Kenni understood. "I'll take care of it."

Numb, I wandered for a bit after that. I spotted Simon, and the familiarity of his pale skin and red hair made me smile. "Simon!"

He jerked his head around and trotted to me. "You all right?"

I nodded. "You?"

"Yeah."

"Have you seen Walela?"

He pointed. "She's outside, helping patch up some of the wounded."

"Thanks." I wound my way toward the door. Nashoba saw me and nodded, but was clearly too busy giving orders to stop. He had a bloody slice across his cheek, but it wasn't slowing him down. I wondered if anything would slow that man down. He moved past, shouting at people to get the bay doors open and get some fresh air flowing.

Stepping outside, I quickly found Walela. She had been crying, closing the eyes of an old woman with a hole in her chest. She muttered something under her breath and wiped her sleeve across her eyes, smearing her face paint in the process. She smiled when I knelt beside her, relief and weariness equal partners in her expression. She leaned into me.

"I love you too," I told her.

She pulled away and looked at me. She smiled but was clearly puzzled. "What?"

"I love you too. What you said back at the conditioned-air place. When you said you loved me."

She snorted. "Really? You think *this* is the right time for that?"

"Yes. You told me you loved me, and I never said it back."

"Because it wasn't the right time or place."

"Yes, it was. It will always be the right time and place. Look around us. What if I had been one of these bodies?"

She hit me. "Don't say that!"

"What if *you* had been one of them? What if we had left things like they were, and I had never told you?"

She nodded sadly. "Okay, point made. So you love me."

"I'm afraid so."

She leaned against me. "I guess I can live with that."

CHAPTER 63
NEW BEGINNINGS

"**M**OM, YOU HAVE THE BLANKET?"

She came out of the adjoining room, smiling. I noticed that for the first time, she seemed to be showing her age a bit. The trip to Oklahoma couldn't have been easy on her, especially with the coming winter dropping the temperature the way it was. "Of course. Here."

I felt a moment of panic as I saw what she held out. It was a beautiful red quilt with bright-yellow, seven-pointed stars spread all over it.

"Did you know that the stars have seven points to represent the seven clans of the Cherokee Nation?" she asked.

"Yes, I did. But, Mom, please tell me this is a joke. It has to be a blue—"

"Settle down. Yes, it's a joke, son." With a playful grin, she laid the quilt on the bed and pulled a plain blue, woven blanket from beneath the pillow. "You need to take a chill pill."

It was another of her Old Days sayings that I'd heard all my life. I'd never known what a chill pill was, but she always said it when she wanted me to calm down. Of course, that was something that was unlikely to happen that day.

Still, she didn't need me snapping at her, either. I took the blanket and hugged her. "Thanks."

She squeezed me tight then pushed me back to arm's length.

"Nice shirt." Reaching out, she gently pulled one of the colored ribbons hanging from the buckskin top I wore. "What are these?"

"I honestly don't know. I asked four people and got four different answers. All anyone could agree on is that ribbon shirts are traditional for ceremonies."

"Well, I like it."

I kissed her on the forehead. "Thanks. Where's Dad?"

She pointed back to the door that led to their adjoining room. "Still getting ready. You want to see if you can hurry him along?"

"No need. I'm ready." Dad came through the door, limping a little but looking very official in his Old Days suit and tie. I'd only seen him wear it on two or three occasions, and it looked like it had seen better days. But he wore it proudly, and I wasn't about to tell him it was anything less than perfect. I smiled. "You look pretty sharp, old man."

He chuckled, deep laugh lines showing around his eyes as he did. "I seriously doubt that. But this is all I had that seemed like it might be appropriate."

"You look great."

By the expression in his eyes, he looked like he wanted to say so much. But he simply asked, "So is everybody ready?"

"We were waiting on you." Mom laced her arm through his and looked at me. "Lead the way."

It was a short walk through the snow to the church, and Walkingstick was waiting outside. Ignoring the fact that it was a "white custom," she extended her hand, shaking my mother and father's hands as I introduced them. "Welcome, Mr. and Mrs. Dawcett. It's an honor to meet you."

"The honor is ours," Dad replied. "I understand when this is over, we may have some things to discuss."

The old woman smiled. "In time. But for now, if you would follow Simon here..."

"Of course."

I looked past her to the pale redhead standing just inside the doorway. He winked at me before leading my parents inside, leaving me out in the cool air with the old shaman. She took my hand, and I felt the strong warmth as she gazed up at me. I was silent as her eyes stared deeply into my own. Maybe I didn't fully believe yet, but I had learned to accept that I couldn't dismiss the abilities that she and Kenni claimed to have.

"Don't forget, medicine touches you too," she said.

I shook my head, chuckling. "You really need to stop doing that."

"Doing what?" But her answering laugh told me she knew exactly what I meant and that my recognition of it was all the acceptance she required for the time being. "Are you ready?" she asked.

I took the blue blanket and draped it across my shoulders. "Yes, ma'am."

"Then would you please escort an old woman out of the cold?" She placed her hand on my arm, and the two of us walked inside.

She gently guided me inside and to the right until we stood against the eastern wall. In the center, a fireplace warmed the room, and past that, on the west wall, Walela smiled at me. My hummingbird wore a traditional tear dress, patterned after those made when her ancestors were being forced out of their lands and weren't allowed scissors for fear they would use them as weapons. The dresses were made from lengths of cloth that they could tear, using hands and teeth.

Walela's was bright red with bands of turquoise on the sleeves and around her knees. Within each band were more of the seven-pointed stars. And draped across her shoulders was a blue blanket similar to the one I wore. Beside her, Elder Black Horse held her arm. He whispered into her ear, and she nodded. Together, they stepped forward even as Walkingstick pulled me toward them.

We met at the center of the building, in the midst of friends and family, and took our places beside the fire. Walkingstick patted my hand and stepped away from me to the other side of the flames. She said something in Cherokee, and there was a loud shout.

Turning to me, the old woman smiled. "We will do this in English today."

"Thank you."

She chuckled. "Well, it's only right that you understand your own wedding ceremony."

I smiled.

Turning to the seated crowd, she asked, "Who gives away this man that he might join our people?"

As rehearsed, my mother stood and walked to my side. "Debra Dawcett, matriarch of the family." The red quilt she had shown me earlier was draped across her arms. A small basket sat on the quilt.

Walkingstick nodded. "Who gives away this woman that she might join her life with this man's?"

Walela's grandmother stood and walked forward. She had a length of buckskin draped over her right arm and held an ear of corn in the left. She looked to be as old as Walkingstick, perhaps older, but stood tall and walked with a confident step. "Edna Kingfisher, matriarch of the *a ni sa ho ni* clan."

"And who stands as *e du tsi?*"

To my surprise, Keith stood and walked forward to stand behind Walela's grandmother. "Keith Dustu, warrior of the *a ni sa ho ni* clan."

Walkingstick nodded. "Walela Walters, do you accept this man to be your husband? Swear to cleave only to him for all your days?"

"I do."

The elder turned to me. "Zachary Dawcett, do you accept this woman as your wife and swear to cleave to her and no other for all your days?"

"I do."

Walkingstick turned to those seated in the room. "Please stand and bear witness."

Walela took my hand, and we turned to face the people gathered around us as we recited a traditional wedding prayer. It had taken me a few days to memorize it properly, but I was able to say it without thinking as I looked out at the faces gathered around us.

Walkingstick's voice brought me back as she asked Walela, "Do you have the belt?"

My bride smiled and held out a wide red and black woven belt. She knelt and tied it around my waist.

Walkingstick turned to Grandma Kingfisher. "Edna Kingfisher, do you give approval, that this woman of your clan might wed this man?"

"I do." Grandma Kingfisher walked to stand before me, handing me the buckskin and the corn. "I give you these that you might know that my daughter will always clothe and feed you, as a warrior of our clan deserves."

I nodded as I had been instructed, and she stepped behind me to unfold the blanket on her granddaughter's shoulders so that it draped over mine as well.

Walkingstick turned to my mom. "Debra Dawcett, as matriarch of your family, do you give approval for your son to join the clan of this woman, that he might join his life with hers?"

Mom smiled. "I do." She walked around to stand before Walela. "I give you this quilt that you might know that my son will always provide you with a warm bed" — she pulled several strips of jerky from the basket — "and meat that you might know that he will always provide food for your table."

Walela smiled, leaned forward, and kissed my mother's cheek. Mom smiled back and stepped behind me, unfolding my blanket so that it also draped across the two of us.

Walkingstick turned to Keith. "*E du tsi?*"

Keith stood before Walela. He took her hand. "As you have no true brother, it is my honor to stand in as uncle to your children. I accept the responsibility of teaching them our ways." He reached over and grasped my shoulder. "And should my new brother fall in battle, I will provide for them as if they were my own."

Walkingstick held up a clay vessel with two necks. Handing it to Walela, she said, "Drink, and share the fruits of the earth with your new husband."

Together, my wife and I raised the pot and drank to the four directions before handing it back to the old woman. Walkingstick raised it once more. "As they have proclaimed their marriage to the four winds, so too do I affirm it to Father Sky" — she took a sip then held the pot down toward the ground — "and to Mother Earth." She took a second sip. Then she held it out toward us. "That they might see this new couple and bless their union."

After raising the vase one last time, Walkingstick threw it into the fire, shattering it against the bricks. "Please remove your blankets."

I took them off our shoulders and handed them to Keith.

"The blue blankets symbolize the old life, the single life. Now, turn and face your friends and family."

When we had done so, she draped a new blanket over our shoulders. I looked at the length of white that enveloped us. "Let this white blanket proclaim that this man and woman are now one."

There was a second of silence, quickly shattered by an ear-piercing whoop as Keith shouted and clapped me on the shoulders. "Welcome to the family, Zach. Let's get this party started!"

———※——※——※——※——※—

In the months since the battle of Burns Flat, much had changed. Kenni had gone back home, taking news of what had happened. A few weeks later, she had returned with Robin. Mr. Roesch had taken her story back to Rejas, and he, his wife, and my parents had arrived only two days ago, just in time for the wedding.

Now, hours after the ceremony, the evening was finally winding down, and Walela and I sat quietly talking with my parents and Elder Walkingstick — or rather, listening as my father and Walkingstick discussed the aftermath of Burns Flat.

"You just let them go?" Dad sounded incredulous as Walkingstick explained that they had set most of the surviving soldiers free, escorting them out of tribal lands.

"Most of them didn't really want to be here, anyway. And their man... what was his name, Zachary?"

"Collins."

"Yes. Collins already held their loyalty and wanted to leave. So we offered the deal, and he agreed to lead them out."

"And if they come back?"

"Oh, I have little doubt that they will. But it will be a few years. We have time to prepare. And in the meantime, we still have the officers imprisoned. The more time I can spend with them, the more I will learn."

Kenni, Robin, and Mr. and Mrs. Roesch made their way to our table. Mr. Roesch was still moving slowly, but he made it look deliberate. If I hadn't spent so much time with him on the road, I might not have noticed.

"Mr. Roesch, please sit."

He waved me off. "Not necessary, son."

"Actually, it is. Since you're technically my boss, custom dictates that I can't sit in your presence until you do."

He looked at me. "Bullshit."

Walkingstick smiled and went along with my ploy. "No, he's right. As a matter of fact, you can take my chair. It's time I put these old bones to rest for the night." She stood and patted Kenni on the shoulder. "And I'll see you in the morning."

Mr. Roesch pursed his lips then finally sat, while Walela stood and coaxed Jennifer Roesch into her chair.

"How are you feeling, Mr. Roesch?"

He shrugged at my question. "Some days are better than others. It's gonna take a while before I'm a hundred percent, but I'll get there. This cold air isn't doing me any favors, though."

I worried for the first time at the realization that this man that I had always seen as larger than life seemed to have lost some of his essence to our journey. I had seen so many reminders of life's fragility, and I hated the realization that it would eventually take everyone I loved.

"Hell, Zach. You can just wipe that sentimental look off your damn face. I'm not going anywhere yet."

We all shared a laugh at that.

"So Kenni told me what all happened here. Told me what you did."

I glanced at Kenni, but she only nodded. "I know you would have probably done things differently—"

"Course I would have," Mr. Roesch said. "We're different people. Different doesn't mean better, though. From what I heard, you walked into a bad situation and handled it the best way you could." He waved his hand around, indicating the revelers. "And while you didn't get the alliance you thought you were going to get, you *did* get an alliance. Personally, I think you did better than I would have on that front." He nodded at Walela. "Hell, you even managed to fool a pretty girl into marrying you."

"Of course, a diplomat's life might get a little tricky."

"No." I chuckled. "I think those days are over. I'm done being a diplomat."

Kenni laughed. "You're just getting started, Zachary."

"Oh no I'm not. I'm through wanting to make my mark in the world. I just want to go home"—I pulled Walela closer to me—"and settle down... live a quiet, normal life."

Mr. Roesch shook his head. "Sorry, Zach. I don't think that's going to happen."

"Why not?"

"Didn't you just negotiate an alliance with the OTA?"

"So?"

"On behalf of the Sabine River Trading Coalition?"

"Oh, crap. I did, didn't I?" I felt a sinking feeling in my stomach. "How do you think Walkingstick will react when she finds out there's no such thing?"

"What?" Walela pulled away, staring at me. "No such thing?"

Kenni chuckled. "Calm down. Do you really think she doesn't already know?"

Shocked, it was my turn to ask, "What?"

"She knows. She told me she has every faith in your efforts to build the coalition and has promised whatever help the OTA can provide."

"Wait. She what?"

"Yep."

"Well, you and Mr. Roesch can do it, then. You're both better qualified than me."

"Not me," Mr. Roesch said. "My wandering days are done." He grabbed his wife's hand. "I made a promise."

"Well then, Kenni."

But she was already shaking her head. "Robin and I are settling down here in McAlester. Walkingstick has insisted I start studying with her right away. She's not getting any younger." Kenni shrugged. "Mama died before she could teach me much. Maybe Walkingstick can do it."

"But I can't do this alone! You're talking about dozens of alliances... getting thousands of people to work together. It's impossible!"

"No, it's not." Kenni raised a hand, waving to someone behind me. I turned to see Keith, Simon, and John walking toward us. "And you won't be alone. Owen's chomping at the bit to help out. And since the Sabine River Trading Coalition already has an alliance with the OTA, it's only right that the tribes have representatives in the mix as well."

Keith slapped my shoulder. His own wounded shoulder was obviously healing up just fine. "I hear we're gonna be working together for a long time, brother."

ABOUT THE AUTHOR

Jeff Brackett is the author of *Half Past Midnight*, *The Road to Rejas*, *Streets of Payne*, and *Chucklers, Volume 1: Laughter is Contagious*, as well as a variety of short stories and novellas published in magazines and anthologies. After having lived almost his entire life in and around Houston, 2014 presented several life changes that brought him, his wife, and two dogs (Bella and Cricket) to Claremore, Oklahoma. There, they found a nice little house with a much larger yard, and are all adjusting to the new lifestyle quite well. Jeff has even begun learning to garden.

His writing has won Honorable Mention in the action / adventure category of the "Golden Triangle Unpublished Writer's Contest", first place in the novel category of the "Bay Area Writers League Manuscript Competition", and was a finalist in the science fiction / fantasy / horror category of the "Houston Writer's Conference" manuscript contest.

His proudest achievement, though, is in having fooled his wife into marrying him more than thirty years ago, and helping her to raise three wonderful children. He is now a grandfather twice over.

And his gardening? Well, let's just say he still has a bit to learn in that area.

You can follow Jeff's blog and sign up for notification of his latest publications at http://jlbrackett.com

Made in the USA
Monee, IL
07 May 2021